Linda Finlay lives on the ~~_____~~ ~~_____~~ author of eight novels. From lace-making to willow weaving, each one is based on a local craft which, in order to write authentically and place herself firmly in the shoes of her heroines, she has learnt to do herself. However, it is people and their problems that make for a good story and, with so much interesting material to work with, it is easy for Linda to let her imagination run as wild as the rugged West Country landscape which has inspired her writing.

Also by Linda Finlay

The Royal Lacemaker
The Girl with the Red Ribbon
A Family For Christmas
The Sea Shell Girl
Monday's Child
Orphans and Angels
The Flower Seller
The Bonbon Girl

The
Girl
with the
Amber Comb

Linda Finlay

ONE PLACE. MANY STORIES

HQ
An imprint of HarperCollins*Publishers* Ltd
1 London Bridge Street
London SE1 9GF

This paperback edition 2020

1

First published in Great Britain by
HQ, an imprint of HarperCollins*Publishers* Ltd 2020

ISBN: 978-0-00-8263003

MIX
Paper from
responsible sources
FSC™ C007454

This book is produced from independently certified FSC™ paper
to ensure responsible forest management.

For more information visit: www.harpercollins.co.uk/green

This book is set in 10.9/16.2 pt. Sabon

Printed and bound in Great Britain by
CPI Group (UK) Ltd, Croydon, CR0 4YY

To my loving husband, Pern,
for his continued support and encouragement

Prologue

Sedge Moor, Somerset. Autumn 1834

The harvest moon hung like a buttery orb, gilding the withies that stood like sentinels alongside the dykes. The smell of apple pressings from a cider house drifted across the land. Beyond rose Aller Moor, the black holes scored by peat cutters staring down on the Droves like watchful eyes.

Suddenly the quietude of the night was broken by a piercing scream that disturbed a heron from its roost. Mary cuddled her daughter closer, wiping the sweat from her brow before bending to ease the sac from her body. Although she worked quickly, she knew in her heart it was already too late. Sure enough, as the tiny form whimpered and took its first breath, Della shuddered and breathed her last. Mary shook her head, hot tears bouncing from her cheeks to mingle with the waters of the rhyne that now ran red with blood.

All she could feel was despair for a young life lost and hatred for the man whose selfish lust had been the cause. Another whimper sounded from the withies and she steeled herself to look. Yet even as she stared, the wail became impatient, its insistence demanding attention. It was just as Mary had thought, but now her worst fears had been realized, did she have the nerve to perform the task she'd sworn she would?

Chapter 1

Sedge Moor, Somerset. Seventeen years later

'Oh Grammer, why didn't I listen to you?' Eliza cried as, oblivious to the dew glistening like stars in the pale light of early morning, she dropped to her knees on the grass. Gently, she placed her posy between the two graves, one recently dug, the other flattened with time. Grammer Mary now united with her daughter Della, the mother Eliza had never known.

'May St Michael give you protection from darkness and evil,' she murmured. The bright blue daisies symbolized fare-well and Eliza knew she wasn't only saying goodbye to the woman who had raised her, but to her own dreams for the future. As the willows rustled their leaves, she dashed away a tear, scarcely able to believe her beloved grammer had gone to sleep the previous week never to wake and greet another new day.

It was now the end of September and the swallows were taking flight from the nearby reed beds on their way to warmer climes and a new life. Eliza wished she was going with them, for winter was fast approaching bringing the wild winds and incessant rains that would batter their home for weeks on end.

Sighing, she got to her feet and stared over the withy beds that glinted yellow in the swirling autumn mist, towards the scattered stone cottages and farmhouses which made up the hamlet of Worth.

'Happy birthday, Eliza.' She started as her gramfer came up behind her. 'Were a time of mixed emotions the day you were born and that's the truth,' he said gruffly. Turning, she smiled and linked her arm through his, for he said the same thing every year. 'You've brought such joy and Lord knows how I'd manage without you now that . . .' his voice cracked and he turned towards the old oak where the two crosses were flanked by the bright flowers.

Although she didn't feel like celebrating today, her birthday had always been an occasion to be marked. A specially baked cake followed by a toast to Della.

'I'm sure Grammer's staring down from heaven to see what you've got for me,' Eliza teased, forcing a smile as she tried to lift his spirits.

'Mary were never one to miss out on anythin'.' His lips twitched, hazel eyes pensive as he stroked his greying beard. 'I might have a little somethin' but you'll have to wait 'til later. Birthday or no, there's work to do first. Old Man Conger's callin' for those eel traps he ordered this art'noon. Mary was that busy she didn't have time . . .' his voice trailed off again.

'I've a basket to make for Mr Batstone then I'll see to them,' Eliza assured him, for the man was a good customer who always paid promptly, sometimes even giving them fish for their evening meal. Besides, their flour sack was almost empty and the money would help pay for another.

'You're a good girl,' he murmured. 'I'll be out checkin' the beds. The cattle have made a good job of clearin' the weeds so hopefully we'll be able to harvest before the first frosts set in.'

'I'll have a brew ready when you return. We can have it with a slice of the bramble manchit I baked yesterday,' she told him, knowing how he lost track of time when he was checking his precious withies.

'Your pastry's almost good as your grammer's,' he grunted, his eyes suspiciously bright. Eliza watched as he made his way slowly down the drove, a stout hazel stick supporting the body that was stooped from a lifetime spent bending over his precious beds.

As a fresh breeze blew in from the moors, Eliza shivered and hurried over to the ramshackle barn that served both as store and workshop. The letter in her pocket crackled, reminding her of the decision she'd had to take. Although she loved helping the school mistress teaching the young girls their lessons, with Grammer gone there was nobody else to fulfil the orders for the quality baskets her family were renowned for making. It was up to Eliza to take over the business. There was no way she was letting Izziah Gliddon get his hands on it. The odious merchant had called with indecent haste the moment he'd heard Mary had been taken, insisting he would be doing Eliza a favour. He'd even insinuated a young girl such as herself wouldn't be able to cope.

However, she'd helped her grammer often enough and would take great delight in proving him wrong. There was no denying the fact that Gramfer had aged considerably over the past week and she couldn't leave him alone all day to manage by himself.

Still, it was no good brooding for, as he was fond of reminding her, time was tucker. And she'd have precious little of that now she also had to look after their cott and continue tending the vegetable plot. With Clem's help, she'd turned it into a profitable concern that supplemented their income.

Settling herself down on the thin piece of matting, she placed their old flat iron on the lapboard between her legs. Then taking up a pliant osier from the pile beside her, she began making a new basket for the baker at Stathe. To lift her mood, she started singing the song she'd learned as a child.

> *One cane round, neat and tight,*
> *insert a decent border.*
> *Upset tight, wale alright,*
> *to keep my stakes in order.*

Once Eliza had finished up-setting the uprights around the base, she began weaving in and out. Despite working quickly, she prided herself on the standard of her work. Competition was fierce and only perfection acceptable. With the body finished, she picked another, more flexible rod and wound it into a rope handle, finally adding the flower twist that her grammer's work was known for, which would now become Eliza's own trademark.

> *Twisting, binding, winding,*
> *willow wand, now fold.*
> *Handle strong, but not too long,*
> *for ladies' hands to hold*

Her fingers weaving to the rhythm of the words, she worked until the basket was completed. Placing it ready for collection, she went over to the stooks stacked along the walls and selected the strong sticks she would need for the eel traps. Firmly holding three of the thicker ones, she made a split in the centre of each of them. Setting these together and inserting another three horizontally through the holes, she took up a thinner cane and began the figure of eight weave that would become the base. *Over and under with another two, pull up the sides*, she chanted, determined to get on with her work. As the basket began to spread out, she took the weaver over and under singly and was just inserting the spokes into the base when a shadow fell across her.

'Marnen, birthday girl.'

'Clem, how did you get here?' she cried, looking up from her work.

'By boat, same as ever,' he grinned, flicking his unruly dark hair back from his head. 'Your gramfer said you needed flour and as I was passing the mill at Stathe it was easy to pick up a sack.'

'But I didn't give you the empty one and you know what Miller's like.'

'Ah, but when I explained it was a special day, he said you could have it with his blessing.'

'That's kind of him but . . .' she stopped, not wishing to sound ungrateful.

'You don't think you should be celebrating,' he finished, as ever picking up on her thoughts.

'Well yes,' she admitted. 'Grammer's only just . . .' her voice trailed away. As she brushed away the tears that rolled unbidden down her cheeks, Clem leaned forward and took her hand. 'She were a fine woman and wouldn't want you grieving,' he murmured.

'I know but I can't help feeling guilty,' she admitted.

'Whatever for? It were a natural passing,' he frowned.

'But Grammer prophesized it,' Eliza burst out, anxious to share the worry that had been plaguing her. 'You know her life revolved around her beliefs in nature, Wicca she called it. Well, the night before she died, she told me that one of the willows had grown so large it had cast a grave-sized shadow over her as she passed by. It was a portent of her death and I took no notice. No, worse than that, I told her not to be so silly.'

'Mary and her superstitions,' he smiled sadly, his grip tightening. 'And that's what it was, Red. Ma's just as bad, mind. Thinks if she gets a double-yolked egg it means a hurried wedding's in the offing. Not that I've seen that happen – yet,' he added, giving her a look that made her feel strangely uncomfortable.

'Well, getting back to that sack,' she said, removing her hand. 'It was a nice gesture and I shall dye it and make a new top. Goodness knows I could do with one,' she added, frowning down at her frayed and well-worn blouse.

'You look good from where I'm standing,' he smiled, shooting her another of those looks that made her flustered. Although they'd been friends since her first day at school when he'd offered her his kerchief after she'd fallen and cut her knee, it was only lately he'd started paying her compliments. 'Well, it's been a long day already and I'm fair parched,' he added, looking at her hopefully.

'When aren't you?' she smiled, pleased to be back on familiar footing. 'I'll go and make us a drink.'

'And I'll unload the flour and put it in the pantry out of the way of those meddling mice of yours. Then I might have a little something for you myself.' Giving her a cheeky wink, he strode back to the flat-bottomed trow he used for transporting goods along the narrower waterways.

Eliza watched as Clem tossed the sack over his broad shoulders as if it weighed no more than a feather. It had been a relief to share her worries with him, but then she'd always been able to talk to him she realized, her mood lifting like the mist in the heat of the sun as she made her way towards the cott.

Indoors was strangely quiet without Grammer's humming. The smell of bittersweet smoke that curled from the smouldering peat fire hung in the air and she grimaced at the cobwebs swinging from the low beams. Still, the sound of the kettle singing was welcoming and Eliza poured water into the pot then set out the crisp pastry filled with her latest preserve.

'Now there's a sight for sore eyes,' Clem murmured, blue eyes gleaming appreciation as his muscular frame filled the doorway.

'I made it fresh yesterday,' Eliza replied.

'Hmm, the manchit looks good too,' he told her, chuckling when her cheeks flushed bright as the berries in the jam. He waited until she'd served their tea then bent and kissed her cheek. 'Happy birthday, Red,' he said, tweaking her Titian tresses as he handed her a small package.

'Thank you,' she cried as, worries temporarily forgotten, she tore excitedly at the wrapping. 'Oh, this is beautiful,' she exclaimed, running her fingers over the polished handle of a wooden spoon.

'Like the girl I made it for,' he said, his gaze holding hers. 'It's for your jam pot, being as how you make the best ever,' he added quickly.

'Not that the damsons were plentiful this year. I had to mix them with brambles,' she told him.

'Well, you've certainly worked your magic,' he grinned, eying the plate hopefully.

'Go on then, but save some for Gramfer,' Eliza told him, pleased he'd enjoyed it, though she knew she had some way to go before she reached her grammer's standards. 'This really is a beautiful piece of carving, Clem,' she said, admiring the spoon again.

'Not as good as those the Welsh carve. Love spoons, they

call them. Idris was telling me they give them to their sweet-hearts as tokens of affection, to show their intentions as it were.' Again, his clear blue eyes bore into hers, making her blush so that she had to turn quickly away.

'More tea or anything?' she asked, her voice unnaturally high.

'Anything, Eliza?' He cleared his throat. 'I . . . well the thing is . . .' he stopped as footsteps sounded outside.

'Gramfer,' Eliza cried, jumping to her feet. 'You're just in time for a brew. Clem's brought us a sack of flour.'

'That's good of you, my boy,' George said, sinking into his chair beside the fire and holding out gnarled hands to the meagre warmth. Eliza, busy filling another mug from the pot, didn't see the look the two men exchanged.

'It was no trouble, sir.'

'You staying for supper? Old Conger's placed an order for two eel traps so I should have the money for Miller later today,' George said, staring knowingly at him.

'Goodness, I'm only halfway through making them,' Eliza exclaimed. 'I'd better get on.'

'Happy to help,' Clem said, trying to keep up with her as she hurried out to the barn.

Chapter 2

'Are you sure you're not too busy?' Eliza asked, still puzzling over his behaviour.

'Got no more deliveries to make and two pairs of hands will work quicker,' he replied. She nodded, knowing he was right. There was no telling what time the fisherman would be calling for his traps, and Old Conger wasn't a man to be kept waiting.

'Well if you're sure,' she said, sinking gratefully onto her stool and picking up the basket she'd started earlier. 'You know what to do?' Clem let out a loud guffaw that almost raised the rafters.

'Been making these since you was in cradlehood,' he snorted, stooping to gather up a pile of withies from the stack in the corner.

'I'll have you know I'm only three years younger than you, Clem Galton,' she spluttered.

'In years maybe, but experience?' he shrugged. 'Travelling the waterways of Somerset, collecting and delivering for Father, I meet lots of people, see what goes on in life. You've not really been away from the Droves, have you, Red?' he asked.

'That's where you're wrong. I've enjoyed spending time

in Stoke helping Mrs Poundsberry at the school, but now of course, I shall have to give that up,' she sighed.

'I'm sorry, I only meant you haven't seen much of life,' he murmured, reaching out and patting her shoulder. Then never one to stay serious for long he added, 'At least those poor little girls have had a narrow escape.'

'Ha ha. I'll have you know they worked well for me,' she retorted.

'Mother Eliza, eh?' he grinned, then sobered. 'Seriously though, is there really no way you can carry on with your job? What about Izziah Gliddon, I'm sure he . . .'

'Don't even mention that man's name to me,' she cut in. 'He called the day after . . . she was taken, offering to take on Grammer's orders. You know how she prided herself on her work with it all coming by recommendation. Gliddon's associated with shoddy tatt and she'd turn in her grave if she thought I'd let him take over her business.'

'She would that,' Clem agreed.

'Besides I daren't leave Gramfer so soon after losing her. He looks so frail and lost without her,' she sighed.

'Still in shock, I suppose. When he's had time to adjust, I'm sure you'll be able to work something out. In the meantime, keeping busy is best.'

'Well there's certainly enough to do,' she sighed, raising her brows. 'Which reminds me, I lifted some more potatoes and carrots from the plot for Mrs Gill the greengrocer in Stoke earlier. The sacks are outside if could you deliver them for me on your return trip?'

'Of course. Usual terms of business, extra tea and cake next visit,' he bartered.

'Thanks Clem,' she smiled gratefully. 'And do you think you could drop this letter into the school, it would save me a lot of time today,' she replied, delving into her pocket for the envelope and handing it to him.

'Certainly madam. Any more orders whilst I'm out and about?' he asked with a grin.

'I'll try and think of some,' she teased. Silence filled the barn as they resumed their work and before long, the slightly astringent smell of tannin and the rhythmic weaving began to soothe her. She couldn't help thinking about the school though.

'It's not just about the money I earned. I really enjoyed teaching those little girls their letters.' she added, picking up the knife and attacking the bottom spokes that would help trap the fish.

'Here, let me. You'll do yourself a mischief hacking away like that,' Clem said, reaching out and taking the basket from her. 'I can understand why you wouldn't want to work for old Gliddon though,' he said, looking up.

'You can?'

'Of course. I wouldn't want to be employed by someone with one eye higher than the other. Bit shifty, don't you think?'

'Oh Clem, that's a dreadful joke,' she groaned.

'Made you smile, though,' he chuckled, handing the trap back to her.

'I'm sorry for being miserable, Clem,' she sighed. 'I really miss Grammer, and know it's up to me to take over her role but . . .'

'But?'

'I feel as trapped as those poor fish swimming into here will be,' she admitted, holding up the basket.

'Handy for dinner though,' he grinned, then looked sheepish when she shot him a look. 'I do feel sorry for those eels actually. There they are happily swimming up our rivers going about their business, when bang they get caught in the trap with no way out.'

'I know it sounds bad Clem, especially after all Gramfer's going through, but that's exactly how I feel at the moment,' she admitted. He was quiet for a moment, then he laid down his basket.

'Come on Red, you're seventeen yet sound as though your life's over. Here you are on the verge of woman—' Embarrassed, he looked down at his hands. 'Earlier when I was telling you about those Welsh love spoons and their intentions, I was hoping you might see what I was getting at, but obviously I'm not very good at explaining myself.' He took a deep breath and turned to face her, his expression unusually serious.

Fearing what he was about to say, and wanting to keep their relationship as free and easy as it had always been, Eliza opened her mouth to reply. However, Clem continued.

'What with it being your birthday and us good friends, well better than that I was thinking. You must know how fond I am of you, and I was hoping you felt the same.'

'Of course, I do,' she cried, for he really was her best friend and, as he helped sell the extra vegetables she grew, her business partner too. Seeing hope flare in his eyes, she knew she had to stop him from saying anything further. 'You're the brother I never had, Willow Man,' she replied, using her pet name for him. There was silence for a moment then he got to his feet.

'That's something I suppose,' he sighed. 'Enjoy the rest of your birthday, Red.'

'But I thought you were staying for supper,' she called, as he made for the door.

'If you want your letter and supplies delivered today, I'd better get going. Tell George I'll have that talk with him next year. It'd probably a bit insensitive now anyhow.'

'What talk?' she asked but he was already outside hefting the sack over his shoulder. Picking up his unfinished trap, she continued weaving, her thoughts running amok. While she had great affection for him, she couldn't even think of furthering their relationship at this time.

'Somethin' smells good,' George said sniffing the air appreciatively as he shuffled wearily into their tiny living room. Throwing his battered felt cap down onto the settle, he noticed the table set for two and frowned. 'No Clem?' he asked.

Eliza looked up from the pan where she was frying the eel Old Conger had skinned and presented to her as a birthday gift. Luckily, she'd just managed to finish both traps before he'd arrived.

'He was delivering my letter and vegetables to Stoke for me,' she replied tipping the sizzling food onto two plates. George frowned again, sinking into his chair and barely giving his supper a glance. He waited whilst Eliza poured tea from the pot then stared at her questioningly.

'Been bossing him about again have you?' he asked, hazel eyes sharp as they bored into hers.

'Not at all, although he was acting strangely today. Kept going on about us being friends when we've known each other since school. Oh, and he said something about having his talk with you next year, whatever that means. Seeing her Gramfer's frown deepen, she changed the subject. 'We might not be able to afford to have the traditional goose for Michaelmas Day but this eel's really tasty with the taiters fried alongside, don't you think?'

To her relief, he nodded and began tucking into his meal. He was looking pensive though, and Eliza had a feeling the subject wasn't over. Sure enough, as soon as he'd finished eating, he pushed his plate to one side.

'That were grand, Eliza.' He sat back in his chair and began stroking his beard, a sure sign something was troubling him. 'Hard to believe you're seventeen, young lady. Did I tell you that your grammer were the same age when we wed? Right bonny she was, flaxen hair curlin' round her head like a halo, lips red as the ripest cherries. Didn't stand a chance when she looked in my direction, I can tell you. We had a good marriage,' he sighed and stared into the fire. Then pulling himself back to the present, he leaned forward and patted Eliza's hand. 'Want the same for you now. And young Clem—'

'Is a friend,' she butted in. 'A good friend, but that's it,' she added firmly.

'And that's a very good foundation on which to base a marriage. It's not all hearts and flowers, you know.'

'Look Gramfer, I'm not ready to begin thinking about marriage. 'It's bad enough I've had to give up the job I loved.'

'Oh yes, sorry, I forgot,' he mumbled, his brow puckering.

'I'm happy taking over the basket business but one day, I want to go out and meet new people like Mammer did.'

'Pastures new aren't always greater or greener. Sometimes they're full of prickles and creeps, folk who take advantage as Della found out, to all our costs,' he sighed.

'Yet you let her go and find out for herself,' she persisted.

'Couldn't stop her. Wilful as an unbroken filly she was.'

'I know you and Grammer have lived here all your lives but—'

'Now that's where you're wrong, young lady,' he exclaimed, cutting her short. 'We haven't always lived in a dank cott like this.' He grimaced and waved his hand around the shadowy, smoke filled room. 'Moved here from Bridgwater when Della got herself . . . well we moved away from the nosebags to spare her reputation. Cors we didn't know there'd be . . . complications,' he shook his head and sighed again.

Assuming he was referring to her mother dying in child-birth, Eliza nodded and remained quiet.

'Started out by rentin' a few withy beds,' he went on a few

moments later. 'And through sheer hard work, managed to buy and increase them year on year. Now our plot extends as far as you can see. Mary, bless her, supported my venture by learnin' the basket-making from old Harry in Worth.'

'I never realised,' she murmured, taken aback by his revelation. She'd never dreamt they'd lived anywhere other than on Sedge Moor.

'There's a lot you don't realise, my girl. Now my Mary's been taken, tis up to me to see you settled before I'm called to join her. When Clem said he wanted to talk about your future, I were that pleased I intended giftin' you my withy beds. Thought it'd give you a good start so you won't have to scrimp and save like we had to. He's a good fellow, one of the best. Works hard making all them deliveries along the Parrett on his father's barge then navigatin' the narrow rhynes on his trow. Which he bought through his own efforts. He'll make a fine husband, girl, mark my words.'

'Some day, maybe,' she agreed, to appease him. 'But just now isn't the time to think about it.'

'Well, don't dally too long, Eliza. I hear young Bethan's set her bonnet at him and her brother's encouraging her. They've only been in Stathe a few months and she's not wastin' any time.'

'Well, not having a brother, I shall have to make my own choice, won't I?' Eliza retorted. Her gramfer winced, clutching at his chest so that she wished she hadn't spoken so brusquely. 'I'm sorry,' she murmured, patting his shoulder. He smiled at her sadly through rheumy eyes.

'Just think on, Eliza. Clem passes by their cottage most days. Happen he'll not wait around for a hurdy 'ead like you to make up her mind.' Eliza grimaced at the reference to her wild red tresses. Although her grammer had insisted they were one of her best assets, she considered them the bane of her life. 'Still, I've no right to expect you to stay here. I'm quite capable of lookin' out for myself,' he declared stoutly.

'Oh Gramfer, there's no need, I'm not going anywhere anytime soon,' she assured him. Even as she uttered the words her heart was sinking lower than the uppers of her well-worn boots as she saw her dream disappearing. But he'd looked after her since she was born and it was obvious that the loss of his beloved wife, along with years of being out in all weathers, were taking their toll. Not that he'd ever admit it. However, she loved him dearly and it was now her turn to care for him. Summoning a smile she patted his hand, and eyes suspiciously moist, he turned away.

'Fire's smokier than ever this night,' he grunted.

Giving him time to collect himself, Eliza pondered on her future. Perhaps when her gramfer had had time to adjust, and the outstanding order from Longstones was fulfilled, she could go and see the school mistress, ask if she'd consider re-engaging her for a few hours a week. Their humble home wouldn't take long to clean, apart from those cursed cobwebs, she thought watching them swaying like filmy ribbons of lace in the draught from the chimney.

'Nearly forgot,' Gramfer said, smiling as she refilled his mug and sat back down beside him. 'Mrs Finch's darter's expecting and she'd like you to make one of them virtue rattles for her future grandchild. Over the moon she is. Must be nice to have something to look forward to,' he smiled, his features softening. Eliza smothered a sigh, all too aware of where his thoughts were taking him.

'Well that is good news,' she agreed.

'And everyone's rallying round to help. Parsonage Farm have placed an order for ten sparrow traps,' he added. 'Not only that, Longstones are fed up with them shoddy laundry baskets Old Gliddon supplies and have transferred all of their orders to us. They've customers all over the county so that should put welcome coppers in the coffers. I only hope we've enough withies to keep us going until we harvest the new ones in December. Perhaps we could start early. I'll check the leaves come mornin'.'

'In that case we are both going to have a lot to do so we'd best have an early night. Good night Gramfer, try and get some sleep,' she said quickly as she bent and kissed his whiskery cheek.

'Night Eliza. Clem's a fine man and thinks the world of you. But he won't wait for ever.'

Up in her room, breath spiralling in puffs before her, Eliza quickly changed into her calico nightgown. Too cold and dispirited to give her hair more than a cursory brush, she dived beneath the covers of the iron bedstead, pulling the patchwork cover right over her head. Her dream of resuming her position at the school had disappeared almost as soon as the idea had occurred, for now it seemed she was going to be busier than ever. Closing her eyes tightly to stop the tears escaping, she hardly heard the birds scrabbling in the old thatch above her or the mice scratching in the walls.

'Oh Grammer, why did you have to die?' she sobbed.

Chapter 3

Next morning with the sun promising to break through the mist, Eliza determined to give their living room a thorough clean. She smiled, recalling her grammer's fierce pride in keeping the place spick and span. *Tidy house, tidy mind*, had been her mantra.

Brushing the cobwebs from the beams, she thought back over the previous night's discussion. It had been a shock to discover her grandparents hadn't always lived here and she wondered what their lives had been like in Bridgwater. If her gramfer didn't look too downcast when he came in for his midday meal, she would ask about it. Talking about the past might be good for him, she thought, dragging the rush mat outside and throwing it over a bush.

Snatching up the beater she gave a fierce thwack sending dust and ash rising into the air, coating the golden leaves grey. A sudden gust of wind shook the branches, dislodging the mat. Eliza cursed as a cloud of the smitch blew back into her face and clung to her curls. No wonder her grammer always covered her head with a mob cap, she thought giving another whack.

'Hey, watch what you're doing,' a voice shouted.

'Sorry Clem,' she called, grinning as he coughed and thumped his chest. 'That'll teach you to sneak up on me.' He snorted then turned to face her, his expression changing to one of mirth.

'You're blacker than a beast from the bogs,' he hooted.

'And you don't look so good yourself,' she giggled, pointing to the dirt clinging to his clothes. 'What are you doing back so soon?'

'George sent a message for me to fill your stack. Reckons weather's on the turn,' he replied, unloading turves of peat from his trow that was lying perilously low in the water. Eliza stared up at the sky, cobalt blue now that the mist had lifted.

'That's odd. It looks to me like this good weather's set to last,' she replied.

'He doesn't usually get things wrong,' Clem muttered pushing his cloth cap to the back of his head. 'By the way, here's the money for the carrots and potatoes,' he said, diving into his pocket and handing over a few coins.

'You haven't taken your cut,' Eliza reminded him. 'We are meant to be business partners after all.'

'Mrs Gill's sent an order for onions and turnips, and Ma's short of some too, so if I can take her a few, that'll square things.'

'Deal. You can dig them up while I fill the sacks. Then I really must get on with making those baskets. I don't think Gramfer realises how difficult it will be for me to fit everything in, for he's accepted yet more orders.'

'We'd best get on then,' Clem replied, following her round to the higher ground at the back of the cott where the vegetable plot stretched halfway across their field to the orchard. Clem looked thoughtful as he took up the fork and began lifting the vegetables. Eliza was loading the pungent onions into the hessian sacking, when he turned to her.

'This ground is very fertile and your vegetables are in demand. I know you're busy but have you thought of extending the plot for next year? It would give you more income.' And more work, Eliza thought, though there was no denying the extra money would be useful.

'Seeing as it's your bright idea, you can help me dig it over next month. After you've helped me pick the apples,' she grinned, nodding towards the laden trees beyond.

'You're a slave driver, Red, do you know that?'

'Bit of hard work never hurt anyone, and think of all those scrumptious pies and crumbles,' she quipped, knowing his fondness for puddings.

'You win, as always,' he sighed. 'Now, before you find me another job, tidy up here while I unload the rest of the peat,' Clem said, putting down the fork, and throwing the full sack of vegetables over his shoulders.

'Suppose you want a drink now?' Eliza asked, when he'd finished restocking their peat stack. He looked up at the sun that was nearly overhead then shook his head.

'Best not, I've more deliveries to make for Father,' he sighed, climbing into his trow. 'I'll make sure I have time to stop next time and we can finish that conversation we began in the barn.' Giving her a meaningful look, he picked up the oars.

She watched as he pulled away from the bank then bent and rinsed her grubby hands in the water. Clem and his talks, she thought, shaking her head then grimacing at the dust that fell onto her shoulders. There was no time for hair washing, she needed to make a start on that rattle for Mrs Finch's grandchild. Bending down, she searched around until she found seven smooth pebbles, then made her way to the barn.

As ever, the tang of tannin in the air focused her thoughts. Selecting seven suitable withies, she dropped down onto her stool and began weaving the rods in and out to create the conical body. Carefully she inserted each pebble as she went; one for pride, another for envy, wrath, sloth, greed, gluttony and lust. Not that the little mite would have a clue what they signified, but superstition was rife around Sedge Moor and tradition adhered to. Taking up the rest of the lengths, she plaited the seven canes so that they wrapped the seven virtues. *Faith, hope, charity, fortitude, justice, prudence and temperance*, she intoned as she wove.

'How lovely to see a maiden reciting her virtues, and a beautiful one with tresses soft as silk.' Eliza's head snapped up, her eyes widening as she took in the tall young man silhouetted in the open doorway. With the sun burnishing his locks golden, she couldn't help thinking how handsome he looked.

'Oh, you startled me,' she cried, jumping to her feet and brushing bits of bark from her skirt.

'Then please accept my apologies. My horse cast a shoe some way back and whilst waiting for the farrier to attend him, I began exploring. Somehow, I found myself inexplicably drawn to all those funny trees standing alongside the water,' he explained, gesturing towards the rhynes. 'I mean, I know they're willows but I've never seen them shaped in such a way.' His voice was cultured and he spoke in a quick tone, quite unlike the local drawl.

'They are pollarded in order to encourage new shoots to grow straight upwards.'

'Gracious, I can see my education is sadly lacking,' the man replied. She stared at him, wondering if he was making fun of her, but although his green eyes were twinkling, his expression was serious. He was immaculately dressed in clothes so well cut, she couldn't begin to imagine how much they cost. Their eyes locked and she felt a tingling down her spine. She could see by the way he stared that he'd felt something too, but before she could think of what to say to dispel the intensity of the moment, his glance lowered to the withies in her hand.

'I'm making a rattle for a baby,' she explained.

'Oh,' he replied, a frown creasing his forehead.

'Hence the virtues.'

'Ah yes. Well, thank you again for the arboreal lesson, er . . . I didn't catch your name?'

'Eliza, sir, Eliza Priddle.'

'A pretty name for a pretty young lady,' he said, smiling so charmingly Eliza felt sparks closing the gap between them. 'As soon as I arrive home, I will make it my business to enquire of our estate manager about pollarding. Now, please excuse me, I must away and collect my steed. He is apt to become more than a little spirited if kept waiting. Good day to you.'

'Good day to you, sir. Do feel free to call by again,' she added impulsively. Heavens, had she really said that? Whatever must he think of her? Yet even as she flinched at her forwardness, he turned.

'Should I find myself around these parts again, I might just do that,' he replied, his eyes locking with hers once more.

'Oh, please do,' she whispered, hugging her body and suddenly feeling more alive than she ever had before.

Humming happily, Eliza picked up the baby's rattle, her thoughts racing as fast as her fingers plaited. What a charming man. And so beautifully dressed. She grimaced down at her old skirt, criss-crossed with snags where the withies had pulled at the threads. How she wished she'd been wearing something smarter and brighter. Even the new dress Grammer had made for her was a sober dove grey, befitting the position of a school helper. If those smart garments were what he wore for riding then she could only imagine how he dressed when formally attired. Where had he come from, she wondered. It was only then she realized that, overawed by his appearance, she hadn't thought to ask his name. Still, he'd said he might call by again, hadn't he? And he knew where to find her.

Staring down at the rattle, her eyes widened in surprise. She'd been so busy musing, she'd finished it without her movements registering. Impulsively, she began singing, shaking it in time to her tune.

Then, once again, Eliza found her light blocked by a figure in the doorway. Her heart flipped only to flop when she saw it was her gramfer.

'Someone sounds happy,' he murmured.

'Oh Gramfer, it's you,' she sighed.

'And who was you expectin', the queen?' he grinned. 'Haven't seen you this chirpy for ages. Why, your cheeks are as rosy as the apples in the orchard.'

'Sorry Gramfer,' Eliza murmured, guilty at being caught singing so soon after her grammer's passing.

'Well don't be. Mary wouldn't want either of us moping about the place. Life won't be the same without her but we has to carry on. I see Clem's delivered them turves. Inside, is he?' Seeing his hopeful look, Eliza shook her head.

'He said he had a lot to do. I don't think he was expecting to be making a delivery here, especially peat on such a sunny day.'

'Ah, well you know how quickly the weather can change this time of year.' He turned away but not before she saw the flush creeping up his neck. So, her suspicions were correct, he had got Clem here under false pretences. 'See you've finished that rattle so I'll drop it into Mrs Finch. Hopefully she'll have been doin' some baking,' he said, changing the subject. 'I need to check how the beds on the northern boundary are comin' along, anyhow.'

'Well you're the expert on all things arboreal,' she told him, the pebbles jangling tunefully as she handed over the baby's toy.

'Yer what? Heavens girl, I don't know where you gets fancy words like that from, I really don't,' he said, shaking his head. She was about to reply but as he shuffled back outside, she saw he was leaning heavily on his stick again and held her tongue.

Knowing he'd be gone for the rest of the day, Eliza decided to wash out the flour sack. She would make a start on her new top, just in case a certain stranger called by again, she thought, her heart flipping at the thought.

Hurrying indoors, she blinked as the peat smoke stung her eyes, then made her way up the steps and through to the tiny lean-to which her grammer had proudly referred to as the scullery. In reality it was little more than a glory hole that housed their dishes and mugs and a chipped sink with the wonkiest draining board alongside. Behind it was a store, grandly called the pantry, where their meagre provisions were set up on bricks to deter the marauding rats and other vermin that shared their damp environs.

Catching sight of her reflection in the old spotted mirror on the wall, she gasped. Her cheeks were smudged with smitch, while ashes and grass still clung to her windswept hair. To think the most attractive man she'd ever met had seen her looking like this. Clearly, it wasn't only the flour sack that needed washing, she thought, lifting the old tin bath from its nails on the wall and dragging it in front of the smouldering fire. Snatching up the jug, she hurried outside to the barrel. It took quite a few journeys before she had sufficient rain water for it to be deep enough. Although it looked brown and uninviting, at least it would be soft.

It felt indulgent bathing in the middle of the day but needs must, she thought, climbing into the tub and laying back in the water. She'd bet her new flour sack that the handsome man never had to bathe in a smoky living room. Goodness, wherever did that notion spring from, she wondered, feeling the heat creep up her cheeks. His appearance had certainly stirred her emotions. Quickly she dunked her head but the cold water did nothing to deter the wild thoughts that were pounding her brain.

Chapter 4

Eliza finished bathing, threw on some clean clothes, then washed out the flour sack. Leaving her hair to dry in the warm air, she went back outside. The sun, lower in the sky but still casting its golden rays, felt pleasant on her bare arms. Spreading the sack out on a bush, she secured the ends so they wouldn't be blown into the waters that were thick with green weed and scum. The leaves on the withies were turning, but it would still be a few weeks before they fell, signalling the tall green wands were ready for cutting. Getting the timing right was vital, she knew that.

Whilst waiting for the sack to dry, she began searching for material to make a suitable dye. Bark from the willow would result in a peachy brown colour but that would be too dull for her newly lifted spirits. Further along the drove, the carpet of dandelions were a riot of colour, but bright yellow would be too summery now winter was approaching. A heron rose from the bushes and disappeared into the tall trees beyond. How lovely to be free to fly or ride on horseback across the fields and up to the moors beyond. Chiding herself for such fanciful thoughts, she turned her attention back to her task.

Crab apples dotted the nearby trees like rosy buds. Their skins boiled up with red leaves and rosehips would make crimson but that would clash with her hair. Spotting a clump of nettles by the bushes, she smiled. Mixed with sorrel and tansy they would make a vibrant green which would complement her skirt. Hadn't Grammer taught her that dressing in the same shades would lengthen her figure, making her look taller? The woman had certainly known about the art of dressing, and despite having had to make do with clothes reworked from old materials, exuded a gentle elegance. Why hadn't Eliza thought to ask what she'd done before she'd married Gramfer? That was another question for him.

Hurrying back to the barn, she ignored the withies waiting to be woven into sparrow traps, and pulled on her grammer's old thick gloves. Immediately, warmth flooded through her and she knew the woman approved. For hadn't she explained the importance of harvesting the earth's wild abundance, showing Eliza how to use it for food, medicine and the dyeing of material? Snatching up her basket, she retraced her steps and as she began gathering the plants it felt as if her beloved Grammer was standing right beside her.

Later that afternoon, as the plants bubbled with the sack in the big pot swinging from the crook over the fire, so did her excitement. What shape top should she make? It would be the first one she'd sewn by herself. Suppose she made a mess of it? However, the image of twinkling green eyes and that devastating smile rose before her instantly quashing any doubt she might have. She needed to look good and look good she would, she thought heading to the pantry for their bag of salt to fix the colour. If she was careful with the amount she used for cooking, she could make their supply last until after the harvest, when hopefully good sales would mean they'd have money to purchase more.

'Eh girl, that stew don't taste very appetisin',' her gramfer groaned when she returned. He was standing by the fire grimacing at the wooden spoon in his hand. 'It don't look too good either.'

'Oh, Gramfer that's the dye I've made for my top, not stew,' Eliza cried, laughing at his look of disgust.

'Thanks be,' he replied, sinking into his chair and fumbling with his laces.

'I know my cooking's not as good as Grammer's yet, but I am trying. Though I've been that busy I haven't given a thought to what we'll eat this night,' she admitted, ignoring his protests as she bent to help him.

'Ah well, happens Mrs Finch sent back a nice leek and taiter pie,' he grinned, gesturing to the table. 'It weren't quite baked when I got there so she packed me and Fred off to the cider house to sample their new batch. Would have been rude to refuse.'

'That explains your rosy cheeks and the liquor fumes,' she laughed, wrinkling her nose. She knew it was good for him to spend an hour in the company of other men but couldn't resist getting her own back for his earlier comments. Although she was still finding her way without Grammer's supervision, her cooking wasn't that bad.

'I'll just take the pot through to the scullery and peg up the sack to dry. When I come back you can tell me all the tattle.'

'I'll have you know we men don't tattle, we discuss business,' he protested, leaning back and closing his eyes. However, by the time she returned, he was awake and studying her carved spoon.

'This is a fine bit of shaping. Must have taken ages to get it smooth and glossy like that,' he marvelled.

'Clem made it for my birthday,' she admitted. 'It's a jam spoon.'

'Well, he wouldn't have spent all that time on it if he didn't care for you.'

'And you know I care for him,' Eliza replied, steeling herself for another lecture, but to her surprise, he struggled unsteadily to his feet.

'Heavens girl, we got so involved with our chin waggle last night, I clean forgot to give you my gift,' he cried, delving into the dresser. Eliza waited, hoping he wasn't going to mention the withy beds again. 'It's just a little somethin' I bought your grammer when we was courtin',' he said, handing her a parcel wrapped in a cloth.

'Why it's beautiful,' Eliza gasped, gazing down at the amber comb. It was studded with tiny green stones that twinkled in the fading light. 'It must have cost a bit too,'

'Yea, well Mary were worth it. She always wore it afore . . .' his voice trailed away but then he swallowed and gave a weak smile. 'It'll look a treat in that red hair of yours. Always supposin' you want to wear it, of course,' he said, suddenly looking uncertain.

'Of course, I do,' she cried, throwing her arms around him. 'I'll love having something of Grammer's and it'll look perfect with the new green top I'm going to make. Thank you Gramfer, I'll treasure it always,' she told him, reaching up and fixing it on top of her head so that her curls swung high above her shoulders. Looking pleased, he sank back into his chair and closed his eyes.

'I do miss her,' he mumbled.

'I do too,' Eliza told him, but he was lost in his own thoughts and didn't answer.

Next morning, as the first streaks of pink were tinging the sky, her gramfer donned his coat and cap and took off for his daily inspection of the withy beds.

'I know you're keen to make that new top, Eliza, but I promised Parsonage Farm they'd have those sparrow traps as soon as we could make them. You know what a pest those birds can be.' Although he looked apologetic, Eliza's heart dropped. She'd hardly had any time to herself these past weeks.

'I'll just cut the sack to shape while the light's shining into the cott and then make a start on the traps.'

'You're a good girl,' he said, patting her shoulder before picking up his stick. 'If I've time later I'll give you a hand.' She smiled wryly, knowing that despite his best intentions he'd spend all day tending his precious crop.

After clearing away their breakfast dishes she spread the now leaf green sacking out on the table. It was the first time she'd tackled anything like this without her grammer's guidance and she felt nervous yet excited. Using her old top as a guide, she marked out the shape in chalk, before taking up the scissors and carefully following the outline. If there was enough material, she intended adding a collar. It would be her first grown up blouse. By the time she'd cut the front, back and two sleeves the sun was high in the sky. Although she was impatient to start sewing the pieces together, knowing Gramfer was relying on her to fulfil their orders, she resisted the temptation. Reluctantly, she pushed the remaining piece to one side ready to shape the collar later. Then snatching up her shawl, she went outside.

Despite the bright day, a stiff breeze tugged at her hair and shook the branches of the withies making the leaves rustle. The air was heavy with the smell of pommy, the remains of the brown apple pulp and straw discarded after cider-making which had been spread on the fields for the cattle.

Entering the barn, she shivered. It was time her gramfer put up the wriggly tin sheet that served as a door, or her hands would be too cold to work the willow. She'd been meaning to make herself some fittens, her own version of mittens without fingers, to replace the ones that had been shredded by the constant snagging on the bark, but had been too busy. Still, she intended finishing her sewing first, for she was eager to have a new blouse to wear in case any visitor should come calling.

Gathering everything she needed for the first trap, she

squatted on the mat, took up her board and began weaving. Having made many cages like this before, she worked automatically, her mind wandering. Would the handsome man come back today, she wondered, her heart flipping at the thought? Although she was dying to see him, it would be nice if she were wearing her new green top, her hair caught up in the amber comb with its emerald stones. Fancy Grammer having something as grand as that? She was beginning to think she hadn't known her at all.

Eliza worked until late afternoon, when the sun disappeared and her hands grew too cold to continue. She'd managed to complete three of the traps and only had another seven to go. Just as she'd suspected her gramfer hadn't appeared. But then, neither had the stranger. She sighed, her heart heavy with disappointment.

Taking herself indoors, she lit the candle from the fire but as she placed it on the table, she frowned. The material she'd left spread out for the collar was not only screwed into a ball, it was smeared with grease. And worse, the rest of the sacking she'd so carefully cut out, had completely disappeared.

'Ee, it's gettin' cold out there,' George said, hobbling into the room where Eliza was still staring at the table in disbelief. 'What's up girl?' he asked, seeing her expression.

'My new blouse, the pieces I cut out this morning are missing,' she wailed.

He gave a chuckle. 'Is that all? I thought the world had ended the way you was lookin'. I moved them over there earlier when I got out the withy hook,' he told her gesturing to the dresser. 'Needed sharpenin' see, and you know how I likes to be prepared for harvest.'

Eliza hurried across the room and, picking up the pieces, turned to him. 'What about . . .' she began but he was continuing his tale.

'That odd scrap you had left over came in useful for greasin' the blade, so now I'm all set. Cors I was careful to move your sewin' so it didn't get messed up,' he grinned, looking so pleased with himself Eliza hadn't the heart to tell him that the left over piece had been intended for a collar. Now she'd have to make another top with a round neck. After supper she'd pin the pieces together, take her sewing things upstairs and work by candlelight. That way there could be no more mistakes.

'How's them traps comin' along?' her gramfer asked as they tucked into the remains of Mrs Finch's pie.

'I've completed three,' she told him, pleased with her progress.

'That all?' he frowned. 'Only I forgot to say that when I saw Ned in the cider house yesterday, he was askin' about them. Said the birds were being right pests. I promised him . . .' his voice trailed away and looking uncomfortable, he stared down at his plate. The ensuing silence was interrupted by a gust blowing down the chimney, making the fire splutter and hiss and sending another cloud of acrid smoke billowing around the room.

'Must brush out that chimney,' George wheezed, when it had settled.

'What exactly did you promise Ned?' Eliza urged.

'That you'd have them ready for young Clem to collect tomorrow afternoon.' Eliza let out an exasperated sigh but he carried on. 'You know how quick you work when you set your mind to it and there's them laundry baskets to make as well. We're already into October and there'll be the rent to find for Christmas quarter day. We can't afford to risk losin' our home, now can we?'

Eliza stared around the dingy room with its tatty bits of mismatched furniture and the stained walls that would run with damp when the rains came, and wondered why not. Surely anywhere else would be better than this?

'If we had to move from here, it'd mean givin' up my beds and you'd have no withies for basket-making. How'd we live then?' he challenged, as if reading her mind. 'Of course, weather permittin', we'll have some to sell come Christmas, but without your grammer the harvest will take longer to sort . . .' His voice trailed away and he stared pleadingly at her.

'It's alright Gramfer,' she interrupted gently as she got to her feet. 'I'll get on with the traps at first light. Now I'll bid you goodnight. I'm going upstairs to make a start on my sewing,' she said, picking up her candlestick and material.

'You're a good girl,' he murmured. With a weak smile he turned to stare into the fire, losing himself in thoughts of the past.

It was only when she was sitting on her bed, pieces in hand, that she realized that having been caught up in her discussion, she hadn't even got around to pinning them together. But with the moon sporadically obscured by scudding clouds and the light from her dwindling candle dimming by the minute, she knew it would be futile attempting the job now. Placing them down on the chest, she vowed to get up extra early and make a start before working on those wretched cages.

Sighing, she got up and stared out of the window. Beyond the night shrouded withy bed, flat fields spread far and wide, each separated by a straight rhyne. Her thoughts turned to the handsome stranger. What was his name? Where had he come from? More importantly, would she see him again? Just then the moon slid from under its canopy of cloud, turning everywhere a silver wonderland. Her spirits rose. Maybe he would call again tomorrow.

Chapter 5

As fingers of light filtered through the window Eliza slipped out of bed and without even dressing, took up the pieces of sacking ready to pin. It was then she saw the smears darkening the neckline. She groaned then saw there were dirty marks down the sides as well. Clearly her gramfer had moved the material after getting his hands covered in the filthy grease. Realising the stains would never wash out, she threw on her clothes determined to tackle him. However, making her way down the stairs, she heard the rasping sound of his coughing, saw his body hunched as he gripped the side of the table. Immediately her mood changed to one of concern.

'Stop starin', girl,' he wheezed, struggling upright. ''Tis only a bit of damp on the lungs. You know full well it's the risk a withy worker takes. Make sure you gets on with those cages.' Knowing pride was making him brusque, Eliza nodded. Heavy hearted, she watched as he shrugged on his heavy coat then rammed the misshapen cap on his head. 'See you later,' he added, snatching up his stick and hobbling from the room. If he was like this now whatever would he be like when the rains came?

Throwing her shawl around her shoulders, she went outside where a stiff breeze was rustling the leaves on the willows. Stooping to pick the last of the marigolds, she made her way to the old oak.

'Oh Grammer, he's lost without you,' she murmured, kneeling beside her grave. 'And I miss you so much.' Talking to the woman helped get things into perspective and suddenly the grease marks didn't seem that important.

Cover them over with ribbon dear, and add a button or two if necessary. As the solution popped into her head, Eliza stared at the grave and smiled.

'Thank you, Grammer,' she whispered. 'I always could rely on you.'

Eliza was placing the flowers in the little jug set between the two graves, when something made her look up. She thought she glimpsed a flash of gold in the distance. Her heart flipped but by the time she'd got to her feet, it had disappeared. Knowing it must have been a trick of the light didn't stop disappointment flooding through her. Once again, she hoped she hadn't been too forward inviting the stranger to call again. She wasn't usually so impetuous, it had just slipped out.

Just then she heard the swishing sound of oars on the water. Her heart flipped again, but it was only Clem paddling his trow towards her. Bending low, he flicked water at her.

'Beast,' she squealed. 'What brings you here this morning?'

'Marnen, Red,' he called, giving his wide grin as he jumped out and tied up. 'Ma baked new bread and thought you might like some,' he said, passing her a warm loaf wrapped in muslin. 'And before you protest, she sends her respects and wonders if you could make a new basket for her grocery shopping. When you have the time that is.' Breathing in the yeasty aroma, Eliza nodded.

'This smells wonderful. Please thank her and tell her I'll make a start on one as soon as I've finished all those orders Gramfer has secured.'

He followed her into the barn, staring down at the three finished cages and pile of withies lying ready on the floor. 'Still working on the sparrow traps,' she grimaced.

'Obviously not your favourite job judging by the look on your face,' he grinned.

'I'd rather be sewing my new top,' she admitted. 'Although I could kill Gramfer. He used the bits I'd set aside for a collar for greasing his withy hook.' Seeing Clem trying not to laugh, she carried on indignantly. 'Not only that, he got it smeared over the other pieces as well.'

'Wouldn't have liked to be in his boots when you found out.'

'I was going to tackle him, but he was having such a bad coughing fit, I didn't like to mention it. He was fretting about these cages last night though and I've still got seven more to make, so I'd best get on.' Then she frowned. 'I thought Gramfer said you were calling for them this afternoon.'

'Guilty as charged,' he admitted, holding his hands up in mock surrender. 'When Ma said she had a loaf for you I offered to deliver it while it was still fresh. Thought we might share it while we finish that chat.'

'Well as you can see, I'm up to my eyes, Clem Galton,' she sighed, staring at the waiting willow.

'I could always help,' he offered, following her look. 'And before you ask, yes I do know how to make a sparrow trap.'

'Then I accept,' she smiled, squatting down on the old matting and drawing the lapboard between her legs. He watched as she started setting the uprights around the base that was weighted by her iron.

'Why don't you sit on the stool?' he asked. 'You'll be more comfortable.'

'It's quicker this way,' she told him. 'You can use one if you prefer.' He shook his head and, snatching up a bundle of withies, hunkered down beside her. Despite his protestation, she saw he was carefully following her every movement. However, grateful for his help she didn't let on she'd noticed.

They worked companionably for a while, and although from time to time the wind gusted through, scattering the shavings across the earthen floor, the familiar astringent smell and rhythmic sound of willow weaving in and out was both reviving and soothing.

'Don't you have any deliveries to make today?' she asked, knowing he was usually busy.

'Started early so I could call on my old pal.' She looked up to find clear blue eyes studying her and realised with a jolt that he was quite good looking in a dark, brooding sort of way. Nothing like the golden god who'd set her pulses racing, but Clem was a close friend and she was grateful for his help.

'Not so much of the old,' she quipped, then frowned. 'As long as you understand the way things are, Willow Man. There's so much I want to see and do before I can even think of anything else.'

'Aye Red, you've made your feelings very clear on that. It helps to have a friend meanwhile though, does it?' he asked, quirking his brow.

'Yes, it does, and I really do appreciate your help,' she told him.

'That's good. You know I can't believe any bird would be stupid enough to fly into here,' he said, holding up his finished cage and studying it.

'They'll be tempted by the food placed inside. Talking of which, I'll nip indoors and get us a hot drink to go with that fresh loaf. Gramfer brought fresh butter back from the farm the other day too.'

'Ah, so the lady is trying to tempt me now,' he quipped.

'Not at all. A good mistress always treats her servants well.'

'Mistress, now there's a thought. Only joking,' he added, holding up his hands in mock surrender as she held up her cage ready to throw at him.

Cheeks flushing, she made her way indoors. Why did Clem have to overstep the mark, she wondered as she hurried through to the pantry. But then he was taking the time to help her so maybe she was being over sensitive.

Determined to make more of an effort, she carried the laden tray into the barn and gave Clem a beaming smile.

'Now there's a sight for sore eyes,' he grinned. Whether he was referring to her happy demeanour or the food, she had no idea. Not having stopped for breakfast, she was starving, and judging by the way Clem tucked in, he was too.

As they sat munching the fresh bread glistening golden with butter, she told him about making the dye for the sack and how her Gramfer had tasted it thinking it was stew. He laughed then began regaling her with tales about customers along his route.

It was late and the sun was already low in the sky by the time they'd completed all the traps and loaded them onto Clem's trow. Turning, he studied the willows alongside before nodding.

'These are coming on well. You should have a healthy harvest if the weather holds.'

'Gramfer's happy with the way things are looking, though goodness knows how he'll manage everything this year.'

'Like he always has, no doubt. I'll help, though of course I'll have to clear with Father that he won't expect me to make too many deliveries during that time. It hardly seems a year since we were last harvesting.'

'Don't,' Eliza groaned, remembering how she'd helped her grammer take refreshments to the men in the fields each noon. After which they'd spent the afternoon cooking vast quantities of supper to satisfy the workers' huge appetites. Surely her gramfer wouldn't expect her to cook for them by herself this year? Beside her Clem was about to climb into his boat, when he hesitated, sending it rocking.

'Careful Clem, or you'll get a dunking you weren't expecting,' she laughed, putting out her hand to steady him.

'I was thinking, Red.'

'And painful it looks for you, Willow Man,' she teased. 'Well come on, spit it out.'

'I'm stopping off at Worth on my way back. There's a get together in the hay barn to celebrate the cider making. Just a drink and some music, nothing fancy but it should be fun. How about coming with me?' His words came out in a rush and then he stood looking nervous as he waited for her answer,

'Oh Clem, I couldn't,' she protested.

'Why not? You've worked hard all day and your gramfer won't mind. I'll see you safely home.'

'It's kind of you but I really need to get his supper. Besides, it's too soon after Grammer died to leave him alone in the evenings, or for me to enjoy myself.'

'I suppose so, but she wouldn't want you grieving for too long, Red. Perhaps next time eh?'

'Perhaps,' she replied.

'Next,' Eliza called, throwing a glossy green apple down to Clem.

'Should be in the cricket team,' he shouted back, triumphantly catching it.

It was the end of October and they'd spent the day stripping the trees, alternating between picking and loading the fruit into sacks. They worked carefully knowing any bruising would result in reduced sales, and Mrs Gill had already placed a substantial order. Even Gramfer was helping by individually wrapping those apples for storing over winter. It was a laborious but necessary job and he seemed happy enough.

'Any more?' Clem called. Eliza began peering through the nearly bare branches, then started as she caught a flash of gold in the distance. Her heart flipped. Could it be him, she thought craning her neck in order to see better, but whatever or whoever had gone.

'Careful Red,' Clem shouted. 'Your neck's worth more than the odd apple. Besides, we should leave some for the birds.' Eliza gave one final look then seeing no sign of the stranger, sighed and slithered down the trunk.

'We've got a goodly yield here,' Clem said, gesturing to the sacks beside him. 'And so have you,' he chuckled, reaching out and removing twigs and bits of leaf from her hair. 'Ma's sent a flask of her ginger beer and some of her cut round, so why don't we picnic by the water?'

'Wonderful,' she replied. 'I'll get Gramfer.'

'He said he was going for a snooze so we'll save him some for later. Come on.' She watched as he heaved a sack of apples onto his back then followed him towards the trow. Flopping thankfully down on the grass, she waited whilst he retrieved their refreshment.

'Your ma's a treasure,' she said, as he passed her the bottle. 'And she makes the best ginger beer,' she added, gulping down the spicy liquid.

'I'm sure she'd give you the family recipe,' he said, giving her a wink. Yet as they sat side by side eating the soft sponge liberally spread with jam, it was the stranger Eliza thought of. She was certain that golden flash had been him. Her insides were fizzing and it wasn't just from the ginger beer.

Chapter 6

By the time the mists of October gave way to the cold, crisp days of November, Eliza had settled into her new routine. With little left to do in the garden, she had more time for basket-making and worked tirelessly to fulfil the orders. Although proud of her work, she missed the company of the school mistress and the little girls she'd helped to teach. Her restless mood seemed to match the falling of the oval leaves that tumbled in golden showers onto the waters of the rhyne.

It didn't help that despite wearing her new green top, grease marks hidden by emerald ribbon she'd found in Grammer's old work basket, the handsome stranger hadn't come back. Certain that he too had felt the frisson between them, Eliza could only think he'd been put off by her bold behaviour.

Clem meanwhile, had taken to visiting more frequently, often bringing gifts of bread or sometimes a pie for their supper. He'd help with any of the heavy work whilst she prepared a snack for their luncheon.

'This is delicious,' he told her one day as they sat on the matting in the barn munching the sausage plait she'd made.

'Good, with all the practice I've had, I should be getting somewhere,' she replied.

'My, that wind's getting up,' he said, frowning as bark shavings skittered across the floor.

'Yes, usually Gramfer would have set up the door by now to keep out the elements.'

'I can do that,' he said, jumping to his feet and brushing pastry crumbs from his lap. 'Where is it?'

'Over here,' she replied, hurrying to the back of the barn and pushing a pile of stooks out of the way. Between them they carried the sheet of wriggly tin and stood it up next to the opening in the front wall.

'I can manage now,' he told her, manoeuvring it into place. But as he stepped back to check his work, he didn't realise she was standing behind him. 'Oops sorry, Red,' he murmured, quickly turning and reaching out to stop her from falling. As his arms tightened around her, a warm, comforting feeling spread through her body. Smiling weakly, she stepped out of his embrace.

'Oh, by the way I've finished your ma's basket,' Eliza told him as, ignoring his look of disappointment, she quickly retrieved the elaborate article from the shelf. She'd added extra roses and a decorative handle and was pleased with the results.

'Ma will be the talk of the town when she goes to market,' he said, recovering his composure and parading up and down with it swinging over his arm.

'It's the least I can do. She's been so good to us since

Grammer . . .' she stopped, still finding it difficult to say the word 'died'. 'You both have,' she admitted.

'Ma thinks of you as family and hopes, well you know . . .' This time it was his turn to let his sentence hang in the air.

'Don't you ever yearn to see more of the world, experience different things before settling down?' Eliza asked.

'Believe you me I sees lots that goes on around these parts,' Clem chuckled.

'No, I mean further afield than the Parrett.'

'Oh Red,' he sighed. 'Everything I want . . .' he broke off and shook his head. 'Better check if George needs anything before I leave,' he mumbled.

Eliza watched him go knowing he'd always be content to carry on in the same way. They'd known each other seemingly for ever but there wasn't that spark she'd felt the day the golden-haired man arrived at the doorway of the barn. But then he hadn't seen fit to return had he?

With the daylight hours decreasing, Eliza found herself spending more time in the cott. She patched the tears in Gramfer's trousers, for he was always catching them on the branches, and knitted fittens for Clem.

Gramfer was working from dawn 'til dusk preparing the withy beds for harvest, constantly checking the weather. A frost or heavy rains at this stage could signal ruin for him.

'Got to save my strength,' he'd say, taking himself off to bed as soon as they'd finished supper, leaving her alone with only her knitting and thoughts for company.

Then one early December afternoon as dusk was falling, he came indoors, hazel eyes gleaming and grinning widely.

'Well girl, they're ready,' he announced excitedly. 'We begin harvestin' tomorrow.'

'We, Gramfer?' she asked, looking up from the broth she was stirring. Surely, he wasn't expecting her to go out to the fields and cut the pliant osiers as well as making baskets for the laundry?

'Yes, we my girl. Can't do all them beds by myself, now can I? Clem will be here at first light and Ned and young Bobbie will come up from the farm as soon as they've finished the milkin'. The women have agreed to see to the cows in the afternoons so there'll be four of us hungry men for supper each night. We all have to pull together this time of year. Mary always put on a good spread as well as bringin' our nuncheon out to the fields. Said it was the least she could do to repay them for their help.' He stared at her expectantly.

'What about the baskets?' she asked, thinking of the materials she'd set out ready for the morrow.

'Priorities Eliza. Longstones know they'll be no withies for basket-makin' if we don't harvest and replenish.' It was true, everyone knew bringing in the crop before the weather broke took precedence over everything else. And it wasn't only their livelihood that would suffer if they didn't get a good yield. Gramfer had built up quite a clientele who relied on him providing stocks for their basket-making.

'Continue making as many as you can in between feeding the workers,' he murmured, sinking into his chair and sniffing the air appreciatively. 'My that smells good. Far better than that green muck,' he shuddered.

Knowing he was trying to lighten the mood, she grinned. 'You'd all better work hard tomorrow then, for I can easily make more dye.'

Remembering how her grammer would never let Gramfer begin harvesting without a good breakfast inside him, Eliza was up before first light making porridge.

'We'll be startin' down by the cut. Clem's meetin' me there. Yer'll bring our noon pieces?' he asked, spoon poised midway to his mouth.

'Of course,' she agreed. 'Now, I've to get on with making stew for supper, so I'd be pleased if you'd get out from under my feet,' she added, adopting her grammer's no nonsense voice.

'Ark at 'ee, you gets more like my Mary every day,' he said, darting her a small smile before scraping up the last of his breakfast. Taking two laces from his pocket, he tied up his old cord trousers above the calf before pulling on his stout boots. Then getting to his feet, he pulled on his coat and cap.

'What about your stick?' Eliza asked, pointing to the stout willow in the corner.

'No need. I'll have me trusty hook to hand,' he grinned, snatching up his sickle.

'May you have the greatest of gleanings.' Whispering the time-honoured tiding, she went over and wrapped his muffler firmly around his neck. His eyes were alive with anticipation and she couldn't get over how hale and happy he looked.

Routine chores completed, she took herself out to the barn and began making the base for a new basket. As ever, as she weaved, her thoughts returned to the handsome stranger. Although it had been so long since he'd appeared and logic told her the chances of seeing him again were rapidly diminishing, somewhere deep inside a glimmer of hope still flickered.

However, she was too busy to waste time dreaming. She forced herself to concentrate on finishing the body before deftly attaching two handles and adding her flower twist. Satisfied, she set it aside and took herself indoors to prepare the men's noon pieces.

Just before midday she packed the food, along with bottles of cold tea, into a large basket and set off towards the cut. The weather was cold but bright and she felt her spirits lift. Hopefully, having time away from her work each day would give the callouses on the side of her hand, a hazard of weaving the willow, a chance to recover. When she reached the withies, the men were so busy cutting they didn't even raise their heads. It was gangly young Bobbie who came running over.

'Ah me stomach thinks me throat's been cut,' he panted, taking the basket from her. 'Bring this back to the cott later, will I?' he asked, eying her hopefully.

'Please. It'll save me another trip and give me time to make lots of dough boys,' she told him. Flashing his boyish grin, he turned and began squelching his way back to the others who were still busy slashing at the osiers, tying each armful cut with a withy bond.

Pulling her shawl tighter, Eliza began retracing her steps. Although it would be different without her grammer, she knew she owed it to her gramfer to make sure the men were well fed. She just hoped all the fresh vegetables she'd added to the broth would eke out their meagre scrag of lamb. Lost in her musing, it was a few minutes before she felt someone watching her. Looking up, her eyes widened in disbelief for standing before her was the golden-haired man who'd inhabited her dreams these past weeks. Except that in this light his hair appeared more auburn, although his eyes had that green intensity she remembered.

'Good afternoon, Eliza,' he said, his gaze boring into her.

'Good afternoon, sir,' she replied, her eyes meeting his. He had remembered her name, she thought, her heart beating so loudly she was sure he would hear.

'Forgive my intrusion,' he murmured, not looking in the least bit sorry. 'I was putting Bodrilly through his paces, when once again I found myself drawn here.' As if suddenly aware he was staring, he broke their gaze and gestured to the bare branches of the willows. 'I was surprised to see all those dead leaves floating on the water. Why haven't the workers cleared them?'

'No need, sir. When all the leaves have fallen it signals that the sap has become quiescent, or dormant and the withies are ready for harvesting.'

'And is that what those men are doing with those funny hook things?'

'It is, sir,' she replied, grateful her voice sounded steady for his closeness was sending shivers through her.

'But why are they standing in all that water?' he frowned. 'It must surely be most uncomfortable, not to say downright wet.'

'That's the only way they can cut them, for they grow with their roots waterlogged,' she told him. They stood watching, listening to the squishing and squashing of the men's stout boots, the swish of their hooks followed by the soft fall of the severed withies.

'And that dark-haired man over there, is your husband,' he said flatly. She stared at him in amazement before looking to where he gestured.

'Clem? He's here to help with the harvest. I'm not married, sir,' she spluttered. Now it was his turn to look astonished.

'But I saw you. You were laughing together as he rocked in that funny little boat thing.'

'You saw us? When?'

'Alas, you have found me out. I felt drawn to you the moment we met,' he admitted, his gaze directly upon her so that she found herself growing hot. 'I know it was wrong when you'd told me you were making a rattle for your baby, yet I wanted, no needed, to see you again.' She frowned, then laughed as realization dawned.

'The rattle was for Mrs Finch's new grandchild,' she laughed.

'Really? Good heavens. That's marvellous.'

Seeing his delighted expression, Eliza giggled. 'Of course, that doesn't mean I haven't been asked,' she couldn't resist teasing. What was it about him that brought out this flirtatious nature she'd never realized she possessed?

'And have you accepted, pray?' he asked earnestly.

'No, not yet,' she admitted.

'Well, then Eliza Priddle, perhaps you would do me the honour of showing me around. I must say I find this terrain most intriguing.'

'Sorry, I'm afraid that's not possible,' she told him, trying not to giggle when his expression changed to one of dismay. 'Gramfer wouldn't like me to be out walking with someone who hasn't told me his name.'

'Gracious, how remiss. Do please forgive me. Theobald Seymour, at your service,' he said, taking her hand and dropping the lightest of kisses on it. 'Theo to my friends.'

'Oh,' she stammered, as tingles travelled up her arm. Endeavouring to compose herself, she pulled it back and tightened her shawl around her. 'What about your mount?' she asked, gesturing to where the glossy golden-brown horse was contentedly munching the grass.

'I think Bodrilly is happily occupied, although Grainger the groom would blow his stack of straw if he found out. He believes in a strict diet and exercise regime.'

'Well, I won't tell,' Eliza grinned. 'I can show you more of the area if you'd like,' she offered, suddenly wanting to be away from the men in the field.

Chapter 7

They wandered on passing fields bounded by the pollarded trees, although Eliza was more fascinated by his shiny leather boots than the familiar scenery.

'For some reason I cannot fathom, they resonate with me,' he said, matching his stride to hers. Suddenly a duck rose from the reedy dyke nearby, its indignant cry at being disturbed making them laugh. 'It must be wonderful living in such wild environs.'

'It can be pleasant during spring and summer,' she admitted. 'But it's another story when the rains of winter come. The fields are flooded for weeks on end and the wind can bend you double.' He quirked a brow, staring around as if trying to imagine such a scene.

'What are those for?' he asked, coming to a halt beside the big oak and pointing to the wooden crosses with the jug of flowers between them.

'These mark the graves of my grammer and mother,' she told him.

'Well I'm sorry for your loss but why aren't they in a graveyard?'

'Gramfer wanted them close to our cott,' she explained, surprised to see an unfathomable look on his face.

'But what about grave robbers. Oh, please forgive me,' he said, when she shuddered. 'There's probably nothing to steal around here,' he murmured, his voice low as he frowned towards the barn and cott beyond.

'I'll have you know some of the richest of men are buried in barrows around these parts,' she told him indignantly. Then seeing his look of surprise, couldn't resist adding, 'Along with coins, bronze pitchers and wine to drink in case they should be thirsty in their travels to the afterlife.'

'Really?' he asked, his disbelief evident.

'Yes, really.' There was silence, and not wishing for there to be any awkwardness, she turned to him. 'So, your departed family are buried in your local churchyard, are they?'

'Well in the grounds of our family chapel actually,' he admitted. 'Look, let's not waste time dwelling on such a morbid topic. Why don't you show me around your home?' Eliza swallowed hard, reluctant to take him inside the shabby cott with its inevitable reek of peat smoke. She didn't think he'd appreciate smuts on his smart clothes or the mess she'd left after preparing the men's food.

'Goodness, it's far too nice to spend time indoors,' she said brightly. 'Now what else would you like to see?' He gave a lazy grin.

'If I were to answer that question candidly, you would slap my face, Eliza Priddle, so I will content myself with following wherever you lead.'

Leaving the withies behind, they wandered on through the fields, empty now the cows had been moved back to the farm.

'Last time I was here there were cattle grazing and there was the strangest smell wafting on the breeze,' he told her, wrinkling his nose.

'That'd be pommy, the remains of apple from the cider pressing. It's mixed with straw and spread on the land as it's full of nutrients.'

'Well, Eliza Priddle, it seems once again I am indebted to you for enlightening me. I'm meant to be learning how our estate is run and shall certainly inform Father my education has been sadly lacking,' he told her, the thought seeming to delight him.

'You can tell him I'd be pleased to share anything he would like to know,' she told him. He turned and stared at her incredulously.

'Oh, er yes, thank you that is most kind.' He continued walking on in silence, and she wondered what she'd said wrong. After some moments though, he seemed to recover and smiled. 'I find myself drawn to both the environs . . .' he said, gesturing back towards the rhyne they'd just left. 'And, well yourself,' he admitted, staring at her so intently, she could see the gold flecks glinting in his eyes.

'But why should you be drawn to someone like me?' she replied, staring down at her simple attire. 'I'm just a plain country girl.'

'With those fiery red tresses and a spirit to match, you are far from plain. I've never seen a girl climb a tree before, or throw apples down with such accuracy,' he admitted, his admiration evident.

'You saw me in the apple tree?' she cried. So, she hadn't imagined that glimpse of gold or the feeling he was nearby.

'It certainly was a sight to behold,' he murmured, slowly leaning towards her so that she caught the smell of his tangy cologne. Her heart fluttered, certain he was about to kiss her but instead he whispered.

'You've bewitched me Eliza Priddle, and I want to know all about you.'

'Time to gather, boys.' As the sound of her gramfer's voice carried from the field, Eliza started, the spell broken. She'd been so enthralled by Theo, she hadn't noticed the shadows lengthening and the short December afternoon drawing to a close.

'Oh no,' she cried, springing away from him. 'The men have finished cutting for the day and I've yet to cook their dough boys.'

'Dough boys?' he frowned.

'Dumplings to go on their stew,' she explained. 'Surely you have them?'

'Well, Cook makes parsley croutons to grace her venison casserole. Would that be the same?'

'Er, similar, yes,' she replied, not having a clue what croutons were. 'Look I must go, they'll be expecting their meal on the table.'

'Of course, forgive me for keeping you so long. I really must rescue poor Bodrilly before he becomes too fat to canter home,' he quipped. Then his expression grew serious and he took her hand. 'May I see you again tomorrow?'

'Well,' she murmured demurely. 'I shall be taking the men their noon pieces tomorrow.'

'I shall see you then, Eliza Priddle,' he insisted, staring at her so intently her heart flipped right over. 'Be sure, I shall be counting the hours.'

And so shall I, Eliza thought as she fled back to the cott.

'That were the best stew and dough boys I ever ate,' Bobbie declared, sitting back and rubbing his stomach. As the others murmured their agreement, Eliza smiled, relief flooding through her. Although she'd left the broth stewing in the crock over the fire, she'd had to hurry to finish the dough boys and knew they could have done with cooking a while longer. However, the weary men had clattered into the cott, sunk down into their chairs and looked at her so expectantly she hadn't dared dally. 'If there were any puddin', I'd not say no,' Bobbie volunteered.

'Yer be grateful for what yer've 'ad yer varmint,' Ned said, cuffing his ear. 'That were a nice drop of stoo,' he added, getting to his feet and smiling at Eliza. 'Come on boy, time we was gettin' back. Make sure the women's tucked them cows abed proper.'

'Cows don't go to bed,' Bobbie scoffed, getting reluctantly to his feet.

'That what you be thinking, boy,' Ned chuckled, ramming his cap on his head. 'See you in't mornin'.'

'T'wer a good day's cuttin'. Thanks for your help,' Gramfer said.

As the door shut behind them, Eliza sprang to her feet, prodded the fire then began clearing the dishes.

'Leave them 'til mornin' girl,' Gramfer said, rising stiffly to his feet. 'I'm away to my bed so you can keep young Clem here company. It's too dark for him to make his way home now, so I've said he can share my room the night.'

'Oh,' Eliza replied, her heart sinking. All she wanted to do was turn in herself and relive the time she'd spent with Theo. It had been hard enough to concentrate over supper, though luckily the men were much too tired and hungry to say much.

'Don't worry, I'll be going up soon too,' Clem assured her, moving the dishes to one side and resting his elbows on the table.

I bet Theo wouldn't do that. Unbidden the thought popped into her head and she jumped to her feet.

'I made you these,' she said, retrieving the fittens from her workbox. 'Thought they might stop you getting sores from the oars.'

'Thanks Red, they're grand,' he said, his eyes lighting up as he tried them on. 'Fit like, well fittens,' he laughed, holding up his hands.

'Good.' Silence fell and Eliza knew she should make conversation but all she wanted was to be alone so she could relive the past few hours.

'That top really suits you,' Clem smiled. 'Couldn't spot

one grease mark and I looked long and hard during supper,' he said, giving her a meaningful look.

'Yes, well, Grammer's suggestion that I cover them with ribbons worked,' she said.

'Hmm,' he murmured. 'So how have you been spending your time alone here?'

'What do you mean?' she asked, her voice sharper than she'd intended.

'Nothing,' he replied, holding his hands up in surrender. 'Although, I couldn't help noticing you were looking lit up earlier,' he added, eying her closely.

'Must be from the heat of the fire when I was cooking,' she said quickly, collecting up the dishes.

'Let me help,' he offered, jumping to his feet.

'No,' she snapped, then smiled apologetically when he frowned. 'You've had a long day and need to be up early again tomorrow.'

'Well, if you're sure, it has been a tiring day.'

'Night, Clem,' she replied, waiting until he'd climbed the stairs. When she heard the door creak shut behind him, she let out a sigh of relief. He was much too observant and whilst she wasn't one for being deceitful, she knew he wouldn't approve of Theo visiting while they were all out in the fields. She'd been on tenterhooks all evening in case she gave something away. Everything was new and exciting and she wanted to hug her secret to herself a little longer.

It took her ages to get to sleep and when she did her dreams were of Theo. Handsome, green-eyed Theo, whose penetrating looks sent shivers of delight shooting through her body. Consequently, she slept late and by the time she went downstairs the men had long left for the fields.

Feeling guilty, she quickly raked the fire, put potatoes to bake, and fetched fresh water in the kettle. Then, conscious of the mounting orders, spent a good part of the morning weaving her willow. This time though, her fingers flew in time to the rapid beats of her heart as she thought about her forthcoming meeting with Theo.

Tossing the finished basket to one side she took herself indoors and set about making ragged rabbit stew with the offering from poacher Pat. Having given the man tea and shelter during a particularly heavy shower a couple of days previously, he'd not only given her two of his prized plunders but also skinned them in return for a dish of broth. Even so, the dissecting and cutting up took longer than she'd anticipated and by the time she'd thrown the pieces into the pot along with onions, roots, bacon cut from their fitch and a healthy glug of the natch her gramfer had brought back from the cider house, it was time to take the men their noon pieces. She filled their flasks, wrapped the potatoes in muslin, along with four good sized chunks of cheese then headed to the fields. As before it was Bobbie who came running over.

'Hey Eliza, did you see a horse? I'm sure I heard one whinny just now,' he said, taking the basket from her. Eliza's heart leapt but she kept a straight face. It wouldn't do for him to alert the men.

'Well young Bobbie, I reckon hunger must be affecting

your ears. How does a baked potato with a chunk of cheese sound?' As ever, the thought of food sent everything else from his mind.

'Ooh yea,' he cried, taking the basket from her. She watched as he squelched his way back to the others, then feeling that she too was being watched, turned to find Theo tentatively emerging from the shadows. Her heart leapt and she patted her hair into place, for in her haste she'd neglected to put on the bonnet she'd intended to wear in order to appear more ladylike.

'You look lovely,' he assured her. 'Although you do seem to work extremely hard.'

'Doesn't everyone,' she quipped. He didn't reply, turning instead to watch the men scything the withies. She took the opportunity to steal a look at him. Today he was dressed in a well-cut tweed jacket, matching breeches with a kerchief at his neck. Whereas Clem wore his knotted on the side, Theo's was draped neatly inside his shirt, the sea green shade bringing out the colour of his eyes. How stylish he looked, she thought, glancing ruefully down at her old, frayed skirt and stout boots.

'How long will it take to cut them all down?' he asked, interrupting her thoughts.

'Not sure exactly as Gramfer bought more acres this year. But it has to be done before the rains come so the men will keep at it 'til Christmas like as not.'

'Good grief, that long?' he exclaimed.

'And it doesn't stop there, you know. The bolts of withies we don't need for our own use will be ferried down river and sold to other basket makers. Any left over, will go to the merchant. We'll have to boil and strip some but all will be stacked and dried before we can use them come spring.'

'That sounds quite a performance.'

'It is. You should see our hands, brown and wrinkled as walnuts they'll be by the time we've finished.' Seeing him shudder, she realized he didn't relish hearing the nitty gritty of her work. 'Come on, let's take a walk before we're spotted,' she suggested.

His eyes narrowed and he stared around as if suddenly afraid of being seen.

Chapter 8

'What's the matter?' she asked. 'Shouldn't you be here?'

'I was thinking of you,' he replied, linking her arm through his and urging her along the path. 'From the way you jumped when you heard your grandfather shout yesterday, I gathered you wouldn't want us to be seen together at this stage.'

'He is somewhat old-fashioned,' she admitted. 'Besides, he works so hard I wouldn't want him to think I'm shirking,' she sighed, thinking that she'd have to be careful in front of Clem now, as well. 'I just have to do everything at double speed in order to have their supper ready on time.'

'Then it will do you good to have a break for a while.' They walked on, his close proximity sending those funny shivers shooting around her body. Eventually they came to a gate beyond which the flat green land spread as far as the eye could see. While above them, the dark, brooding moors gazed silently down.

'I've never seen fields with so many ditches,' he told her, appearing more relaxed now.

'We call them rhynes and they carry the water away. With these fields lying so low and rain running down from the hills, they'd be waterlogged all year otherwise. Mind you, when the river bursts its banks it's a different story, especially when water streams through the cott. But we won't talk about that,' she added quickly, when he grimaced. 'What about you? I suppose you live in a castle high on a hill and your water is the moat that surrounds it,' she teased.

'Goodness no. Although our manor does overlook the lands and forests below.'

'And do these lands and forests extend far?'

'Our estate spreads into Dorsetshire.' He shrugged as if it was no consequence. 'But, let's talk about you Eliza. What do you do when you're not making babies' rattles?' he asked, leaning back against the gate and giving her a searching look.

'Well, since Grammer died I've been keeping the basket-making business going, supplying vegetables to the green-grocers, looking after Gramfer, keeping house and cooking,' she replied. Even as she spoke, she was thinking how boring it all sounded. And that she'd have to rush to catch up with everything when she got back.

'So what are you cooking for supper tonight?'

'Ragged rabbit.'

To her surprise he burst out laughing.

'What's so funny about that?'

'Sorry Eliza, I just had this vision of little rabbits hopping around the fields in ragged clothes.'

'Ha ha, very funny,' she grinned. 'It's just a way of making the meat go further. I suppose I could have wrapped the pieces in the bacon to look like pink jackets,' she added, getting into the spirit of things.

'That's better. You look all relaxed and happy when you laugh.'

'I suppose your mother or Cook never prepares rabbit?' she asked, eager to hear more about his family life.

'Mother never prepares anything and I can't remember Cook serving up rabbit. Pheasant in Madeira is one of her specialities at this time of year, and very nice it is too. Goodness, it's getting a bit chilly, shall we head back?' he asked, as the watery sun disappeared behind the building clouds.

'I suppose we'd better,' she agreed reluctantly as they fell into step once more. 'So, what does your mother do with her time?' Dying to find out more, she only hoped her questions didn't sound rude. Luckily, he didn't seem to mind.

'Oh, she arranges soirees, balls, dinner parties that sort of thing. On such occasions she will consult with Cook on the menu, although Father organizes the wine. Poor Mother doesn't have a clue as to which vintage should be served,' he replied nonchalantly.

Oh yes, poor Mother indeed, Eliza thought, stifling the urge to laugh.

'And I suppose you get to meet lots of pretty young ladies,' she said lightly.

'I do and believe you me, it's such a bore. They're not half as spirited as you and most certainly wouldn't dream of dirtying their clothes climbing trees,' he grinned, shooting her an admiring look. 'Usually I sneak off to the library and lose myself in a book, much to Father's disgust. Got to make a suitable marriage son,' he intoned, clearly imitating the older man. 'I'm only just seventeen for heaven's sake.'

'Oh, the same as me,' Eliza exclaimed. 'Do you have any brothers and sisters?'

'No, that's the trouble. Just me, the heir, and no spare. What about you Eliza?'

'Mother died giving birth to me, so no siblings.'

'And did you mean it yesterday when you said you had no followers?' he asked, turning to face her.

'Yes, I did,' she replied, gratified to see his eyes light up.

'Then, would you consider walking out with me?' he asked, his expression serious as he waited for her to reply.

'Why, Theo I thought that was what we were doing now, walking out in the fields,' she quipped. Gently he traced his fingers down her cheek. Then, as quivers of delight ran through her, he leaned forward. She caught the tang of his cologne then lost all sense of reason as he placed the lightest of kisses on her lips.

'I hope you don't think me presumptuous, especially when we have only spent a short time together, but I want you to know how much you already mean to me. It's strange, I feel animated in your presence, and it's as if I've known you for ever.'

'Oh Theo,' she murmured, not sure how to answer for she too felt herself come alive in his company.

Then, as if from nowhere, a sudden squall blew up, the

wind nearly buffeting them off their feet, heavy hailstones stinging their heads and drenching their hair.

'Come on, we should have heeded those dark clouds,' he said, taking her hand and dashing back the way they'd come. But, as often happened at this time of year, the storm stopped as soon as it had started, and by the time they reached the drove leading to the cott, the setting sun was streaking the horizon crimson.

'I don't suppose you want me to come inside?' he asked, his voice coming in breathless gasps.

'Better not. That squall might have stopped the men working and they could be in soon. Besides, I've still masses to do,' she told him regretfully.

'I would love to continue meeting, although I think we need to find somewhere that affords a degree of shelter,' he said, giving the cott a dismissive look. 'Leave it with me.'

'Tomorrow?' she asked.

'Wild horses, or at least Bodrilly, won't keep me away from you. However, tomorrow I have a prior engagement,' he grimaced. 'Like you Eliza Priddle, I have obligations to fulfil. However, be assured I shall return as soon as I can.'

'Oh,' she murmured, her spirits sinking. Forcing a smile, she waited hopefully for another kiss. But he gave a nod, turned and headed briskly towards the wood.

She watched him for a few moments then realizing she was wasting time, rushed along the track and pushed open the door to the cott. Although the peat was still burning and there was an appetizing aroma wafting from the crock, she couldn't help peering sadly through the ever-present cloud of acrid smoke at their dingy surroundings. It didn't matter how hard she tried to keep the room looking nice, it still looked shabby.

By the time the men came in, the living room, by flickering candlelight at least, looked passable and the supper was ready. However, she noticed her gramfer frowning as he ate his meal. Clem too, kept darting her inquisitive looks but to her relief, didn't ask any awkward questions.

But, as ever, Gramfer had only been biding his time. He waited until the men had departed, Clem with his ma's basket under his arm, assuring them he'd be fine guiding his trow by the light of his lantern, before turning to her.

'Is everything alright?' she asked.

'Mm,' he murmured, non-committedly.

'I've been thinking Eliza. It's too much expectin' you to manage everythin' here by yourself. I'll get Flo Chambers up from the village to help out while we're harvestin'. She'll jump at the chance to earn a few extra coppers. It'll mean cuttin' back a bit, but Mary would never forgive me if I didn't look out for you.'

'There's no need Gramfer,' she protested, her heart sinking. Mrs Chambers had eyes everywhere and would soon notice if Eliza disappeared of an afternoon. The thought of not seeing Theo the next time he visited was more than she could bear. Her heart was already singing with love for him and she now understood how her grammer could have fallen for her gramfer at seventeen. 'Give me a bit more time for I'm just getting used to the extra cooking and cleaning. Grammer taught me well, and I couldn't bear the thought of letting her down.'

'Well if you're sure,' he said doubtfully. 'But if it gets too much you must promise to let me know.'

'Yes Gramfer,' she replied, swallowing down her guilt and vowing to be up extra early to fit everything in.

Determined to keep her word and prove she could manage, Eliza was dressed before the sky had lightened to grey the next day. She carried out her chores, settled to her basket-making then took the men their noon time pieces. Despite what Theo had said, she couldn't help turning towards the woods before she returned to the barn. However, the heaviness in her heart told her he wasn't coming. Determined to make up for lost time, she threw herself into her basket-making before taking herself indoors and giving the cott a clean then preparing the men's meal.

'Ah I thinks maybe you're getting' the hang of this,' her gramfer said, staring at the gleaming dresser after the men had left. 'Still, you just tell me if it gets too much to cope with and we'll call Flo in to help.'

'Thank you Gramfer, but like you say, I think I'm getting the hang of fitting everything in,' Eliza replied, unable to stifle a yawn. 'But if you don't mind, I think I'll call it a day.'

The next morning, heart skipping at the thought of seeing Theo, she bounded out of bed. But as she hurried outside to the privy, she was met by a bank of cold, thick fog. At any other time, she would have enjoyed the eeriness of being shrouded in silent mystery. But today all she could think of was the effect it might have on the harvest. If it was deemed too damp and dangerous to cut, the men would stay home and she would be unable to meet Theo. Of course, he might not be able to make it himself, she thought, her heart sinking. After all, he hadn't told her which direction he came from, and even if he got near Sedge Moor, the foul weather might prove too hazardous for him to ride Bodrilly through the wood and along the narrow paths that led here.

''Tis meant 'twill happen. Another of her grammer's mantras popped into her head, lifting her spirits and spurring her into action. Quickly she filled the kettle from the water barrel. Back indoors, she banked up the fire and set it to boil. With the porridge cooking, she set about preparing the evening meal for the men. Always supposing they were able to turn out in this weather.

'Mornin' Eliza.' Lost in thought, she hadn't heard her gramfer making his way slowly down the stairs. 'My, you're up early.'

'I'm determined to manage everything like Grammer did during harvesting,' she told him. He nodded then disappeared outside to the privy. Eliza poured tea into his favourite brown mug, dished up a generous dollop of porridge and set a pot of her plum and bramble jam on the table.

'Pushin' the boat out, aren't we?' he asked, eying her suspiciously as he came back indoors.

'Got to keep your strength up for the harvest, Gramfer,' she told him.

'This fog'll have to lift before we can do much,' he grumbled. 'Still, it shouldn't stop Clem continuing stacking withies on the high ground behind the shed.'

She looked at him in alarm, her knees going weak. If Clem had already been delivering boat loads from the fields, he would know she hadn't been in the barn working on her baskets. In future, she'd have to ensure the door was pulled tightly closed.

'*Be sure your sins,*' the voice sounded in her ear.

'So, what would you like for supper?' she asked, blotting out her grammer's reproving tones. Or had it been her own conscience talking?

'You means we got a choice?' he spluttered, staring at her in astonishment for the second time that morning.

'Well, I could stew up the rabbit carcasses, add some barley and roots.'

'Ah, variation on a stoo. Make a bit of suet crust to go on top, could you? Haven't had that since my Mary passed,' he murmured, looking downcast. 'Always said a man needed rib stickin' food at harvest, she did.'

'And so you shall,' Eliza agreed, her stomach dropping to her boots, for despite her grammer's careful teaching, she was no good at making the savoury pastry. Besides it would take time she didn't have. Still a promise was a promise and she'd have to find time to work on her baskets later.

Just as she feared, in spite of getting the stew into the crock in good time, the pastry seemed to have a mind of its own, first being too dry to stick and then too wet to roll.

Finally, after much frustration, she managed a passable, if somewhat lumpy effort, and set it aside for cooking later. Peering anxiously through the window, she saw that while the fog was still hanging, it had at least thinned.

Excitement tingling her veins, she threw the men's noon pieces into her basket then did her best to make herself look presentable. She toyed with the idea of pinning her hair up with Grammer's comb before realizing Gramfer would be suspicious if he saw it, and settling for her usual bonnet. Trimming it with the same green ribbon she'd used to hide the grease marks on her top had lent it a new lease of life, although she knew she couldn't compete with the glamorous ladies Theo associated with. Whatever did he see in her she wondered? Apart from being spirited, she grinned remembering his words.

The cold air nearly took her breath away as she hurried towards Lower Field, where the men were now harvesting. You couldn't get any lower than the levels, but her gramfer assured her it was so named because it was lower down his parcel of land.

'My, it's so cold and murky, I'm surprised you can cut in this,' Eliza told Bobbie as, like an eager puppy, he came bounding over.

'Father says we just got to get on with it,' he shrugged resignedly. 'But I sure am starved.'

'Well, this should keep you going and there'll be a hot meal waiting when you finish,' Eliza assured him, handing over her basket to the ever-hungry boy. She waited until he'd disappeared into the murk then peered around, hoping to find Theo waiting. Her heart sank when she could see no sign of him. Well what had she expected, she thought as she began retracing her steps.

Chapter 9

Suddenly a shrill whistle made her turn and there beckoning to her from the edge of the woods, was the tall figure that so stirred her emotions. Her heart flipped and lifting her skirts, she ran over to join him.

'I thought you weren't coming,' she said, her voice sounding breathless.

'Nothing could keep me away today,' he murmured, staring at her intently so that her stomach flipped. 'Although it wasn't an easy journey. Luckily Bodrilly is sure footed for the paths leading here aren't very defined, are they? Anyway, it's too cold and damp to stay out here.' Her heart flopped again. Surely, he wasn't leaving straight away?

'Don't worry, I've found us the perfect place. Come on,' he said, hefting a leather bag over his shoulder then holding out his arm for her to take. Side by side, they tramped through the trees, laughing as they kicked up the soggy, rotting leaves. Finally, at the edge of the wood, they came to a stile.

'Nearly there,' he assured her, taking her hand and carefully helping her over. Loving his attentiveness, she didn't tell him she'd leapt over it many times before. Besides, she didn't suppose the elegant ladies he knew would ever jump over stiles. Or climb trees, she thought, stifling a giggle. 'Ta da,' he trilled, pointing to the wooden hut that stood in the empty field beyond, its roof of wriggly tin glistening through the fog. 'It's quite safe, there are no sheep in here, I checked,' he grinned, mistaking her hesitation.

'That's because the flocks have been moved to higher ground before the rains come.'

'Well then, it can be our perfect haven for today. Come on.'

Why not, Eliza thought, following him into the shadowy interior, not daring to enquire whether he'd sought the farmer's permission. As Theo knelt and deftly lit the tiny stove, she watched surprised he should do something so domestic. But as the sticks caught, oblivious to her thoughts, he opened his bag, drew out a plaid blanket and spread it along the bench that served as a bed for the shepherd at lambing.

'Best if we divest ourselves of our wet outdoor things or we might catch a chill. Don't worry, it won't take long for the fire to warm the place,' he said, mistaking her shocked expression. He moved towards her and slowly unwrapped her shawl from around her shoulders before hanging it carefully on a nail by the door. His touch sent those delicious tingles shooting around her body again and she watched eagerly as he shrugged off his heavy jacket. Seized by a sense of recklessness, she took off her sodden bonnet and shook out her curls. 'You are so beautiful,' he murmured, admiration shining from his eyes. Feeling self-conscious, she gave a laugh that reverberated round the empty room.

'Let's make ourselves comfortable,' he suggested, settling himself on the blanket and drawing her down beside him. 'I got Cook to prepare us a picnic. But we'll have that later.'

'It sounds as if you've come prepared,' she murmured, finally finding her voice. Looking serious, he turned towards her.

'Dearest Eliza, may I have permission to put my arm around you?' He was gazing at her so intently, her heart beat faster, her mouth went dry and all she could do was nod. With a sigh he pulled her close and her senses swam as she caught the tang of his scent. She nestled against the soft wool of his jumper and they sat in contented silence for some moments, listening to the crackle of the fire as the sticks began to blaze.

'You can't know how I've dreamed of being with you like this,' he whispered, placing the lightest of kisses on her hair. 'Since I first saw you reciting those virtues, your copper curls dancing around your shoulders like flames, I've felt incredibly drawn to you. Yearned to get to know you.'

'Really?' she asked. 'I can't think why. I mean, whatever do you see in me?' There, she'd voiced the very thing that had been worrying her.

'What do you mean?' he asked, moving so that his face was level with hers.

'Well, you obviously come from a different background. You wear fine clothes, mix with beautiful ladies for whom dressing in silk is an everyday occurrence,' she told him, finally meeting his eyes. 'Whereas if I want even as much as a new top, I have to make it from an old flour sack.' He frowned, his glance sweeping lower as if taking in her clothes for the first time. She couldn't tell from his expression if he was disgusted or delighted by her revelation.

'Believe you me you have a natural beauty that outshines any of those ladies you mentioned. Pampered, powdered and preened like peacocks on parade they are,' he shuddered. 'Whilst you are sweet and kind and look lovely just as you are,' he murmured, kissing her hair again. 'I know this probably sounds trite, corny even, but I feel as though you're the one I've been waiting for all my life.'

'Oh.' It was all she could manage, for hadn't she been feeling the same about him?

'You're so lucky living beside all those wonderful willows.'

'You must be joking,' she spluttered. 'It's so remote, cut off by the rhynes. I can't wait to escape.'

'Really?' He stared at her in surprise. 'I can't imagine anything better than being secluded. It's so frantic back at the manor.'

'My heart bleeds for you,' she murmured, rolling her eyes.

'You might mock but although it's only the first week of December, Mother is already in high dudgeon about Christmas. Invitations being sent and received seemingly by the hour. Servants rushing hither and thither. I couldn't imagine anything more pleasant than a peaceful place with time to ponder. So much more liberating than having every day, or the rest of one's life even, mapped out,' he sighed.

'Well my days are definitely mapped out, as you call it. When I've finished keeping house and feeding the men, I have a hundred or more baskets to make.'

'Poor Eliza,' he murmured, lifting a strand of her hair and running it between his fingers. 'Soft as silk,' he sighed. 'I feel drawn to you as I have never been drawn to anyone else before, Eliza Priddle. You are beautiful and fun to be with so I'll not hear another word to the contrary.' Turning her face to meet his, he lowered his lips in a gentle kiss that became so passionate, she felt her entire body tremble in response. He too, seemed dazed for drawing away, he gave a rueful smile. 'I think we'd better eat,' he whispered.

Getting shakily to his feet, he delved into his bag. Like a magician he drew out two individual pies wrapped in snowy linen napkins, pâté and slices of white bread, spreading them out on the blanket between them. Then he produced a flask and two glasses carefully wrapped in soft cloth. Eliza had never seen anything so splendid and, to her embarrassment. her stomach rumbled noisily.

'Not a minute too soon by the sound of it,' he laughed and the tension between them vanished like dew in the sun. Pouring golden liquid into one glass he held it out to her. She took a sip, her eyes widening in delight.

'Delicious,' she murmured, her insides fizzing with warmth.

'Cook's cordial. It's her speciality,' he grinned, chinking his glass against hers. 'Here's to us and a happy future, if I might be so bold.' He gave her a searching look and as their eyes locked, she felt immersed in a glow of warmth.

Not feeling the need to speak, they sat together enjoying the fine food and drink. The fire had almost died but suffused with emotion, she hardly noticed. It was only when she glanced out of the tiny window that she saw the fog lowering again.

'I have to go,' she cried jumping to her feet.

'Stay a bit longer,' he pleaded. Looking at his earnest expression she felt torn, but her conscience was pricking and she shook her head regretfully.

'I wish I could but I daren't. I must get back before the men finish work,' she said, snatching her shawl from the nail and throwing it around her shoulders. 'Gramfer has already threatened to get help in from the village, and if that happens, I'll never be able to get away,' she told him as she placed her bonnet on her head and stood looking at him. 'Always supposing you want to see me again.'

'Of course, I do. I think you've put a spell on me Eliza Priddle,' he cried, covering the distance between them and pulling her close. She could hear the beating of his heart and wished she could stay enfolded in his warm embrace for ever. It took all her will to pull away and he let out a long sigh. 'I'll walk you back.'

'No don't worry. I'll run back.'

'But I can't leave you to find your own way. It wouldn't be gentlemanly,' he protested.

'Maybe not but it'll be quicker,' she told him.

Tenderly he tied the ribbons of her bonnet in a bow under her chin. Then taking her face in his hands, he lowered his lips to hers. It was gentler than his previous kiss but still set her pulse racing.

'Meet me here again, say in two days' time?' he asked.

'Yes,' she agreed, her heart jumping. 'But now I really must go.'

Then before he could protest, she let herself out of the hut and started running. It was only when she'd leapt the stile that she thought to see if he was watching. Luckily though he was still inside the hut.

Hurrying back through the woods, she hardly noticed the chill of the thickening fog. Her body still tingled from Theo's touch and she wished she could have stayed with him for longer. However, she knew the men had a right to expect a good meal after working hard all day and she owed it to her gramfer not to let him or them down. How difficult it was being torn between desire and duty.

It was further back to the cott than she'd realized and by the time she arrived the men were already preparing to leave the field. Grateful for the cover the fog afforded, she ran as fast as she could and just managed to have the candles lit and the stew covered with its pastry lid cooking over the fire by the time her gramfer lifted the latch. Standing in the doorway, he sniffed the air.

'That don't smell nowhere near ready yet, girl,' he grumbled.

'Supper won't be long Gramfer, it's the first time I've done that topping you wanted, don't forget,' Eliza replied truthfully, as the others clattered into the room.

'I tell you, I definitely 'eard an 'orse again,' Bobbie declared. 'An' Rueben down't village said a well-to-do stranger's bin spotted riding through the woods. Looking all furtive like this he were,' he added, screwing up his face and peering around the room. Eliza felt her mouth grow dry but luckily the others just laughed at his antics.

'Don't be daft boy. All the animals is back at the farm. And it's too dark for any strangers to be out. They'd not see nothing, there be no stars this night,' Ned, said rubbing his hands together.

'Not outside, no,' replied Clem, looking quizzically at Eliza. 'Seems to be a funny whiff in here Red,' he said, lowering his voice. Her heart nearly stopped. Surely, he couldn't smell Theo's cologne on her? 'More like wood smoke than peat smoke, I'd say.' This time Eliza's mouth felt so dry she could hardly swallow. Clem was too observant by far.

'Tea's brewed,' she said brightly, turning away from him and praying he said nothing more to her gramfer. 'And there's some cut round and jam to keep you going until supper.'

'That's unusual . . .' her gramfer began, only to be interrupted by Bobbie's whoop of delight.

'Yeah, cake afore stoo!' he cried, throwing himself down on his chair and looking expectantly at Eliza. As the others followed suit, she busied herself spreading the buns thickly with jam and passing them round. Then she poured tea into their mugs, studiously ignoring Clem's searching stare.

Chapter 10

'I don't know what you're up to Eliza but I sense it ain't no good.' The men had gone home and Eliza, thinking her gramfer would go straight up to his bed, had taken the dirty dishes through to the scullery to wash. However, when she went back into the living room he was still sitting in his chair by the fire.

'Sorry Gramfer, I don't know what you mean,' she replied, ignoring his penetrating look and hoping the smoke curling from the fire would hide her flushed cheeks.

'I may be old and slow but I'm not so daft as not to know when a woman's tryin' to pull the wool.'

'Wool, that reminds me, I must ask Clem to pick some up from Stoke when he's next passing. You'll be wanting a new muffler for Christmas and there's not enough left in the basket.'

'Nowt wrong with the one I got, nor my senses neither,' he grunted. 'You're hidin' something from me, Eliza Priddle. Just remember, I'll be waitin' when you decide to share whatever it is.' As he got slowly to his feet and made his way to the stairs, Eliza breathed a sigh of relief.

'Somat's goin' on and Clem do feel it too. I see the way he's bin lookin' at you,' her gramfer called over his shoulder. 'And I trust it ain't got anything to do with that stranger young Bobbie was mutterin' about.'

'I'm sure that's just one of his stories, you know what he's like,' she said quickly.

As Eliza lay in bed, thinking back over the wonderful time she'd spent with Theo, she couldn't help smiling. The shepherd's hut was a cosy meeting place, especially after Theo had lit the fire. He'd said he found her more attractive than the posh ladies he met and hadn't seemed to mind the way she dressed. Recalling the way his kisses had sent shivers of delight shooting all round her body, she wrapped her arms around herself, trying to relive the warmth of his embrace. She'd never really been kissed before, unless you counted the odd peck from Clem and that wasn't like anything she'd experienced today.

Yet how much longer could they get away with these secret meetings? Especially with this rumour going around. Obviously Theo had been spotted, so they'd have to be more careful, for nothing could keep her away from him.

Although with carefully planning her time, and sheer hard work, she was managing to carry out her chores, someone was bound to spot her slipping away sooner or later and put two and two together. Neither of them could understand why they were so strongly drawn to each other, but they were, and she would cut off her arm rather than not see Theo again. However, she'd never hidden anything from her gramfer before and hated going behind his back.

Eliza threw herself into her chores, but all the while her head was buzzing with thoughts of Theo and their next meeting. To make matters worse, her gramfer had darted her funny looks over the breakfast table so that she was tempted to tell him about Theo.

'I thought you were never coming,' Theo murmured, pulling her close the moment she shut the door of the shepherd's hut behind her.

'Gramfer's getting suspicious,' she blurted out. 'And Bobbie heard Bodrilly again and mentioned a stranger's been seen in the woods.' Theo frowned as he led her over to the blanket covered bench.

'Then I shall have to be more careful. Look Eliza, I can't understand this feeling I have for you. All I know is it's so strong I wish, no I need, to keep seeing you. Do you feel the same?' As his green eyes studied her intently, she nodded.

'Yes, I do.'

'Then it's time we did something about it. I'll seek his permission to walk out with you and then we can meet freely without skulking in the shadows. It might not be what you wanted initially, but it's got to be the way forward, surely?'

'I know,' she sighed. 'But Gramfer's on edge until all the withies have been safely harvested. Let's wait until then. It'll only be another couple of weeks at most and then he'll be more relaxed.' *And amenable*, she added under her breath. For Gramfer was protective and she wasn't going to risk being confined to the cott.

'As you wish, Eliza,' Theo agreed. 'I just thought it would be easier for you, but I'll bide by your decision.'

'What about you, Theo. Do your parents know you come here to see me?' His glance slid away from hers.

'No,' he admitted. 'Like you, I know I shouldn't be here and yet, God help me, I cannot keep away.'

He pulled her close and for a moment they sat there united, yet lost in their own thoughts. Then he turned to her, a determined look in his eyes.

Eliza's heart lifted. Although she hated the subterfuge, she was pleased he wanted to continue meeting. They might come from different backgrounds, yet their feelings for each other were the same. And after harvest, he would speak to Gramfer and they could walk out together properly.

However, that evening after the men had eaten and retired to their own homes, her gramfer remained at the table.

'We're two thirds the way through the cuttin' now and, as you know, your grammer always gave the men a present to show our gratitude for their help. Ned was saying his wife would like a new shoppin' basket for Christmas and as she's taken on the extra farm chores whilst he's been comin' here, he'd like to give her a nice fancy one. Bobbie, bless him, wants to give her a new besom, said hers is sheddin' like a moultin' pup.'

'That's nice,' Eliza replied as she gathered up the dirty dishes.

'Glad you agree cos time's short so you'd best make a start on them tomorrow.'

'What?' she gasped, spoons clattering to the floor as she turned to look at him.

'By the time you've made them and given this place a decent clean, the harvest'll be in and we'll be invitin' everyone to celebrate. You've a lot to do my girl.'

'But . . .' she began.

'Now look Eliza, it was you who insisted you could manage everythin' so I'll not expect you to let me down.' He shot her one of his uncompromising looks, and she swallowed hard.

'I've already planned things for tomorrow but I'll make a start on the presents the day after,' she promised, her heart sinking at the thought of having to tell Theo she wouldn't be able to meet him for a few days. However, if he intended seeking permission to walk out with her, it wouldn't do to upset her gramfer.

'I don't know what you been doin' whilst we been out in the fields but this place is beginnin' to show signs of bein' neglected,' he said, running a finger along the dresser and frowning.

'Sorry, Gramfer. The fire's been smoking more than usual in the damp air.' Although it was true, her heart was heavy with the thought of having to stay here and make presents. She knew where her duty lay, but the thought of not seeing Theo was like a knife in her stomach. 'I'd better see to these,' she said, turning to take the dishes through to the scullery.

'I know it's been hard on you without your grammer, but things will be easier once we've got through Christmas,' he said, patting her arm as she passed. 'Though Lord knows, we'll not be of a mind to rejoice,' he sighed and stared into the fire.

The next morning, mindful of what she had to tell Theo, Eliza sped through the chores even quicker than usual. The men were always so hungry they bolted down their supper almost without tasting it and she was sure they wouldn't notice the extra roots she put in the stew rather than making dough boys or a crust for the top. Anyway, she'd do better the next day, she resolved, tidying her hair.

However, Theo was quiet when she arrived at the shepherd's hut. Although the fire was burning and he'd laid out the plaid blanket, he seemed pre-occupied.

'Are you alright?' she asked.

'Yes, why shouldn't I be? Oh, come here Eliza,' he groaned, pulling her close. He kissed her hair then her cheeks before claiming her lips. Flames of fire tore through her body and she clung to him, carried away by the intensity of her feelings. Then his lips were at her throat and as he began to trail little butterfly kisses lower, she felt as if she'd died and gone to heaven. She heard a moan and was shocked to realize it had come from her.

'Forgive me, Eliza,' Theo gasped, reluctantly pulling away from her, leaving a chilly void where moments before she'd been enveloped in pleasurable heat. 'I had no right. My only defence is that you fill me with such desire, I yearn to get as close to you as I can. But that is no excuse . . . forgive me, please?' He sat there looking so contrite, her heart went out to him. He was saying nothing she didn't feel herself.

'Oh Theo, of course I do.'

'I just wanted to make the most of our last afternoon together . . .'

'Last afternoon?' she repeated, her heart almost stopping as she stared at him in dismay.

'Well, until after Christmas,' he amended, so that she was able to breathe again. 'Mother and Father have all these dashed balls and parties arranged and I am expected, no have been ordered, to attend each and every darn one of them. Oh, please excuse my bad language. Whatever must you think of me?'

'I understand how frustrating it is not being able to do what you want, for I am being confined to the barn to make a fancy basket and besom.'

'What on earth is a besom?' he asked, frowning.

'It's a brush – you know for sweeping the floor?'

'Oh, I guess the staff would know,' Theo said. Eliza sighed, again conscious of the difference between them. 'As soon as these wretched festivities are out of the way I shall call at your cott and speak with your grandfather.'

'Always supposing you don't get swept off your feet by some sultry princess sheathed in silk,' she told him, only half teasing.

'Well I don't actually get to meet many princesses,' he told her gravely. Then his demeanour changed. 'But let's not dwell on our respective duties. We'll devote the rest of our precious

95

time to us, starting with your Christmas present.' Excitedly, he jumped to his feet and picked up a package from the little ledge that ran the length of the hut. 'Joyous felicitations, Eliza,' he said, bending and kissing her cheek before handing her the most beautifully wrapped parcel.

'But I don't have anything for you,' she cried, staring down at the silver embossed paper.

'The delight of your company is the only present I want. Now, go on, open it, see if you like it,' he urged. Eagerly she folded back the paper, gasping as she lifted out the most beautiful blouse she had ever seen. It was made of emerald green silk which shimmered in the light of the fire and had a row of tiny pearl buttons leading from the neck down to a sash around the waist. However, it was the full sleeves gathered at the wrist and decorated with more of the tiny pearls that fascinated her.

'It's absolutely gorgeous,' she gushed, running a finger over the shiny buttons. 'But it must have cost a fortune.'

'Luckily Father doesn't question how I spend my allowance. I'm glad you like it. Now come here and thank me in that way you do so well,' he added, puckering his lips suggestively.

'You are terrible, Theobald Seymour,' she told him, raining a shower of little kisses all over his face. With a groan, he put his arms around her and pulled her close.

'Promise me you won't go off with any dark-haired boatmen in my absence,' he whispered.

'I'll try not to,' she teased. 'But only if you promise to return as soon as you can.'

'Ah, so you'll miss me, will you?'

'Goodness me no, I shall be far too busy,' she paused teasingly. 'Weaving willow baskets,' she chuckled. Although she kept her manner light, her heart was heavy at the thought of not seeing him again for so long. Miss him? That was an understatement but even she knew a lady should never let on.

'At least I shall know where to find you. Perhaps you'd tell your grandfather I wish to speak with him as soon after Christmas as I can get away. Until then, pretty Eliza,' he murmured, leaning forward and giving her the sweetest of kisses.

Chapter 11

But when Christmas came it brought with it the heaviest of rains and winds. The fields of Sedge Moor flooded so that the rhynes overflowed across the Droves, cutting them off from the rest of Worth. Eliza, used to water streaming into their living room, had already removed their few belongings along with the rag rug, to the two upstairs bedrooms. Thankfully, with the scullery and pantry being at a higher level, her provisions should stay dry on the shelves.

She'd wrapped her treasured blouse from Theo in muslin and hidden it at the top of her chest. Yet under the cover of darkness, when the wind howled through the cott and screeched down the chimney, she couldn't resist taking it down and running her fingers over the soft material. Although she couldn't ever imagine having occasion to wear anything so glamorous, it didn't stop her dreaming she was at one of Theo's grand balls, his arms holding her tight as they swayed in time to the music.

It was the only light in a period of darkness, for downstairs the walls oozed foul-smelling water and the dull bloom of dampness covered the sticks of furniture she'd been unable to move. Gramfer became fretful as he waited anxiously for the floods to recede so that he could check his beloved withy beds.

'Never be able to plant me new sets,' he groaned, staring morosely out of her bedroom window. 'Can't stand havin' nothin' to do.'

'You could always help me,' Eliza told him. Determined to keep busy, she'd brought in the iron, lapboard and a bolt of withies. Although orders had slowed down, she hoped that once things returned to normal, they would pick up again. He grimaced, down at the swollen joints on his hands.

'Think my days for weavin' willow are over,' he mumbled.

'Have you been rubbing in your salve?' she asked but he'd turned away and was shuffling back to his own room.

Knowing it was useless to pursue the subject, Eliza took up her lapboard. As she began making the base for a new basket, she recalled how Grammer, with her belief in harnessing the goodness of nature, had lovingly blended a concoction of willow bark, lavender and marigold flowers with herbs and oil. Maintaining it would only work if done on a new moon, she'd stirred and blended outdoors at night by the waters of the rhyne. Despite Gramfer scoffing at her notions, amazingly the resulting balm had eased his suffering even reducing the swelling.

With the up-setting of uprights completed, she began weaving in and out, her thoughts turning to Theo. How she hoped he'd find a way to reach them soon, for she missed him so much it hurt.

Although she'd set aside a good store of food, supplies were depleting by the day and now it was more a case of what they had rather than what they'd like to eat. Daylight hours might have been at their shortest, but the days seemed long as each one dragged by.

Then, as December turned to January, they heard the sound of oars lapping along the overflowing waters of the rhyne. Eliza's heart flipped wildly, Theo had arrived at last. Rushing down the rickety stairs, she lifted her skirts in one hand and heedless of the water swirling around her feet, rushed outside. She couldn't help the feeling of disappointment that flooded through her when she saw it was Clem.

'Marnen Red, long time no see,' he grinned, hefting a sack over his shoulders. 'Thought you'd be running short of supplies by now so I stopped off at the mill. Knowing you'd probably be struggling to cook at the moment, Ma sent some of her baking.'

'That's very good of her,' Eliza replied, forcing a cheerful note.

'Ah lad, that's really kind,' Gramfer called from the upstairs window. 'Don't know how we'd manage without people's generosity.'

'You've done many a favour for them in the past George. So, how's things?' he asked, pushing his cap to the back of his head.

'Mustn't grumble. Bit of rheumatics and a chesty cough but what else can I expect in this weather? Bit of a natter would be good though. Seem to have run out of chatter these past weeks,' he added, shooting Eliza a meaningful look. She turned guiltily away knowing she'd been lost in her own thoughts recently. Although thinking about it, what had there been to talk about apart from the weather.

''Fraid I can't stop, George,' Clem told him. 'This is the first time I've been able to get out in the trow and there's many others running low on provisions too.'

'Ah well,' George replied, trying to hide his disappointment. 'Weather done much damage down the way?'

'No more than it usually does. Everyone's been sitting tight waiting for the waters to go down. I'll be back in a couple of days if the weather holds. We'll have a good tattle then,' Clem called up.

'Here, you take this,' he said, turning to Eliza and passing her an overflowing bag. As the aroma of fresh bread wafted before her, Eliza's stomach rumbled and she was tempted to take a bite there and then, but Clem was already hefting a sack onto his shoulder and didn't notice. He followed her indoors to the pantry asking, 'You all right?'

'We're fine, although Gramfer's getting tetchy being stuck indoors.'

'Sorry I couldn't stop and chat with him but, like I say, the people in the hamlets further down are cut off too. Their only hope of getting any provisions is by yours truly and his trusty trow,' he told her.

'Do you want a hand with your deliveries?' Eliza offered.

'Now, that would be helpful,' he nodded. 'With you hopping ashore and dropping off supplies, I won't need to moor up each time we stop. It'll mean we can get around to more of the outlying cottages today,' he said. 'Best go and tell George where you're going and put on some warmer things whilst you're about it.'

Eliza did as Clem bid and returned just as he was picking up his oars.

'Careful,' he called as she went to jump onto the edge of the trow. 'Remember to place your foot in the middle or you'll have us both in the water along with all that food.'

As Clem carefully navigated across the flooded fields, Eliza became used to the gentle rocking of the little boat. Although she'd seen everywhere swamped before, it was the first time she'd actually been out on the water and couldn't help feeling a frisson of excitement as she stared around the vast lake. Clem followed the course of the rhynes, wherever he could make them out, using the pollarded willows as a guide and before long they were making the first of their deliveries to the grateful customers of Worth. After they'd repeated the process in Stathe and Burrowbridge, he gestured towards the empty bottom of the trow.

'Thanks to you I've visited twice as many cottages as I expected to today. If you're still happy to help, we'll need to stop off and restock.'

'Of course,' beamed Eliza. It was good to feel useful and she'd enjoyed handing out much-needed supplies to neighbours and to some she'd never even met before, whilst Clem kept the trow as close to the cottages as he could. They'd nearly reached Stoke when Clem pointed to a deep gouge in the bank of a rhyne.

'Someone tried to manoeuvre a large boat across the flooded fields, there,' he told her. 'It didn't even have a flat bottom,' he tutted in disgust. 'Ended up well and truly stuck in the mud and had to be rescued. As if our boys haven't got enough to do.' Despite Clem's disdainful expression, Eliza's heart skipped. Had Theo been trying to reach her?

She hadn't time to dwell on the matter for Clem was mooring up a gully close to the village. Having replenished supplies from the local shops, they were struggling under the weight of full sacks when Eliza spotted the school mistress.

'Good afternoon Mrs Poundsberry,' she called. 'I hope you are well.'

'Thank you, yes,' the woman responded. 'I was sorry to hear of your loss.'

'And I'm sorry I had to give up my position. I've really missed the girls and was wondering if, now Gramfer's coming to terms with things, I might return for a few hours each week.'

'I'm sorry Eliza,' replied the school mistress. 'But the girls' education couldn't be interrupted so I have already appointed another.' Smiling apologetically, she went on her way, taking with her Eliza's hopes for the future.

'I thought you were too busy to even think of going back to the school,' Clem said, helping her into the trow.

'I know,' she sighed. 'But being out amongst people again today has made me realize just how lonely it is back home. As soon as the floods disappear, Gramfer will be out amongst his beloved withy beds and I'll be back to weaving baskets in the barn. I mean, I enjoy making them but . . .' her voice trailed away.

'You like having company,' Clem finished shooting her a knowing look.

'Well, I did enjoy teaching the girls,' she murmured, turning away so he didn't see her flush. Had he noticed her absence from the barn during harvest?

It was almost dark and mist was rising from the waters by the time Clem dropped her off. Although she was chilled to her bones, it had felt good to see other people and feel she'd made a difference too.

Another week passed and just when Eliza thought she'd go mad with only Gramfer's muttering and moaning for company, the water slowly began to recede. Although fields and paths began to emerge, to Eliza's consternation, Theo didn't. She couldn't help worrying some glamorous lady had caught his attention at one of the grand parties and balls his family had held. One swathed in a silk dress, she thought, glancing hopelessly up at the line strung over the fireplace where she'd tried in vain to dry their coarse clothes these past weeks. It was a seemingly never-ending task, and by the time they were ready to wear, they reeked of peat smoke.

The flood waters had receded from the cott, leaving behind a thick layer of dirty sludge which coated the floor and lower walls of the living room and scullery as well as covering the fields with a fine layer of silt. Resigned to spending the best part of the day cleaning up, Eliza waited until her gramfer had left to check his stacks of newly-cut withies and beds, before getting out the besom and filling a bucket with water and the lye her grammer had saved for such occasions. Pulling on her mother's mob cap, and donning an old apron, she opened the door and began cleaning. It was hard work sweeping the slimy, sticky muck out of the cott then giving everywhere a thorough scrubbing. By the time she was satisfied she'd got rid of the worst, her back was aching and she was hot and dirty from her exertions.

Picking up the bucket of filthy water, she traipsed wearily outside and was about to empty it into the rhyne, when she heard a whinny. Her heart flipped and looking up, she saw Theo trotting towards her.

'Excuse me, Miss,' Theo called.

'Theo,' she replied, letting her bucket fall to the ground.

'Gracious Eliza, is that you?' he asked frowning as he dismounted.

Chapter 12

She stared down at her mud stained apron in dismay. He couldn't have seen her looking worse, she thought, snatching off the cap so that her curls cascaded over her shoulders. Immediately, his lips curled into a wide grin and heedless of her damp garments, he held out his arms and pulled her close.

'Dearest Eliza, it's been an absolute age and I've missed you so much. Have you missed me too?' he asked, releasing her and gazing at her intently.

'Why yes, although we've been up to our eyes in water,' she told him. 'Well not literally but the floods did sweep through the cott, which is why I've been cleaning out the silt,' she added, pointing to the dirty trail behind her.

'You've been flooded?' he asked, his astonishment evident as he peered out over the fields that still gleamed silver. 'Gracious, you poor thing.'

'You didn't know?'

'Had no idea. Father insisted I join him for a hunt on Exmoor. Then the party decided to go shooting. It went on for ages. Only got back last night.' So, he hadn't tried to reach her, she thought. 'As you can see, I came as soon as

I could,' he went on oblivious to her thoughts. 'I spent the whole time dreaming about you,' he added, frowning as he took her red hands in his. 'Goodness, they look really sore.'

Eliza sighed, for the constant damp, weaving and cleaning had left them chaffed. However, all thought of her hands were forgotten when he pulled her closer. As his lips grazed hers, she felt tingles darting through her body like millions of shooting stars.

'Oh, it's so good to see you,' she murmured as she smiled up at him.

'Well, Eliza Priddle, I'm here to formalize our liaison. Let me tether Bodrilly here and you can introduce me to your grandfather.'

'And who wishes to be introduced to me?' They spun around to find George, leaning on his stick.

'Gramfer, this is Theo, Theobald Seymour and he would like to speak with you. Theo this is my grandfather, George Priddle.'

'Good to make your acquaintance, sir,' Theo said, proffering his hand. To Eliza's dismay, her gramfer ignored it and continued staring at Theo, shaking his head in disbelief.

'Where're you from?' he suddenly barked. His voice was so harsh, it broke the quietude of the drove, sending the water fowl squawking as they sought refuge further down the rhyne.

'Montacute Manor, sir. It's just the other side of—'

'I know where 'tis.'

'Then perhaps you'll permit me to come inside and explain the reason for my visit.'

'I'll have no Seymour on my land let alone in my home. Be off with you,' he shouted, shaking his stick at Theo.

'But sir . . .' he began.

'Gramfer . . .' Eliza gasped. They spoke in unison but George ignored them both as he advanced on Theo, waving his stick threateningly.

'You're to have no further contact with my granddarter, understand? Now get off my land and don't come back.'

'You can't do that,' Eliza protested.

'I can and have. You're only seventeen and my ward until such time as you gain your majority.' He turned to Theo. 'Come here again and I'll have you up in court for pursuin' a minor. Do you hear me?' he asked, again brandishing his stick.

'But sir, I mean no harm—' Theo began.

'Then you'll do as I say and leave right now, afore I gets me gun,' he snarled, incandescent with rage. 'Come along Eliza,' he ordered, making his way indoors.

'I don't know what's come over him,' she exclaimed, shaking her head in bewilderment.

'I'll try to speak with him again,' Theo said, taking a step towards the cott.

'No,' Eliza said, putting her hand out to detain him. 'Best wait until he's calmed down. I've never seen him like this before.'

'If you're sure,' Theo frowned.

'I'll find out what's got into him,' Eliza replied, then hesitated not wanting to let Theo go.

'Eliza, I said get yourself in here,' George bellowed.

'I'll wait for you at the shepherd's hut,' Theo said, throwing himself onto Bodrilly's back. 'Perhaps he'll see reason if you speak with him alone.'

'I'll join you as soon as I can,' she whispered, torn between wanting to go with him yet needing to find out what had got into her gramfer.

'Did you have to be so rude?' she asked as she entered the cott. 'That was the most embarrassing situation I've ever found myself in,' she told him.

'Pah, you'll find yourself in a much worse one if you don't heed my words, girl,' he hissed, eyes narrowing as he stood facing her. 'Carryin' on like that and on my land too. I won't have it.'

'But Gramfer, Theo came here to ask your permission to walk out with me.'

'Over my dead body,' he barked, his cheeks flushing red as beetroot.

'What do you mean?'

'Just what I say.'

'But why Gramfer?' she asked. 'Theo's a fine man. He's from a good family and—' She came to a halt as the old man snorted. Slowly he made his way over to his chair, dropping down with such a thud, a cloud of smoke billowed from the fire setting off his coughing. Eliza clenched her fists in frustration yet could only stand there and wait until the spasm had passed. The mood he was in, if she offered him a mug of water, he'd probably throw it over her. Finally, his spluttering stopped.

'Just do as I say, girl. It'll be for the best, mark my words,' he wheezed.

'But why can't I walk out with Theo?' she persisted, determined to find out why he'd taken against him.

'Because you're too young,' he muttered.

'For heaven's sake Gramfer. You were telling me only recently how you married Grammer when she was my age.'

'That were different, we was of the same class. Trust me, no good can come of it. You're not to see him and that's an end to it,' he muttered, leaning back and closing his eyes. Eliza stared at him in disbelief. Never before had he forbidden her to do anything. But she was grown up now and could make her own decisions.

She waited until snores filled the room, then jumped to her feet. Snatching up her shawl and bonnet she quietly let herself outside. Quickly she rinsed the worst of the silt from her hands in the water butt, then sped towards the wood. She was seventeen, old enough to decide for herself who she had as a follower. And she wanted Theo. Already she knew she loved him and nothing or nobody was going to stop her seeing him.

'You came,' Theo cried, jumping to his feet as she let herself into the shepherd's hut. He'd lit the fire but she hardly noticed as she threw herself into his arms and the warmth of his embrace radiated through her.

'Did you doubt that I would?'

'Well, I know how fond you are of your grandfather so I can only presume you managed to talk some sense into him.

Come and sit down and tell me about it. I felt terrible leaving you to sort things out, but my presence seemed to enrage him.'

'I don't know why,' she sighed. 'I did tackle him but he was having none of it. All he'd say was I am too young, although Grammer was the same age when they wed. Oh yes, and that no good would come of it because you were of a different class.'

He stared at her for a moment then frowned. 'If he didn't agree, does your being here mean you have gone against his wishes?'

'Yes. I'm old enough to make my own decisions and I wish to be here with you,' she told him defiantly.

'You're beautiful when roused,' he murmured, running a finger over her hot cheeks. 'The question is, what do we do now?'

'Perhaps we could continue meeting here until I can talk him round,' she said, looking at him hopefully. He pulled her closer and all was quiet save for the beating of their hearts and the crackling of the fire. 'You do want to carry on seeing me?' she asked, realizing he hadn't replied. He pulled away from her and she feared she'd said the wrong thing.

'Of course, I do,' he admitted. 'Although Father too would have an apoplexy. But then . . .' he grinned and sank to one knee. 'Marry me, Eliza Priddle.'

Heart thudding, she stared down at him in astonishment. Suddenly the door of the hut was yanked opened and a gust of icy air swept into the hut. They jumped as a weather-beaten face almost hidden beneath a woollen hat, peered at them in astonishment.

'Aye up, what be goin' on in 'ere?' the man muttered, staring from one to the other. Theo jumped to his feet.

'We were merely seeking shelter,' he replied.

'Well I'm afraid you'll have to seek it elsewhere,' the man told them, climbing inside and glancing appreciatively at the crackling fire. 'I use the 'ut for the lambin', see?' he told them, holding up the blood streaked squirming body he'd been cradling. 'Just began it has, so I'll be needin' to keep an eye on things.'

'Yes of course,' Eliza said quickly when Theo hesitated. 'We're just going.' Straightening her bonnet and shawl, she hurried towards the door.

'Good day to you,' Theo replied, pulling on his coat and stuffing the blanket into his leather bag.

'Best get the girl home, there be snow on that there wind,' the shepherd grunted, hunkering down in front of the fire and rubbing the little lamb briskly with a cloth.

Outside the sky was already beginning to darken and Eliza shivered. Theo put an arm around her and, snuggled into his warmth, they made their way towards Bodrilly.

'It's too cold for you to walk,' he said, helping her over the stile. Before she could protest, he sprang nimbly into the saddle and patted the space in front of him. 'Jump up and I'll take you back . . . no not right to the cott,' he added, when she hesitated. 'We'll stop behind it so your grandfather doesn't hear.'

Eliza felt her earlier confidence seep away as Theo helped her up. She could only imagine what mood Gramfer would be in. As Theo tugged on the rein, all thought of her gramfer disappeared. She'd never been on a horse before and found the sensation of trotting up and down exhilarating. However, it was nothing like the thrill of Theo's arms holding her firmly in place. Lost in the wonder of it all, she hardly noticed when they came to a halt behind the cott.

'So, Eliza Priddle,' he said, as he handed her down then slid to the ground beside her. 'You have yet to respond to my proposal. Do you have an answer for me?'

'Is that you out there Eliza?' As the querulous voice of her gramfer interrupted them yet again, Eliza groaned. Why did he have to spoil such a magical moment?

'I must go or he'll come out and get me,' she whispered.

'God Eliza, we can't carry on like this,' Theo groaned. Her heart flopped and she stared at him in dismay. Surely, he wasn't giving up now?

'Eliza, get yerself in here now.'

'I've a good mind to throw you back on Bodrilly and ride off into the night with you,' Theo declared.

'There's nothing I'd like better,' she giggled, thankful he wasn't giving up on her. 'But Gramfer'll be out here with his gun if I don't go in now.'

'I'll not let you go until you promise to meet me tomorrow. I'll be here waiting for your answer.'

'I will meet you, but better make it in the woods. Gramfer will be out checking his withy beds so could be anywhere along here,' she told him, gesturing to the willows.

'Eliza!'

'I'll try and talk to him,' she promised. Then on tiptoe, she crept around the back of the cott until she came to the privy. 'Honestly Gramfer, can't a girl attend to her toilette in peace,' she called, emerging from the gloom.

Chapter 13

'Been waitin' for my supper,' Gramfer grumbled. 'Suppose you've been out in the barn catchin' up on them laundry baskets.' As he fixed her with his gimlet eye, she busied herself pouring hot water into the teapot.

'The orders are up to date,' she soothed. 'Now, it'll have to be hash,' she added, throwing leftover meat and potatoes into the skillet.

'Mary always added an egg,' he grumbled, when she set it before him.

'Well, we haven't any left so you'll have to make do without,' she said lightly, determined not to let him nettle her. 'How are the withies looking?'

'They'll bounce back. Be a while 'til I can sow me sets though, looks like we might get snow.'

'Well that's not unusual this time of year, is it? And you usually wait 'til spring anyhow,' she told him only to receive a doleful look. 'Look Gramfer, can we talk about Theo . . .'

'No,' he shouted, slamming his fist down on the table. 'That man's never to darken our door again. And what's more, I'll make sure he don't,' he said patting the gun beside his chair.

'But . . .'

'There's no buts, girl. You'll not mention that name in here again.' Seeing the set of his chin and the way his eyes glittered, Eliza knew it would be futile continuing the conversation. Getting to her feet, she began clearing away their dishes. 'Believe me, it's for your own good,' he added.

Nothing or nobody would stop her from seeing Theo, but she knew better than to pursue the matter. It was strange Gramfer should be so upset when only recently he'd wanted to see her settled. She couldn't remember him ever being this incensed before. Was it because he had his heart set on her marrying Clem? Although she hated deceiving him, if he wouldn't discuss it with her, he left her no choice. She loved Theo and intended giving him her answer in the morning.

'So, what do you think?' Theo asked, his breath rising like mist as he pulled her closer. They were sheltering in the woods; the one place she knew they'd be safe from prying eyes. Although the threatened snow had only resulted in a light sprinkling, the temperatures had plummeted and there was a bitter wind howling through the trees. A shiver ran through her, whether from the cold, Theo's closeness or what he'd just proposed, she wasn't sure.

'But how would we get there?' she asked, excitement tingling despite the enormity of what he was suggesting.

'We'll catch the staging post,' he grinned. 'It shouldn't take too long for Gretna's only just over the Scottish border.

Please say yes, Eliza.' He looked at her so lovingly she felt her heart melt.

'But what about Gramfer? I can't just up and leave him by himself, he'd never manage.'

'Look I understand your dilemma but think of the longer term. There are plenty of nice dwellings around our estate. Once we're married, I'll sort something out, both for us and your Grandfather. It'll certainly be an improvement on that damp hovel you're living in at the moment,' he shuddered. Eliza's hearted lifted. With his rheumatics getting worse, Gramfer would benefit from living somewhere better.

'Oh Eliza, you remind me of a little bird the way you put your head on one side as you consider the whys and wherefores of everything. Remember, as your husband, it will be up to me to take care of you.'

'Oh,' she gazed at him in wonder, thinking how lovely it would be not to have to worry. 'But I must leave a note for Gramfer, he'll worry else.'

'Best not to. We'll write when the deed is done. By that time, it will be too late for him to do anything about it. He doesn't have any transport here, does he?'

'Gramfer always uses shanks's pony.'

'He has a horse?' His brows lifted in surprise.

'No silly. That means he walks everywhere. The only transport here is Clem's trow, and he keeps that up on the Parrett.'

'Oh, I see,' he replied, clearly not understanding at all. 'Of course, if you think it's all too much . . .' His abrupt manner had her turning to him in dismay.

'No, of course not,' she said quickly. It's just that since Grammer died, I've been looking after Gramfer. But you're right, I should be concentrating on us,' she agreed, leaning into the warmth of his chest and breathing in the citrusy smell that was him. There he was making romantic plans for their future and all she could think of was practicalities.

'We'll need to be away at first light so meet me by the woods as usual and Bodrilly can take us to pick up the coach at the staging post.'

Back at the cott, Eliza could hardly contain her excitement as she packed a few belongings into the carpet bag that had belonged to her mother. She thought about wearing the silk blouse then realized her gramfer would be suspicious should he get up early and see it. Besides, she needed it for her wedding ceremony. Heart flipping with anticipation, she folded it carefully then added the amber comb noting that the emerald chips matched it perfectly.

It was difficult to act normally over supper. Though her gramfer was amiable enough, Eliza felt a pang of guilt shoot through her every time he smiled at her. She hated the thought of going against him, and yet a decent cottage, free from damp, would be good for him, wouldn't it?

'You wool gatherin' girl?' Realizing her gramfer was speaking, Eliza looked up from her plate. 'I was asking how the orders are?'

'They've slowed down since the floods Gramfer, but I'm sure when everything's back to normal we'll get more.' In truth, she was feeling relieved she wouldn't be letting anyone down. 'I think I'll turn in,' she said, bending and kissing his cheek.

Upstairs in her room, she penned a quick note, for despite what Theo had said, she didn't want Gramfer worrying.

As the first streaks of grey lightened the sky, Eliza stole from the cott. Anxious in case her gramfer woke, nervous Theo wouldn't show and fearful she was doing the right thing, she hurried towards the woods. Just as he'd promised he was waiting astride Bodrilly and his eyes lit up as soon as he saw her.

'Come along,' he whispered, taking her bag then helping her up into the saddle. As soon as his arms closed around her, any lingering doubt vanished like the morning mist. Theo was a competent rider and it wasn't long before they'd gained the road where he urged the horse into a canter.

Eliza was filled with excitement, clinging to the front of the saddle as she was bounced on Bodrilly's back, the wind nearly lifting the bonnet from her head. In the gloom of the overcast morning, blurred images of isolated cottages, farmhouses, hedges and stunted trees swept past. She'd never experienced anything like it before and in seemingly no time they came to a cluster of buildings beside a crossroads. Theo turned Bodrilly into the courtyard and Eliza saw a brightly painted coach with four dapple grey horses waiting. As he dismounted and reached out his hand to help her down, ostlers came running to assist. One took Bodrilly's reins and Theo handed over some coins. Then retrieving their bags, he turned towards another man wearing a heavy leather coat and hat.

'If you could stow your luggage in the box, sir,' the man said. Theo did as asked, just as a group of travellers swarmed out of the hostelry eager to get on with their journey.

'Come on,' urged Theo, taking her arm and all but pushing her inside the coach. They'd only just sat down in the corner when other passengers squashed in beside them and judging from the thuds, others were clambering on top. A large woman wearing a dark blue cape with matching hat positioned herself noisily opposite and gave Eliza a piercing stare then turned her attention to Theo. Nudging her companion, she started to say something but whatever it was got lost in a loud blast from the coaching horn, and with a rattle and judder they began to move.

As they made their way back onto the road, the woman in blue gave Eliza a knowing look before turning back to speak to her friend. Judging from the nods in their direction, it was obvious she and Theo were the topic of conversation. When she'd become used to the rocking and rattling of the carriage and the exhilarating sensation of a world she'd never seen before speeding past the windows, she turned to Theo.

'I still don't understand why we have to go all the way to this Gretna place,' she murmured, careful to keep her voice low.

'The laws are different there. Regrettably, since the English

Marriage Act, clandestine marriages have been outlawed in this country.'

'Clandestine?' she frowned.

'Secret, which ours will be, as we have no parental permission,' he grinned delightedly.

'You mean your parents don't know either,' Eliza exclaimed, only for Theo's eyes to widen as the others in the coach turned in their direction. He smiled graciously before turning back to Eliza.

'Good heavens no,' he said in hushed tones. 'Father would have an apoplexy if he knew I was marrying someone without an estate, or at least a dowry to bring to the union. I can just imagine his horror if I were to say you came with withy beds. Not that there is anything wrong with them,' he added quickly when he saw her expression. 'I still find myself drawn to them as I was to you that first time.'

'Yes, I know what you mean,' she admitted, recalling how she'd felt she'd been waiting for him all her life. Trite or not, it was true. 'But we will be properly married, won't we?'

'Heavens, yes. They are more liberal in Scotland and, as I said, Gretna is only just over the border. All we'll need are a couple of witnesses and I'm sure we will have no difficulty finding them.'

'Oh, I see,' she said, although she didn't fully understand. Smiling reassuringly, Theo squeezed her arm and she felt her worries dissipating. Having been too excited to sleep the previous night and with the carriage rocking from side to side, she felt her eyelids growing heavy. As the woman opposite shot her another curious look, Eliza closed her eyes.

'Wake up sleepy head.' Her eyes snapped open to find Theo smiling down at her. 'We're stopping to change the horses.'

'Change them?' she asked, her brain still befuddled. 'Change them for what?'

'Fresh ones. These have travelled a fair distance and need food and rest.'

As the doors opened and the others began climbing out, she peered out of the window, surprised at the activity going on around them. Men were rushing out of stables, some leading the new horses, as they headed across the straw strewn yard towards them.

'Do you need to, er, refresh yourself?' Theo asked. Eliza shook her head. The sight of the imposing brick building and the throng of noisy people all going about their business looked intimidating and she had no wish to leave the safety of the coach.

'Cook packed a picnic,' he said, looking pleased.

'Doesn't she ever ask where you eat all these lunches?' Eliza enquired.

'Good heavens no. It's not the staff's place to question our wishes,' he exclaimed, staring at her in astonishment before reaching into his leather bag and drawing out a package.

'Tonight, we will stay at a coaching house en route so you will have the opportunity to change and refresh yourself before we dine,' Theo told her.

'I didn't realize we'd be away so long,' she sighed. 'I thought we'd be home again by tomorrow.'

'Well unless you can miraculously get this carriage to fly in the sky, I'm afraid you're in for a long journey. Gretna is some 300 miles from Somersetshire you know.'

'Oh,' she gulped, feeling stupid. She thought of Gramfer. He would have found her note by now, and she hoped he'd understand. Although she knew deep down, he wouldn't.

'Now come on, tuck in,' he said, handing her a pie glistening with red berries. Worried about Gramfer, she had little appetite but not wishing to offend Theo took a tentative bite. 'Oh goody, game,' he announced gleefully, not noticing her reluctance as he bit into his.

As they sat munching in silence, Eliza stared out of the window. They were in the courtyard of another hostelry flanked by stables, similar to the first one they'd left. Then seemingly moments later, the travellers re-emerged and, with much pushing and claiming of space, clambered back inside. With a sound of the horn, the carriage began to move.

Soon they'd left the buildings behind and seemed to be passing tree after tree, hedge after hedge, as the flat landscape of the levels gradually began to change. The coach slowed as the horses climbed a long gradient, and Eliza could see rough scrubby land rising to a row of high hills on one side, and a glimpse of a wide expanse of muddy water in the distance on the other. So, this is what the outside world looks like, she thought, her heart hammering with excitement. There was a hypnotic rhythm to the rocking which she found strangely comforting, however, the journey seemed to go on for ever. As the sky darkened, the temperature in the carriage plummeted but she noticed that the wind was coming from the east, so at least it was unlikely to snow. She hoped Gramfer had stoked the fire and heated the stew she'd left for him. Pushing down the feelings of guilt, she shifted awkwardly in her seat.

'A few days travelling is a small price to pay for our being able to marry and spend the rest of our days together, is it not?' Theo murmured, moving closer. Ignoring the frown from the woman opposite, Eliza nodded. Put like that, it did seem reasonable. She must have dozed again for the sudden lurching of the carriage as they pulled to a stop jolted her awake.

'This is where we are staying for the night,' Theo told her, just as the door opened and the steps were lowered. Taking her arm, he led her into the coaching house. 'I'm afraid it's quite modest but looks clean. Let's hope the food's edible.' Eliza stared around. Even in the gathering gloom, she could see the tall building looked quite palatial compared to the cott she was used to.

'Good evening, sir, madam,' the landlord greeted them cordially. Aware of the glances they were attracting from the other travellers, Theo leaned forward and spoke in hushed tones. As money changed hands, the landlord's demeanour changed.

''Ere Nancy, you show the lady to her room,' he shouted, nudging the bosomy woman beside him who was making eyes at Theo.

'Coo blimey, he's a chunk. However did you net 'im?' the woman asked, looking Eliza up and down, before leading her up the stairs. 'He asked for two rooms but I've put you next door to each other. I'm sure you'll want to see to 'is comfort.' It was only when the woman laughed raucously that Eliza got her meaning.

'Oh, but we're to be married,' she stuttered, anxious the woman should understand.

'Cors you are dear,' the woman snorted. 'Still it's no business of mine. Gets all sorts 'ere we do.'

Chapter 14

If Eliza was shocked by the woman's reaction, she was to become used to it for it was the same in all the establishments they stopped at. While landlords treated Theo with deference, she was given knowing looks and nudges by the landladies. Just wait until their return journey, Eliza vowed. She'd take great delight in flashing her wedding ring in front of them and calling Theo, *husband*.

She'd wanted to see something of the world and now she was. She'd never realized how big it was or how many different people she'd come into contact with, for seemingly the passengers were different every day. Some were pleasant, some curious, some smartly dressed whilst others looked scruffy and smelled decidedly less than fragrant.

Throughout the seemingly never-ending journey, her thoughts were in turmoil. Never for one moment had she envisaged being away for so long and she wondered if Gramfer was taking care of himself. She hoped Clem had called by, though what he'd think of her behaviour was another matter entirely. But then Theo would catch her eye, squeezing her arm so that excitement soared again.

Finally, after seven interminable days of travelling through rolling green countryside, noisy, dirty and smelly towns, past towering snow-capped hills and vast shimmering lakes, they arrived in the village of Gretna. Eliza's excitement soon turned to bewilderment when she saw it was nothing more than a huddle of low stone cottages and old buildings. Surely it should look more romantic than this?

'Well, here we are,' Theo announced. Bound up in his excitement, he didn't notice her frown. As they alighted by a limewashed cottage and blacksmith's forge, heedless of the other passengers, he leaned forward and kissed her gently on the lips. Tingles of desire shot through her body and she realized it didn't really matter where they were as long as they were together.

'Now my wife-to-be, let's see where we can refresh ourselves before our wedding,' he grinned. With Eliza's frayed carpet bag in one hand and his own smart leather Gladstone, embossed with his initials, in the other, he led the few steps to the cottage where a tiny woman dressed in a plaid shawl and green dress waited.

'Welcome to Gretna, come away in, I'm Mrs McTavish,' she greeted them. Although it was dim inside, the smell of beeswax and heather gave it a homely feel after the impersonal coaching houses that reeked of horses, ale and tobacco. After a quick discussion with the woman and more exchange of money, Theo turned to Eliza and smiled.

'Mrs McTavish will show you where you can get ready then has kindly agreed to be a witness,' he told her. 'Meanwhile I shall find another and will be waiting for you when you're ready.'

'Aye, away yer go,' she ordered him, with a wave of her hand. 'Now my dear, you come with me. Luckily you were the only passengers to disembark from that coach but you'd do well to make the most of a wee bit of quiet before the next stage gallops in from Carlisle. Then, it'll be all chaos and confusion with more couples desperate to wed before it leaves again,' she sighed, throwing open a door.

Inside the tiny room, a fire burned in the shiny black grate and next to it was a chair with a folded towel on its wooden seat. A washstand with porcelain bowl, soap and steaming jug of water stood in the corner.

'There's some *sal volatile* should you feel faint. I know what nerves can do,' the woman said, gesturing to a small bottle on the shelf above. 'If there's nothing else, I'll leave you to get ready.'

'Thank you, Mrs McTavish,' Eliza murmured, but the woman had already bustled out of the room. Grubby from her travels she washed, then changed into the green blouse. Then she brushed her hair but as she arranged her curls in the amber comb that had been her grammer's, she was seized by a feeling of guilt. How she wished the woman was here to reassure her. But then Eliza wasn't sure she'd approve and she definitely wouldn't be pleased she'd simply upped and left Gramfer.

But she hadn't come all this way for nothing. This was her wedding day, she reminded herself, smoothing down her frayed skirts in front of the mirror. She didn't know if she was suitably attired but had little choice. Then it hit her. Not only was she about to be married, tonight would be her wedding night. Butterflies skittered in her stomach so that she had to hold on to the back of the chair and take a deep breath. Everything would be alright, for dearest Theo had shown her nothing but the utmost courtesy on their long journey. A knock on the door made her jump, rousing her from her musings.

'Yer looking right bonny, lass,' Mrs McTavish crooned, bustling into the room. 'Now, yer just needs heather for luck,' she said, handing Eliza a sprig of white flowers bound with ribbon. 'Come on, yer young man's waiting with the anvil priest. All of a dither, he is. Keeps looking this way and that. Not that that's unusual, minding the circumstances.' It was hard to imagine confident, self-assured Theo being nervous, Eliza thought, following the woman out of the room.

'What do I have to do?' she asked, her voice shaking. The woman stopped and gave a sympathetic smile.

'Yer just stand one side of the anvil with yer young man on the other so the blacksmith, also known as the anvil priest, can join yer hands in matrimony. There's nothing to be—' But the rest of her sentence was lost as the front door burst open so violently it shook on its hinges. 'What the—' she began as a dishevelled man staggered into the tiny hallway and stared wildly around.

'Gramfer!' Eliza cried, her eyes widening as she recognized the figure before them. 'What are you doing here?'

'I could ask the same of you but I fear I know the answer. Where is he?' he demanded.

'The young man is waiting in the forge,' Mrs McTavish replied, seemingly unflustered. As her gramfer rushed outside, Eliza stared helplessly at the woman for a moment, then ran after him.

'Gramfer, Gramfer,' she called but he was already disappearing into the building next door. Dashing after him, she entered a low room where Theo and a large man in a black coat, his face grimy with soot, were standing by the large black anvil.

'This weddin' cannot and must not take place,' Gramfer roared, rushing over to the blacksmith.

'I say, I must protest,' Theo began, but both men ignored him. 'You have been paid to marry us and I insist that's what you do,' he added, addressing the blacksmith.

'Be quiet Seymour,' Gramfer roared, before turning back to the blacksmith. 'I repeat, this marriage is not to take place.'

'Gramfer please,' Eliza cried.

'Be quiet, there's things you don't know,' he replied in a voice that brooked no argument. 'Come with me, boy, you need to hear what I have to say or so help me, you'll be committin' a crime against God.'

'Take your hands off me, old man. Just who do you think you are?' Theo asked, shaking Gramfer's hand off, then flicking an imaginary speck from the shoulder of his jacket.

'Come here and I'll tell you exactly who I am, scoundrel.'

Shocked, Eliza could only stare as her gramfer took hold

of Theo's arm again and dragged him over to the other side of the room where an assortment of iron tools was lined up alongside the white-washed walls. As Theo's glance slid to the axe he was standing beside, Eliza's heart almost stopped beating. Oh goodness no, surely, he wouldn't? She started to go over to them but her gramfer held up his hand in warning. Edging Theo away from the lethal looking blade, he leaned in closer and began speaking urgently, pointing to Theo's abdomen. What on earth was he doing Eliza wondered. Then, she saw Theo glance down and nod slowly, sheer disbelief followed by indignation crossing his now ashen face. Slowly, as if on leaden legs, he walked back to Eliza.

'I really don't understand this Eliza but before we proceed, I must consult with my father urgently,' he muttered.

'But why? What's the matter?' she asked, finding her voice at last.

'Your grandfather has made a serious allegation,' he exclaimed. 'I'm sure he is mistaken but I need to make certain before we can be wed. Don't worry, my sweet,' he said as she gasped in dismay. 'I will come and see you as soon as I can.' He kissed her gently on the cheek, then strode towards the door. As he reached the black anvil, the anvil they should have joined hands over, Eliza could stand it no longer. But as she made to follow him, her gramfer put his hand on her arm to restrain her.

'What's going on?' Eliza demanded, tears streaming down her cheeks. But he let his arm drop and leaned back against the wall as if all the energy had drained from him. Mrs McTavish glanced at the blacksmith then came bustling over.

'Sir, there's going to be a rush for the anvil priest shortly. Best you come away back to the but and ben and I'll make a pot of tea,' she said, ushering them outside.

To Eliza's dismay, she saw the coach disappearing, the horses kicking up mud in their wake. Theo had gone, leaving her behind, and she felt like screaming. Two excited couples who'd just disembarked, stared curiously at her then eager to proceed with their own plans turned to Mrs McTavish.

'Away inside the forge, the blackie will see to yer,' she said, shooing them away. 'Come with me,' she told Eliza and her gramfer. Numbly, Eliza followed her back inside the cottage.

'Come away into the scullery, you can talk in there,' Mrs McTavish said gently, leading them into a cosy back room. As the woman bustled around pouring hot water into a pot, Eliza turned to her gramfer, bewilderment turning to anger.

'I suppose you're happy now you've stopped my wedding and sent Theo away,' she cried. Bleakly, he shook his head.

'The last thing I wanted to do was upset you Eliza but . . .' his voice petered out and he closed his eyes.

'But what?' she persisted.

'I know yer upset lass,' Mrs McTavish said, pouring tea into two mugs. 'But yer grandfather looks all in. Would you like a wee dram to go with that, sir?' she offered.

'Thank you, that's very kind but the tea will revive me,' he said.

'Well if you're sure. We keep a wee stock for such emergencies.'

'Well I'm glad someone realizes that's what this is,' Eliza

gulped. 'He's just ruined my wedding day. My betrothed has left without me, and I'm broken-hearted,' she cried.

Suddenly, the room spun before her and she slumped back in her chair. Mrs McTavish snatched a little blue bottle from the table and wafted it under Eliza's nose. Immediately, she began to cough and splutter.

'That's better,' the woman said. 'Look, I'll leave yer awhile.' Giving George a pitying look, she bustled from the room.

'Well, are you going to tell me what all this is about?' Eliza demanded, her strength returning. Her gramfer sighed.

'This will come as a shock, but I swear to God every word is the truth,' he murmured.

'For heaven's sake, just tell me why you stopped me marrying Theo?' she burst out, unable to contain herself any longer.

'Because he's your brother. Your twin brother, in fact.'

'What?' she laughed incredulously. 'Oh, come on Gramfer, that's ridiculous even for you.'

'I swear to God it's true,' he reiterated, then to Eliza's frustration, he paused and took a sip of his drink. 'Your mother died in childbirth, not givin' birth to you but your brother who came along minutes after you took your first breath.'

'No, that can't be true,' Eliza spluttered, staring at him in disbelief. The long journey must have affected his brain. And yet she'd never known Gramfer to lie, and from the pained expression on his face, it certainly looked as if he was being honest with her.

'I swear it's the truth Eliza. Your grammer guessed by your mother's size she was carryin' two babies and swore she'd take care of the second. But for all her bluster, she was a tender woman and when it came to it, couldn't bring herself to harm him.' He shuddered then took another sip of his drink.

'So what happened . . .' Eliza began, then almost screamed when Mrs McTavish appeared in the doorway.

'Excuse me interrupting, but yer'd best be making yer way outside for the last staging coach heading south has just pulled up.'

Chapter 15

Once again Eliza found herself crushed into the corner of a coach, only this time it was Gramfer beside her. Ignoring the other travellers, she turned to him.

'What happened to this so-called brother of mine?' she burst out impatiently as the horn sounded and they began to move.

'Better wait until we stop for the night,' he replied, staring meaningfully at the other occupants. 'Dirty linen and all that.'

'Dirty linen?' she cried, causing the man opposite to raise his brows.

'Try and restrain yerself,' Gramfer chided, sitting back in his seat and closing his eyes. Fuming with frustration, Eliza turned and stared out of the window. Fat flakes of snow were fluttering down from the darkening sky and everywhere looked still and cold.

'Leave him be, he looks exhausted. Whatever's ailing you will be better sorted when he's rested,' the man said quietly. The others murmured their agreement and Eliza knew she had no alternative.

As the carriage rattled and rolled its way south, she put her hands in her pockets to keep warm, then winced as something sharp jabbed her finger. It was the sprig of white heather. Some luck that had brought her, she thought, taking it out and shredding it into pieces. How could Theo have just left her like that? Why hadn't he stood up to Gramfer? She'd heard of being jilted at the altar but the anvil? At the very least he could have waited and accompanied them back home.

Turning to her gramfer, she felt a pang of guilt. He was white with fatigue and for the first time she realized the long journey had taken its toll.

Finally, as they pulled up outside the coaching house in Kendal her gramfer woke. As they stepped from the carriage, Eliza felt a fluttering of hope. Perhaps Theo had stopped here too. She stared frantically around hoping to catch sight of his auburn head in the crowd. But all she could see were the weary faces of her fellow travellers. She turned to her gramfer but before she could say anything, he patted her hand.

'I know yer impatient to hear the rest, but it will take time so we'll snatch a bite to eat first.' Eliza could have screamed. The last thing she wanted was to eat.

Later, having toyed with the ham and eggs before her, she stared expectantly at her gramfer. He pushed his empty plate to one side, ordered hot drinks to be brought then led her to a quieter corner at the back of the smoke-filled tap room.

'So, if this is true, why didn't Theo and I grow up together?' she asked, eager for him to continue where they'd been interrupted in Gretna.

'Times were hard.' His voice was low and she leaned

forward to hear. 'With your mother gone, Mary and I were at our wits' end as to how we would cope. Then we got word from the manor that Lord Seymour's son had been stillborn. The birth left her ladyship damaged and unable to bear any more children. Lord Seymour needed an heir and as Theo or Jack as we'd named him, was half his, he offered to bring him up as his own in return for a consideration and the promise of secrecy.' Eliza frowned as she tried to take everything in.

'You say Theo was half his? Does that mean . . .' He nodded.

'Whilst workin' at the manor, your mother fell in love with Lord Seymour. He swore he loved her too, but when she told him of her plight, he denied all knowledge and she was sent home in disgrace.'

'Oh, that's terrible,' she sighed. Then realization dawned. 'So, if Lord Seymour is Theo's father and you say we are twins then . . .'

'He's your father too,' he finished for her.

'You mean I have a rich father and yet live in a hov—' Realizing she was bordering on being rude, she grimaced. 'Sorry. It's just such a shock. I mean there's us having to count every farthing while Theo's been raised in the lap of luxury.'

'Life is unfair sometimes,' he agreed. 'But, if you're thinkin' of making contact, yer can't. We had to sign a declaration, so nothin' could ever come of it. Seymour's a ruthless man and will stop at nothin' to prevent his name being besmirched.'

'I can't believe Theo's like that.'

'We'll see,' her gramfer said, the doubt in his voice evident.

'He might have no choice. Them nobles live by their own rules.'

As Eliza tried to take all this in, he reached across the table and took her hand. 'Mary and I did what we thought was best at the time. You may not have had the luxuries money can buy but you were raised with love and have been like a darter to us. But I see now we should have told you sooner,' he sighed. 'Although, never in our wildest dreams did we expect this Theo to turn up on our doorstep.'

'I really love him, Gramfer,' she cried.

'I know,' he said sadly. 'But be sure that in time, you'll see it is the love of a sister to a brother.'

'Yet we felt so right together.'

'Oh blimey, you never er, you know?' He stopped, looking so aghast that even in the dim light of the tap room she saw colour flooding his cheeks.

'No, Gramfer, of course, we didn't,' she cried.

'Well, thank the Lord,' he murmured, letting out a long breath.

'From the first time I saw him it felt as though he was the other half of me,' she confided.

'That's because he is, what with you being twins. Surely you must have seen the likeness between you?'

'Not really,' she frowned, but it was true, they both had the same green eyes, red hair, although his was fairer.

'It were the first thing I noticed that day he called. Knew immediately who he was. When I saw the way you looked at him, I knew I had to save you from doin' something stupid. Except I went the wrong way about it.'

'If only you had told me,' Eliza sighed, a lump rising in her throat as she thought of what could never be. She took a sip of her drink then choked as the bitter liquid hit the back of her throat. 'But what did you say to make him leave so quickly?' she asked, still hurt by what she saw as his indecent haste.

'I simply asked if he had a strawberry birthmark on his abdomen. Mary saw it when he was born. Said it was the work of the devil, and perhaps she was right.'

'I don't believe that. Theo is a fine man and he's promised he'll come and see me once he's spoken with his father,' she told him, still hoping that somehow her Gramfer had got things wrong.

'I wouldn't hold your breath,' he muttered. 'He might have good intentions but once his father finds out, he'll put a stop to things. Like I said name and standing is everything to Seymour.' Eliza's heart sank like a stone. She'd been hoping there'd been a mistake for, despite everything, she loved him so much it hurt. But now, well it didn't seem likely, did it?

'Now let's call it a night. We have a long day ahead of us tomorrow,' he said, getting wearily to his feet.

Whereas the journey to Gretna with Theo had been exciting and full of anticipation, the one home was filled with disbelief and heartbreak. After the shock of her gramfer's revelation, Eliza desperately needed to speak with Theo and each passing mile saw her growing ever more impatient to see him. A love that would always be, yet never could be. Like the wheels on the carriage, the words kept going around and round in her head.

At each stop, she found herself searching the crowded hostelries for a glimpse of his auburn hair. It was futile though, and to make matters worse, the landladies seemed to delight in commenting on the fact that she was travelling with a different man this time.

Then the weather turned even colder with frequent hail and snow showers lashing against the windows and churning up the mud on the roads. Their slowed progress made the other travellers tetchy. Her Gramfer, exhausted by his travels, slept most of the time, leaving Eliza alone with her thoughts. How was Theo getting on with his father? How had he felt when he'd found out he was her brother? Suddenly, like a slap in the face, came the realization that Gramfer had been telling the truth. And if it hadn't been for him, she would have been married by now. To her brother.

Her face grew red, her throat constricted. Far from being cross with Gramfer she should be grateful to him. A wave of love engulfed her, but as she snuggled into his reassuring body, the coach suddenly gave a lurch then tilted. As the passengers were thrown against each other, the lady opposite screamed, waking her gramfer with a start.

'What the . . .' he stammered, his eyes snapping open. Before Eliza could say anything, the door was wrenched open and they were assaulted by a rush of cold air. The driver, collar turned up against the gusting wind that was blowing huge feathery flakes of snow into the coach, looked grim.

'Everybody out,' he announced. 'We've gone in a ditch, so mind the mud.' There were cries of consternation and mutters of dissent, but ignoring them, he held out his hand and helped each of them from the coach.

'Blimey, where the hell are we?' a rotund man, buttons straining over his middle, enquired, peering around the desolate landscape.

'Between Gloucester and Bristol, somewhere near to Dursley.'

'And what happens now?' a querulous woman asked, tying a scarf over her bonnet to prevent it from blowing away.

'We're going to try and get the coach out, so I suggest you take shelter under those trees,' the driver said, pointing to the line of elms ahead. 'Any of you gentlemen willing to lend a hand?'

'You must be joking,' the man protested, his florid face growing redder by the moment.

'I'll help,' George volunteered.

'No Gramfer, you can't,' Eliza protested.

'The lady's right,' agreed a smartly dressed gentleman who'd stayed hidden behind his newspaper since they'd left the last post. 'You look after the ladies, sir, I'll go and help the drivers. Otherwise I fear we shall have to wait for the next coach to come along.'

George smiled gratefully and let Eliza lead him over to the stark trees, which at this time of year would only afford minimum shelter. Still it was better than standing in the gusting wind that was showering them with snow. Shivering and silent, they watched while the drivers coaxed the horses and the men heaved and pushed as they endeavoured to drag the stricken carriage from its resting place.

'If only I'd thought, we could have returned by railway. Much quicker and safer,' Gramfer muttered.

'You mean you travelled to Gretna by train,' Eliza gasped, staring at him in astonishment.

'Clem helped. He was that worried about you, he wanted to come with me,' he admitted. Eliza frowned. Although Clem worked hard, he didn't earn that much and rail travel was prohibitively expensive for the likes of them, surely?

'We could only afford the one ticket especially after—' George began, but was interrupted by an almighty creak followed by a cracking sound as the coach was righted. The little crowd cheered then fell silent when it became evident that one axle had snapped and they would be going no further until it had been repaired. The gentleman gestured them over.

'Regrettably we'll be delayed for some time, but, as long as we don't move around, we can return to the coach and take shelter from this wretched weather,' he told them. 'One of the drivers is setting off to get help. Apparently, the next staging post is only a few miles away,' he explained, wiping mud from his hands with his handkerchief.

'Come on Gramfer,' Eliza said, their conversation forgotten as she guided the frozen man back to the coach. It was as cold inside as it had been out, but at least they were sheltered from the wind, and could wrap the coach's heavy, if somewhat soiled, blankets around them. The rotund man sank into his seat, pulled a hipflask from his pocket and gulped greedily. Then, noticing the others watching, he gave a rueful smile.

'Snifter anyone?' he asked, waving it around. There was a murmur of polite refusal before they all lapsed into silence.

Hearing a jangling sound, Eliza looked out of the window and saw the drivers unhitching the team. Then, one clambered onto the bare back of a large horse, and shoulders hunched against the thickening snow, began plodding his way down the road that now glistened white.

It was growing dark by the time they heard the rattling of the replacement coach. Eliza's feet were frozen and she could hardly feel them as they were transferred. Then with lanterns lighting their way, they set off again in the gathering gloom. The landlord, warned of their plight, had hot broth waiting, but her gramfer only managed a few sips before retiring for the night. Thank heavens the next day would see them home again, Eliza thought, noting his pallor as, ignoring the barmaid's smirk, she helped him up to his room.

She had so much to ask him still, and so much to thank him for.

Chapter 16

By the time they eventually arrived back at the cott, they were chilled to the bone and utterly exhausted. Although Eliza lit the fire, it took time to catch and they sat silent and shivering in their frost stiffened clothes. Even when it finally began smoking, it gave out little heat and the water took an age to boil. It was only when she'd made them a hot drink and they'd begun to thaw that she turned to her gramfer.

'I'm really sorry for all the trouble I've caused,' she murmured.

'We all make mistakes, Eliza. Thing is to learn from them then move on. Cors yours was more spectacular than most, but then what else would you expect from a hurdy 'ead,' he grinned wryly. 'Had Mary been here, happen she'd have handled things better.' Sighing, he stared into the fire.

'I've been wondering how you managed to fund the train fare for the long journey north?' she asked, for the question had been plaguing her. As he turned to face her, she saw his eyes were moist.

'Sold . . .' Seized by a sudden fit of coughing, he was unable to continue and Eliza stared helplessly, wishing she hadn't asked. Then he rallied. 'This . . .' he gestured around the room. 'My withies,' he wheezed. Her eyes widened in horror, but before she could say anything, another fit of coughing wracked his body.

As Eliza topped up his mug with water and waited for the spasm to pass, she pondered this revelation. That he'd sold up for her was shocking. And who could he have sold to so quickly? Guilt hung heavy in her chest that he should have done such a selfless thing for her, and it was only then that she realized the implication of her hasty actions. If it hadn't been for him, she would have been married to her brother by now. The very idea filled her with abject horror, yet she wasn't to have known, was she? If only she'd made more of an effort to explain her feelings for Theo her gramfer might have explained the situation before they'd eloped. Still, she'd never know now, would she?

'I'm so cold,' her gramfer shivered, breaking into her musing.

'Let's get you to bed, you'll be warmer under your blanket. A good night's rest and you'll feel much better,' Eliza assured him.

He was all in, and it took Eliza some time to get him up the stairs and onto his bed. She covered him with his pitifully thin blanket then as he lay there wheezing and shaking, quickly fetched her grammer's cover, adding his coat on top too. Finally, he fell into a restless sleep and she hurried down to the living room to prepare him another hot drink.

By the time she returned, he was bathed in perspiration and

muttering to himself. Gently she sponged his forehead with a damp cloth and whispered words of reassurance. Yet despite her best ministrations, the fever took hold and he spent the long night muttering and moaning, grunting and groaning. Then, just as the new day was breaking over the moor, he opened his eyes and reached for her hand.

'Eliza . . .' he croaked. She leaned closer.

'I'm here Gramfer. Just rest and you'll be better in no time.'

'Too . . . late,' he gasped.

'No, it isn't,' she said, clutching his hand. 'I'm sorry you had to come after me and when you're better, I'll make it up to you. I promise.'

'Nothin' to make up,' he muttered. 'Look after . . .' But the effort was too much and his eyelids fluttered closed. Fear clutched at her heart.

'Gramfer?'

'See . . . Clem . . .' he wheezed, and then the room was silent.

'No,' she wailed. Tears coursing down her cheeks, Eliza stared at the still figure in disbelief. There hadn't even been time to summon help, although she knew in her heart there was nothing anyone could have done. Heart heavy, she opened the tiny window to let his soul fly free. Then, as the sound of the dawn chorus flooded into the room, she stared towards the woods as if expecting Theo to appear on Bodrilly.

Knowing Gramfer's passing had been peaceful did nothing to assuage her overwhelming feeling of guilt. How would Theo feel when he arrived and found the man, whom he'd only just learned had been his gramfer too, was dead?

*

Bereft, Eliza knelt and placed a wooden cross bearing the name George on the newly dug grave beneath the oak tree. Her eyes were red rimmed with crying and lack of sleep, her conscience racked with remorse. As if tuning in to her thoughts, Clem put down the shovel and placed his arm around her.

'Don't blame yourself Red,' he murmured, pulling her close. 'George was riddled with rheumatics, his lungs congested. He knew he could go anytime.'

'But if I hadn't gone off like that, he wouldn't have come after me and got soaking wet. And where is Theo?' she cried. 'Surely, he should have spoken to his father and returned by now,' she blurted, automatically looking towards the woods.

'Don't know, Red,' Clem murmured, his lips hardening into a line. Then as if checking himself, he gave a wan smile. 'As Ma says, hindsight's a wonderful thing but makes not a h'appeth of difference. George had a good life, but it wasn't the same for him since Mary was taken. Take comfort that he is now gone to join her and his daughter.' Eliza nodded and smiled at him weakly. Dear Clem, always doing his best to make her feel better. 'Come on, you're frozen, let's go and get a hot drink,' he murmured, ushering her indoors.

Gently he eased her into the chair before the fire then placed a steaming mug in her hand. Smiling gratefully, she turned to him unable to keep her thoughts to herself any longer.

'I feel so terrible. He had to sell up to pay for his rail fare north. I didn't even get the chance to ask who to. Do you know? Please tell me it wasn't Izziah Gliddon?'

'Calm yourself Red. He might have been desperate but he'd have sold them to the devil rather than that merchant. Now, drink your brew else I'll have to force it down you,' he told her. Duly she sipped her drink, and slowly the warmth spread round her body replacing the numbness that had engulfed her.

'Where would I be without you,' she said, making an effort to smile.

'Well that's the thing, you don't have to be,' he murmured, staring at her in that direct way of his. Embarrassed, she looked away.

'You need to understand about Theo and I. You see we . . .' She sighed and shook her head. 'Incredible as it may sound, it seems we're twins.' There she'd admitted it. To her surprise though, he didn't seem shocked at all.

'I know, Red. George told me. Oh, he didn't want to,' he admitted when he saw her frown. 'But he was desperate. Swore me to secrecy...' he shrugged.

'Ironic isn't it? she said. 'I fell in love with Theo who wanted us to marry only to find out he's my brother. While you, who I've always thought of as a brother . . .' her voice trailed away as she realized how ungracious she sounded.

'Wants to marry you.' There was an awkward silence as his words hung in the air. 'Well Red, at least I'm eligible. You do realize that if your wedding to Theo had gone ahead, you'd have been in real trouble,' he said quietly.

'I know,' she sighed and stared into the fire.

'Well, I'd best be going,' he said, jumping to his feet. 'There's bread and stew from Ma in the pantry and I'll bring more peat when I next call. Look after yourself,' he added.

'Thanks Clem, for everything. I just wish . . .' she began but he shook his head.

'Don't Red,' he murmured, closing the door quietly behind him.

Desperate to keep her dark thoughts at bay, Eliza spent the next few days sorting through Gramfer's things, although there was pitifully little to show for his sixty years on earth. She then set about the onerous task of clearing the bedroom he'd shared with her grammer, her trinkets bringing back memories of happier times.

Finally, she gave the cott a thorough clean in readiness for Theo's visit. Yet still he didn't appear. *A love that would always be, yet never could be.* Seemingly from nowhere, the words that had haunted her on the journey back from Gretna, surfaced. Although they could never marry now, she and Theo were twins and would always share a special bond.

When there was nothing left to do indoors, she took herself to the barn where the withies were waiting. Their familiar, slightly astringent tang was comforting and selecting a suitable bundle, she settled herself onto her mat. Automatically, she began weaving, turning as she went, adding more to reinforce the hoop. Then with eight for the ribs she turned the frame upside down and wove more withies across them until the base was completed. She cut the butt ends and, using her iron to weigh the base down, began up-setting the uprights. Unbidden, the words to her grammer's song sprung to her lips:

> *One cane round, neat and tight,*
> *insert a decent border.*
> *Upset . . .*

A lump rose in her throat and she could sing no more. The tears that were never far away these days, streamed down her cheeks, but whether she was crying for her beloved gramfer, Clem's kindness, or the fact Theo hadn't appeared, she wasn't sure.

It was a pattern that was to repeat itself over the coming days. Although the weather was still cold, she kept the make-shift door open in the hope she'd look up from her work and see Theo standing there. While her fingers wove, her ears would listen for the sound of Bodrilly's hooves. But another week went by and he still didn't appear. *A love that would always be, yet could never be.* Like the rounds on the baskets, the words just wouldn't go away.

'Marnen Red. How're you doing?' Startled, she looked up to see Clem peering at her from the open doorway, turves of peat balanced over his broad shoulders. Lost in thought, she hadn't heard his paddles on the water.

'I'm fine, Willow Man,' she murmured, trying to sound convincing as her pet name for him came unbidden to her lips.

'Long as you are,' he murmured. 'Just go and put these in the stack. Guessed you'd be running low.' As he disappeared into the store, she wiped her cheeks and made an effort to compose herself.

'I thought I'd get back to the baskets, although I don't have any orders at the moment,' she said when he reappeared.

'That's cos you're a victim of your own success. You make those baskets so well they'll last for ever. Specially the ones I helped with,' he grinned, making her smile for the first time in days. 'Good that you're keeping busy though.'

She nodded, not wishing to tell him that even as she worked remorse cut through her like a blade through butter.

'Want a brew?' she asked, eager for his company. He shook his head.

'Wish I could but I need to check on Father's barge. It's moored up at Burrow with a load of sails from Martock. The men are waiting for the morrow's tide to take them up to Bridgwater. No peace for the wicked, eh? Not heard from Theo yet?' he asked casually.

'No,' she sighed. 'I expect it's taking longer than he thought to sort things out.' He stared at her for a long moment.

'Well Red, I wouldn't hold your breath. To my way of thinking, if he were coming, he'd have been here by now. Which he should have, being as how he all but abducted you.' She looked at him sharply and he shrugged. 'If that were me, I'd have been back making sure you were alright ages ago. You need looking after Red,' he called over his shoulder as he climbed into his trow.

Sadness settled on her shoulders like a big black cloud for hadn't she been thinking the same thing about Theo?

Although in fairness, she hadn't needed much persuading to run off with him. Finally, she acknowledged what her heart had refused to accept. Theo wasn't coming. With Clem voicing her doubts, she could deny it no longer. Even though they were unable to marry, had Theo truly loved her, he would have returned to check she was alright. They would have talked things through, moved forward as brother and sister. Evidently, he neither wanted that nor cared enough for her. Although that hurt, it was nothing compared to the remorse she was feeling for all she'd put her gramfer through. Perhaps it was the divine retribution her grammer used to speak about.

She took herself into the cott and stared bleakly around the room, empty now save for echoes of happier times. There was nobody or nothing here for her anymore and she wasn't waiting around for the landlord to evict her.

Clem's words had struck a chord. He might think she needed looking after, but she could take care of herself. Before she could change her mind, she hurried up the stairs and changed into her soft green blouse. Carefully, she packed her few things into the carpet bag she'd only recently put away. It was time to make her own way in life, perhaps even find out about her grandparents' past.

Downstairs, she snatched up the remaining bread and wedge of cheese and placed them in her bag. Then ramming her bonnet on her head, she shrugged on her shawl and, before she could change her mind, placed the key on the table and hurried outside to the big oak.

'Goodbye,' she whispered, her eyes filling with tears as she knelt beside the three forlorn crosses. 'I'm sorry for all the trouble I've caused.'

'*We'll be waiting when you return.*'

Telling herself it was the wind whispering in the willows, Eliza didn't reply. Instead, she picked up her bag and walked purposefully away.

Chapter 17

It was a fair trek across fields still sodden from floodwater but for the first time in ages Eliza felt her spirits lift. She'd been looked after all her life and now needed to prove she could make her own way.

Finally, having squelched her way up the muddy bank, she saw the River Parrett gleaming before her. Squinting in the dimpsy light, she could just make out the barge moored beyond the bridge, its cargo of sails setting it low in the water. She edged her way closer but could see no sign of its crew. Guessing they were spending the evening in the cider house further along the tow path, she gingerly climbed aboard and hid between the big sail bags stowed under the barge's canvas cover.

All that walking had made her ravenous, and quietly so as not to draw attention to anyone passing by, she pulled out her bread and cheese and ate. Replete, she lay back and listened to the soothing sounds of the water lapping against the wooden hull.

The gentle rocking must have sent her to sleep for she was rudely woken by the sound of a man shouting. As the boat began to move, she peered out from a gap between the side planking and canvas cover then watched the scenery slowly pass by in the pale morning light. It wasn't long before the few ramshackle brick buildings of the hamlet, gave way to flat, open moorland. They drifted downstream with the tide, leaving the pollard willows, withy beds and rhynes in their wake. She was seized with a mixture of excitement for what was to come and sadness that she was leaving her home behind.

Lulled into a torpor by the gentle bobbing of the barge, a horrible clattering noise made her jump. Her eyes widened as she saw a long cloud of smoke rushing across the fields towards them. A huge machine with strange coaches attached appeared from under the smoke. Then, with a screaming whistle, the whole frightening effigy rushed past them and disappeared into the distance. The ensuing peace was broken by the honking of a flock of geese that having been disturbed by the noise, circled the barge before settling back onto the marsh.

'Train from Taunton's on time this marnen,' the bargee shouted.

'What that we could go as fast as that,' his mate shouted back. 'Get our load delivered in next to no time, we would.'

So that's what a train looks like, Eliza thought. No wonder Gramfer had said it would have been quicker travelling back from Gretna on one.

She settled back down on the sails and watched the ever-changing landscape. It was completely different to what she'd experienced on her journey to Gretna, she thought, her heart leaping as they came to the outskirts of a large town. She could see a sprawl of tall brick buildings and many other vessels on the water. Men were yelling from the dockside as ropes were thrown to them from the bank. Splashing and scraping was followed by a jolt as they came to an abrupt halt against the dock wall. Her excitement turned to alarm when she noticed the deck of the barge was far below the top of the quay, tall warehouse sheds and long armed cranes towered menacingly overhead. How was she going to get up to the dockside? she thought, staring frantically around. Then she noticed a steep flight of brick steps leading up from the water.

Clutching her bag, she slipped out from her cover between the sails, slid over the gunwale, and jumped from the boat. Then, fearful she would be spotted and stopped, she hurried up the steps and onto the wharf.

'Hey, you, what do you think you're doing?' a sharp voice called, as a filthy hand snaked out to stop her. Dodging past the big, burly man, Eliza sped along the quay, her bag flapping against her side. Shouts and catcalls from roughly clothed men rang in her wake, but she paid no heed.

Finally, just when she thought her lungs would burst, she came to a street of imposing buildings and collapsed against the wall. She tried to listen for footsteps chasing after her, but it was impossible for everywhere was so noisy. The rumble and clatter of wheels mingled with clip-clopping of hooves and ringing of boots on the cobbles as people hurried about their business. To her relief, nobody took any notice of her, and once she'd regained her breath, she quickly made her way up the wide street. Keeping to the inside of the pavement, she began looking in the shop windows for anyone advertising for help. She passed by greengrocers, bakers, butchers and all manner of other businesses but nobody seemed to be hiring.

With the shadows lengthening, nowhere to stay and precious little money in her pocket, she grew evermore disheartened. Then, as she turned into a tiny back street, she spotted a notice on the door of a grocer's shop and hurried inside.

A large lady in a voluminous apron looked up and nodded before returning to the thick rashers of bacon she was slicing from a flitch. The smoky fragrance made Eliza's stomach rumble, reminding her she hadn't eaten since the previous evening. To distract herself, she peered up at the shelves that were neatly lined with jars containing dried beans, peas and all manner of foods she'd never seen before. As the customer placed her purchase in a wicker basket, Eliza noted it was far inferior to those she made.

'Sorry to keep you waiting, dear,' the shopkeeper smiled, looking her up and down.

'I've come about the position,' she explained, gesturing to the sign.

'I'm afraid it's been filled,' the woman said. 'Meant to take that down but I've been rushed off my feet all day. Not that I'm complaining, mind.'

'Oh,' Eliza sighed, her spirits sinking. 'I don't suppose you know of any other vacancies. I'm willing to try anything and am good at making baskets.'

'Can't say I know of any work of that sort around here. There's the brickworks, they always need people, but that's messy work for a pretty girl like you.' As Eliza let out a long sigh, the woman gave her an assessing look. 'I suppose you could always try Lavender House. That's if you don't mind looking after gentlemen, of course.'

'Now that's something I do have experience of,' Eliza replied, her spirits lifting. 'Where is this Lavender House?'

'West end of the town. I'm sure Mrs Goodtime would be interested in someone like you.'

'Are her positions live-in do you know?'

'Well, er yes, I suppose they must be,' the woman murmured, busying herself putting the bacon back inside the glass counter.

'Thank you so much. How do I find this place?'

'Carry on up the hill, past the parish church, until you come to the big houses. It's right at the far end of the lane with tall chimneys and a mauve door. Backs onto the old priory, it does.'

'Nice views then,' Eliza replied, eagerly.

'Oh yes, definitely,' she smirked. 'So I've heard, anyhow.' She turned and popped a cube of cheese into her mouth, making Eliza feel hungrier than ever. Then, as the bell tinkled and another customer came in, she turned away before Eliza could ask any more questions. Anxious to secure a position and hopefully a bed for the night, she thanked the woman and set off up the hill.

Eliza's feet were aching by the time she reached Lavender House. It was a large imposing building, three storeys high and surrounded by a high brick wall. Quickly, before her courage failed her, she clicked open the wicket gate, mounted the steps. The door was opened by a maid in a black dress and lace trimmed apron.

'What are you doing using the front entrance? Who've you come to see?' she asked, frowning as she looked Eliza up and down.

'Mrs Goodtime,' she replied. 'The lady in the grocer's said she might have a position available.'

'Did she indeed?' To her surprise the girl giggled. 'That might be what Madam's known as in town, but you'd best not let her hear you call her that. Come on, I'll show you to her office,' she said, wiggling her way along a patterned tiled hallway. There were pictures on the wall but, in the dim light, Eliza was unable to make out what they were. The maid gave a sharp rap on the door and waited.

'Have you worked here long?' Eliza ventured.

'No, I haven't and I'll be late if Madam doesn't hurry up and answer,' she cried, knocking again.

'Come,' a husky voice rasped, making Eliza jump.

'Give as good as you get if you want a position. You need to show you can stand up for yourself,' the maid said, nudging her inside, before tip-tapping back down the hallway.

A spicy fragrance pervaded the large room which was bathed in a rosy glow from the fire crackling in the ornate marble fireplace. Eliza stared around, her eyes widening in amazement as she took in the glass covered gaslights on the wall, purple velvet drapes hanging from the tall windows and the elaborate furnishings. Finally, her gaze came to rest on a woman of middle years who was studying her through eyes dark as sloes. Dressed in purple silk, ebony hair styled artistically on the top of her head, she was elegantly reclining on a matching chaise longue.

'Good afternoon, Madam. I've come to . . .'

'You are seeking employment,' the woman interjected.

'Well yes, how did you know?' Eliza asked, staring at her in astonishment. The woman gave a throaty laugh.

'You have a testimonial for me?'

'Well, er no,' Eliza admitted, realizing she should have asked the school mistress for one.

'But you come recommended?'

'Oh yes, the lady in the grocer's told me you might have a position for someone who can care for gentlemen.'

'Did she now?' The woman quirked a brow, her lips curling in amusement. 'And, you are good at taking care of gentlemen?'

'Yes, I cared for my gramfer before he died.'

'Did you indeed. Well then, er . . .'

'Eliza, Eliza Priddle,' she replied, trying to keep her voice steady. The woman grimaced.

'Well Eliza Priddle, if this gramfer died you can't have taken very good care of him, can you?' Eliza stared at her in horror. Position or not, that really was below the belt.

'I'll have you know Mrs—' she began.

'Just my little joke dear. And do call me Madam.' She leaned forward and in confidential tones, added, 'The gentlemen who come here require a different sort of looking after, if you get my meaning.'

'Why, do they have some particular disease?' Eliza asked, remembering her grammer once saying something about disease and isolation.

'Gracious, we trust not,' she shuddered. 'They are all esteemed. Now, take off that terrible bonnet and shawl and let me take a proper look at you.' Eliza did as she was told and as her hair tumbled over her shoulders, the woman's look changed to one of admiration. 'Oh yes,' she purred, giving a little clap of her hands. 'Eyes like a cat, hair like fire and high cheekbones on porcelain skin. Perfect. Though how you come to be wearing such a fine blouse, albeit creased, with the rest of that tattered ensemble is beyond me.'

'Well, you see . . .' she began but the woman held up her hand.

'We ask no questions here,' she chuckled, giving Eliza an outrageous wink. 'Well, I'm happy with what I see, apart from those dreadful hands.' She grimaced then gestured to a high backed button wing chair with antimacassars edged in lilac lace. 'Take a seat over there.' Surprised, Eliza did as she'd been asked, sinking right down into the soft leather. 'Sit up straight and cross your legs at the ankle,' the woman ordered.

Eliza shifted forward and did as she'd been asked. Although she hadn't been interviewed formally by the school mistress, this seemed a strange way to be carrying on.

'Now all my girls have glamorous names so from now on

you will be known as Eliza Beth and I will get Angelique to give you a little lesson in the art of diction. Where do you hail from?'

'Sedge Moor.'

'Hmm, that explains it,' the woman grimaced. 'Now you will be expected to work most weekends and weekday evenings, plus some afternoons if called for. My terms are generous, but I demand discretion at all times. Most of our gentlemen don't wish it known they come here, although the occasional one likes to be seen at the theatre with a pretty girl on his arm. We have reception rooms at the front of the house for the gentlemen's entertainment. Private ones are on the first floor, with most commanding a good view of the gardens and Priory Park beyond, not that our clients will be looking out of the window much,' she laughed. Goodness, they certainly looked after their gentlemen in this home, Eliza thought.

'Will I be sharing one of these rooms?' she asked, carefully folding her things back into her bag.

'Gracious,' the woman exclaimed, quirking an immaculate brow. 'Well, I never would have thought . . . Still, it's none of my business how you girls see fit to please and sometimes there is a request, so who knows? I'll get Angelique to show you where you'll be staying.' She picked up a silver bell from the table and shook it. Almost immediately, a tall woman, her head wreathed in a halo of golden curls, glided gracefully into the room. Dressed in a blue satin dress with matching slippers, she glanced curiously at Eliza before turning her attention to the older woman.

'You rang Madam,' she asked in a soft voice that sounded foreign.

'Ah Angelique, I'd like you to show Eliza Beth upstairs. Familiarize her with everything she needs to know, but don't show her into the reception rooms until she has bathed and changed. She needs to slather her hands with ointment until they are soft and presentable. We can't have our gentlemen thinking they have come to the wrong place. Oh, and teach her to enunciate properly, she drags her vowels like a cat on heat.'

'Yes Madam. Come with me Eliza Beth and I'll show you where everything is,' she said quickly, as Eliza opened her mouth to protest. However, as soon as she'd pulled the door closed behind them, the girl dissolved into hysterics.

'You should have seen your face,' she spluttered, all pretence of her accent disappearing.

'Well, did you hear what she said about my voice?' Eliza cried. 'Who does she think she is?'

'She's the boss and you'd do well to remember that if you want to stay. Madam runs a good house and, as long as you bide by her rules, you'll be handsomely remunerated. Disobey or question and . . .' Angelique ran a finger across her throat. 'Now, come upstairs and I'll show you where you'll be sleeping.'

Chapter 18

Eliza followed the young woman further down the hallway and through a door which led onto a dingy corridor. Then lighting the candle that was on a ledge she led the way up two more flights of stairs. The further up they went, the darker and narrower it got. By the time they reached another steeper flight of stairs, the flame was flickering in the draught and she could see their ghostly shadows on the walls as they climbed.

'Here we are, Eliza Beth, welcome to your new home. Not quite what you expected from downstairs, I'll be bound,' she said throwing open a door.

Eliza stared around in dismay. The stark room housed two rows of iron bedsteads, each covered with a honeycomb bedspread that looked clean yet worn. Squeezed alongside each one was a cabinet. It was as desolate and basic as her room at home, without affording the benefit of privacy. By the slope of the roof, she guessed it was an attic room too. Wasn't that where servants slept?

'This will be your bed,' Angelique explained, her dress rustling as she glided over to the farthest side of the room and patted a bed beside the window. 'It's a bit basic I know, but play your cards right and you'll be spending more time in the luxurious rooms below,' she winked.

'But where will I keep my things?' Eliza asked, holding up her carpet bag as she eyed the rickety cabinets.

'Come and have a look,' she replied, leading the way into the next room which was lit from the window in the roof. The walls were lined with shelves piled high with fancy hats, leather gloves and all manner of accessories. Eliza's eyes widened in astonishment for she had never seen such luxurious items, but before she had time to study them properly, Angelique was urging her further into the room. There was a bank of large wardrobes and as the young woman threw open the doors to one, Eliza gasped at the array of gorgeous silk and satin gowns draping languidly from padded hangers. The next revealed rows of full skirts and frilled blouses, the one adjacent had elegant coats and mantles with hoods lined in the softest fur. The final one contained a row of black dresses and snowy white aprons which Eliza realized were identical to the outfit the woman who'd let her in had been wearing.

'Oh my, how many maids work here?' she asked, dropping her bag to the floor in astonishment. 'I saw the one who let me in, but had no idea this place needed so many.'

Angelique giggled.

'This is what we wear to welcome the men, silly.'

'Welcome them?' Eliza frowned.

'We take them through to the reception room, serve their drinks and if required, keep them company. Though I doubt any self-respecting maid would wear anything that permitted a glimpse of her décolletage. Oh, my you've gone all white, are you sure you've looked after gentlemen before?'

'Only my gramfer,' she admitted.

'Your grandfather!' Angelique squeaked, her eyes widening in shock.

'Yes, I cooked and cleaned our cott after Grammer died. Now he's dead too so I've come to Bridgwater to make a new life.'

There was silence as the young woman digested this. She seemed about to say something then shrugged.

'Well, Madam must think you're suitable. Now, see this wardrobe here?' She went over to the far end of the room and opened the door of the shortest cupboard which fitted snugly under the eaves. 'This is where we keep our own things. Usually we'll be dressed up in one of Madam's outfits even on our days off. She insists we look like ladies at all times and luckily, for sometimes we need to change two or three times a day, she employs a woman to do all the laundry. Now stow your bag and outerwear in here, I've just time to show you the boudoirs,' she winked.

'Boudoirs?' Eliza frowned.

'You'll see,' Angelique giggled.

Her head still reeling, Eliza followed her back down the narrow staircases. This time though, Angelique led the way through a different door which opened onto a wide carpeted hallway hung with chandeliers. Blinking in the sudden light Eliza could only marvel at the difference in their surroundings.

She stopped beside one of the gilt framed pictures that lined the walls but before she'd had time to look at it, Angelique was nudging her into another room.

'Right now, tell me, what do you think of this for a boudoir?' For the second time that afternoon, Eliza gasped in amazement. With its high ceilings, ornate cornicing and gaslights on the wall, the room was nothing less than palatial. It was dominated by an enormous bed draped in red velvet with tables on each side adorned by gold candelabra. Red velvet drapes hung from the windows while the floor was covered in a sumptuous carpet patterned in red and gold.

'My, I've never seen anything like it,' she spluttered.

'Surprisingly this is known as the Red Room,' Angelique said with a grin. 'It's my favourite, but the Gold, Green, Blue and Purple and Silver ones are all quite impressive too.' She moved over to the window and peered out.

'It's getting too dark to see now, but the gardens back onto the Old Priory and there's a disused Friary to one side so the neighbours are quiet.' Her soft laughter was drowned by a persistent banging sound.

'What on earth's that?' Eliza cried, covering her ears with her hands.

'That's the supper gong. Come on, I'll introduce you to the others. We all eat together in a dining room off the kitchen. Well, it's called the dining room although it's a bit basic. Still Mrs Brown's a good sort and prides herself on her cooking. She gets irate if anyone's late and her food spoils, so make sure you're always on time. Of course, we're not served the best cuts like the upper crust but the food is tasty, and as long as we earn our money, we don't have to pay out anything for bed and board.'

Well that sounded good, Eliza thought. She'd save as much as she could so that on her days off, she'd be able to explore Bridgwater and enquire about her grandparents' family.

'As you can see, the staff quarters are somewhat different,' Angelique told Eliza as they retraced their steps. 'We are only allowed in the main areas of the house when we're working. I'll show you the other rooms later. Now, I don't know about you but I'm starving.'

Eliza nodded eagerly, for she hadn't eaten all day and was beginning to feel quite faint. She followed the young woman along another corridor and down more stairs until finally, when she felt hopelessly lost, they arrived in a windowless basement room. As the appetizing aroma of cooking wafted her way, Eliza's stomach rumbled. Then she saw four women already seated at the long table watching her curiously.

'This is Eliza Beth, everyone,' Angelique announced. 'She has come to join our happy house. I'm sure you'll all make her welcome.' Eliza couldn't help noticing how she emphasized the word all, and stared in the direction of an attractive lady with hair black as a raven, who was eying her up and down through narrowed eyes.

'Of course, we will. Nice to meet you dear. I'm Eva,' said a slender brunette with the reddest lips Eliza had ever seen.

'Hello Eliza Beth, I'm Veronique,' smiled the blue-eyed girl with flaxen tresses, coiled around her head to reveal a long slender neck.

'Clodah,' said a cheery voice, with a lilt. 'Wish my hair was smooth like yours. To be sure mine's as bristly as a badger's backside.'

'Really Clo,' Eva chided, then turned to Eliza. 'You'll have to excuse her she's bog Irish.' They all laughed, then as silence descended, they turned to face the remaining girl. To Eliza's dismay, she was still regarding her with contempt.

'And this is Sophia,' Angelique said brightly when it became obvious the woman had no intention of speaking. Sophia gave a toss of her head then began studying her nails, managing to look both sultry and sullen at the same time.

'Come and sit by me, Eliza Beth,' Clodah invited, patting the chair beside her. As Angelique took the seat on her other side, the Irish girl turned and whispered. 'Don't you be minding Sophia. Considers herself to be queen bee she does. She won't like you competing in the looks stakes, if you get my meaning.' Before Eliza could ask exactly what she did mean, a stout woman in white cotton cap and apron bustled into the room. She was carrying an enormous steaming casserole dish which she carefully set down on the table.

'Right girls, supper,' she announced breezily. 'Thank you, dearie,' she added, taking a dish of vegetables from the tiny young girl hovering behind her.

'Ah, a new face,' the woman said, smiling at Eliza.

'This is Eliza Beth, Mrs Brown,' Angelique told her.

'Well dearie, I hope you'll be happy here,' she said, sounding as if she thought this was highly unlikely. 'Now, do you want me to serve?'

'Of course, that's what you're paid for isn't it?' Sophia snapped.

'Oh dear, at home to Miss Sulky this evening, are we?' the cook said mildly, as she picked up a plate and began ladling out sizable pieces of meat in glistening gravy. Eliza's eyes widened in anticipation. If these weren't the best cuts, she didn't know what were.

'I do wish you'd stop serving up this stodge,' Sophia said, staring disdainfully down at her platter. 'You know we need to keep in shape.' Eliza stared at the slender girl in astonishment.

'Seen more meat on a sparrow's leg,' the cook sniffed as she continued serving the others. 'Tell Monique I've left her some in the kitchen for later,' the woman said, bustling back out again.

'Thank you, Mrs Brown,' Eliza called after her.

'Gracious, we don't thank the servants. That's what they're here for. To attend to people,' Sophia told her loftily.

'Same as us then,' Eva chortled.

'Peasant,' Sophia snapped. 'Where do you hail from?' she asked, pushing her plate away untouched and turning to Eliza. Her eyes were as hard as the flat iron Eliza used back home, and her appetite vanished like morning mist.

'Sedge Moor,' Eliza replied, trying to sound friendly.

'Good heavens. That explains your dreadful accent. You'll have to do something about that before you can even think of mixing with the upper echelons,' she trilled.

'The what?'

'Don't worry Sophia, it's all in hand,' Angelique told her.

'And what exactly did you do at this Sedge Moor?' Sophia persisted. Although her lips formed a smile it didn't reach her eyes.

'I was a willow weaver. Made laundry baskets, eel and sparrow traps,' she said proudly.

'Gracious me, how frightful,' Sophia tutted, raising an immaculate arched brow. 'I suppose that explains those awful hands. I've seen smoother, whiter ones on a washerwoman.'

'That's not nice, Sophia,' Angelique told her.

'But true. We have high standards here at Lavender House and don't want anyone lowering the tone,' Sophia said looking pointedly at Eliza as she got to her feet. 'Still, the acid test will be if you pass Madam's criterion. I mean, for example, do you understand the importance of froufrou?' Seeing Eliza's blank look, she sighed and shook her head. 'I thought not.'

'What did she mean?' Eliza asked the others as with a rustle of her silk skirts, the woman swept regally out of the room, heels click clacking on the bare boards.

'That is a fine example of froufrou,' Clodah giggled.

'You'll soon learn to ignore siren Sophia,' Eva told Eliza. 'Just because she's popular with men and earns the most, she thinks she rules the roost. Now, who's at home tonight?'

They all nodded and Eliza's spirits rose. Apart from Sophia, they seemed friendly and it would be good to spend the evening getting to know them. However, her hopes were soon shattered.

'That's the polite way of saying we're booked,' Angelique explained. 'If someone wants to know if you're free to entertain, they will ask if you're at home to visitors. Subtle difference of words but huge difference in meaning.'

'But we all know the meaning of the word late,' Veronique said, squealing as she caught sight of the clock on the shelf.

'We need to go and get ready for our guests,' Angelique explained as they all jumped to their feet, clattering their chairs back into place. Automatically, Eliza began collecting the dishes only to see Angelique shaking her head. 'That's the maid's job. She's been taken on from the workhouse so you'll not want to do her out of a position, will you?'

'No, of course not,' Eliza said, putting them down again.

'I'll ask Mrs Brown to see the tub is filled for you and suggest you spend the evening bathing and preparing for tomorrow. Madam is sure to want you working the room and serving drinks until you've been passed.'

'Been passed?' Eliza frowned.

'Yes, we all have pass our checks or Madam will throw us out. Now, you'll need to be looking your best tomorrow so I'll see if Mrs Brown has something for those poor hands of yours. The stillroom is full of her magic lotions and potions. And if you can remember to clip those vowels a bit, it would help.' Seeing Eliza frown, she smiled.

'For example, say room, not rooom, hello not heello, good afternoon, not good art'noon, get it? We'll practise tomorrow at breakfast. Now, I may or may not see you later,' she winked.

Eliza sat in the empty room, her head spinning. Something

about these checks was niggling her, yet she couldn't put a finger on it. What exactly was this place and what had she got herself into? She'd always thought she spoke normally yet now it seemed she didn't. She stared down at her rough hands. There was no denying they needed something to soften them, but callouses were the price you paid for weaving willow.

Later, refreshed from her bath and wrapped in her calico nightdress, Eliza sat on the bed she'd been allocated, gently rubbing salve into the cracked sores on her hands. What a strange day it had been and what a peculiar place this was, with its narrow stairways and tiny attic rooms upstairs, the more opulent surroundings lower down. And whilst Angelique had referred to the dining room as basic, the room was larger and grander than the whole of the ground floor of their cott back home. Earlier, when she'd plucked up the courage to ask Mrs Brown what exactly her duties would be, the woman had told her quite bluntly that if she didn't know she'd be better off leaving right away.

However, it was late and she was too tired to go anywhere tonight. Yawning she climbed into bed but when she closed her eyes, thoughts of the day kept going around and round in her head. Had she been impetuous leaving home on the spur of the moment? Perhaps she should have thought things through more but so much had happened recently her head was in a muddle. She didn't know if she was angry or hurt that Theo hadn't thought enough of her to honour his promise to come and see her. But she did know that with Gramfer gone, she couldn't bear staying alone in the Droves with only her conscience for company. Although Clem had been his usual kind self when he'd said she needed looking after, it had made her realize it was time to make her own way in the world. When he'd mentioned the barge was travelling to Bridgwater it had seemed as if it was meant, and if she could find out more about where her family had come from it might help her make some sense of her past. As for this place, Lavender House, she couldn't help feeling she'd been hasty applying for the first vacancy she came upon. Tomorrow, she'd get up early, go back into the town and find another position, she vowed.

Chapter 19

'Come on sleepy head.' Someone was shaking her arm. Snapping her eyes open, it was some moments before Eliza realised it was Angelique standing over her. Wearing a simple gown of palest pink, her hair modestly tied back in a band, she gave the appearance of an elegant young lady. Eliza despaired that she could ever aspire to look the same. Then her heart sank. Despite her good intentions, she'd obviously overslept and if Angelique was up then the others would be too. 'For heaven's sake Eliza Beth, the gong sounded ages ago and if you want breakfast you need to go downstairs right away. We have to eat before any of the guests surface.'

'But the dining room's down in the basement so they won't know,' Eliza pointed out, stifling a yawn.

'Like all good children, we are to be seen when our attendance is requested. Now, do hurry, I've chosen this for you to wear,' she said, holding up a green gown with pleating in the bodice.

'That's a bit grand for breakfast, isn't it?' Eliza asked, thinking it would be far too extravagant for one of the get togethers at Worth.

'We are expected to look like ladies at all times, so you'd better wear these instead of those old boots you arrived in,' she added, placing a pair of tan mid heeled slipper shoes by her feet. 'Now do come on, I'm starving even if you're not,' Angelique sighed. Reluctantly Eliza climbed out of bed and with the girl's help, was dressed in record time.

'So many layers,' Eliza groaned.

'And you still need suitable lingerie, but we'll have to sort out that out later,' Angelique said, trying her best not to grimace at Eliza's thick torn stockings as she slid into the shoes.

The appetizing aroma of cooking greeted them as they made their way down the flights of stairs. It certainly beat the smell of porridge and at least she could ensure she had a good breakfast before slipping away. However, just as she was about to enter the dining room, Monique, the girl who'd let Eliza in the previous day, announced that Madam wanted to see her straight away.

'Must be important for her to summon you this early,' Eva cried. 'She doesn't usually surface before noon.'

'For heaven's sake don't let her see your stockings,' Angelique murmured.

What a lot of fuss, Eliza thought, nevertheless hurrying back up the stairs and along the ornately tiled hallway, hoping she could remember which was the door to Madam's room. In the light of day, she could clearly make out the pictures adorning the wall and she stopped in her tracks, her cheeks growing hot. Each one depicted a lady reclining on a chaise longue, the bodice of her dress cut low so as to reveal rather than conceal. With their half-closed eyes and smiling red lips the overall effect was quite shocking.

'Admiring the view?' She jumped as Sophia appeared beside her. 'Women inclined to embonpoint hold a fascination for some gentlemen. Not that I can understand it myself,' she added, running her hands over her slender hips. 'But then, men are funny creatures with their penchant for white meat.' Thinking the woman was being friendly, Eliza turned to smile at her only to feel a stab of fear when she saw the gloating look in her eyes. 'Madam and I were just discussing your er, potential, shall we say, so I'd look sharp if I were you. It doesn't do to keep her waiting.' Looking like the cat who'd cornered her prey, she gave a brittle laugh as she tip-tapped down the hallway. Swallowing hard, Eliza knocked on the door.

'Come.' This morning the woman's voice sounded harsher. Wishing she'd taken the time to at least put her hair up in a comb, she entered the room. Busy at her escritoire, Madam did not look up. The spicy aroma Eliza had thought exotic the previous day, now seemed overpowering, making her feel nauseous. She waited politely, but the woman continued with her writing. Apart from the scratching of her nib and ponderous ticking of the long case clock in the corner, all was silent. Finally, Eliza could bear it no longer.

'You wanted to see me, Madam?' she asked, pulling her skirts down to cover her stockings.

'Not particularly, but Sophia has voiced concerns about your suitability for a position here,' she said, carefully putting down her pen and staring candidly at Eliza. 'I know you are a bit naive but that can be an advantage. And even a girl from the moor can serve a drink with a smile, can't she?'

'Yes, of course,' Eliza replied, thinking that if she reassured the woman, she would still have time to break her fast. But Madam didn't respond. 'I did say I was used to looking after people . . .' her voice trailed away when she saw the woman frowning at her skirts. Hastily, she pulled them lower.

'For heaven's sake girl will you stop fiddling with your attire. I can't bear one who fidgets. Now, did you get something for those hands?'

'Yes, Mrs Brown gave me a large pot of her special salve,' Eliza told her.

'Good. See that you use it religiously,' Madam replied, turning and writing something on the paper before her. 'Now, where was I? Oh yes, before we go any further, I need you to sign your indenture.'

'My what?'

'It is a paper that sets out the terms by which you repay your loan,' the woman smiled.

'My loan? But I haven't borrowed any money from you?' Eliza replied indignantly. The woman's frown deepened, her lips pursed into a crimson slit.

'Are you or are you not wearing my dress, my shoes and heavens knows what else?'

'Well, yes but . . .'

'And by your own admission you have purchased salve

from Cook. I also know for a fact you ate supper with the others, slept in a comfortable bed upstairs.'

'Comfor . . .' Eliza began, then realized it would be better not to argue. 'Well yes, but of course I can always return the clothes.'

'Fair enough, we'll just make a nominal charge for wear and laundry. So, all in all that comes to . . .' she looked down at her paper and began counting under her breath. 'Twenty guineas?'

'Twenty guineas. But I don't have anywhere near that amount,' Eliza cried in dismay.

'In that case my dear, you have no alternative other than sign this paper,' she replied, holding it out in front of her. 'Pay up or put up, as they say.'

Heart thudding, Eliza took the paper and stared down the row of figures until she finally arrived at the extortionate total of twenty guineas. She couldn't believe it, she'd been here less than a day and somehow managed to spend more money than her grandparents had in ten years or more.

'I don't know why you're looking like that. The finest clothes and good tuition cost money,' Madam told her. 'And you'll get none better anywhere else I can assure you.'

'Tuition?' Eliza frowned, still reeling from the shock of discovering she'd inadvertently incurred an enormous debt.

'My dear Eliza Beth, your voice needs schooling, your movements are clumsy in the extreme and although naivety is a quality some admire, you won't get far here if you don't understand the needs of our clients.'

'But if I'm that bad then surely it's better I just leave?' Eliza pointed out.

'Not so fast, Eliza Beth. I saw your potential as soon as you entered the room yesterday, and I'm certainly not one to waste time. It is money after all,' Madam told her in a voice that brooked no argument.

'Gramfer always said time was tucker,' Eliza agreed, hoping to appeal to the woman's better nature.

'Then he was a sensible man,' she conceded. 'Now, I have instructed Sophia to tutor you. Of course, she too has a living to make and will require recompense. However, she is my top earner and well respected by our patrons. Follow her guidance and you will not only repay the modest cost of your indenture, but build a tidy sum for your future.'

'I have dec—' Eliza began, thinking to appeal to the woman's better nature.

'Please do not interrupt. Good manners are a prerequisite here,' Madam admonished. 'Now, where was I? Ah yes, the one draw-back of our profession over that of the common street women, is that generally only the services of younger girls are required. The men who work at the docks or in factories aren't that choosy, but our clientele is discerning, and once one reaches twenty-five . . .' she shrugged.

'But I'm only seventeen,' Eliza said.

'Then I'd advise you to make the most of the years you have. Now, if you'd hurry up and sign before you reach twenty-five, I'd be obliged,' she said, holding out the pen.

'Of course, there's always the workhouse, if you prefer,' she added, when Eliza still hesitated.

Shuddering at the thought, but realizing she had no choice, Eliza scribbled her name then jumped as the woman snatched the paper back with indecent haste.

'Now let me explain a little about some of our other services,' Madam said, sitting back in her seat with a satisfied smile on her face.

'Other services?' Eliza asked, wishing she understood what the first one was.

'Indeed. There are those for whom marriage is one of convenience whilst others, who do not, er shall we say, wish to be married, need the respectability of being seen in public with a female on their arm. It allays any suspicions their peers might have. It is also an easy way for you to make money for merely being entertaining. These men pay handsomely for the decency it provides.'

'Decency?' she frowned. 'I don't understand.'

'Heavens above girl, can you really be that simple?' Madam tutted, waving her hand as if batting away a bothersome fly. 'You came here seeking employment after all. Where else would you get a live-in position that provides fun, frivolity and endless opportunities for advancement?' Eliza had to admit that, put like that, it did sound tempting. As if reading her thoughts, Madam smiled.

'Now, I have a gentleman who wishes a pretty girl to escort him to the theatre this afternoon.'

'So soon?' Eliza whispered, her spirits sinking even lower.

'Don't look scared, girl. This will be your ideal debut. You'll get a lovely outing safe in the knowledge that nothing more will be asked of you. Which reminds me, I must make an appointment for your examination, which foolishly I have omitted from your indenture,' she tutted.

'Examination for what?' Eliza asked, staring helplessly as the woman scribbled another figure down on the paper.

'It's vital all my ladies are clean,' Madam replied, narrowing her eyes.

'I had a bath last night,' Eliza smiled, expecting the woman to delete the sum. Instead, her eyes narrowed as she shook her head.

'Don't take me for a fool, young lady,' she warned. 'I run a strict house and you will have regular checks like the others. Now, where was I? Ah yes, not only will you get a delightful outing, you have the opportunity to begin repaying your loan right away.'

Well at least that was something, Eliza thought. And, it would be a good way to familiarize herself with the layout of the town. Having been intent on securing a position, all she could recall was a maze of streets crammed with tall buildings. She became aware that Madam was eying her impatiently.

'I said that when you return, I'll get Sophia to show you how we greet and treat our clients.'

'Thank you,' Eliza replied, hoping she could now escape. However, it seemed Madam had other ideas.

'Now we really must do something about your deportment. Despite wearing the lightest of slipper shoes, you manage to walk like a constipated duck. First, lengthen your neck like a swan thus.'

Eliza bit back a giggle as the woman got to her feet and demonstrated, her wrinkles miraculously disappearing as if someone had taken an iron to them. Obediently, she copied.

'Imagine you have a pile of heavy books on your head and walk towards the window, turn gracefully before returning to me. Off you go.' As she gave a little clap of her hands Eliza duly made her way towards the French doors. Beyond she could see tall trees edging an immaculate lawn and she had the sudden urge to throw them open and run. But then Madam would surely send someone after her, for having signed that stupid paper, she now had a horrendous debt to repay. Groaning inwardly, she realized she was as trapped as those poor eels back home.

'And turn,' Madam's voice ordered, cutting through her musing. Duly she spun around and began walking back towards the woman, her thoughts still running wildly round in her head.

She'd never been to a theatre before, and if she had to stay and work off this indenture thing, then she might as well make the most of it. Besides, knowing her luck, the French doors would be locked anyway.

'No, no, no, I've seen daintier soldiers on parade.' Madam's strident tones cut through her thoughts. 'Point your toes forward so, then glide as if you're skating on ice.' As she bent and moved Eliza's feet into the correct position, her eyebrows shot up and she let out a howl of outrage.

'Whatever are you wearing, girl?' she cried, grimacing at Eliza's woollen stockings which were caked with dried mud and riddled with holes. 'You will purchase three pairs of silk stockings immediately.' Eliza watched as she strode over to her escritoire, took out a package and counted out the flimsy items. Then to her dismay, yet another sum was added to the total on her indenture paper. 'And ask Mrs Brown to burn those, those . . .' She wrinkled her nose. 'Disgusting things. Now once more across the room and then we really must start on your diction.'

Eliza lost track of time as the woman, finally satisfied with the way she 'carried herself', began coaching her in the art of speaking the King's English.

'Your vocabulary is actually quite good,' Madam pronounced. 'But the way you elide your vowels makes you sound like a half-wit. Our gentlemen expect a woman with a cultured speaking voice, although it has to be said, they like to do most of the talking themselves.'

'Oh, you mean you wish me to speak like this,' Eliza replied, giving a fair imitation of Theo. Madam grinned and clapped her hands in delight.

'That is exactly how I wish you to speak. Well done, Eliza Beth. I know I'm a good teacher but, even so, you have learned impressively quickly.'

Just then the long case clock in the corner began chiming the noon hour and she picked up the silk stockings and thrust them in Eliza's hands. 'Ask Angelique to help you dress appropriately for the theatre. She will then show you where to meet your client. His name is Lord Levine but no doubt he will tell you how he wishes you to address him.' The woman returned to her escritoire and Eliza knew she was dismissed.

Chapter 20

Head buzzing with instructions, Eliza made her way down the hallway to find Angelique waiting for her.

'I can't believe you've got a theatre trip on your first day,' she squealed. 'Well done you.' Eliza frowned, then shook her head.

'You've been listening.'

'And you'll soon learn to keep your ear to the ground, or at least the keyhole, if you want to know what's going on around here. Actually, we've all been worried since you were summoned. Sophia's been boasting about having seen Madam to advise her of your unsuitability.'

'But why?' Eliza asked, shaking her head.

'Cos she's jealous of your youth and beauty, silly. Being the top earner here, she sees you as a threat. However, it would appear Madam's taken no notice. She's going to be livid when she hears you're escorting Lord Levine to the theatre this afternoon.'

'Why?' Eliza asked as they made their way up the back stairs to the attic.

'Because she thinks he's exclusively hers and always makes herself available for him,' Angelique giggled. 'Apparently he buys chocolates and refreshments in the interval then tips her handsomely for her company when they return.'

'But isn't he meant to pay anyway?'

'Of course, but Madam deals with the financial side of the business. You keep any tips you earn and she invoices each client for your services at the end of the month. When she receives their money, she pays us our share, minus board and any sundries we owe. Like those for example,' she said, gesturing to the stockings in Eliza's hand.

'I hadn't realized it was all going to be so expensive,' Eliza sighed.

'Don't worry, it seems daunting at first but you'll be surprised how quickly your earnings mount up. It beats serving in a shop or working in the brick factory that's for sure, and if you save your money wisely, you'll set yourself up nicely for the future. Without having to rely on any man,' she grinned. 'That's what I'm doing. Now, come on, we've less than an hour to make you look presentable,' she said, pushing open the door to the dressing room.

'What's wrong with what I'm wearing?' Eliza asked, staring down at the beautiful green gown.

'One simply cannot be seen out in public wearing a house dress. That would be so infra dig, darling.'

'What does that mean exactly?' Eliza frowned.

'Beneath one's dignity,' she trilled in a passable imitation of Madam that set them giggling.

'What on earth is going on in here?' They looked up to see Sophia glaring at them from the doorway, and abruptly stopped laughing.

'We're getting Eliza Beth ready for her outing to the theatre,' Angelique told her demurely.

'Oh, and whom might that be with?' The girl's eyes narrowed as she stared condescendingly at Eliza through long, dark lashes. But Eliza had put up with enough of Sophia's superior attitude.

'Actually, I am escorting Lord Levine,' she replied, doing her best to imitate Theo's cut-glass accent. Sophia blanched and stood there looking shocked.

'Over my dead body,' she finally hissed, turning on her heel and clattering back down the stairs.

'Goodness Eliza Beth, I didn't know you could speak like that,' Angelique told her, looking at Eliza with respect.

'It's a long story,' Eliza sighed, thinking of the wonderful time she'd spent with Theo. But those days were over. This was her new life and she was determined to make a success of it. No man would ever make a fool of her again. 'I'll tell you about it one day when we have more time.'

'Sounds intriguing and I can't wait to hear. Seems there's more to you than meets the eye, Eliza Beth,' Angelique said, looking at her speculatively. 'Still it doesn't matter how you managed it, Lord Levine's going to love you,' she added, pulling open the door to the largest wardrobe. 'Now you'd look charming in this.'

Eliza stared in wonder at the amethyst dress she was

holding up. It had sloping shoulders and pagoda sleeves, the soft material of its full overskirts shimmering in the light. Handing it to Eliza, she ran her fingers along the shelves, selecting a velvet stole and matching hat. 'Oh, and these are de rigueur,' she announced, triumphantly holding up a pair of ivory kid boots.

'Isn't it all a bit, well dressy for afternoon wear?' Eliza said, dubiously eying the lavish ensemble.

'It's the theatre darling. Besides, the colour means he'll know he's not expected to, well you know, take things further. He'd scuttle off faster than a ferret down a rabbit hole otherwise,' she laughed. But Eliza had other things on her mind.

'Heavens, what with the special way we have to say things and the certain colours we have to wear, well it's more like a school, isn't it?' To her surprise the other girl burst out laughing. 'Come on, let's get you ready or we'll both be expelled. Now how about . . .' she leaned forward and lowered her voice, 'corsets. Have you a suitable one to go under this dress?'

'I don't have any,' Eliza admitted.

'Cripes whatever have you been wearing then?' she gasped, her blue eyes wide. 'Oh, never mind, let's see what we can find. Time's getting on so you'd better start undressing,' she added, quickly sorting through a pile of ghastly looking contraptions, that to Eliza looked just like the sparrow cages she wove out of willow.

Finally, after much tugging, squeezing and moaning, Angelique stood back and eyed Eliza critically. 'You'll do,' she pronounced. 'Now let me braid your hair around your head so this hat sits neatly on top.' Minutes later she stood back and nodded. 'Blimey you look like some gorgeous lady. See what you think,' she said, gesturing to the mirror on the wall.

Eliza peered into the glass, hardly able to believe the reflection staring back was her.

'Stunning or what? Sophia's going to have to look to her laurels,' Angelique grinned. 'Now here's a velvet reticule. You'll find a purse with coins inside, for Madam always insists we take enough money for a hansom cab home should we get stuck. Not that it's happened to any of us yet, but best to be prepared.' As Eliza reached out to take the bag, Angelique grimaced.

'Crikey, we've forgotten gloves. You'd best cover those hands or the man will run a mile. Very particular about appearances is Lord Levine,' she said, handing Eliza a pair of ivory kid gloves, chuckling as she watched her struggle into them. 'Right, now let's go, I'll show you where to wait.'

Once again Eliza found herself following the young woman down the stairs, only this time they went through a heavy studded door that led outside to the garden. Blinking in the sudden brightness of the spring sunshine, she just had time to glimpse the square immaculate lawn that was so different to the scrub of the moors, before Angelique turned down a path to her right. They passed a couple of outbuildings that looked like stables and out through a little gate that was concealed in the high, dense hedge. The driveway was edged with bright yellow daffodils, bluey-mauve crocuses, and an abundance of hyacinths in pink, red and white.

'This is beautiful,' she said, admiring the riot of colour. 'Are there parks near here we can walk around on our days off?' she asked. Angelique gave a sigh.

'There might be but we don't get to leave the premises unless we are being escorted. Madam is very protective and watches our every move.'

'But . . .' Eliza began.

Before she could say any more, they heard the sound of hooves approaching. Eliza's stomach turned over. Whilst she was looking forward to her first ever visit to the theatre, the thought of being escorted by someone she didn't know filled her with dread.

'The carriages pull up here away from prying eyes, although I can't say I've met any monks recently,' Angelique laughed. 'Now I'd better leave you to it or I'll get a telling off. Remember to address him as Your Lordship, unless he says otherwise,' she instructed, turning and retracing her steps.

Her head swimming with all she had to remember, Eliza swallowed hard as she watched her new friend go, but there was no time to fret for moments later a fancy yellow horse-drawn coach, its hood pulled up, turned into the driveway.

There was a clatter of heels from behind. One minute, Eliza was watching the carriage approach, the next she was being thrust violently into the hedge.

'Nobody usurps me,' Sophia hissed, dark eyes glittering

with hatred. Taken aback by the woman's vehemence, it took Eliza a moment to collect herself. However, before she could reply, the strident tones of Madam reverberated down the path.

'Sophia, get back to the house this minute.' As the order hung in the air, they turned and saw the older woman striding towards them, a murderous look on her face.

'But you know I always accompany Lord Levine to the theatre,' Sophia wailed, shooting Eliza a mutinous look.

'Do as I say right this instant. I will not tolerate you fighting like a common cur at any time, let alone when the arrival of an important client is imminent,' the woman remonstrated. Eliza now recovered, had to hide a smile as the girl, like a dog reluctantly obeying his mistress, slunk back to the house.

'As for you girl, you've leaves on your shoulder,' Madam tutted, removing the offending greenery and flicking it onto the ground. 'And smooth down your skirts.'

It wasn't an instant too soon, for just at that moment the carriage drew to a halt and the liveried driver jumped onto the path, opened the door and let down the steps.

As a jovial looking man dressed in top hat, black tailed coat and grey trousers alighted with his silver topped cane, Madam gave a regal smile.

'How lovely to see you again my Lord.'

'The pleasure is all mine, Madam,' he replied, tipping his hat.

'Permit me to present Eliza Beth, the newest addition to my humble establishment,' she proudly announced, drawing

Eliza forward. 'As you can see, she is young and beautiful and will make the perfect escort for your excursion to the theatre.'

'Pleased to meet you, Your Lordship,' Eliza greeted him, adopting her poshest voice, and dipping a little curtsey. As he smiled, she noticed the fan of wrinkles around his eyes and realized he was older than she'd expected.

'Delighted to make your acquaintance my dear,' he said, gallantly handing her up into his landeau. 'We will return at five of the clock Madam,' he added, turning and giving her a pointed look.

'And everything will be ready for you as usual, my Lord,' she replied, with a conspiratorial smile.

As soon as he'd climbed into the seat opposite, the driver shut the door and Eliza felt butterflies skittering in her stomach. Her grammer would surely turn in her grave if she knew her granddaughter was riding off into the sunset with a strange man, albeit it was early afternoon and they were going to the theatre. She settled herself on the leather banquette, neatly crossing her ankles as she'd been taught, glad that the reticule gave her something to do with her hands.

They set off at a sedate pace enabling Eliza to take in the unfamiliar scenery. They passed a church, its tall spire towering over a large graveyard regimentally lined with grey and black sculptured tomb stones, then by contrast, grand houses with their red tiled roofs, ornate limestone quoins and manicured gardens.

'Beautiful architecture, don't you think?' Lord Levine's voice broke into her thoughts as he gestured to the buildings.

Although his hands were encased in soft buckskin, his movements were graceful, his timbre soft. 'I find the Double Roman roof tiles and ornamental gable ends quite pleasing to the eye. Tell me Eliza Beth, do you live in a similar property?' She stared at him in astonishment. Surely, he was having a laugh at her expense? However, the man looked quite serious as he waited for her answer.

'No, my Lord, I was brought up in a small cott on the Sedge Moor.'

'Really?' he exclaimed, soft brown eyes staring at her in surprise. 'Well in that case you must find the topography of Bridgwater decidedly different. I have visited Exmoor, Dunster to be precise, and found the scenery to be spectacular, especially in the autumn with its changing colours.' He smiled as if he'd mentioned somewhere she frequented, and Eliza realized he was trying to make her feel at ease. Then she recalled Theo mentioning he'd been hunting and shooting there and guessed Exmoor must be somewhere the nobility met. To her surprise, although she still felt a pang when she thought of him, it wasn't as acute as it had been. It was a shame Theo hadn't thought it worth continuing a relationship as brother and sister but from now on, she would move forward with her life. Feeling more positive, she smiled politely at her host.

'Well my Lord, should you ever visit Sedge Moor, you'd best make sure it's not during the winter for the land floods and all you'll see is the murk of grey water.' To her surprise, he threw back his head and laughed.

'Thank you for the advice, my dear. Now, if we are to

enjoy one another's company, I think we should dispense with formality. May I call you Eliza Beth?'

'Why, yes of course,' she replied, amazed that he should even ask.

'Then you must call me Louis,' he said, reaching across and tentatively patting her gloved hand before quickly staring back out of the window. What a strange man, Eliza thought.

Chapter 21

As they slowly promenaded through the town, Eliza watched the long terraces give way to tall shops and other commercial premises the town had to offer. Everywhere was so noisy with market traders crying out their wares and costers shouting to each other as they pushed their rattling carts between the people scurrying about their business. She couldn't equate this place with her gentle, peace-loving grandparents at all.

'Ah, here we are,' Louis smiled, when a few moments later they turned into another broad street and drew to a halt outside a marble colonnaded building set back from the road. As they alighted, a man in red jacket and black trousers bustled down a wide flight of steps to greet them.

'A pleasure to see you again my Lord, welcome m'lady,' he added, darting Eliza a probing look whilst still managing to smile politely. 'This afternoon's performance is Shakespeare's tragedy of *Hamlet* which I'm certain you will enjoy. Permit me to escort you to your box.'

'Thank you, Ponsonby,' Lord Levine replied, holding out his arm for Eliza to take. Nervously she slipped her own through his then, trying to remember Madam's instructions, picked up the front of her skirts and endeavoured to glide up the steps without tripping.

As they entered the brightly-lit foyer, the well-dressed patrons fell silent, their polite smiles doing little to disguise their curiosity. Eliza was pleased to see that despite her earlier misgivings, she was perfectly dressed for the occasion and silently thanked Angelique for her guidance. To her surprise, instead of merely following the theatre manager, her escort seemed to delight in stopping and acknowledging everyone he passed, all the while smiling gently down at her. Judging by the looks and nudges, she guessed they must be providing eagerly sought gossip. The manager stopped by a stall selling lavish boxes of beribboned confections, and looked enquiringly at Louis.

'Well Eliza Beth, what tickles your fancy?'

'Pardon?' she frowned.

'Do you prefer candies or chocolates to nibble on during the play?'

'Oh, er chocolates, please,' she replied, staring in amazement as the manager plucked the largest from the display and tucked them under his arm. As they proceeded along a maroon carpeted hallway, where framed pictures of artistes gleamed ghostly green in the flickering light of the gas lamps, Eliza noticed how the manager slowed his pace to accommodate the daintier steps of her escort. Then, after climbing a few steps, he grandly threw open a door and Eliza found herself entering the most elaborate surroundings she had ever seen.

'If there is anything else your Lordship requires, then please ring,' he told him, indicating the bell on a shelf beside the two cushioned seats.

'Thank you, Ponsonby,' Louis smiled, taking the proffered confections. Then as the man gave a bow and withdrew, he waved flamboyantly to those seated in the box on the other side of the stage before turning to acknowledge people in the stalls below. When he was satisfied their presence had been noted, he gestured for Eliza to take her seat. Smiling, he handed her the box of chocolates then folded himself elegantly into the chair beside her. Eliza stared uncertainly from the chocolates to her ivory clad hands. Should she remove the gloves before selecting one or keep them on? Not wishing to risk marking the pristine material, she discreetly placed the box beside her seat, hoping he wouldn't notice.

Eliza then gazed curiously around at her surroundings, from the soft red seats with gilt frames, the curved gold painted box front and the theatre ceiling which was so high it seemed to disappear into the darkness. A decorative wooden arch framed the stage from which hung a plush maroon curtain. It was surprisingly noisy in the auditorium, the gaslights casting ghoulish shadows over the audience's faces as they sat laughing and talking. Then a bell rang and as silence fell, her companion turned and whispered.

'I find anticipation of what's to come almost more exciting than the play itself.'

Luckily, she was saved from responding as the heavy curtain was lifted to reveal luridly painted scenery that Eliza presumed represented a forest. An actor dressed in fancy tunic and breeches stood mid stage and moments later, what looked to Eliza like some kind of ghost, appeared. The audience began mocking so that Eliza only caught snatches of what was being said. She tried to follow but became so confused with all the obscure phrases, she gave up and let it wash over her.

'Jolly good play what?' Louis asked as the coach rocked them along the streets in the dimpsy light.

'Oh, er yes,' Eliza replied politely.

'So, what did you think of the actor's portrayal of Hamlet?'

'Erm well, it was good,' she murmured. Then as he gave her a knowing look, she shrugged. 'Sorry, I didn't understand it at all. I mean what does "doubt thou the stars are fire" mean anyway?' she asked. To her surprise, he sat back in his seat and laughed.

'You are quite something,' he chuckled. 'Sophia would have hotly debated the merits of such a fine performance.'

'I'm sorry,' she murmured, feeling she'd let him down.

'Well you shouldn't be, the play is undoubtedly fine, but the language is, and I'm sure Shakespeare would forgive me, a little archaic for this day and age. It's refreshing to hear someone speak so frankly. You should continue, and again I'm sure the bard would excuse my quoting his eloquent words, "above all, to thine own self be true".'

'And are you?' she ventured. 'True to thine own self?' He let out a long sigh.

'I try to be, but it is certainly not easy,' he told her. His eyes momentarily took on a haunted look before he gave a sad smile. 'However, I would much prefer to talk about you.'

'Why? I'm sure I'm quite boring compared to your usual companions.'

'That is not true, I assure you. In fact, you intrigue me, my dear. You're not like the other girls who work for Madam and are certainly completely different to Sophia. I mean, you haven't even opened your chocolates,' he said, gesturing to the box on her lap.

'I thought I'd take them back and share them with the others,' she said, thinking quickly to avoid offending him.

'That is an admirable thought. Sophia would not only have scoffed them all but requested another box to take back with her. You are like a breath of fresh air, Eliza Beth,' he told her, then leaning forward, added, 'Tell me, are you enjoying life at Lavender House?'

'Well, yes, of course,' Eliza replied, anxious lest he should report her to Madam and refuse to pay the fee. Not that he looked as if he would, but she couldn't risk incurring the woman's wrath on her first outing.

'I'm pleased to hear that, although I'm not totally convinced. Have you acted as er, hostess yet?'

'No, but I've been told I will be shown what to do in the lounge tonight,' she told him, her spirits sinking.

As if he too felt the weight of the world upon him, Lord Levine sat back in his seat and fell silent. Every so often he took out his pocket watch and studied it and then, as if he were nervous, began fiddling with the cuffs of his shirt. Eliza was perplexed by the change in his demeanour and the nearer they got to Lavender House, the more unsettled he became. Despite his reassurance, had she disappointed him?

'Well, here we are,' he said as the coach lurched to a halt. 'Thank you for the delight of your company. I shall ask Madam to reserve you for one afternoon next week. There is a new play that has received glowing reviews. You might find that more to your taste.'

'Thank you,' Eliza replied, her spirits lifting that he wanted to see her again for it meant she could begin repaying her debt.

As the door was opened and the steps lowered, he gracefully alighted and handed her out. She felt the press of coins against her palm.

'Good afternoon, Eliza Beth,' he murmured, then stood there looking nervously around.

'Are you not coming inside?' she asked, remembering his earlier conversation with Madam. To her surprise, he flushed and looked away.

'Er, not into the house, no,' he mumbled. 'You'd better hurry along though. I hope you have a good evening.'

'I hope you do too,' she replied. He nodded, the flush spreading across his cheeks. Knowing she'd said something wrong but not sure what, she hurried down the path. Pausing by the gate, she couldn't help looking over her shoulder and was just in time to see him peering furtively around, before scurrying into the stable building.

'Whatever are you doing standing out there like that?'

Eliza jumped as Madam appeared behind her, spicy fragrance wafting in her wake.

'I was just making sure Louis, I mean Lord Levine, was alright.'

'Why? What do you mean?' the woman asked, eyes narrowing as she peered intently at her.

'Instead of coming back to the house, he went into the stables,' Eliza told her, gesturing to the building behind her.

'Stables? What sta—? Oh, you mean the—' her voice came to an abrupt halt. 'Well never mind that now, go inside and get changed. Sophia is waiting to show you how we receive and entertain our gentlemen in the lounge. It simply wouldn't do to keep either her or them waiting. They pay handsomely and expect the best service so you'd better make sure you give it to them, understand?' As those dark eyes burned into hers, Eliza nodded.

'Yes Madam,' she replied, her heart sinking to the soles of her ivory kid boots.

'And not before time,' Sophia hissed as Eliza scuttled through the door. She was wearing the maid's outfit and revealing more shapely calf than Eliza deemed decent. 'Ah Louis clearly missed me,' she added, snatching the chocolates from her hand. 'I don't imagine you were able to discuss the finer points of the play,' she laughed.

'Actually . . .' Eliza began, but Sophia had picked up a napkin covered plate and thrust it at her.

'We are particularly busy tonight so there will be no time to go to the dining room. Mrs Brown has prepared a snack for you,' the woman said, ignoring Eliza. 'Go upstairs and eat it in your room before getting ready. Your things are laid out in the dressing room, but for heaven's sake don't get any marks on them. Change and be down here in twenty minutes for inspection.'

'Inspection?' Eliza asked. Was this what Madam meant when she'd spoken about her examination? But then why would she have to pay? It didn't make sense. But Sophia was clucking impatiently.

'Do pay attention. All hostesses are reviewed before entering the lounge, especially new, naive ones,' she added, dark eyes glinting. 'Now hurry along, you've already wasted two of those minutes arguing.' Arguing? Eliza bit down a retort. Clearly the woman hadn't forgiven her for accompanying Louis to the theatre and was spoiling for a disagreement. Well, she wasn't going to give her the satisfaction of rising to the bait. Besides, she was ravenous.

The attic room was empty and Eliza counted the coins Lord Levine had pressed into her hand, gratified to see he had been very generous. Quickly she secreted them under her nightdress in the rickety cabinet beside her bed. If she carried on at this rate, she would soon make a healthy dent in that stupid indenture thing.

It was a far cry from Sedge Moor and as she peeled off her gloves and kicked off the ivory boots, she couldn't help wondering what Clem would say if he'd seen her all dressed up in her finery. Fleetingly, she wondered if he'd called by and noticed she was missing yet. Perhaps she should have told him she was going. But he would have tried to change her mind and after the mess she'd made of things recently, she needed to prove that she was capable of coping by herself.

She settled herself on her bed, plate on her lap, and tucked into her food. The bread was freshly baked, the ham succulent and she ate heartily, thinking back over her afternoon. Lord Levine had been good company and despite not understanding the play, she had enjoyed her first trip to the theatre.

From somewhere she heard a chiming of a clock and mindful Sophia would be waiting, reluctantly took herself into the next room where her outfit had been laid out. Her eyes widened when she saw the purple lacy under garment with tiny gold buttons all the way down the front. Clearly, she was expected to change her corsets as well. Beautiful it might be, but what was the point of wearing such a thing, when no one would see it? she thought, struggling out of her daywear.

Sitting down, she pulled on the black silk stockings and black dress which revealed a glimpse of décolletage at the top and was shorter than anything she'd ever dreamed of wearing. However, the white apron was bibbed at the front and she was able to hitch it up, although the shiny black heeled boots which she was unable to lace tightly enough to hide the stockings beneath, only served to accentuate legs she'd never before revealed. Sighing, she pulled on the little white lace gloves then stared helplessly at the scrap of lace that was the only thing remaining on the bed. What on earth was that for? Conscious that time was galloping by and knowing Sophia would delight in having an excuse to remonstrate, she stuffed it in the pocket of the apron. Balancing precariously on the high heels, Eliza tapped her way as quickly as she dared down the stairs to find Sophia waiting.

Chapter 22

Eyes narrowed, she surveyed Eliza from head to toe before gesturing for her to turn around. With a deep sigh, she pulled down the front of Eliza's apron until she was satisfied.

'You need to show some décolletage; the punters expect it. They're here to be entertained by women not nuns,' she hissed. That's what they pay good money for. And for heaven's sake what have you done with those laces on your boots?' Letting out a sigh of exasperation, she bent and loosened them. 'The whole idea is to reveal a tantalizing glimpse of what's beneath. Some men have a thing for fetching feet. And you've forgotten your pill,' she said, straightening and giving Eliza a disdainful look.

'My pill?' Eliza frowned.

'Your hat. It was left with your uniform,' Sophia snapped impatiently.

'Oh, so that's what this is,' Eliza said, producing the scrap of lace from her pocket. The woman snatched it from her and arranged it deftly on top of Eliza's head.

'Right, now for your lips,' the woman said, snatching up a phial and dabbing crimson liquid onto Eliza's lips. 'Tonight, you will shadow me, which means doing exactly as I say. Watch what I do, speak only when spoken to, understand?'

Eliza nodded, her stomach turning over for she felt like one of the painted people she'd seen on the stage that afternoon.

'Come along,' Sophia urged. She followed the woman down the corridor and through a door that led into the much grander hall hung with the splendid chandelier she so much admired.

As Sophia pushed open a heavy studded door, Eliza found herself in a room with cherry wood panelling. Plush-looking chairs upholstered in burgundy fabric were arranged around small circular tables with crystal ashtrays in the centre. The windows were covered in heavy drapes the same fabric as the chairs and fringed with gold-coloured silk ropes and tassels. Cigar smoke hung heavily in the air and there was the overwhelming smell of liquor fumes. As Eliza tried not to shudder, she became aware that the room had fallen silent. Gentlemen dressed formally in evening attire turned in her direction, their eyes alight with curiosity as they looked her up and down.

'Good evening gentlemen,' Sophia purred, skirts rustling as she slowly circled the tables, taking time to smile seductively at each of them in turn. Eliza was relieved to see Clodah and Angelique smiling encouragingly at her. Although they were seated with gentlemen at tables in the corner, it would be comforting to know they were close by. Her attention returned to Sophia who was commanding everyone's attention.

'I would like to introduce Eliza Beth. Now I know just how naughty you boys can be,' she paused as a ripple of mirth ran around the room. 'However, this is her first night so please be kind to her.'

'Of course, we will Sophia darling,' one gentleman called.

'Bring her over to my table and I'll be pleased to show her just how kind I can be,' another suggested with a salacious wink that made Eliza cringe.

'All in good time, Dickie darling. I have to teach her the ropes first,' Sophia purred, sashaying towards the bar at the back of the room leaving Eliza to follow. 'Now the idea is to make as much money as possible,' she said, keeping her voice low. 'When a client orders a drink, he will ask that you join him. Mostly they drink spirits so you place his glass on a silver tray, along with a flute for yourself and a bottle of the champagne here. It's imperative you remember to take a bottle from this side of the shelf for these are filled with carbonated water which, in the dim lighting, appears the same.'

'So, what's the point?' Eliza asked.

'The point you little imbecile is that they pay top price for a bottle of the best champagne.'

'But that's—'

'Business,' Sophia interrupted. 'And if you're clever with your promises, you can persuade them to buy another later,' she added, scanning the room then nodding. 'Of course, until you have been examined, you will serve or sit and chat to customers in here.'

'But—' she began, for hadn't Sophia just inspected her?

'There are no buts, that's Madam's ruling,' Sophia hissed. Swallowing hard, Eliza peered through the fug, her heart sinking when she saw Clodah and Angelique rising to their feet. They were followed moments later by the two gentlemen. 'Are you listening?' Sophia hissed.

'Er yes,' Eliza murmured.

'I said, you can start with William over there. We dispense with titles here in the lounge. Calling everyone by their first names helps preserve their reputations. William's a card but quite undemanding, has a thing about feet so remember to wiggle yours enticingly,' she instructed, picking up a tray set with glasses and a tall green bottle. 'Now, the men are out to have fun so it's froufrou all the way. Madam insists on high standards, so watch how I act and do the same. Oh, and for heaven's sake keep your gloves on. Luckily for you, some men find that attractive.'

Dress rustling and heels clicking, Sophia led the way over to a corner table where an older man, hair greying at the temples, was already nursing a drink.

'Sophia,' he said, rising to his feet and bowing gallantly. 'You are looking divine as always.' He gave Eliza an appraising look, his eyes glittering as he took in her stockings beneath the loosely laced boots. 'Your first evening, what? Well why don't you take a seat and tell me all about yourself.'

'Oh, I . . .'

'Will be delighted,' Sophia finished, shooting Eliza a warning look. 'Now make sure you look after William, he is one of our most distinguished guests.' She turned to the man and gave him a dazzling smile. 'You will have to excuse me, I'm afraid. It is Madam's night off and she has asked me to oversee the girls in her absence.'

'And she couldn't ask for a more capable assistant,' the man replied, smiling at her briefly before pulling out a chair for Eliza. Nervously, she took a seat and watched as he poured a glass of the pretend champagne for her. He took a sip of his liquor and glanced down at her boots, his eyes lighting up. Remembering her instructions, Eliza shook her foot, then when his gaze continued to linger, said the first thing that came into her head.

'Do you come here often?' she asked.

He threw back his head and roared. 'I do as it happens. Although I must say in all my visits, I've never been asked that question before. Now, more to the point, what brings a pretty girl such as yourself here?' He gave her a searching look as he edged his chair closer.

Eliza had to steel herself not to move hers away as she cast around for a satisfactory answer.

'Secrets eh?' he gave a mirthless laugh. 'Well, we all have plenty of those. Now let's just relax and get to know each other.'

To her relief, he began regaling her with stories about his racehorses. An obvious passion for him. In between glances down at her feet, he moved from the state of the economy to the latest show he seen in London. Eliza sipped her drink, nodding every time he paused to take a drink or replenish her glass. The bottle seemed to be emptying at an alarming rate and she slowed her pace. Then she saw Sophia glaring and quickly downed her drink. The speculative gleam in the man's eye grew brighter and he leaned closer.

'Are you wishing for more refreshment?' Eliza asked quickly.

'Well, now here's a thing. I would love another glass. However, at my age it would be ill-advised. Besides I think Sophia needs your help,' he added, pointing to the crowded bar where the woman was gesturing in her direction.

'So how did you get on last night?' Clodah asked Eliza as they sat over breakfast in the dining room.

'Oh, er fine,' she replied, helping herself to the eggs and offal from the serving dishes in the centre of the table.

'Well good for you. Of course, once you've been passed you can begin earning real money,' Clodah added. Before Eliza could ask the question that had been niggling her, the girl reached for her cup, her sleeve rising so that Eliza saw the livid bruises on her arm. Seeing Eliza's shocked expression, she shrugged. 'Goes with the territory.'

Suddenly Eliza had no appetite. What had she got herself into? And more importantly how soon could she get out again? She stared around the windowless room as if it would somehow give her the answer.

'You'd better watch out. Too much of that greasy food will make you fat and no man will find you attractive,' Sophia sneered, gliding into the room and staring down at Eliza's full plate. It appeared she saved her foreign accent and sultry manner for the clients. 'Mrs Brown, will you please bring me something more appetising. I've told you before, I simply cannot stomach this stodge,' she called. Immediately the woman came bustling out of the kitchen and placed a plate before her.

'Perhaps these lady finger biscuits and mousse au citron would be more to your taste,' the woman said, her voice dripping with sarcasm. The girls stared at each other waiting for Sophia to retaliate. However, she seemed placated and merely nodded.

'One up to Mrs B,' Angelique whispered.

'What's everyone doing this morning?' Clodah asked.

'Madam's asked me to help Eliza Beth with her diction and dress,' Angelique replied.

'Well make sure she's ready to present herself in the lounge this afternoon. Her serving technique left much to be desired last night and she needs extra tuition,' Sophia retorted, talking over Eliza's head.

'I am here if you wish to speak with me,' Eliza told her.

'Actually, I don't,' the woman sneered, elegantly nibbling on a biscuit. Then a gleeful expression crossed her face and she turned to Angelique. 'The gold dress will suit her colouring so make sure she's wearing that.' There was a horrified silence as the girls stared from one to the other.

'But that's the one Rosa Marie wore . . .' Monique began.

'So? Not here to object now, is she? Remember, Eliza Beth you are to wear the gold dress, and that's an order.' With a satisfied grin, she got to her feet and swept from the room.

As silence descended again, Angelique turned to Eliza.

'Go and grab a couple of capes from the dressing room and meet me by the side door. We'll take a walk in the garden, get some fresh air and work on your diction at the same time. Although after the classy voice you adopted yesterday, I'm not sure I can teach you much,' she said quickly.

Knowing this was her opportunity to get some answers, Eliza tripped lightly up the stairs. The atmosphere in the dining room was oppressive and she really couldn't care less what she wore that afternoon. In fact, she didn't care if she never entered that horrid lounge with its fug of smoke and stink of liquor, ever again. Snatching the nearest cloaks from the dressing room she hurried back downstairs. Away from the others, she intended asking the questions that had been concerning her.

As they strolled along the path that bordered the lawn, Eliza breathed in the fresh air and listened to the birds singing. The trees were beginning to blossom while golden daffodils bobbed their bright heads in the borders. She couldn't help thinking of her vegetable plot back home and the seeds she'd so carefully saved last summer ready for sowing for the new season. But that was her old life and she'd been longing to see what was beyond Sedge Moor hadn't she?

'This is much better than being indoors,' she sighed.

'It's a bit early to be outside really,' Angelique yawned. Eliza stared at her in surprise. Back home, she would have done half a day's work by now. But then everyone kept late hours here.

'I couldn't help noticing those bruises on Clodah's arm,' she said, stopping and turning to face her companion. Angelique stared anxiously from side to side, then took Eliza's arm and hurried her further down the garden.

'Be careful. Madam has her spies everywhere,' she whispered.

'Spies?' Eliza cried, her head spinning round. Sure enough, a burly man was leaning casually against the far fence smoking a cigarette, his eyes fixed in their direction.

'Keep walking and talk quietly,' Angelique murmured. 'Madam runs this place with a rod of iron. She employs men to keep an eye on the patrons and us too. None of us escape surveillance.'

'Well if they're here to look out for us, what about that bruising of Clodah's arm then?'

'Well obviously they can't intrude in the chambers. Most clients are considerate in their dealings but some get a bit carried away. And, of course, they are of a different class and some consider it their right to dominate. It goes with the job, I guess.'

'But why do you stay?' Eliza asked.

'We all have our reasons,' Angelique said, taking the path along by the hedge. 'Obviously money's the primary driver. As I said before, none of us could earn what we do anywhere else.'

'But money's not everything,' she replied.

'Easy to say if you have plenty, which none of us do.' Angelique gave a harsh laugh. 'Clodah sends nearly all her money home so her mother can feed her brothers and sisters. There's eleven of them, can you imagine,' she shook her head in astonishment. 'Apparently, her father having kept his wife almost permanently pregnant, upped and left one day never to be heard of again.'

'Oh, that's terrible,' Eliza cried.

'We women do have our problems. Neither Monique nor Eva can read or write properly so that narrows down their choice of work. Then there's Sophia. Her betrothed jilted her days before their wedding. She's so bitter she spends her time making as much money as she can out of the men while venting her hatred on us.'

'I suppose that explains her jealousy to a degree. But what about you Angelique, you are so pretty.'

'My stepfather obviously thought so too, for he turned to me for his satisfaction. As soon as I could, I upped and left,' she shook her head, so that her halo of curls lifted in the breeze. 'No decent man's going to want me now, so I'm saving every penny I earn to set up my dressmaking business. What about you Eliza, you said your grandfather had died, is that what brought you here?'

Eliza was silent as she tried to make sense of her feelings. Her grandparents had always treated her well and after what Angelique had told her about the others, running away from an empty house seemed absurd. Of course, there had been that devastating revelation about Theo which could so easily have ruined her life. And the terrible guilt for what she'd put her gramfer through still haunted her. Although Clem had said he'd been old and ailing, it really wasn't any excuse and she knew he'd placed the blame on Theo to make her feel better. Dear Clem. Recalling his candid blue eyes and easy-going nature, she realized with shock how much she'd always taken him for granted. And with sudden clarity, she saw how Theo and she having been brought up in completely different circumstances, were poles apart. He might have wanted to meet Gramfer but he'd never mentioned introducing her to his own family and friends had he?

'You don't have to say, if you'd rather not,' Angelique said, breaking into her thoughts.

'I came to Bridgwater to try and find my grandparents' family. Madam did say I'd only be working evenings and weekends so I thought I'd have plenty of time,' she replied.

'Hmm, well they might be your official hours but she'll keep you busy the rest of the time, believe you me. Besides, getting away from here, unless on an officially escorted trip, is simply not permitted.'

'Oh, come on,' Eliza said. 'She can't really stop us.' Angelique nodded towards the man at the end of the garden. Even if you managed to leave the premises, they'd find you. 'Only last month one of the girls gave them the slip. She was found the next day in the canal – dead.'

'That's dreadful,' Eliza cried.

'Not as dreadful as if she'd lived. Her body was so badly mutilated she'd never have worked again.' As Eliza gasped in horror, Angelique broke into peals of laughter.

Chapter 23

'How can you laugh at such a dreadful thing?' Eliza asked, looking aghast.

'Madam's watching so smile and look as though we're just chatting. We don't want to arouse suspicion,' Angelique hissed through the side of her mouth.

'Girls,' Madam called.

'Too late. Come along,' she sighed, hurrying over to the French doors where Madam was waiting.

'I'm glad you have time to enjoy yourselves,' she said, her smile not reaching her eyes. 'Eliza, I wish to speak with you. No, no girl,' she tutted, as Eliza went to step through her open door. 'Present yourself properly when the clock chimes the half hour.' With that she snapped her doors closed leaving the girls outside.

'If she wanted to speak with me, why couldn't I just walk in?' Eliza exclaimed.

'That's her way. Besides, she wouldn't think you properly attired like that, so you'd better run upstairs and change into a morning gown. I suppose I'd better as well,' she said, frowning down at her simple dress.

Upstairs, Angelique threw open the wardrobe doors and drew out a turquoise silk gown with matching cape.

'That's a bit much just to speak with Madam, isn't it?' Eliza spluttered.

'We all have to be ready to be presented to any of her guests at any time. Now hurry up, you're not wearing corsets I'll be bound.'

Eliza groaned, then her attention was caught by the golden dress hanging alone at the end of the rail.

'Is that the dress Sophia was talking about earlier?' she asked, reaching out to stroke the sheeny material.

'Don't touch it,' Angelique all but shrieked, making Eliza jump back.

'But why?'

'If it was up to us, that garment would have been burned, but Madam refused, saying it had cost too much. Now come along, you mustn't keep her waiting,' Angelique urged, holding out the corset. 'Get into this whilst I sort out suitable slippers.' Seeing she wasn't going to be swayed, Eliza duly wriggled into the horrid contraption that made her feel as confined as those sparrows, then slipped the dress over her head. The slinky material felt so much nicer than the rough sacking she was used to, and the cape was welcome for the air was chillier up here in the attic room than it had been outside.

'Lips,' Angelique reminded her, holding out the phial of crimson liquid.

'Oh really, it's not even the middle of the morning,' she exclaimed.

'Madam expects it,' Angelique reminded her. 'Now hurry along or you'll incur her wrath.' Heavens, Eliza thought, this place was worse than school had ever been.

It was only when she reached the hallway that she realized she hadn't got to the bottom of the mystery of the gold dress. She'd ask one of the others later, she thought, smoothing down her skirts and knocking on Madam's door.

'*Entrez*,' the woman's husky voice replied. Obviously, Madam had clicked into French mode in the last thirty minutes, Eliza thought, opening the door. Perhaps this was the time to tell her she'd made a mistake and see if they could come to some agreement about this stupid indenture thing.

'*Bonjour* Eliza Beth, we have *un visiteur important*,' Madam announced grandly, all but curtseying to the figure sitting incongruously on the chaise longue. He was a thin man of late middle years, with greying hair and watery green eyes that gleamed gold with interest as he rested on his ivory topped cane. Silently, he looked her up and down as if she was a racehorse he was considering purchasing.

'Oh yes, nice, very nice indeed,' he finally pronounced with a leer. His voice was loud, his manner so condescending it caused a shudder to creep down Eliza's back. Impatiently, he gestured for her to turn around; she was about to refuse but saw the look on Madam's face. As she did as she'd been asked, she felt his gaze burning through her dress. What a revolting creature she thought, when he nodded to Madam.

'*Merci*, Eliza Beth. *Allez-vous-en*,' she purred, beaming widely as she waved Eliza away.

Odious man, Eliza fumed, stamping back up the stairs. And she had no idea what that had all been about. Or why Madam had looked so delighted.

'Oh, I didn't expect you back so soon,' Angelique said, looking uncomfortable when Eliza reappeared. She'd changed into a more formal afternoon gown and the cerise colour matched the flush on her cheeks. 'What did Madam want?'

'Haven't the faintest idea. She had some old man with her who looked me up and down as if I was up for sale,' she sniffed.

'Well that's what these people pay good money for, and why we take it,' Angelique replied, shrugging. 'It's a funny world when you think of it. These men think they are taking advantage of we females, when really it is us who are using them to further our futures.'

'Hmm,' Eliza replied, thinking that didn't sound funny to her at all. All it did was strengthen her resolve to find a way to leave this place as soon as she could. She stared out of the slanted windows but couldn't see beyond the roof of the stables.

'You're not still thinking of leaving, are you?' Angelique asked, following her gaze. 'You won't get away you know. Madam, or her men, will be keeping their eyes on you, at least until you've brought in some decent money, so you might as well accept it.'

'I went out with Lord Levine yesterday,' she said, remembering how he'd said he wanted to book her again. 'That should have earned me something towards that indenture thing.'

'Not much though, not with him being the way he is. You'll probably earn more in the lounge later.'

'Ah yes, that reminds me. Why do I have to wear a dress and not the maid's uniform I wore last night?' she frowned.

'Because you get a different type of man visiting in the afternoons. They expect a bit more refinement, and you only wear a black dress when you are acting as hostess for the evening as you and Sophia were last night.'

'If I'm meant to wear that gold dress, you could at least tell me what's wrong with it. Who was Rosa Marie and what happened to her?'

'Well . . .' Angelique began, looking distinctly uncomfortable. 'I suppose you have the right to know as it's another hazard of the job. But with our checks and everything we didn't expect it to happen here, yet it did.'

'What did?' Eliza almost shrieked. 'For God's sake will you please tell me what happened.'

'Rosa Marie caught syphilis from one of the punters. She was wearing the gold dress and it's said the infection in the sores can stay in material and . . .'

'And we all know what a fallacy that is,' Sophia said, appearing beside them. 'So, you will wear that dress this afternoon, Eliza Beth,' she added, her lips curling in triumph. 'However, before that, I have come to escort you downstairs.'

'For heaven's sake I've only just come back up,' Eliza cried.

'Am I to tell Madam you're disobeying her instruction?' Sophia asked, raising an immaculate brow.

'Has that ghastly, er I mean, her visitor gone?' Eliza asked.

'Yes, he has.' She paused then gave another supercilious smile. 'But she has another man for you to see, so I would look sharp if I were you. She hates being kept waiting and . . .' she left the rest of her sentence hanging in the air but her meaning was clear.

'Oh, very well,' Eliza sighed, following the woman down the stairs. All this trailing up and down three flights was tiring not to mention a waste of time. Sophia gave her a gloating look then knocked on Madam's door.

'Come.' So, the woman was back to speaking English, Eliza thought, then jumped as Sophia all but pushed her inside, quickly closing the door behind her.

'Really,' Eliza began, only to hear Madam cough. Standing beside her was a dapper little man with a moustache that seemed to curl as far as his ears.

'Ah Eliza Beth, Doctor here has come to carry out your inspection.'

'Actually Madam, I have . . .' she began, desperate to let the woman know she had decided to leave.

'Good, good, I will leave you in his capable hands, so to speak,' Madam said, ignoring Eliza. 'The room is prepared Doctor,' she said, gesturing to an open door in the corner of the room.

'But I've decided . . .' Eliza began again, desperate to make her feelings heard.

'I do hope you're not going to be tiresome,' Madam snapped, all pretence of civility gone. 'The doctor is a busy man and I hope I don't have to remind you of this . . .' She picked up the dreaded paper from her escritoire and shook it in front of Eliza.

'I want to speak . . .'

'Well don't. Over to you Doctor and you know what to do if she doesn't oblige.'

The man gave a curt nod then gripped Eliza firmly by her arm, his strength belying his diminutive stature. He all but dragged her into the smaller room, gesturing towards the daybed which was spread with a white sheet.

'Lie down,' he ordered.

'There's been a mistake. I've changed my mind,' Eliza squeaked, certain she was about to be sick.

'I said lie down and close your eyes,' he growled, pushing her backwards so that she collapsed onto the bed. She began to struggle but his hands pinned her firmly down. She made to bite his wrist but he snatched up a cloth and held it over her face. The foul-smelling fumes made her gag and then all went black.

Groggily, Eliza forced her heavy eyelids open. Where was she and why did she feel so sore? She tried to sit up but the room swam before her and she fell back onto the bed again. As she lay there trying to focus, Madam appeared beside her. Grinning from ear to ear, she helped Eliza to her feet. 'There, that wasn't so bad was it? I knew you seemed naive but . . .

well, this is simply marvellous,' she crowed. 'I shall spread the word. Lord S— er, Edward, the man you saw earlier, has a penchant for red hair and already declared his interest, but now . . . I have sent my men to spread the word and soon we'll be in the money,' she rubbed her hands together enthusiastically. 'Oh, and I'll keep this as proof,' she added, snatching up the soiled sheet.

Still woozy, Eliza tried to take in what the woman was saying. Then, as her head began to clear, everything began to click horribly into place.

'Look, there's been a mistake. I must leave right now . . .' she pleaded.

'I will arrange for a tub of hot water to be prepared,' Madam continued, ignoring her. 'Take that ribbon from your hair.'

'You don't understand . . .' Eliza began.

'No Eliza Beth, it is you who doesn't understand,' the woman retorted, her eyes narrowing to slits as she reached out and tugged the ribbon from Eliza's hair.

'Ow!' she cried, tears springing to her eyes.

'Hmm, just as I thought, ends as rough as rats' tails,' the woman said, lifting a handful of Eliza's locks and grimacing. 'As my *pièce de résistance* you will need to look elegant and poised. Eva is proficient with the scissors so I'll get her to cut off at least two inches and loan you some of that really bright, shiny lip colour she's fond of applying. Right, make yourself comfortable, I've things to arrange.' And for the second time, Eliza felt herself being pushed back onto the bed.

As soon as the woman had left the room, Eliza jumped up. Ignoring her throbbing head, she straightened her clothes and hurried to the door only to find it was locked. This couldn't be happening, she thought, staring frantically around for another means of escape. To her horror, she saw the room had no windows, the only light coming from a gas lamp on the wall. Slumping back onto the bed, she shook her head wishing it would stop pounding. That dreadful doctor had obviously used something to knock her out.

What a bizarre world she'd inadvertently become mixed up in. Only a short time ago, she'd been weaving willow wondering what life was like beyond Sedge Moor. Well she'd certainly found out, hadn't she? Clem had said she was inexperienced and how right he'd been. Now to her abject horror, she found herself all but imprisoned in this disreputable house and up to her eyes in debt. She simply had to escape before she was made to . . .

As bile rose in her throat, Eliza heard the key turn in the lock.

Chapter 24

Eliza jumped to her feet then swayed as the room span before her. Falling back on the bed, she groaned, certain she was going to be sick this time.

'Better not to fight it,' a soft voice advised. Slowly opening her eyes, she saw Eva standing beside her, scissors in hand.

'Please, you must help me escape,' she pleaded, her voice croaky as a frog.

'Eva is here to see to your hair so do not make things difficult for her,' Madam retorted, appearing in the doorway. 'Now sit up and sip this,' she added, proffering a glass. As Eliza stared suspiciously at the liquid, the woman sighed. 'For God's sake girl do as you're told, it will calm you down and make you feel better. We can't have you feeling faint for your debut.'

'My what?' Eliza whispered, her throat dry and rough.

'Drink up, then shut up so Eva can get on,' Madam said, forcing the glass to Eliza's lips. Too thirsty to resist any longer, she opened her mouth and felt the cool liquid slide down her throat. Within moments she felt that fuzzy feeling returning and shook her head trying to clear it. Madam gave a satisfied nod then turned to Eva.

'Trim as little as you can get away with. That red hair is her main asset and will command a high price.'

'You're going to sell my hair,' Eliza mumbled, sure she'd misheard.

'We are going to sell all of you girl,' Madam replied, triumphantly. 'Right, I have things to arrange but time is of the essence so I'll be back in ten minutes,' she said, addressing Eva before crossing the room. Again, Eliza heard the door being locked behind her.

'You've got to help me,' Eliza beseeched Eva, but her speech was slurred and as the woman's face swam before her, she sank back on the bed.

'For God's sake sit up, if you don't let me cut your hair I'll be in trouble. Like you, I have my indenture to pay off.'

'But you've got to help me,' Eliza stuttered, trying to make her meaning clear as she struggled to sit up.

'We have to help ourselves here, and that's something you need to learn if you're to survive. Now keep still or I won't be responsible if these scissors stab you.' Stunned by her harsh voice, Eliza did as she said.

'You don't realize how lucky you are,' Eva told her, moments later as she snipped into Eliza's hair.

'I don't feel lucky,' she muttered, then feeling the cold blade on her neck, fell silent.

'Lord Seymour has many enemies and if he's offering for you then there are bound to be others who'll be desperate to outbid him. You could be fortunate enough to clear your indenture in one fell swoop. Unlike the rest of us who . . .'

'Did you say Lord Seymour?' Eliza squeaked, her mind suddenly clear although her movements were clumsy as she spun round to look at the woman.

'For heaven's sake, I nearly cut your ear there,' Eva tutted. 'Yes, and he's got pots of cash.'

'The Lord Seymour from Montecute Manor?'

'That's the one. Now I'm not answering any more questions until your hair's done or Madam will have my guts for garters – or worse.'

But Eliza hardly heard her. She was to be auctioned and Lord Seymour, Theo's father, her own blood father, was going to bid for her. Her stomach churned. She had to get out of here. The question was how.

'There, all done,' Eva announced, just as Madam reappeared.

'I need the privy,' Eliza announced.

'Very well, Eva will escort you. I have men posted everywhere so no funny business,' she said, giving Eliza a knowing look. 'After that you will go downstairs where the tub has been filled for you.'

'But I had a bath the day before yesterday,' Eliza protested.

'I shall not even credit that statement with a reply. Remember, you are representing my establishment and I have a reputation to uphold. Now, there is still much to prepare,' she added sweeping out with her head held high.

On legs that wobbled and shook, Eliza staggered into the privy where she wretched and heaved until her stomach had nothing left to offer. As she leaned weakly against the slats of the wall, she heard Eva speaking with someone but when she stumbled from the wooden hut, she was alone. A quick glance down the garden revealed the man she'd seen that morning, watching her from his position by the fence. He looked even more menacing and Eliza knew he meant business. But what could she do?

But there was no time to think, for she spent the rest of the afternoon being primped and preened. Not for one moment was she left alone, not even in the privacy of the tub. Her hair was washed and rubbed dry, her curls anointed with some kind of aromatic oil. Her hands were slathered in salve, her lips were coloured in carmine. Then just as her corsets had been laced, Sophia appeared triumphantly bearing the gold dress aloft on its hanger.

'This will set off your colouring well,' she announced. Eliza gasped and turned to Eva for help. The girl shrugged but Eliza saw she'd gone very pale.

'No, not that one Sophia,' Madam announced as she bustled into the room. 'Eliza will wear this tonight. The symbol of purity, is it not?' she grinned, holding up a white satin gown with matching slippers.

'I really think . . .' Eliza began, determined to say her piece as her head began to clear.

'That it is the most exquisite thing you have ever seen,' Madam finished for her. 'So, hurry, hurry, it is nearly time,' she urged, placing the garment over Eliza's head then indicating for her to step into the shoes. Then she stood back and studied Eliza closely. '*Magnifique*,' she cried, clapping her hands in delight. Then she frowned. 'We need something to clip up those curls so they dangle enticingly over your shoulders. Flames of temptation hovering above an innocent face as it were.' Seeing her opportunity, Eliza forced a smile.

'Why Madam, I have a beautiful amber comb in my bag upstairs. I'll go and get it.'

'No,' the woman shouted, as she turned towards the door. 'Nobody outside this room must see you yet. Eva go and bring Eliza's bag down here, quickly now, quickly.' As the woman hurried away, Eliza's heart sank to her slippers. She needed to think of something else for time was running out. As if reading her thoughts, Sophia shot her a satisfied look. Intercepting the glance, Madam frowned.

'Sophia, my men have spent the afternoon spreading the word and things promise to be very busy. You will be in charge of the bar tonight so please go and prepare – now,' she added when the woman hesitated. No sooner had she grudgingly left than Eva appeared carrying Eliza's bag.

'Right, let's see this clip,' Madam ordered, watching closely as Eliza delved through her old clothes. No sooner had her fingers closed over the amber comb than it was snatched from her hands.

'*Magnifique*,' Madam crooned admiringly. 'You have had an admirer, no?' Before Eliza could explain, the woman turned to Eva. 'Fix it,' she ordered. When it was fixed into place, her eyes gleamed and she rubbed her hands together. 'Perfect. Never will there have been such an event as we are putting on tonight. We will be the envy of the town, if not the county when word gets out.'

Obviously, she was on a mission and that was to make money, Eliza thought. Desperately, she made one final plea.

'Look Madam, if I promise to pay you for—' she cried jumping to her feet, only for the woman to push her back down again.

'Drink,' she ordered, holding a glass to Eliza's lips. Only too aware of what it contained and needing to keep her wits about her, Eliza refused. Not to be thwarted, Madam pinched her nostrils and as Eliza gasped for breath, tipped the liquid down her throat. 'Silly girl, it is only a little sedative to keep you calm,' she grinned.

Chapter 25

The air was heavy with excitement and expectation, as what felt like a hundred pairs of male eyes turned in Eliza's direction. With Madam next to her whispering instructions, she circled the room and made her way to the gold chair that was set on the raised platform.

Clasping her gloved hands tightly in her lap, she stared down at the lace pattern, willing the debacle to hurry up and be over. Sick with nerves and her head still woozy from the sedative she hardly heard Madam's address.

'Welcome, my esteemed guests, to what can only be described as the grandest event ever to be held here at my humble establishment.' She paused and smiled graciously as the men demurred. 'Now you all know why you are here and will agree, I am sure, that it is indeed a rare opportunity on offer tonight.' Theatrically, she gestured to Eliza then called for opening bids. Eliza's mouth went dry as the men began calling out amounts that made her gasp. The loudest and most insistent voice she recognized as belonging to the loathsome man who'd looked her over that morning whom she now knew to be Lord Seymour.

Then, all went quiet, and she heard Madam announce, 'The highest bid lies with Lord Seymour. Do I hear any advance?' She paused and Eliza's heart almost stopped. 'Gentlemen, the bidding is over. The lady's virtue goes to Lord Seymour.' She waited for the hubbub to subside before smiling graciously at the man.

'We will conclude our business and drink a toast in my office, my Lord,' Madam purred. 'Come along Eliza Beth,' she ordered, ushering Eliza from the room. In the doorway, as if suddenly remembering her manners, she turned and thanked the men for coming. 'If, no, *when*, I am fortunate enough to get another innocent on my books, I'll be sure to let you know.'

She swept her way grandly through the hall and along the corridor, a gloating Lord Seymour by her side. Sick to her stomach, Eliza could only follow them into Madam's room. The effects of the sedative were wearing off now and as she watched Madam deftly pop open a bottle of champagne, she noticed her bag behind the chair. There was a clinking of glasses and then the odious man turned to Eliza, his hand going to her bottom. Repulsed she made to move away but Madam gave a raucous laugh.

'I think we'd better conclude our business before you claim your prize, my Lord.' As the man turned and leered lasciviously at Eliza, she let out a cry.

'I need the privy urgently.'

'Don't be ridiculous Eliza,' Madam growled, her eyes hard. 'We went through all this earlier. It's just nerves my Lord,' she said, turning back to the man whose hand snaked its way over Eliza's bottom once more. Enough was enough and remembering a trick from her childhood, she leaned forward and began heaving and retching. Lord Seymour jumped back, staring aghast at his spattered trousers.

'I'm most awfully sorry,' Madam cried, dabbing ineffectively at the material with her handkerchief. Then she saw the state of Eliza's dress.

'Go and get yourself cleaned up at once,' she ordered, giving her a stern look. 'And don't try anything funny. I will get my men to shadow your every move and if you are not back in ten minutes, I won't be responsible for their actions. Do I make myself clear?'

'Yes Madam,' she replied meekly although her mind was working overtime.

As the woman picked up her bell, Eliza hurried from the room, snatching up her bag as she went. Knowing she had precious little time, she hared up the staircase and tugged open a door, praying she'd got the right one. If her earlier calculations were correct, this room was directly beneath their dressing room and also overlooked the stable. Heart in mouth, she prised open the window, letting out a sigh of relief when she saw the outline of the roof below. Throwing her bag onto the parapet, she jumped down after it and leapt to the ground. Then she heard voices and, heart thumping, darted into the cover of the hedge. There was laughter, the slam of a door followed by the sound of a carriage pulling away. All went quiet apart from the pounding of blood in her ears. With eyes and ears alert for Madam's men she edged towards the entrance. She might only have been on Bodrilly with Theo, but how hard could riding a horse be?

Except there were no horses inside the building, just rows of boxes and baskets. Clearly it was a storeroom of some sort and not stabling at all. But then why had Lord Levine come in here? And why had he looked so furtive? The sound of footsteps and murmur of voices made her jump, and scuttling over to the farthest corner, she crouched behind the largest box. It wasn't a moment too soon for two heavy set men stood in the doorway swinging a lantern around. Eliza trembled and held her breath.

'She wouldn't 'ave come in 'ere. Right den of iniquity.'

'Even worse than the 'ouse itself. We'd best search the gardens again, ask the drivers if they've seen 'er. Not that they'd 'ave seen anything, of course.' With a guttural laugh, the men continued on their way.

Eliza waited until their footsteps had died away, then desperately looked around for another way out. It was then she saw a door slightly ajar and crept cautiously towards it. There was a flight of stairs leading down to some sort of cellar which seemed to be lit by candlelight. On tiptoe she started to descend then stopped short when she heard the sounds of men making merry. There was the strangest of sickly smells, not dissimilar to the one in Madam's room. Then her eyes widened and she stood transfixed as through the haze of smoke, she saw bodies sprawled on cushions and realized what was going on. Bile rising, she fled back up to the storeroom. So that was why Lord Levine had come here and why he was anxious not to be seen. Clutching her bag tighter, she hurried to the entrance and peered out only to see two more men built like stevedores making their way purposefully towards her. Without pausing to think, she lifted the lid of the nearest tall basket and clambered inside, nearly gagging at the stench. Peering between the gaps in the weave, she could just make out their figures shifting things about as they searched the building.

'No sign of the wench here but we'd best get this lot shifted.'

'Madam's goin' to be livid if she don't turn up, wouldn't be in her shoes when she's caught.'

'Well, she won't be standing in them, that's for sure.'

They gave a nasty laugh, then Eliza heard the sound of boxes being dragged along the floor.

'Might as well get this one down to the docks an' all while we're at it. It'll get us out of the way 'til the rumpus dies down. Seymour's that livid, he's threatening all sorts.' She heard a grunt and groan then to her horror felt the basket she was hiding in being lifted into the air.

'Blimey, this one's heavier than the rest. Must have a really good stash this time,' one man muttered.

'Best get it away before the moon comes up then.' There was a thud as the basket landed on something hard, the rustle of a cover, then a judder as the two men climbed up.

'Keep yer eyes peeled Bones. The girl seems to have got away. Hope for her sakes she gets out of the county. Seymour's threatening to have every inch of Somerset searched, he's that mad. Offering a good reward though so could be worth taking her back alive if you find her.'

'Will do,' another man with an even deeper voice called back. 'No doubt Madam will have us all out searching too.'

The cart began to move and Eliza didn't know whether to laugh or cry. She'd got away from Lavender House but now there was a price on her head. The cart was heading to the docks but how was she going to escape from the basket without being seen? And where would she end up if she didn't? As the wheels rolled so did Eliza's brain. She might have had one narrow escape but it seems she'd got herself into yet more trouble. Although the men were talking, she couldn't make out what they were saying above the rattling and rumbling of the moving vehicle. She grew ever hotter and the disgusting odour of whatever was in the basket, mingling with the smell of stale sick on her dress, was becoming increasingly overpowering. Then, just when she thought she was going to pass out they jerked to a halt.

The cart juddered as the men jumped down and she heard the cover being dragged back, then a grunt as they hefted one of the other baskets. Gingerly she lifted the lid and peered out. They were pulled up on the wharf which, even at this time of night was noisy, with gaslights casting ghostly shadows over the water. She thought of the poor girl whose mutilated body had been found in the canal and shuddered. Please God let her not end up the same way. But then being returned to Lord Seymour would be as bad, if not worse. Hearing harsh voices, she squinted to see where the men had gone and spotted them talking to a bargee. There was laughter, a flash as cigarettes were lit and then pin pricks of light as they leaned back against the vessel smoking. Eliza knew this was her one chance. Easing her cramped body from the basket, she clambered down from the cart and darted towards the shadows of a tall building.

Creeping round the back, Eliza crouched down in the doorway and pondered her next move. She could beg a lift on one of the many vessels, but the men all looked rough and by now they could have heard she'd escaped. And would no doubt be delighted to return her to Lavender House and receive their reward. There was the rumble of carts arriving and leaving, but word would probably have spread to the drivers too. As the silvery moon rose higher in the sky, the temperature dropped and she began to feel cold and stiff.

Knowing the longer she stayed the more likely she was to be discovered, she got to her feet and, keeping to the shadows, stole from the quay. The towpath was empty and she could hear merriment coming from the nearby tavern. While the men were busy revelling, she took the opportunity to steal past. Walking as quickly as she could in the flimsy dress slippers, and mindful of what Angelique had told her, she hugged the hedgerow keeping well away from the water.

Eliza lost all track of time as she headed away from the lights of Bridgwater. Although anxious to get as far away as possible, she couldn't help feeling sad she hadn't had time to explore the town her grandparents had come from and where her mother had been born. She walked on trying to ignore the stones and sticks that pierced the soles of her feet, passing the brickworks and rows of houses until they petered out and there was just the odd farm cott set back in the fields. The water was low and the lack of passing traffic made her feel a bit easier.

Eliza jumped as an owl swooped low, how lovely it would be to fly like that, she thought grimacing down at her blistered feet. She was desperate to change into her old boots but didn't dare stop until she was far away from the wharf and those big, burly men. Bats squeaked as they flew close by and she recalled how afraid she'd been of them until Clem explained their innate senses meant they would never actually hit her. Dear Clem, with his common sense and playful pranks. What she wouldn't give to have him beside her now. She had a sudden urge to return home but knew he'd ask what she'd been up to and could just imagine his expression when she told him. Shuddering at the sordid existence she'd so easily become entangled in, Eliza knew she now needed to prove to herself that she could make something of her life.

Finally, the path petered out and with her feet blistered and aching, and her eyes gritty with tiredness, she knew she could go no further. Wearily stumbling over a stile, she slumped down in the hollow of a large elm. Her last thought before she fell asleep was that it was strange how it was Clem's dark hair and blue eyes that sprang readily to mind and not the red-haired, green-eyed Theo. Fickle, red-haired, green-eyed Theo. She'd been so drawn to him, she'd not given much thought about the difference in their social class. How naive she'd been. And what if he turned out like his father – their father, the odious Lord Seymour. She gave a shudder knowing she'd had more than one narrow escape.

The sky was beginning to lighten, the moon lowering, when she woke and she knew she needed to be on her way again. She had no idea where she was and hoped she would come across a way marker showing where she was heading. Her nose wrinkled at the odour of stale sick that rose from the now filthy dress and she tore it thankfully from her body along with the cape and hateful corset. Delving into her bag, she pulled out her old boots, skirt, top and shawl. Never in her wildest dreams would she have believed she'd feel thankful to be wearing them again. Placing her precious amber comb in her purse next to the few coins she possessed, she reflected on the generous tip money that lay hidden beneath her nightdress in the rickety locker in the attic room. She trusted it would help pay off some of that dreadful indenture. She hardly dared think of what Madam was feeling about the outstanding debt and the loss of earnings her 'innocence' was to have secured.

Shuddering at the thought, Eliza realized she'd soon have to find a way of earning her living, but respectably this time. Snatching up the hateful clothes and slippers, she buried them deep in the dirt, where they belonged. Rubbing her hands in satisfaction, she picked up her bag and began making her way across the field towards the line of hedging.

She'd just reached the open road when the rumble of an approaching wagon made her jump. Glancing around, she saw there was nowhere to hide and kept walking, hoping the vehicle would pass by. However, it pulled up beside her, the glimmer from its lantern dimly lighting up the highway ahead. Suppose it was some of Madam's men or even Lord Seymour's, she thought, willing her legs to stop shaking.

'You alright, Miss? Here, don't ee be scared, I ain't goin' to hurt ee.' The thick set driver leaned out and smiled. Combined with his gentle voice that was her undoing, and unbidden she felt tears welling. 'You look all in and this air's right nippy. Why not jump up beside me. I got a nice drop of tea 'ere and one of the wife's butties.' It sounded tempting and she was about to accept when she remembered what the men searching for her had said.

'Where are you heading?' she asked.

'I be takin this load of wool to a mill at Culme in the next county of Devonshire,' he told her, gesturing to the back of his wagon.

Devonshire! Eliza's heart lifted and she nodded.

'Thank you, I will,' she said, climbing into the seat beside him.

'The name's Bob and we'll have to eat as we travel 'cause I have to be at the mill afore they start work.' He whipped up the horses and slowly the heavy load began to move forward. After a few moments he delved into his capacious pocket and drew out a muslin package. 'Should find summat nice to eat in there,' he said, passing it to her. Inside were two slices of soft white bread and chunks of ham. The smell was delicious and Eliza's stomach rumbled in anticipation. 'Thought I recognized a fellow hungry traveller,' Bob grinned knowingly.

Eliza sat back against the seat and munched happily as they trundled along. And the further they travelled the more she felt an overwhelming sense of relief to be away from the weird environment she'd found herself in. Pulling her old cloak around her, she breathed in its familiar smell, and comforted, leaned against the canvas cover. Although her eyelids grew heavy, she jerked herself awake for she knew she daren't fall asleep. Bob might seem friendly, but if Eliza had learned anything these past few days, it was that it didn't pay to trust anyone.

Chapter 26

Despite her resolve, the rocking motion must have sent her to sleep for she was jolted awake by the cart lurching to a halt. Early morning sunshine was filtering through the trees, and from the front of the canopy she saw they had pulled up next to a tall, brick building with lots of windows and a huge wheel on the side. It was steadily turning, its cages dipping in and out of the waters of a leat that ran alongside.

''Ere yer be,' announced the jolly old man. In the daylight she could see he was dressed in a thick woollen jacket, a battered cap pushed to the back of his head.

'Where am I exactly?' she asked, frowning as she stared around at the unfamiliar scenery.

'Culme Mill, Miss. I do believe they're hiring if you be lookin' for work,' he told her, staring down at her bag.

'Well, I hadn't thought but yes, I certainly do need to find employment. Who owns this mill?' she asked, her eyes lighting up at the possibility of securing a job.

'Well, Mr Wolfe, he do own this mill and most all the others round here too. But 'tis Grange who does the hiring.

Although . . .' he paused and stared at her as if he was uncertain he should continue.

'Although what, Bob?' she asked.

'Well, if you'll pardon me for saying so Miss, you could do with havin' a bit of a wash afore you sees the gaffer. Anyhow, I'd best get me load down t'hatch to the combing shed afore the maids do clock on.' Whistling, he jumped down then held out his hand to help Eliza.

'Thar yer go, Tricky and Dicky, wander off and have a nice drink,' he said fondly as he unfastened the horses. It was obviously part of their routine, for obediently they ambled further upstream where the water was clear and the grass was lush. Bob clambered up on the rear of the wagon, pulled back the cover and began throwing down heavy sacks. How lovely to see a normal man happy in his work, Eliza thought, reflecting on the fancy men who despite their cut-glass accents and apparent wealth, never seemed content with their lot.

'How much do I owe you?' she called, delving into her bag for her purse.

'Why bless you, it's been good having some company even if you were asleep for most of the journey,' he quipped.

'Thank you so much Bob,' she cried. 'You 've been so kind.'

As the carter got on with his job, she peered around taking in the tall poplars beyond the leat, with bluebells, primroses and flag iris lining it. Rows of identical stone cottages stood to one side of the mill, and apart from the water babbling as it wended its way and the soft pulse of the wheel as it turned, everywhere was tranquil.

Picking up her bag, she walked over to the water and splashed her face and hands. Then feeling cool and refreshed, she leaned back against the wall and stared around. Everywhere looked so serene and pretty. It would certainly be a lovely place to work. Although if she was taken on, she'd need to find somewhere to stay. Her musing was rudely interrupted by the loud clanging of a bell that made her jump. Then, as the jangling persisted, doors of nearby cottages opened and people of all ages began streaming towards the building.

Eliza stepped back against the wall to avoid being crushed as, like bees, the workers swarmed into the building. Some were chatting, others yawning, but all seemed intent on getting inside as quickly as possible.

'You alright, dearie?' an older woman, hair hidden beneath a cloth cap, asked.

'Actually, I am looking for a Mr Grange,' Eliza told her.

'Wanting a start, are you?' she asked. 'You'll find his eyrie or highry as we call it, up there,' she chuckled, gesturing to a flight of steps beyond the entrance. 'Gotta go and get clocked on or me pay'll be docked.'

'Thank you,' Eliza said, but the woman had already joined the line that was snaking its way through the open doors.

As Eliza made her way up the steps, the bell finally stopped its jangling only to be replaced by the even noisier clanking and clacking sound of machinery. In an effort to be heard, she knocked hard on the metal frame.

'Yes?' a voice barked. Gingerly, Eliza pushed open the door and found herself in a musty room with the only light coming from a dirty window. There were papers and samples of cloth piled seemingly everywhere. At first Eliza didn't notice the thin man dressed in a grey woollen jacket who was staring through an internal glass panel to the floor below. She just had time to glimpse huge, metal machines topped with big reels when he turned and appraised her with eyes as steely as the water wheel outside.

'Good morning sir,' she said, ignoring his scowl. 'I hear you might be hiring?'

'Who says?'

'Well Bob, the carter,' she murmured.

'Don't suppose you have a testimonial?'

'No, but I am honest and a hard worker,' she told him, meeting his stare head on.

'So says you,' he snorted. 'I'll give you a start but you'll begin in the grading and sorting shed like the others. See if you're so keen then.'

'Thank you, Mr Grange, sir,'

'Stop calling me sir. It's Master to you.' Quickly he scribbled on a ticket and thrust it at her. 'Give this to Mrs Tucker downstairs,' he barked, gesturing to the window. 'She'll tell you our terms and get you started. Like a happy family here, we are,' he intoned, his severe expression belying his words. 'But if you want to get on, you'll do well to remember our maxim is "Minimum Waste, Maximum Profit".'

'I will, thank you,' she replied, grabbing the docket and

hurrying out of the oppressive room with its equally oppressive master. Wherever had she ended up now? Yet anywhere would be better than Lavender House, she thought as she made her way back down the steps.

Inside the mill, the noise was even more deafening and the very ground itself seemed to vibrate. As Eliza stood dithering inside the doorway, a tiny, birdlike woman came scurrying over.

'New girl?' she asked Eliza, beady brown eyes boring into her. 'I'm Mrs Tucker, the overseer, although Barney Beer would have you think he was. Just cos he's male. However, he is the foreman,' she acknowledged, gesturing to a burly man in overalls who was shaking his finger at a young lad. 'Do as we both say though, and you'll not go far wrong. Now let's get you started,' she said, taking the proffered ticket and ushering Eliza over to the big clock-like machine that was on the wall just inside the lobby. 'Name?'

'Eliza Priddle,' she replied, watching as the woman noted it down on a lined card. 'Address?'

'Oh, I don't have one. I've just arrived you see,' Eliza stammered, fearful the woman would ask awkward questions. She gave Eliza a searching look, glanced down at her carpet bag, then shrugged.

'It's vital you let me know when you've found somewhere. People like Dolly Lacey or Prudence Sutton are always happy to rent out a room. I'll point them out later.'

'Thank you.'

'Now you clock on by putting your card in here, like so,' the woman explained, inserting it into the slot and pulling down a lever. 'Do the same when you clock off and then put your card in here,' she said, placing it in a tall rack hanging beside it that was virtually full with other cards. 'We work from six in the morning til six at night, except Sundays. The bell is rung five minutes before clocking on time and you can hear it all around the village, so there's no excuse for not being here on time. Anything up to ten minutes late and you'll be docked half a day's pay. Anymore and you're down the road. Wages are 9d a day and paid out on Saturday afternoons. Any questions?'

'Will there be any deductions for training?' she asked, remembering Madam and her awful indenture.

'Good grief, no, we're not tyrants. But you will be earning your learning,' the woman said brusquely. 'Now let's find somewhere for your things,' she added, gesturing to Eliza's bag. 'Of course, I should have done that before clocking you on but I won't tell if you don't and you'll find it useful if you can keep your mouth shut round here.'

'Right, I'll remember that,' Eliza replied, anxious to please. Dutifully, she followed the woman into a room off the entrance hall where a shelf running the length was stacked with snap boxes. The walls were hung with rows of hooks and nails from which cloaks, shawls and mufflers draped.

'You can hang your things on this peg here and stow your bag beneath. You'll need to wear a pinafore and cover your hair as well,' she added, holding out a huge white apron with pockets together with a soft cap, similar to the one the old woman had been wearing. 'Can't have your hair getting tangled up in the machinery. Seen a couple of accidents like that. One poor girl would have had her whole head mangled too, if they hadn't managed to stop the spinner in time.' Although she grimaced, Eliza couldn't help feeling she relished telling the story. 'Take those garments home on a Saturday evening and bring them back freshly laundered on Monday morning. Forget your things and there's a deduction for borrowing, understand?'

'Yes, Mrs Tucker,' she replied, then wondered if like Grange she was meant to call her something else. However, the woman seemed satisfied.

'Now, let's get you down to the grading and sorting floor. It's a messy job but do it well, don't complain and when the next person gets taken on, you'll be moved along. That's the way we work here.'

Wearing the voluminous garment that was a far cry from the frilly little apron she'd had to wear at Lavender House, Eliza followed the woman down another flight of the steep stairs. Her eyes widened as she saw the huge piles of fleeces stacked from floor to ceiling along the entire length of the room. In front of the nearest heap, a woman sat seemingly picking at a skin while others, spaced at intervals, appeared to be doing the same. They gave Eliza a curious look before quickly resuming their work.

In the middle of the room stood two enormous tanks filled with liquid that smelt decidedly less than savoury. As Eliza wrinkled her nose, the overseer sniffed.

'Acid baths. They're filled with urine and water to wash or

scour the fleece. You'll find buckets placed in the privy ready, for we provide our own.' Seeing Eliza grimace, she turned to the young boy who, standing on tip toe so he could reach, was vigorously stirring one of the baths.

'You soon get used to it, don't you, Joe?' she called.

'I pretends it smells of bread and jam,' he grinned. 'Trouble is it makes me hungry, and it's still ages to nuncheon.'

'But he's so young,' Eliza exclaimed, thinking of the girls she'd helped to teach back in Stoke.

'He's six,' Mrs Tucker snorted. 'Mills further down start them at four or five. That's young. We care about our children's welfare here. Now come and meet Sally,' she said crossing to the woman who appeared to be cutting with great concentration. However, when she saw the overseer, she jumped to her feet and smiled.

'Sally here does the skirting and a very important job it is too,' she said, her voice softening. The woman beamed with pleasure. 'Sally dear, this is Eliza and I'd like you to show her how we cut off the tags.'

'Like this, snip, snip, snip,' the woman grinned, snipping at the air with her large scissors.

'That's it, now can you show us how it's done on the fleece.' Immediately the woman squatted down and began cutting at the edge of the wool with glee.

'Snip, snip, snip.'

'Splendid, well done,' Mrs Tucker exclaimed. She turned back to Eliza. 'The fleeces are called grease wool because of all the lanolin in them. There is also much vegetable matter and manure to be removed before it can be moved on to the cleaning process. I admit it is mind numbing, laborious work but that is why Sally is able to spend all day every day doing it. She's known as Simple Sally, if you get my meaning,' she added in hushed tones. 'Now grab a pair of shears and follow her example. The more tag ends you cut off, the more of the fleece can be processed. Minimum Waste, Maximum Profit. I'll be back to see how you're doing later.'

'Oh, er right,' Eliza replied, hunkering down beside Sally on the floor and following her example.

'Have you worked here long, Sally?' she asked, carefully snipping off the tag ends.

'Yes. Snip, snip, snip.'

'Do you like it?' Eliza asked.

'Yes. Snip, snip, snip,' the woman grinned.

'That's all she says,' Joe called. 'Snip, snip, snip, ain't it Sally?'

'Snip, snip, snip,' the woman said, grinning inanely.

'Don't worry, yer'll be doin my job soon, when I'm moved onto willowing,' the boy grinned delightedly.

'Willowing?' Eliza asked, excitedly. Was this something to do with withies?

'See them machines over ther',' he said, pointing to the other side of the room, where dimly through clouds of dust, Eliza could just make out figures pulling and pushing. 'Yer puts the fleece through to untangle the wool and get out all the dirt and sand and things. Cors in me grandad's day they used to use willow sticks to beat the muck out.'

'Really? Well, I've never seen withies used for that before,' Eliza murmured, trying not to breathe in the tufts of wool, fluff and dust that seemed to fill the air. It was noisy, hot and smelly down here, but with nowhere else to go and the little money she had needed for food and lodgings, Eliza knew she had no option other than begin her assigned task.

'Look sharp, old Beer's on his rounds,' the boy called before bending back over his tank and swirling the fleeces round even more exuberantly than before.

As Eliza sat on the hard floor snipping at the lumps of earth, excrement and goodness knows what else, a shadow loomed over her. Her heart began beating wildly in her chest. She'd been so sure she was safe here.

Chapter 27

'Ain't done much yet, 'ave yer?' Eliza looked up to see the foreman frowning down at her. Her relief was so great she nearly smiled at him. 'Yer'll need to work harder and faster if you want to stay. Like our Sal here,' he added, his voice becoming less gruff.

'Snip, snip, snip,' Sally intoned, grinning up at him.

'That's it lover, yer snip away to yer heart's content,' he told her, patting her shoulder.

To the accompaniment of Sally's incessant chanting, the clattering of machinery and stench of the acid baths, Eliza cut and snipped, yet seemingly as soon as she'd finished one fleece, another was placed beside her. She lost count of the number of men, women and children who came and went. They all knew what they were doing, scurrying about their work like ants, seemingly without the need for discussion, which was just as well, she supposed, for it was hard to hear yourself think let alone talk.

It was certainly a contrast to the seemingly refined atmosphere that surrounded Lavender House. And yet, despite the privations and conditions, she felt safer here. It would be a long time before she forgot the previous day's events. Still here she was, pride dented but virtue intact. All she had to do was remember to talk in her own voice and she'd be fine.

Her musing was interrupted by the clanging of the bell. Immediately some of the workers began filing up the stairs. Others remained and continued working.

'You new?' She looked up to see one of the girls who'd been sitting further along the room, grinning down at her. Eliza nodded. 'Well, hurry up, we're on early nuncheon so it's time for our break, not that we get long.'

Smiling back, Eliza got stiffly to her feet and followed the girl back up the stairs where workers of all ages were grabbing boxes and bags from the cloakroom.

'Come on, let's go outside and breathe in some decent air. I'm Rose by the way, but everyone calls me Rosie.'

'That's cos she's dozy,' another young woman chortled, following them out into the sunshine. 'Come on let's bag a space,' she added, ignoring the others who were filing into the yard and pulling herself up onto the low wall that ran alongside the outbuildings. 'I'm Jenny.'

'Aptly named cos she's always in a spin, spinning Jenny, get it?' Rosie grinned.

'And I'm Eliza,' she told them, trying not to stare as they eagerly pulled out their noon pieces. She breathed in the fresh air and stared at the babbling water instead. It was such a contrast to the gloom, dirt and noise of inside the mill.

'Ooh goody, jam today,' Rosie beamed, holding out a crust

with a scraping of red in the centre. Eliza's stomach rumbled and she thought longingly of the thick damson and bramble preserve she'd made last autumn. 'Aren't you hungry?' Eliza shook her head but with a knowing look, Rosie tore the bread in two and held out one. 'Go on take it,' she insisted. 'Auntie Flo always says you can't live on fresh air.'

'Well, if you're sure,' Eliza said, hunger weakening her resolve.

'And you can have some of my mine too,' Jenny told her, generously breaking off a piece of her bread that was thinly spread with paste.

'Oh, I couldn't,' Eliza demurred.

'It'll cost yer mind?' Jenny grinned, waving it under Eliza's nose until she weakened and accepted. 'You can tell us where you've come from and what you're doing here.'

'Yea, we're starved of news from outside the village,' Rosie mumbled through her crust.

'I come from the moors,' Eliza told them, carefully editing her story.

'What on earth made you come to a place like this?' Jenny asked, scowling at the tall building of the mill.

'Work,' Eliza replied. 'I need to earn money and find somewhere to live. Which reminds me, Mrs Tucker said Dolly Lacey and Prudence Sutton take in lodgers and . . .' She was interrupted by peals of laughter.

'Devout Dolly and Purity Prudence. Yeah they take in lodgers alright. And think just because they've got tied cottages next to the mill, they own the place. You'll have no fun there, nor freedom either. And you'll be banned from the social club in the village cos they're abstainers,' Jenny said.

'Jen's right. You'll be at their beck and call and all the Mill will know your business.'

'But I need somewhere to stay so I'd better go and see them.'

'Or you could speak to Auntie Flo. They put up our rent recently and she's been finding it hard to make ends meet so she might be pleased to take in another lodger. It'll mean a squeeze but we wouldn't mind, would we?' Rosie asked her friend.

'The more the merrier,' Jenny grinned. 'Come home with us and see what she says. You can liven up our evening by telling us more about yourself.'

As the bell that seemed to rule their lives began its insistent tolling, Rosie and Jenny jumped down from the wall.

'Come on, before Beer appears and tries to dock our pay.'

'Oh, was I meant to clock off?' Eliza asked.

'Old Grunge doesn't have the monopoly on maximum profit,' Jenny chuckled, giving a broad wink as they joined the throng surging back inside the mill.

When the bell finally rang at six o'clock, it was with a deep sense of relief that Eliza collected her things then joined the queue to clock off. Her back was aching from bending over the fleeces, her bottom numb from sitting on the cold floor, while her ears were ringing with the noise from the machinery and Sally's constant chanting. Placing her card in the rack, she saw Mrs Tucker deep in conversation with

Mr Beer, and from the glances being thrown in her direction knew she was the subject of their discussion. However, when she saw her, the overseer scuttled over.

'I hear from Mr Beer that your work fell short of the required amount. You'd do well to pick up speed tomorrow or . . .' her voice trailed off, but her meaning was clear. 'Also, I saw you sitting on the wall outside during your midday break. Please be aware the correct place to eat is in the yard. Merchants often visit the weaver's floor to check on their finished cloth before it is transported, and we do not want them being discouraged by workers littering the place. It's not professional. Of course, Jenny and Rosie know better, but . . .' she sniffed, leaving Eliza in no doubt as to what she felt about the matter.

'Yes, Mrs Tucker, I'll make sure it doesn't happen again,' Eliza assured her.

'Good because we're fair here and give everyone a chance. Now, off you go, I can see Prudence Sutton waiting for you over there,' she said, gesturing towards the clock.

'Thank you, Mrs Tucker, but you see . . .' But the overseer had already disappeared and Eliza had no choice but to go and explain to the waiting woman.

'Miss Priddle, I take it,' the woman sniffed, making the wart on her nose wobble as she looked Eliza up and down.

'Yes, and you must be Mrs Sutton. It's very kind of you to—' Eliza began only for the woman to interrupt.

'Kindness is written in the scriptures is it not, so I do what I can.' She sighed, giving Eliza a long-suffering look. 'I keep a clean, honest house. Front door is locked each night at eight o'clock sharp, breakfast of bread and a scrape at 4.30 a.m. after which we will read from the scriptures until it is time for work. Absolutely no male visitors and rent paid in advance.'

'Well the thing is Mrs Sutton . . .' Eliza began, hurriedly trying to think of an excuse, for there was absolutely no way she could stay with this insufferable woman.

'Of course, my rooms are highly sought after. In fact, I have a waiting list,' the woman crowed gleefully.

'Well in that case it wouldn't be Christian for me to push in, would it? Thank you so much for your kind offer though,' Eliza said, smiling brightly.

As the woman scowled and hurried away, Eliza felt she was being watched. Looking up, she saw Mr Grange staring down from his office. His countenance was stern and Eliza felt a shiver prickle her spine. However, she had no time to dwell on the matter for Jenny was shouting through the doorway.

'Do get a shifty on, Eliza.'

'We've been waiting ages for you,' Rosie added, as she joined them outside.

'Sorry, Mrs Tucker wanted a word,' she told them.

'Well we'd better get a move on if you want to speak to Auntie Flo before supper,' Rosie said, linking her arm through Eliza's.

'I do hope she agrees to my lodging with you,' Eliza said, realizing that she had well and truly burned her boats with Mrs Sutton.

As they began following other workers past the rows of

mill cottages, Eliza noticed some of them turning into front doors that stood open onto the street. The sun was beginning to set and apart from the sound of boots on cobbles, the early evening was peaceful after the mayhem at the mill. She was tired after her long day, her throat was full of fluff, while her ears still resounded with the noise of machinery and poor Sally's jabbering. Whilst she understood the woman couldn't help herself, it had become more irritating as the afternoon wore on.

'Gosh my ears are still ringing,' she murmured.

'Ah, you'll be getting your cloth ears,' Jenny told her.

'Pardon?' she asked, only for the two girls to dissolve into hysterics.

'Mill workers are renowned for going deaf,' Rosie explained. 'Hazard of the job, only it probably won't hit you properly 'til you're really old. I'm nearly fifteen, how old are you by the way?'

'Seventeen,' Eliza replied, hardly able to believe it had been six months since her birthday. So much had happened since then she thought, as they turned up the hill. They passed a couple of shops, their blinds already pulled down and an inn from which the sound of laughter and the smell of liquor fumes exuded. Eliza wrinkled her nose, but as they continued on their way, Jenny nudged her, looking quite animated.

'The new curate, James Newman, lives there,' she told Eliza, blue eyes sparkling as she pointed to a tiny cottage next to the grocer's, that was still open.

'She'll be going to church next,' Rosie grinned.

'Along with Mrs Sutton then,' Eliza replied without thinking.

'You've already spoken to her about a room?' Rosie asked, staring at her in surprise.

'I think it was her speaking to me, or rather preaching. Let's just say it wouldn't be a suitable arrangement,' Eliza replied as tactfully as she could.

'Good thing if you want to have any chance with the fellows here. Her witch-like warts and sermons on the evils of the flesh, scare the life out of them,' Jenny giggled. 'Or have you already got a fellow?' Eliza shook her head, then seeing they expected more, added.

'I did have once but, well it didn't work out.'

'So, you ran away and came here,' Rosie squeaked. 'How romantic. Perhaps he'll realize he can't live without you and come calling.'

Jenny snorted. 'You'll have to excuse Rosie and her notions. She's always got her head in one of those Penny Bloods, and thinks real life is the same,' she said, with a shake of her head.

Rosie's answer was drowned by the sound of a carriage approaching. Eliza jumped, her eyes widening in alarm. Supposing Lord Seymour had found out where she was and come after her? Although this wasn't Somersetshire, he might have extended his search. Or maybe Madam had sent someone to find her? As the horses drew closer her heart began to pound faster, and she dived into the shop doorway out of sight. When she realized it was only the staging post, she let out a long sigh of relief and, on trembling legs, re-joined the others.

'Blimey you look all shaken. Did you think that was him?' Rosie squeaked, excitedly, pointing to the disappearing coach now hidden in a cloud of rising dust.

Before she could reply, the door of a nearby cottage flew open and a woman, hair tied up in a scarf, bright pinafore covering her clothes, stood on the step frowning.

'I'd just about given you two up for lost. Supper's ready an' all. Oh, pardon me dear, and who might you be?' she asked, staring curiously at Eliza from her face down to her carpet bag.

'Good evening, my name is Eliza Priddle and I was wondering . . .'

'Coo blimey, we don't stand on ceremony here,' Rosie chuckled. 'She's come to work at the mill and is looking for lodgings, Auntie. We thought the extra money would come in handy now your rent's been put up.'

'Oh, you did, did you? Full of bright ideas as usual then.'

'We don't mind sharing,' Jenny assured her. The woman laughed.

'Just as well when we've only got the two room upstairs, and there's no way I'm sharing mine,' she said, good naturedly. 'Well come in, we don't want the whole of Culme knowing our business, although they probably already do,' she added, staring up and down the street before closing the door. 'And mind you leave those dirty pinnies and caps on the mat. I don't want you bringing fluff and muck into my clean house.'

'Can't wait to be rid of the wretched things,' Jenny muttered, tearing off her cap and revealing dark hair that tumbled over her shoulders. Rosie, following her lead, shook out her fair curls then gasped as Eliza's Titian tresses swung free.

'I'd give anything to have red hair like that.'

'Just be glad you've got some with all that dangerous machinery they've installed,' Flo retorted. 'Now come on in.'

The door led straight into the living room, which although shabbily furnished with a colourful rag rug on the floor, mismatched chairs and a long wooden table set for supper, felt comfortable and more welcoming than any of the grand rooms in Lavender House.

'Well sit yerself down and take the weight off your feet, not that there's much of you,' the woman said, looking Eliza up and down before grimacing down at her own ample hips.

'Auntie Flo's a great cook,' Rosie said.

'And it shows,' the woman laughed. 'Now tell me how you come to be seeking lodgings.'

'Well, Mrs . . .?'

'Flo dear, just Flo. Mrs makes me sound ancient and I ain't thirty yet. Well not much past it anyroad,' she added as Rosie and Jenny spluttered.

'Well Flo, I arrived by cart this morning and started work at the mill.' Shrewd eyes regarded her steadily for a moment then she smiled.

'She ran away from a failing love affair,' Rosie exclaimed, clutching her hand to her heart.

'Blimey if you've got a tale to tell, we'd best eat and then talk,' the woman chuckled, not unkindly.

'Do you work at the mill too?' Eliza asked politely. The woman shook her head.

'No fear. I cook for Willie Winson at the Lamb down the road. The hours suit, pay's fair and I get to bring home any leftovers. Talking of which, it's meat pie and mash tonight, girls.' She smiled at the resulting cheers and took herself through to the kitchen.

'I couldn't help noticing there were more women than men working at the mill. It's good to see females getting a fair chance, isn't it?' Eliza said, her stomach rumbling at the appetizing smell emanating from the next room.

'You what!' Jenny shrieked. 'The only reason they employ us women is because they can get away with paying us much less. If we complain, they say men get more cos they have to provide for their families, but we have bills to pay too, don't we?'

'And they get a subsidized house as well,' Flo told her, appearing with dishes in hand. 'Not like me who has her rent put up whenever the landlord thinks fit.'

'I hadn't realized that's why they employed so many women,' Eliza murmured, jumping up to help. 'It hardly seems fair . . .'

'Life often isn't and of course, most of the women have had no educatin' to speak of,' Flo muttered. 'Leave the door open so the heat from the kitchen fire can warm the room,' the woman told her, setting plates down on the table. 'Now tuck in.'

'Blimey, I'll have to charge you extra if you eat like that,' Flo remarked, when Eliza, having eaten heartily, began scraping her plate clean. Seeing her look of alarm, the woman shook her head.

'Only joking dear.'

'You'll soon get used to Auntie's weird and wonderful ways,' Rosie sighed.

'Less of your cheek or you'll be out on yer ear, niece of mine,' Flo told her, pretending to look stern.

There was an easy atmosphere as the others, having forgiven her faux pas about women workers, joked and talked about the day's happenings. Although names of people and references to the various spinning procedures were unfamiliar to Eliza, she listened with interest. There was obviously much more to the wool process than she'd realized. When they'd all finished eating, Flo turned to Rosie and Jenny.

'Right girls, you can clear away whilst Eliza and I have a chat.' She waited until the table was cleared and they'd shut the door behind them then turned her all seeing gaze on Eliza. 'So then, young lady, any run-ins with the law resulting in convictions or anyone got a party out searching for you?' Was the woman psychic? Eliza thought, staring at her in alarm.

'Sorry dear, my little joke. Now, I can tell by your accent you're not from Devonshire, so how come you've ended up in Culme?'

'I'm from Sedge Moor and have come to work at the mill,' Eliza said, determined to be truthful yet sparing with detail.

'Well that's your choice, of course although as I said earlier, it wouldn't do for me. Too many rules and regulations. Our Rosie's only been working there a couple of months and I'd feel happier if someone could keep a weather eye out, if you know what I mean. Jen's a scream but Rosie is easily led.' She lowered her voice and leaned closer.

'Her mother, my sister, took up with one of the casual workers. Right Jack-the-lad he were, but she thought the sun shone out of his backside. Ran off with him taking Rosie with her. Wasn't long before the oaf started paying Rosie er, unwanted attention, would be the polite way of putting it, when her mother was out. Ran back to me she did, in a dreadful state she were.'

'Oh, poor Rosie,' Eliza murmured, her own predicament fading by comparison.

'She's a good kid and bright too, but even after what that scum tried, she still has, well let's say, romantic delusions. Sure a handsome young knight will gallop in on his white charger and carry her away to the land of happy ever after.'

'Hmm,' Eliza muttered. Having recently experienced what men could be like, handsome or not, she vowed never to become involved with one again.

'Precisely, I can see you are of the same opinion as me,' Flo said, giving her a knowing look. 'So, are you prepared to keep a look out for young Rosie?'

'Yes, of course,' Eliza told her, pleased to feel she could be of use.

'You'll do,' Flo said, happy with her scrutiny. 'You're welcome to bunk in with the girls if you think you can bear it.'

'Oh, thank you,' Eliza cried, relieved to have somewhere to stay.

'Same rent as the others, which is half your weekly wage. In return you get your bed, two meals and a snap box each day, and we all muck in with the chores on Sunday. Some say it's the day of rest, but for us workers it's the only time we can get anything done,' she said, looking up as the door opened. 'Right girls, take Eliza upstairs and show her where she's sleeping. That's if she can get any with you yacking on half the night.'

Whooping with glee, they ran up the stairs and threw open one of the two doors. Eliza stared around the compact space, her heart sinking. Where would she sleep, for there were only two beds, one on each side of the room. Seeing her puzzled look, Rosie bent and slid another from underneath one of them.

'Never seen a truckle bed before?' she asked. 'You can put your things in the bottom drawer of the chest then your bag can go underneath Jennie's bed.' Eliza unpacked her few remaining clothes along with the amber comb and purse.

Ten minutes later, with Eliza's bed made up and her things stowed away, they took a satisfied look around.

'I reckon we'll manage just fine,' Rosie said. 'Now we'll go outside and show you the privy. We keep a bucket there for collecting our wee cos we get paid extra for it.'

'Hang on a tick,' Jenny grinned, standing over her bed and lifting up her blouse. To Eliza's surprise a pile of wool fibres floated down onto the blanket. 'Phew that's better. Itching me like mad all afternoon that has. Been on the rover today and the bloomin' wool kept breaking.'

'But why did you bring it home?' Eliza asked.

'Easy peasy. We get an allowance for wastage see. Any more and our money's docked. Can't afford that,' she sniffed. 'Besides it makes nice stuffing for pillows,' she winked, packing the wool into hers. 'Don't worry, we all do it, you just have to be careful old Beer doesn't catch you. And it's not our fault if they've bought in cheap fleece from further up country, is it? Best not to mention it to Flo though. She might be no angel, but she's always trying to instil a sense of honesty into us.'

That night as she lay in bed listening to the girls' gentle snores, Eliza reflected back over the day. She knew she'd been fortunate to secure a job, even if it did mean cutting off lumps of sheep dung and goodness knows what. She liked it here in this little house as well, even if it was something of a squash. Flo was a hoot yet for all her witty ways, had a heart of gold. Rosie was a darling and Jenny good fun, if somewhat mischievous. The rent was manageable and with judicious economy, would enable her to save enough to have her boots resoled.

It was a long way from the glamorous façade of Lavender House and she'd surely be safe here in the Devonshire countryside.

Chapter 28

Although the girls were friendly and Flo had made her welcome, Eliza found the work at the mill monotonous. It had been three weeks since she'd arrived, yet she still couldn't get used to the arid, airless room with the constant clouds of fluff that rose from the grading and sorting which caught in her throat and made her eyes itch.

It was a far cry from the moist, spring air on Sedge Moor, and as she mindlessly cut the tags from fleece after fleece, her thoughts turned to home and days gone by. Her gramfer sowing the new season's sets, her weaving the willow. It might have been cold in the workshop at times, but at least she'd had a mat to sit on rather than this hard, bare floor. Suddenly, she envied Clem, out in the fresh air plying his trade along the River Parrett and rhynes in his trow. Straight as a die Clem, so different from the toffs with their wheeling and dealing ways. Was he walking out with Bethan now? A pang cut through her at the thought. As for Theo, she didn't suppose for one moment he had called by. Surprisingly, she found she hardly cared now. The way he'd left her to face her gramfer that day at the cott when he'd come to meet him and ask permission to walk out with her, should have alerted her to the fact he shied away from the difficult things in life. To think she'd had to come away to appreciate all she'd had back home.

But now Gramfer was dead and his beloved withy beds along with the only home she'd ever known, belonged to someone else now. Knowing he'd had to sell them because of her actions filled her with remorse, and yet she couldn't help wondering who'd bought them. So much had happened and all she could do was learn from her mistakes, she thought, tossing yet another trimmed fleece onto the pile. Suddenly, a shadow loomed, making her jump.

'Yer meant to be wool pickin' not bloomin' wool gatherin'.' The rough voice of Beer bellowed, his eyes narrowing as he glared down at her. 'I've bin keepin' me eye on yer, my girl, and if yer don't buck up yer be down road. Understand?'

'Yes, Mr Beer,' she replied, turning back to her work and making an effort to cut off the tags even faster. The man's rough voice and uncertain temper kept them all in fear of their jobs, but it did seem he'd taken a particular dislike to her, seeking the slightest excuse to berate and belittle her.

With Rosie recently having been moved onto the acid baths, Eliza had found herself shifted to the other end of the room. Although it was good to be away from Sal and her constant chanting, it meant she was trapped in the corner and at the full mercy of the man's moods. As he strode away, Rosie shot her a sympathetic look. She was flushed as red as her name from all the stirring with the huge paddle. It was a thankless job that required being careful, for the strong solution that scoured the dirt, grease and dried sweat from the fleece could also strip human skin. Eliza shuddered, knowing that would be her next task.

When the bell finally rang at noon, ignoring her cramped limbs, she jumped thankfully to her feet. Twenty minutes wasn't long and she didn't intend wasting a moment. Being moved meant Rosie was now on the second shift, and the girl shrugged ruefully as Eliza passed by. Apparently, work didn't stop unless there was a malfunction of the machines or someone got caught up in one, and the remaining operatives had to cover three or more machines each throughout the breaks. Seemingly, the motto, "Minimum Waste, Maximum Profit" applied to everything here, she thought as she took herself outside and gulped in the fresh air.

Mindful of Mrs Tucker's instruction and ignoring Jenny's taunting, she'd taken to eating her noon time snack in the yard. Having heard that merchants sometimes visited, Eliza felt safer in the shelter the terrace afforded, although it meant vying for a space to relax on the grass.

'Anyone sitting here?' a voice asked. She looked up to see a young man smiling down at her. His twinkling blue eyes and cheeky grin made a change from the dour expressions of the other mill men and she found herself smiling back.

'Not that I can see,' she quipped, making a pretence of checking the space beside her.

'Well there is now,' he smiled, hunkering down beside her then holding out a hand politely. 'Peter.'

'Eliza,' she replied, taking it briefly.

'Well Eliza, care to share half a mutton butty?'

'Only if you agree to share my jam one.' Eliza couldn't believe her luck when he nodded. A scraping of jam hardly compared to mutton. However, he was holding out a neatly cut sandwich and gave another cheeky grin when the swap was made.

They sat savouring their food in contented silence, watching the squeaking wheel going around, the splash of the water as its cages dipped in and out.

'Well, that'll be me working late tonight,' Peter grimaced. 'Grange will have apoplexy if he hears the wheel whining like that. I'm an engineer, well trainee one at any rate. Can't wait to get a look at all those spinning machines and looms. The boss says they need servicing now but Grange won't have anything interfering with production.'

'It sounds more interesting than cutting dirt off fleeces,' Eliza told him.

'All jobs have their challenges,' he sympathized. 'If you're in the cutting shed you can't have been here long.'

'Three weeks going on three years. How long have you worked here?' she asked, ignoring the curious looks of the people sitting nearby.

'Long enough to know I can't do anything until the machines stop tonight. The owner's a good man who insists all his mills be self-sufficient in repairs but Grange has his own ideas about saving money. Still that wheel will have to be fixed tonight before the weather changes,' he said, staring anxiously up at the sky.

'But . . .' she began, only to be interrupted by the jangling of the bell. 'Oh, not already surely,' she groaned, getting reluctantly to her feet.

'No rest for the reprehensible, as my nan always said.' He gave a rueful look. 'Nice to have met you Eliza. Make sure you wrap up tomorrow, there'll be a sharp frost.'

'Oh, er yes, thank you,' she murmured, joining the press of workers pushing their way into the mill. 'Do you really think . . .' she began, but he'd already gone. She stared up at the sky but it was buried by the sea of faces as she was swept inside.

'A word Priddle.' The booming voice of the foreman carried across the room as she made her way inside. His bushy brows were knotted together as he stood, hands on hips, glaring at her. High above she could see Grange staring down from his office and understood what the woman had meant about it being his eyrie.

'Yes, Mr Beer?' she asked, trying to sound polite when all she wanted was to put her tongue out at the disagreeable man.

'You've bin seen talkin' to a higher.'

'Pardon?'

'There are no pardons, Missy. A common mill worker like you doesn't mix with the skilled workers, do I make myself clear? Now get back to work and I mean work, not the half-hearted attempts you've bin makin'.'

'Old Beer's really got it in for Eliza,' Rosie told Flo as they sat eating their supper of leftover rabbit stew eked out with crusts of bread. 'He gave her a right telling off for talking to one of the trainee engineers today.'

'Oh?' Flo said, frowning at Eliza.

'He said common mill workers like me didn't mix with skilled ones,' Eliza sighed.

'Since when?' Jen cried. 'Look, the mill owner only cares about profit and wouldn't give a fig who talks to who as long as his machines keep turning. I mean, we know they all need servicing but that's got to wait until the mill closes for Culme Cease, and that's weeks away,' she said, pulling a face.

'Maybe you should be careful who you are seen talking to, though Eliza,' Flo said thoughtfully. 'Don't fan the flames, so to speak.'

'But why should she have to worry?' Jen spluttered. 'It's bad enough we have to keep out of the way of visiting merchants cos they pay for the cloth we make. Let's face it, if they did deign to talk to us it would only be cos they was feeling frisky and thought they was in with a chance, if you get my meaning.'

'I do, my girl, and you'd do well to remember that you've already been given a chance. Or have you forgotten the work-house?' Flo asked, giving her one of her level looks.

'Yeah, sorry Flo,' she murmured, turning her attention back to her food.

'It does sound like Beer's looking for any excuse to pick on you,' the older woman said, turning back to Eliza. 'Always been a nasty bit of work that one, but he's got much worse since Mrs Tucker was made overseer instead of him. Thinks women should know their place. You'd best be careful though.'

Next morning, just as Peter had predicted, they stepped outside the front door to be greeted by a world of white.

'Bit of a shock after all that sunshine,' Jenny moaned, pulling her shawl tighter round her shoulders.

'Perhaps the acid baths will be iced over,' Rosie said hopefully, her breath spiralling in the cold air.

'Wee doesn't freeze stupid,' Jenny told her. 'Blimey I'm not going to be able to feel my fingers let alone thread the machines,' she grimaced, blowing on them in an effort to get them warm.

'You needs some fittens,' Eliza replied.

'Some what?' they chorused.

'Fingerless mittens. You can wear them while you work. I used to knit them back home,' Eliza explained.

'Never heard of them,' Jenny muttered. 'And where exactly is home? Despite us telling you all about our lives, you still haven't explained how you came to be here.' Eliza looked away from the girl's prying gaze. It was true, she had been evasive but that was because she was trying to forget her time at Lavender House. She might not have been there long, but it had left a lasting impression.

'I could always make you some,' she offered, in an effort to deflect the subject. 'Always supposing we can get hold of some wool.' Realizing what she'd said, they burst out laughing, which drew curious looks from the other workers stamping their way to work through the crunchy frost. It was hard to think that the lengthy processes they carried out led to the spinning of wool.

As the bell began its insistent clanging, forgetting the

slippery path beneath their feet, they automatically hastened their steps. Eliza noticed that the ice in the leat had been broken and the wheel was turning smoothly. She was pleased Peter had been able to carry out his work. He'd seemed a friendly young man and she'd enjoyed chatting with him.

Then she was entering the mill and as she joined the queue to clock on, her heart sank. The thought of spending another day sitting on the cold floor filled her with dread. She was bone weary, having spent a restless night going back over the foreman's warnings, trying to pinpoint any reason for him singling her out. She couldn't afford to lose this job. Her boots leaked and desperately needed mending. And now she needed to purchase wool to make the fittens she'd promised her new friends.

'Where do you think you're going you two?' As the harsh voice of Beer boomed down the steps, Eliza and Rosie stopped and stared at one another.

'Don't you listen to anything?' Although he addressed them both, his eyes bored into Eliza. 'I told you last night that we've got a new order and you're being moved. So, you, upstairs to the spinning frame,' he barked, waving Rosie away. 'And you Priddle, can earn your living by stirring the fleeces in the bath. Make sure you put your back into it or it will be my duty to inform Mr Grange that you have failed to make the grade – again.' He strode away, leaving her in no doubt as to his meaning.

As she began loading the heavy fleeces into the tank, the smell of urine and other muck made her retch.

'Think of bread and jam,' Joe shouted, as he went by. He was pushing a wicker trolley laden with the cleaned wool and could hardly see over the top, but seemed happy enough. Giving him a nod, she picked up the enormous paddle and began stirring the sodden fleece. Round and round, up and down.

'I said put your back into it Priddle.' She heard the foreman yell but didn't look up. She couldn't fathom out why he'd singled her out, but during the long, wakeful night, had come to the conclusion that if she kept her head down, she might minimize his unwelcome attentions. Seeing a lump of fleece sticking up from the liquid, she imagined it was Beer's head and began whacking it as hard as she could.

It was so exhilarating, she got quite carried away until she saw Beer bearing down on her again.

'You're meant to be taking that seriously, not enjoying yourself,' he growled. Whether it was the unfairness or from lack of sleep, Eliza turned to him, eyes narrowed.

'I work hard Mr Beer and all you do is pick on me. Well, I've had enough,' she cried, throwing down her paddle.

'And I've had enough of your high-handed attitude, Priddle,' he bellowed, making sure everyone could hear him above the noise. 'If we hadn't won this important order, you'd be down the road. Get yourself over to the willowing machine. I want double the usual amount of fleece untangled and ready for upstairs by six o'clock tonight. Even if that means working through your break.'

Striding over to a lady in the corner, he pointed to Eliza and she knew she was being replaced. Well, she couldn't afford to be out of work and it would make a change working on a machine. As Rosie had said, it would be an improvement on the stench of urine. The woman operating the willower stopped as soon as Eliza approached.

'I'm Anne and I'll show you what to do and then I'm away upstairs.'

'Sorry if I'm pushing you out,' Eliza said, for the woman looked like she enjoyed what she was doing.

'Don't be. Got five bairns to raise so the extra money will be welcome. Now, you need to feed the fleece through the machine like this to untangle the wool. Mind your fingers though, this one has a tendency to jump and the metal teeth are sharp as tacks.' As the fleece moved through the machine, she grimaced. 'As you can see it also removes any impurities left from the scouring while it's at it.'

'Wouldn't have thought anything could survive that mixture,' Eliza said. As she nodded her head towards the tank she'd just left, she saw her place had already been filled by the large lady who didn't seem to mind the stench at all.

'Old Betty's used to mucking out stables so she's used to odious smells,' Anne said, following her glance. 'I see they've pulled in labour from the workhouse too,' she added, gesturing over to the grading and sorting area with her spare hand. Eliza saw two young girls hardly more than five or six years of age, crouching down with huge shears almost bigger than they were.

'Shouldn't they be in school?' she asked, raising her voice to be heard above the machine.

'Mind your own business, Priddle,' Beer boomed, appearing beside her. 'Those girls are grateful for the work, which seems more than can be said for you.' He turned to Anne. 'Right you, get upstairs and start on spinning frame one. The lass there will show you what to do.'

'But Rosie only went upstairs a short time ago will she . . .' Eliza began, only to receive another glare.

'I'll be back shortly to see how you've done.'

Eliza barely refrained from poking her tongue out as she began feeding the fleece through the willower. It was a simple job and watching the roller with metal teeth, creating a soft, fluffy mass of fibres, she began to feel like she was at last doing something worthwhile.

'I thought I told you to get a move on.'

As the dreaded foreman bore down on her once more, Eliza stiffened. Couldn't he leave her alone for more than ten minutes?

'I said . . .' but the rest of his sentence was drowned by a piercing shriek, so ear splitting it could be heard above the noise of the machinery.

Chapter 29

Slowly the machines on the floor above ground to a halt. As an ominous hush descended, the workers stared at each other in horror. Then, as one, they rushed towards the stairs.

'Get back to your work,' Beer blustered, before hurrying up them himself.

Although Eliza was desperate to know if the poor girl who'd screamed was alright, she knew arguing wouldn't help matters. Turning back to the willower, she resumed feeding the fleece through it, looking up from time to time to see if anyone had discovered what had happened upstairs. After a short lull, there was a clunk and grating above them as the spinning machines started up again. Although the noise seemed even more deafening after the silence, she hoped it meant the poor person who'd screamed wasn't badly hurt.

To her surprise and relief, the foreman didn't reappear and she began to relax into the rhythm of the willower. When break time came and there was no jangling of the bell, they all shrugged and continued working. Stopping before it rang meant instant dismissal.

'Poor Rose.' She jumped as an ashen faced Joe appeared

by her side. 'I were upstairs unpacking me trolley when she got . . .' Seeing Mrs Tucker heading briskly towards them, he stuttered to a halt.

'You mean it was Rose who screamed? Is she alright?' Overseer or not, Eliza needed to know, but Joe hastily bent down and busied himself replenishing the trolley.

'How is Rose?' Eliza burst out.

'If you could come upstairs please Miss Priddle.' It was a command and not a request and feeling sick and anxious, she followed the woman back up the stairs. All the machines appeared to be running, but the workers were looking shaken. Heads turned in her direction as Mrs Tucker led the way up the back steps and ushered her into Mr Grange's office. The foreman, his face red, was shouting and thumping his fist on the table.

'Wait outside Beer,' the master ordered, cutting across his tirade.

'But I told you, it was her fault . . .' the foreman spat, jabbing his finger at Eliza.

'I said outside.' This time the command brooked no argument. With a final glower, the foreman, like a dog with its tail between its legs, slunk out of the door. Mr Grange, looking grim, gave Eliza a searching look.

'You will have heard there was an incident with one of the machines this morning. The unfortunate operative,' he stared down at the paper before him, 'Rose Brice, got her hand caught when a thread broke.'

'So, it was Rosie? How badly hurt is she?' Eliza blurted out. The master glanced at his overseer before continuing.

'Luckily, an engineer was on site and able to stop the machine before she lost it entirely,' he continued as if she hadn't spoken. 'As it is, she has been dismissed and taken home.'

'Dismissed,' Eliza cried. 'You mean you've sacked her for having an accident?' she asked incredulously.

'That is the procedure when such an incident occurs,' Grange said, stressing the word incident. 'She won't be able to work the machine again for some while, if at all, and we've others waiting to take her place. This is a business, you know,' he added, staring down at his desk. 'And we did permit . . .' again he consulted his paper, 'Miss Jennifer Smith to accompany her.'

'I know this is upsetting for you Miss Priddle,' the overseer interjected, placing her hand on Eliza's arm. 'But, in the interest of our workers' safety, it is vital we get to the bottom of things.'

'Then, in the interest of safety, perhaps you can tell me why . . .'

'It is my job to ask the questions, Miss Priddle,' the master cut in, eyes as hard as flint as his head snapped up. 'It is customary when a member of staff is moved onto a new machine, that our foreman, Mr Beer stays with that operative until he or she is conversant with its workings. In this case, I have been informed that although Miss Brice had only just started on the spinning frame, Mr Beer was downstairs on the grading and sorting floor, attending to what he refers to as your . . .' Again, he glanced down at the paper before him. 'Persistent protracted working, inattention and disregard for orders, which he claims was holding up production.'

'That's not true,' Eliza replied, her eyes narrowing at such unfairness. 'From the day I arrived, I have done everything Mr Beer has asked of me, despite him constantly singling me out for criticism.'

'And why would that be?' he asked, cold eyes scrutinizing her closely.

'I wish I knew,' Eliza sighed.

'I think I might shed some light on that,' Mrs Tucker said. 'Mr Beer has been er, morose, since his wife left him. It is my belief, that Miss Priddle with her red hair and green eyes, reminds him in some way of her.'

'Never heard anything so ludicrous,' Grange sneered. 'No decent man would ever permit a woman to influence either him or his work.' It was patently obvious from his tone that he would never let a female affect him. Not that any decent woman would contemplate having anything to do with such a cold-hearted man.

'But it's Rosie we should be discussing. I must find out how she is,' Eliza cried. The master stared at her, incredulous that his discourse should be interrupted, but Eliza was past caring. 'I lodge with her aunt and was entrusted with her care. I need to find out how she is,' Eliza repeated impatiently.

'I think under the circumstances, we might let Miss Priddle leave early,' Mrs Tucker ventured. 'She clearly won't be able to concentrate until she's established just how badly injured Miss Brice is, and we don't want to risk another acc— er, incident. Besides, anytime I have had occasion to be downstairs, Miss Priddle has been working diligently so . . .' she shrugged, and let her words hang in the air.

'Very well, Miss Priddle, you may take your leave. To show we are not the hard-hearted people you seem to think, provided you and Miss Smith are back at your machines at six o'clock in the morning sharp, your pay will not be docked for early departure. Tell Miss Brice, we wish her well for the future.'

Not sure whether to thank him or smack the self-righteous expression from his face, Eliza gave a curt nod and hurried from the room. Outside, the belligerent foreman sneered.

'You'll be down the road Missy. I saw you sucking up to the bosses, but they'll not believe your word over mine.' Intent on getting home as quickly as possible, Eliza ignored him and hurried outside. To her surprise, Peter was waiting.

'I've just got back from seeing Rose home,' he explained.

'How is she?' Eliza asked, impatient for news.

'Her aunt has bandaged her hand and stemmed the blood as best she can, but it is badly crushed and of course, she's in shock.'

'Oh, poor Rosie,' Eliza cried, trying not to shudder at the stains on his jacket.

'I did offer to go for Dr Jarvis, but Flo refused. To be honest, I don't think she can afford his fee,' he added, lowering his voice.

'But surely, the mill will pay for that. They more or less admitted it was their fault,' Eliza told him.

'But they won't in public. Grange will have to report to Mr Wolfe, but you can be certain he will couch things in such a way the mill won't be implicated.'

'But that's so unfair.'

'Yet the way things are. I mentioned to Burrows, my boss, that those machines needed servicing a while back, but he told me in no uncertain terms, that it wasn't my place to interfere. He even intimated I would lose my job if I did. Now, I feel terrible,' he murmured.

'It's not your fault,' she sighed, patting his arm. 'But I must go and see how Rosie is.'

'Let me know how she gets on, won't you,' he called after her but she was already hurrying up the hill.

Quickly unlatching the door and dashing into the cottage, the first thing that hit Eliza was the unnatural stillness. Where usually there'd be laughter and banter, there was silence. Finding nobody in the living room, she tore up the stairs. A harassed looking Flo was leaning over the bed, sponging Rosie's brow. The scene was so reminiscent of her gramfer's last illness, that Eliza froze in the doorway.

'How is she?' she murmured through the lump in her throat.

'Not good,' Flo whispered. 'We've stemmed the blood but her temperature's gone sky high. Eliza glanced at the stained sheets that had been used as bandages and grimaced.

'I've brought more cold water,' Jen said, appearing with a

bowl in her hands. 'You go and rest Flo, I'll take over here.' Flo shook her head but Jen turned to Eliza. 'Take her downstairs and make her a hot drink. Try to get her to eat something, she's almost out on her feet.'

'Come on Flo, you need to keep your strength up or you'll be no good to Rosie,' Eliza urged, putting an arm around the woman's trembling shoulders and leading her towards the stairs.

In the little kitchen, the fire was lit and the kettle set to boil. Seeing Flo shiver, Eliza gently pushed her down onto the chair and threw a shawl around her shoulders. Being the end of the week, they were down to reusing old tea leaves, and in an effort to make a strong brew, Eliza poured boiling water over the lot of them then stirred the pot vigorously.

'Poor Rosie. What will I tell her mother? I promised to look after her,' Flo sobbed, her pitiful cries filling the tiny room.

'You're not to blame Flo,' Eliza assured her. 'Now drink this while it's hot,' she said, placing a mug in the woman's hand. 'Are you sure we shouldn't send for the doctor? I saw Peter and—'

'No,' Flo said, shaking her head vehemently. 'I'll just drink this and go back to her.' But the woman had only managed a couple of sips before they heard Rosie cry out. Flo was on her feet and back up the stairs in a flash.

'Them bleeding misers,' Jen said, appearing moments later and flopping into the seat Flo had vacated. 'If they weren't so penny pinching and worried about their profit this never would have happened.'

'Exactly what did happen?' Eliza asked.

'We're not really sure,' Jen admitted, letting out a long sigh. 'Yarn snapped and when Rosie went to rethread it her hand got caught. She's in a real bad way,' she wailed, tears running down her cheek. Never having seen Jen without a smile or cryptic remark on her lips, Eliza was taken aback. But as she comforted the young woman, she felt her own tears welling.

'If only there was something we could do,' Jen cried.

'Surely we should send for the doctor?' Eliza asked.

'And pay him with what, the buttons from our blouses?'

'But we can worry about that later, when she's better,' Eliza insisted.

'Jarvis knows the likes of us can't afford his fee and insists on cash in his hand before he'll turn out,' Jen spat. 'You should know it's one rule for the toffs and one for us.'

Arms around each other, they lapsed into silence, the only sound coming from the occasional crackle as the burning sticks shifted in the grate. The evening wore slowly on, the room growing ever darker, but neither had the energy to move. Eliza was staring at the flickering patterns on the wall, fighting off the memories of that terrible night her gramfer had taken ill, when they heard Rosie cry out.

Rushing up the stairs, Eliza could feel the heat emanating from the small body as soon as she entered the room. Rosie was gibbering wildly as, despite her fever, she lay shivering. But it was the colour of her face that sent the prickle of alarm creeping down her back. As Flo stared helplessly, Eliza knew what she had to do. Pulling her bag out from under Jen's bed, she snatched up her purse and Grammer's amber comb.

'I'm going for the doctor,' she said.

'But we can't . . .' Flo began.

'We must,' Eliza said firmly. 'Come on Jen, show me where he lives.'

Chapter 30

'But where did you get an expensive comb like that?' Jen asked, the next morning as they made their way blearily to work.

Remembering the look of astonishment on her friend's face when she'd offered it to the doctor in return for him visiting Rosie, Eliza couldn't help giving a sad smile. Although she'd had an inkling the stones were worth something, she'd had no idea of its true value until she'd seen the reaction on Madam's face that fateful day of the auction. The woman's eyes had positively gleamed with greed when she'd seen it sparkling in Eliza's hair.

Frost rimed the roofs and paths, silvering the branches of the trees along the leat while their feet marched in time to the summoning of the bell. Everywhere looked cold but beautiful, and it was hard to think that, only a few short hours ago, Rosie's life had hung in the balance.

As Eliza sat in the kitchen with Jen the previous evening, all she'd been able to think of was her gramfer on the night he'd died. Would his life have been saved if she'd summoned the doctor? Reason told her that it probably wouldn't have made any difference as age and infirmity were against him.

But Rosie was young and healthy, and upstairs in Eliza's bag lay the wherewithal to engage the services of Dr Jarvis. When the girl's condition took a turn for the worse, she knew she had to act. And it appeared they'd only just been in time.

'Well, hurry up spill the beans,' Jen urged, but they'd reached the entrance to the mill and were inundated with enquiries about Rosie.

'Tell you later,' she called, as they rushed to clock on.

'And how is Rosie today?' the overseer enquired, pushing her way through the press of the crowd.

'Improving but no thanks to you lot,' Jen spat. 'The doctor has disinfected and dressed her arm. He's also given her powders to bring down the temperature.'

'The doctor?' Mrs Tucker echoed, her surprise evident.

'The fever has broken and we are hopeful Rosie's turned the corner,' Eliza cut in quickly, anxious to avoid any awkward questions.

'That's good,' the woman nodded. 'Well, the bell has stopped ringing so off to your machine Jenny. Eliza come with me. We need to conclude yesterday's conversation,' she added, leading the way to a small room behind the cloakroom. Eliza's head began to pound. She was exhausted after the events of the previous day and night, and had no desire to be questioned about how she'd bartered her grammer's comb for the doctor's services. However, Mrs Tucker smiled and gestured for her to take a chair.

'Firstly, I can't tell you how relieved I am about Rosie. She is a lovely young girl.'

'Yes, she is very young and the young need guidance, don't they?' Eliza burst out, still reeling from the shock of finding out Rose hadn't been supervised. Mrs Tucker looked at her with those beady eyes that seemed to see and understand at the same time.

'They do,' she agreed. 'And such instruction has been given to the new foreman.'

'You mean . . .?' Eliza asked, her spirits rising.

'Mr Beer has been dismissed and Mr Carter engaged in his place. He is a competent foreman, deployed from one of our other mills. I'm sure you won't have any trouble with him. From today, you will be working upstairs on the skein winder. I am sure you will find it a much nicer job and of course, your pay will be increased by another halfpenny a day. Any questions?' Eliza looked at the woman wondering if she dared voice the thing that had been niggling her since her first day.

'Well, Miss Priddle?' The overseer's eyes narrowed. Clearly, despite her words, she'd thought the interview over.

'I don't understand why such young children are employed here when surely, they should be at school.'

'Your concern for the youngsters is commendable. However, the families of these children are poor and need every penny that can be earned. We here at the mill realize this, and also recognize that in order to get anywhere in life, boys need educating, at least in writing and arithmetic. That is why we pay for a gentleman to come in and tutor them after work three evenings a week. We are not the callous, unfeeling people you seem to think, Miss Priddle,' she said with a tight smile.

'But what about the girls? They need educating too,' Eliza cried.

'Of course. In the running of a home, which they receive from their mothers.'

'But that's archaic. Girls should learn their lessons too. Why back home I taught—'

'If that is all?' Mrs Tucker interrupted. Eliza hesitated then remembered the way Rose was suffering.

'There is one more thing. I would like to ask about the servicing of the machines.'

'Well don't. You really cannot expect me to waste time listening to the views of someone who has no experience in these matters,' she said, waving her away.

'But . . .' she began.

'We have wasted enough time and have work to do. You will find the skein winder just inside the mill doors.'

'Yes, Mrs Tucker,' she replied, getting to her feet. Obviously what Peter had said about the bosses banding together was true. She just hoped she was given sufficient instruction and didn't end up like poor Rosie. Thankfully, it looked as if they'd been prompt enough to save her hand, but it had been a close thing and would still take a long time to heal completely. Then it would be months before Rosie could return to work. Another halfpenny a day might not be a lot, but it would help make up the shortfall she reminded herself as she took up her position in front of a long, metal machine topped with various, ominous looking spools.

While most of the workforce asked about Rosie as they passed, there were a couple who made scathing remarks.

'Think you're better than the rest of us, eh, bypassing the spinning frames?' one mean looking woman shouted.

'Most of us have to work our way to get to there,' another pointed out.

'Now ladies, to your machines please,' a man of middle years told them.

'Oh yeah, and who might you be?' the first one called.

'Mr Carter, the new foreman,' he said mildly but his direct gaze left them in no doubt that he meant what he said. He turned to Eliza. 'I understand you have never worked this before,' he said, gesturing to the skein winder. 'You'll be pleased to know that once it's threaded, all you really need to do is keep turning the handle until the wool from the bobbins has wound onto the slats of wood at the front which form the drum here, see,' he told her, showing her what he meant. 'When the bobbins run out, you remove the skeins from the drum, replace the bobbins and just feed the threads over like they are now.'

'Well, it seems quite straightforward,' Eliza told him.

'It is, and as the machine is hand driven there should be no risk of an incident,' he told her, eyes twinkling.

He made it sound simple and demonstrated so clearly that Eliza was soon able to take over.

'Signal if you need any help,' he told her once he was satisfied that she'd mastered the movements. 'No point in saying call me with this racket going on, is it?' he grinned and wandered off. What a change from the overbearing, bossy Beer she thought. And it was better being up here for although it was noisier, light flooded in through the windows and there was no overpowering stench of stale urine. Determined to do well, she threw herself into her work, looking up in surprise when the bell rang at noon and Mr Carter came over to inspect what she'd done.

'Admirable Miss Priddle, you may go and enjoy a well-earned break,' he told her.

Although it was cold outside, Eliza welcomed breathing in the fresh air. Who would have thought April would turn out to be so bitter after the mild weather of March, she thought pulling her shawl tighter around her. Seeing Peter leaning against the wall of the yard, she wandered over.

'How's Rosie?' he asked, his expression brightening as she approached.

'Dr Jarvis has treated her hand and given her something to bring down her temperature,' she told him.

'You summoned the doctor but I thought . . .'

'She took a turn for the worse. Thankfully, she was sleeping peacefully when we left this morning,' she cut in, anxious not to enter into any awkward discussion about how they'd settled his fee. 'Which is what I wish I was doing,' she added, stifling a yawn. 'Roll on six o'clock.'

'Or eight in my case,' he grimaced. 'Got to service the spinning machine Rosie was using yesterday. Apparently, the owner is paying Grange a visit.'

'Just wait 'til I see him, then,' she growled.

'Better to keep quiet if you value your job. I mean, Flo will be short enough not having Rosie's pay packet,' he said, giving her a meaningful look.

'Alright, I take your point,' she sighed. 'But one of these days I shall make my feelings known,' she declared.

'Goodness, such determination, Miss Priddle,' he chuckled. 'Better find yourself a rich husband or another job first though.'

When Eliza and Jen arrived home that evening, Flo came wearily down the stairs saying that Rosie had woken earlier, taken a few sips of water with another powder, and was sleeping once more.

'But the fever has broken and her temperature's much lower,' she added, stifling a yawn.

'Well you stay down here and put your feet up. We'll take over now,' Jen told her. 'We was passing old Tom Churley's shop when he came out and asked about Rosie. He says to tell you not to worry about his account this week and gave us some beef bones to stew up,' she added, holding out a wrapped parcel. 'I'll just pop them in the kitchen then go up and see Rosie.'

'That was kind of him. People have been calling by all day with gifts and offers of help. Willie brought a whole dish of that rabbit stew so we wouldn't have to cook tonight,' she told them, flopping gratefully into a chair.

'I'll make us a drink while it's heating then, shall I?' Eliza asked.

'In a moment, Eliza, I'd like a word first.' She waited until Jen had disappeared up the stairs then. 'Now young lady, Dr Jarvis paid Rosie another visit this morning and it seems we have you to thank. Although I'm right grateful, his visits don't come cheap so what I'd like to know is why you'd do something like that for us. It's not as if we're family or you've known us that long.' She fixed Eliza with her shrewd gaze.

'You told me to look out for Rosie and I failed, didn't I,' Eliza sighed, relieved to hear the doctor had checked on Rosie again.

'Lordy above,' the woman cried. 'Jen explained things, and as I understand it, you was on different floors. Now many's the time I've raised my eyes to the ceiling but I'm blowed if I've ever been able to see through it.' Despite herself, Eliza couldn't help smiling at the woman's facetiousness. But Flo wasn't going to let the matter drop.

'You've hardly known us five minutes, so why should you part with your expensive comb? It was yours to part with, I take it?' she asked, narrowing her eyes.

'Of course. It belonged to my grandmother,' Eliza explained.

'Well then, that was a right kindly thing to do,'she smiled wearily then became serious again,' but you still haven't told me why?'

'You've all made me so welcome here. It's the first time I've felt at home since Grammer and Gramfer died and I've become fond of you all,' she admitted.

'Well, I'm glad you feel at home, cos we like having you here. But, there's more to it, isn't there?' She fixed Eliza with her candid gaze and waited.

'I felt so guilty after Gramfer died. If I'd sent for the doctor he might still be here,' Eliza admitted. 'Knowing I had something to barter with I couldn't stand by and let Rosie suffer or . . .' her voice trailed off and remembering the unnatural pallor on the girl's face, she shivered.

'Die too,' Flo finished for her. 'Look Eliza you're a kind, sensitive girl and I'm sure you did everything you could for your gramfer. He wouldn't want you suffering for something that was probably inevitable. People get called when it's their time, you know.'

'Thank you,' Eliza murmured. She'd never feel totally free of guilt but the woman's words did help a little.

'It was a generous thing you did for our Rosie and I want you to know you'll have our everlasting gratitude. For what it's worth, this is your home for as long as you want,' she told her.

'Thank you,' Eliza whispered again, a feeling of warmth spreading throughout her body.

'Yeah, you can't beat a lodger who knows when to put the kettle on and heat up the dinner,' Flo quipped. 'Now I'm just going to shut my eyes for five minutes while you get on.'

As her gentle snores echoed round the room, Eliza took herself into the little kitchen. What her grandparents had told her was true. Family and friendship were worth far more than money or valuable trinkets. Flo, Rosie and Jen had all welcomed her into their home and she knew Grammer would understand why Eliza had parted with her amber comb. She was still disappointed that during her short spell in Bridgwater she hadn't had time to find out about her grandparents' past. But now it was time to look forward rather than over her shoulder. If Lord Seymour or Madam had intended coming after her, they would have been here by now, wouldn't they?

A knocking on the front door made her jump. Hoping it hadn't disturbed Rosie, she hurried to open it only to find herself face to face with a tall stranger dressed in a top hat and long black coat.

Chapter 31

'Eliza Priddle, we meet at last. I have heard so much about you.' As the man's lips split into a grin revealing enormous white teeth, Eliza felt her heart miss a beat. Reeling back in horror, she began to slide down the wall just as two strong arms reached out and grabbed her.

The next thing she knew, she was sitting in a chair, a strange smell wafting under her nose. She coughed and spluttered, then opened her eyes.

'She's coming around. You must have scared the life out of her Reverend. It's alright Eliza, it's only the vicar calling about Rosie.' Flo's voice seemed to come from a long way off and then finally, her face swam into focus.

'Sorry, I thought he'd come to get me,' she stuttered.

'My dear girl, I might try and persuade people to come to church, but I have yet to kidnap anyone,' he said indignantly.

'Sorry it was the tall hat and black coat,' Eliza murmured, taking a sip of water from the glass Flo proffered. 'Thanks, that feels better,' she added, feeling foolish for now she could see the man was actually wearing a cloak above which poked his clerical collar.

'Ah, the hat,' he murmured, taking it off and staring at

it. 'Saw it in a junk shop when Mrs Topper and I were on vacation in Torquay. I'd just heard I was to move here and thought it would break the ice with my new parishioners and help them remember my name.'

'Well Reverend you certainly made an impression on our Eliza, though why a top hat should scare her I have no idea,' Flo said, looking sideways at the girl.

'My sincere apologies, Eliza. I merely called round to enquire after Rosie and to see if there is anything I can do.'

'She's sleeping at the moment, but that's the best thing for her,' Flo told him. 'Do sit down, so that I can.' The man nodded, looked around the small room then folded his long legs under a vacant chair at the table. 'That's better,' Flo said, sinking into the one next to him. 'All these shocks aren't good for my nerves, I can tell you, but it's good of you to call.'

'I heard Dr Jarvis has been to see Rosie?' The Reverend said, phrasing it as a question.

'Twice in fact,' Flo told him. 'He put something on her hand and dressed it all professional like. Said he thought that would stop any infection setting in. It was his powders that brought down her temperature and made her sleep easy.'

'Then it was indeed fortunate you were able to fund the services of a medic,' the man replied casually, whilst his eyes took in the shabby curtains and ill matched furniture.

'We had an angel benefactor, Reverend,' Flo told him, matching his serious tone.

'God moves in mysterious ways,' he nodded. 'I understand Rosie is your niece, Flo. I may call you Flo?' he asked.

'Well it's me name, though Lord knows what others call me. Oops forgive me Reverend, I'm not used to visitors from on high dropping in,' she laughed, then her expression became serious again. 'But you're right, Rosie is my niece. Why do you ask?'

'It occurred to me that perhaps her mother should be informed about the accident,' he replied. 'I would be pleased to write a letter if . . .'

'I can write, thank you,' Flo said quickly. 'Although it's kind of you to offer, Reverend. I'll send a note by mail coach tomorrow.'

'I'm sure she would wish to know; whatever the circumstances,' he added, giving a knowing look.

'I can see the grapevine's been gossiping,' Flo muttered.

'People often impart knowledge they think I should know,' he admitted. 'Now, let us offer up a prayer for Rosie's recovery.' They closed their eyes while he intoned a few words and had all joined in the amen when Jen came thundering down the stairs.

'Rosie's awake and asking for something to eat,' she shrieked.

'Blimey Reverend that was quick,' Flo gasped, staring at the man in astonishment. 'I'll just pop up and see her,' she gabbled, jumping to her feet.

'Nice to see you Reverend,' Jen said so sweetly, Eliza stared at her in surprise. 'How is Mrs Topper?'

'She is quite well, thank you Jennifer. I'm pleased to hear young Rosie's awake. It must have been a terrible shock for you all.'

'It was,' Jen said quietly. 'It's at times like this you appreciate people calling in to offer their support.' She paused, then asked casually, 'How is your new curate getting on?'

'James has settled in very well,' he replied. 'Mrs Topper is baking a cake for Rosie. She had intended dropping it round tomorrow, but perhaps James could bring it after morning service on Sunday instead,' he grinned sagely, revealing teeth that were big but not as enormous as Eliza had first thought.

'That'd be flipping marvellous,' Jen cried, then remembered who she was talking to. 'I mean that would be very kind, if he could spare the time.'

'I'm sure he would be pleased to. Now if you'll excuse me, Mrs Topper will have my supper waiting,' he said, getting to his feet. 'Once again, my apologies for inadvertently scaring you earlier, Eliza.'

Jen saw him to the door then turned to Eliza, her eyes dancing.

'He's sending James round,' she sang. Then she glanced around and grimaced. 'We'll have to get this place cleaned up before he arrives.'

'Before who arrives?' Flo asked, coming back into the room.

'The new curate. Reverend Topper said his wife was going to drop a cake round tomorrow but he's going to get James to bring it around on Sunday instead. Isn't that marvellous?'

'No Jen, it flipping well isn't,' Flo cried, then chuckled when the girl looked shocked. 'We've got to wait another 'flippin' day to eat it now, haven't we?' the woman chided. 'Anyhow, Rosie's looking much better so Eliza, you can keep her company while I heat the stew. Only she could think about food so soon after surfacing.'

'I'll go up now,' Eliza smiled, running up the stairs. 'Alright to come in?' she asked, putting her head around the bedroom door.

'Yeah course,' Rosie replied, wincing as she tried to prop herself up on her pillow.

'Here let me do that.' As she made her friend comfortable, she was pleased to note the girl's colour was almost back to normal. 'Does your hand hurt much?'

'A fair bit, but don't tell Auntie, she's worried enough as it is.'

'Well, you did give us all a fright you know.'

'Yeah, but you should all be grateful to me. I mean it got rid of beastly Beer, didn't it,' she chuckled, then fell back against the pillows. 'Still a bit weak. Must be all that food I've missed. You do the talking. What's the new foreman like? Jen said he spent ages showing you how to use the skeiner.' She grinned impishly.

'None of your romantic ideas now, young Rosie. Mr Carter is at least thirty-five and for your information, he was only doing his job.' But Rosie's eyes had fluttered closed. Eliza smiled down at her little friend who, even after her recent trauma, had a head filled with starry eyed notions. She'd buy the girl one of those little romantic booklets when she got paid tomorrow, along with wool to make some fittens.

Then she could knit whilst keeping Rosie company during her convalescence.

Knowing the mill workers all got paid on Saturday afternoons, the shops stayed open until late. Since arriving in Culme Eliza had been too busy to see all they had to offer. In fact, with the weather turning so bitter and then Rosie's accident, she hadn't seen much of the hamlet at all. It would be a good opportunity to have a proper look around, she thought, making her way back down the stairs.

'Rosie's sleeping,' she told the woman as she joined them at the table where the aroma of rabbit stew reminded her it had been ages since she'd last eaten.

'Probably the only way she could escape your sparkling conversation,' Flo retorted making Eliza smile. It was good to see the woman happy again, she thought, tucking into her meal. However, as she put down her knife and fork, she saw Flo looking thoughtful.

'Something worrying you?' she asked.

'Just thinking about what the Reverend said about writing to Rosie's mother. I suppose she would want to know but . . .'

'Well mine wouldn't,' Jen retorted, breaking into the conversation. 'Couldn't care less about me if she tried. What about you Eliza, would yours want to know?'

'My mother died in childbirth so I never knew her,' Eliza said, quickly gathering up the dishes in the hope of avoiding the question she knew would follow.

'Hence that bond with your grandparents,' Flo murmured, reaching out and patting her hand. 'Do you have any siblings?'

'Like I said, I was raised by my grandparents who both died recently,' she told them, taking their things through to the kitchen and hoping that was the end of the matter.

'So, you're an orphan,' Jen exclaimed, as soon as she returned. 'Were your grandparents from the upper classes then?'

'Heavens no, whatever made you think that?' Eliza asked, staring at her in astonishment.

'Well, that fancy comb was worth enough to pay for Dr Jarvis. Then you go and faint when you see the Reverend, muttering about his top hat and black coat. Well that's what toffs wear so . . .' Jen shrugged, leaving the sentence hanging in the air.

'Gramfer gave me that comb on my birthday. It had belonged to Grammer and he thought I'd like something of hers to remember her by. Not that I needed anything for that,' Eliza explained.

'He didn't wear a topper like the Reverend then?' she continued, staring at Eliza curiously.

'No, he didn't,' she replied, thinking of Gramfer's old woollen hat.

'Well, I'm going to marry someone like him,' Jen announced.

'Who the Reverend?' Eliza gasped. 'But he's already married.'

'Not him, his curate, silly,' she grinned. 'He'll have a huge stone manse on the edge of the village like the Rev. Have you seen it? It's got a massive garden with apple trees, fancy lace drapes hanging from the window. Imagine swanning around the parlour, spying on all the passersby without being seen. You'd know everything that went on.'

'As if everybody doesn't already. Why you've only got to go for a pee in the privy and yer neighbour's pilfering yer pail for an extra penny from the mill,' Flo scoffed, her Devonshire accent becoming more pronounced. 'Anyway, back to Rosie's mother. I know I should send her a letter, but what if she turns up with that oaf in tow.'

'Then I'll wrap his fancy braces round his dangly bits, hang him from the mill wheel and set it turning,' Jen declared so hotly the woman smiled.

'Still, the Reverend is right, I am going to have to let her mother know,' Flo yawned. 'But I'll write to her in the morning. I'm crackered and that's a fact. Lord knows you must be too after being up half the night. I'll bunk in with Rosie and you two can have my room.'

'What sleep in your fancy big bed, Flo? Yes please,' Jen cried.

Eliza's head was throbbing and her throat tight with wool fibres as she waited in the queue for her pay. It seemed to take for ever to reach the front and then they had to check the contents of their packets before signing for them. Once they'd left the office there was no going back if an error had been made. Finally, clutching her precious money, she made her way out into the open air where Jen was waiting impatiently.

'Blimey at last. You need to learn how to get to the front quicker,' she told Eliza. 'Come on, Saturday evening's the best night of the week,' she added, doing a jig. 'Two nights of freedom from this hell hole.'

'Apart from us engineers,' Peter muttered, falling into step beside them. 'How's Rosie?' he asked.

'Sleeping a lot, but Flo says that's good,' Jen told him. 'Surely you've not got to work tomorrow?'

'No, the bosses won't allow us to come in on the Sabbath. They'll just make us work on tonight until the machines are oiled and running freely, ready for Monday. My first job is to check the wheel's not icing up as the temperature falls,' he grimaced, dipping his hand into the leat. 'Feels freezing even if it isn't actually.'

'Well, we'll leave you to your fun,' Jen laughed.

'See you on Monday, Peter,' Eliza called.

'I think he's sweet on you Eliza, all them sly little looks he darts you from under his cap,' Jen said, giving her a nudge.

'Peter's nice, but I'm not in the market for a man,' she told her friend firmly.

'You must be joking,' Jen cried, looking at Eliza as if she'd grown another head. 'What'll you do for fun?'

'Well, first of all I want to get some wool from the shop here. I understand they sell it cheap to workers.'

'Blimey, you call that fun? But if you mean is this where they try and get rid of their substandard stuff, then yes, it is.'

'Well it'll do for fittens. Has Flo got any needles do you know?'

'Flo knit, you must be joking,' Jen spluttered, leading the way into the little hut that served as a shop. It was teeming with workers rummaging through the finished skeins. Spotting a suitable one of red, Eliza went to pick it up at the same time as someone else.

'That's mine,' the woman snarled, tightening her hold, as she stared coldly at Eliza. 'I saw it first, didn't I Maggie?'

'Yes, you did Bertha,' her friend nodded. 'Besides, you always have first dibs, everyone knows that.'

'I didn't realize,' Eliza replied, letting go of the wool as the two women closed in menacingly.

'Well you do now. And make sure you remember. If you can afford to pay for a medic you don't need to snatch discounted supplies from us poor workers,' she spat, hurrying over to the counter with her prize.

'But . . .' Eliza began. Shaking her head, Jen pulled her away.

'She's a nasty bit of work so choose something else,' she hissed. Puzzled at the usually gutsy Jen giving in to a bully, Eliza shrugged. It wasn't that important anyway, she thought spying another, similar one.

'This one's better quality and the hank's thicker,' she said, snatching up a pair of needles and taking her purchases over to the woman sporting a huge pinafore, who'd been watching the exchange.

'Nicely handled, dear,' she whispered, as Eliza paid. 'Don't you rise to Big Bertha's bait, you're worth ten of her.'

'Thanks,' Eliza murmured, before turning back to an impatient Jen who was hovering outside the door. 'What was that all about?' she asked.

'Big Bertha works for Paton, he's the master pattern maker upstairs on the weaving floor.'

'I didn't even realize there was another floor,' Eliza murmured, staring back up at the tall building, with its bank of large windows.

'Paton reigns supreme. Even Grange kowtows to him, especially when merchants call to discuss a new pattern for cloth they wish to purchase. Bertha helps him thread his machines and thinks she rules the roost. She's a wicked woman and we all stay clear.'

'Must be mean if you avoid her Jen,' Eliza said, frowning at her friend. 'Anyway, let's forget her. It's Saturday night and we've just been paid. We'll go down to the store and choose one of those stories Rosie is so fond of.'

Arm in arm they made their way through the thronging street. With money in their pocket, and a whole day off to look forward to, everyone was in good spirits.

Chapter 32

'How about stopping for a quick drink at The Lamb?' Jen suggested. 'Flo will be at home so she won't see us.'

'I'd rather see how Rosie is,' Eliza said, wrinkling her nose at the fumes emanating from the open door as they passed. 'Besides, I can't abide the smell of liquor.'

'Oh lordy, first she don't do men and now she don't do drink,' Jen cried, raising her eyes to the sky. 'I hope you're not turning out to be a pious prig, Eliza Priddle.' Jen pouted.

'Well at least it won't be me breathing alcohol fumes all over the curate when he calls,' Eliza retaliated. Jen stared at her then let out a hoot of laughter, causing others to turn and look.

'You're funny when your dander's up girl. Well don't stand there with arms both the same length, let's get Rosie's romantic drivel and go home. I've to wash me hair, press me frock and get everywhere spick and span,' she said, her mood changing in an instant, as only Jen's could.

'How's Rosie?' they asked in unison, as soon as they walked through the door.

'Sleeping again. She managed some of the beef stew I made with them bones. She says her hand doesn't hurt much but I've seen her wince every time she moves. Still, it's early days,' Flo murmured.

'We've got her one of those Penny Bloods,' Jen told her. 'And Eliza's volunteered to read to her when the curate calls.'

'I have?' Eliza asked. 'Oh, yes, I have,' she amended, seeing her friend's pleading look.

'Well you needn't think you're entertaining him by yourself, young lady. I shall be sat in this chair chaperoning. Don't want any hanky-panky in my house, thank you,' Flo sniffed, wagging her finger as Jen pouted. 'Now girls, the kitty's empty so do you have your rent money?'

Unusually, Jen was the first one up on Sunday. After they'd tidied the house, Eliza coaxed Rosie to drink some beef tea while Jen got herself ready for her visitor.

'Would you help me wind my wool?' Eliza asked Flo when Rosie had fallen asleep.

'Good idea, it'll mean I can take the weight off my feet,' the woman said, sinking into a chair and holding out her hands. Eliza slipped the skein over them and began to wind.

'Have you heard anything from Rosie's mother?' she asked.

'No, so I'm pleased I didn't tell Rosie I'd written to her.'

'But surely, she'll want to see her daughter?' Eliza frowned.

'Depends on *him*, I suppose,' Flo scowled, emphasizing the word him. 'So, you said you had a feller back home?' the woman asked, eying her curiously.

'Don't you think this is a lovely colour,' she replied, nodding at the ball of wool that was growing bigger by the minute.

'Alright Eliza, I can take a hint,' the woman sighed. 'But sometimes I catch you with a certain faraway look in your eye and that usually means some chap's involved. If you ever want to talk you know I'm here, and surprising as it may seem, I can keep me mouth shut.' Eliza stared at her in astonishment, again wondering if the woman was psychic, for these past few days she'd found her thoughts returning to the Droves, wondering how the withies were, her little vegetable plot, Clem. Clem with his impish sense of humour yet always ready to listen or help. As time passed, she found she was really missing her good friend. As if following her train of thought, Flo shook her head.

'It might surprise you to know that I had a fella once. Not that I appreciated him at the time. No, I wanted more than this sleepy little hamlet had to offer. Or at least I thought I did. But the bright lights weren't that bright after all and by the time I realized and came back, my fella had upped and left himself.'

'Oh,' Eliza murmured. 'That must have been tough.'

'It was. Some said it was no more than I deserved though.' She was quiet for a moment, a faraway look in her eye. Then she shrugged. 'Still it was all a long time ago. Now, being as how you asked, I do think this wool's pretty, although I never got the hang of this knitting lark meself,' Flo said. 'How long will it take to make these fitten things?'

'The wool's quite thick and these needles are large so I

could have this pair done by tomorrow if I get a shifty on. Poor Jen's hands get so cold, I thought they might help her operate the spinner.'

'You mean you bought that wool for me?' Jen cried, coming into the room and stopping dead. 'Well I'll be. Nobody's ever made me anything in me life before.'

'Steady on,' Eliza cried as the girl flew over and threw her arms around her.

'Blimey you look lovely dressed up like that,' Flo said, gazing at her admiringly. 'If you'd only remember to act like a lady, you'll have young James eating out of your hand.'

'Do you think so?' Jen asked, looking uncertain as she smoothed down her skirts. It was then Eliza realized that under that brash exterior, she was actually vulnerable.

As Jen went around bashing the thin cushions into submission, Eliza finished winding the last of the wool. She'd just begun casting on her stitches when there was a loud knock.

'I'll go upstairs and see if Rosie's awake,' Eliza offered. But Flo was already opening the door.

'Come in gentlemen,' she cried, opening it wider to admit James carefully carrying a cake, followed by Peter.

'Good afternoon, ladies,' James beamed. 'Look who I found littering the road.'

'I hope I'm not intruding?' Peter said, his eyes seeking Eliza's.

'Of course not, welcome both of you,' Flo said, ignoring Jen's look of dismay as she took the proffered plate. 'Take a pew, if you'll forgive my pun, curate. Kettle's coming to the boil so I trust tea will be acceptable?'

'That would be delightful thank you Mrs . . .?' James replied, looking askance.

'Flo, everyone calls me Flo.'

'Flo. How is Rosie?' Peter enquired. 'We understand she likes to read so we brought her a periodical,' he said, placing it on the table.

'That's very kind of you both. Rosie is better than she was a couple of days ago, I can tell you. Mind you, with all the sleeping that girl's doing she should be quite beautiful by now. Except Rosie got her hand pricked by a blinking machine and not a spinning wheel,' she added in case they didn't realize she was alluding to the fairy story.

'It must be a worrying time for you,' Peter said politely, as he perched on the chair beside Eliza.

'Yes, it is. Now I'll make the tea and Jen you get a knife and slice this lip-smacking cake. Please tell Mrs Topper I'm most obliged,' said Flo.

'These are so beautiful and warm,' Jen cried, holding up her red fittens admiringly. 'And it's still blooming freezing, an' all,' she added.

'Even the trees don't want to unfold their blossom,' Eliza sighed, staring bleakly at the tightly closed buds.

'Can't say I blame them,' Jen muttered.

It was Monday morning and they were making their way towards the mill, their feet ringing in time to the bell. After a pleasant hour in the boys' company the previous afternoon, Eliza had gone upstairs. She'd read a few pages about a woman seeking thrills with a dashing dandy who then realizes that real love is gentle and enduring, only to find Rosie had fallen asleep. Chuckling at the ridiculous notions of the heroine, Eliza had crept back downstairs and returned to her knitting. With Jen asking every few minutes how much longer they'd take, she knew she'd get little peace until the fittens were finished. She'd sat up well into the night sewing them up, and now felt bleary eyed.

'Funny how Peter came along with James. I said he fancied you, didn't I?' Jen grinned, her breath spiralling in the frosty air.

'Rubbish. James said he met him on the street,' Eliza protested, wishing her friend would be quiet.

'How convenient, and Peter just happened to know where James was heading, I suppose,' Jen winked. 'He'll be asking to walk out with you next.'

'Look Jen, I told you I'm not interested in . . .' she began, but the rest of her sentence was lost as they were swept into the building by the press of people impatient to clock on.

'That's Paton the Pattern Maker,' Jen hissed, nudging Eliza's side. She looked up, just in time to see a neat little man wearing a pin striped suit, gold rimmed glasses perched on his long nose, disappear through a side door. 'Course, he don't have to clock on. His weavers used to do their work on wooden framed looms in their cottages before they installed the mechanized ones here. It must have been nice working at home,' Jen sighed, stamping her feet in an effort to warm them as she inserted her time card into its allocated slot on the wall. 'Oh well, here we go.'

Making her way towards the skeiner, Eliza saw Grange staring down from his eyrie and wondered if he ever actually did any work himself. But then the bell stopped jangling and the machines thrummed into action. Across the room, Jen waved her bright red hand and gave her the thumbs up. Obviously, the girl was able to operate her spinner with them on.

In the corner of the room she saw Joe trundling his trolley onto the wooden platform of the lift. Watching as it rose to the floor above, Eliza couldn't believe she hadn't realized there were even more machines in this building. But then it made sense that the cleaned, spun and combed wool should be turned into finished cloth on the premises.

She shuddered, recalling the hostile encounter with Big Bertha and her compatriot. That she should think Eliza rich because of her grammer's comb was ridiculous. How Clem would laugh at such a notion. Clem. Increasingly her thoughts seemed to turn to him and home. He'd probably given up calling at the cott once he realized Eliza had left. Surprisingly, she missed weaving her baskets too, for whilst working the skeiner was an improvement on the work downstairs, it was repetitive and hardly creative. Still it was a job and she needed to earn a wage in order to live, she reminded herself.

'How are you getting on?' She turned to see Mr Carter beside her. 'Hmm, good,' he murmured, inspecting what she'd done. 'The mill has secured a lucrative order and the weavers are calling for more yarn. I'm not going to be popular with the spinners when I tell them they have to work faster.'

'I'm not sure I can go much quicker,' Eliza replied.

'No, you misunderstand me. These skeins,' he gestured to the finished ones beside her machine, 'are sold to outworkers. I'm here to ask if you'd be prepared to help in another area.'

'Oh, er yes, of course,' she replied, looking askance.

'Good. I'll be back later. First, I need to speak to the spinners.'

He strode away and Eliza resumed her turning. As she worked, she watched the foreman walking around and talking to the others. Seeing their looks of dismay, she wondered what exactly she would be expected to do.

Then, as if they'd been galvanized into action, the machines began to whirl faster and the noise increased to an unbearable level. Eliza saw the operatives wiping the sweat from their faces as they endeavoured to keep up with the spinning bobbins.

Seeing the envious glances darted her way and feeling she ought to be playing her part, Eliza began turning the handle as fast as she dared so that the wool from the bobbins wound onto the slats of wood at the front at an alarming rate. However, it meant the bobbins ran out much quicker and she had to keep stopping in order to remove the skeins from the drum and replace the bobbins. It was back breaking work and when her arms felt as if they were dropping off, she knew she had to slow down before she fell down.

As the bell jangled for the noon break, Eliza sighed with relief. Snatching up her snap box, she was on her way outside, when she noticed Joe leaning against the wall of the entrance to the lift shaft.

'You alright Joe?' she asked, hurrying over to him. He shook his head, tears running down his cheeks as he gestured to the trolley from which full cones of wool had spilled out onto the floor.

'It got caught on the ledge as the lift came down and the wicker tore. Look there's a blimmin' great hole in it now. I was meant to be taking this lot up to Big Bertha but it all keeps falling out. I'll be down the road if she sees all this mess,' he gulped. Feeling sorry for him, Eliza put down her box, righted the trolley then inspected the torn willow.

'But this can be mended Joe,' she told him.

'Can it?' he asked, staring at her incredulously. 'How?' Seeing the curious looks they were attracting from workers filing outside to the yard, she patted his shoulder.

'Look, you pick up those cones and I'll trundle this through to the cloakroom and have a look at it,' she smiled, attempting to wheel the wonky trolley away from prying eyes. Settling herself down on the narrow bench, she studied the withy cage. It was shoddily made and she could see where the willow had broken. After ten minutes of judicious twisting and weaving, she had affected a passable repair. In fact, she'd found the feel of willow along with the rhythmic movements quite satisfying.

'You is clever,' Joe cried, his face relaxing with relief, as she trundled it back to where he was standing guard over his stock. 'You'd never know there'd been a hole there.'

'I've seen you going up and down in the lift many times Joe, so what was the problem today? Did you trip on something?'

'I kind of shot into the lift,' he sighed, then seeing Eliza's frown admitted, 'Big Bertha boxed my ears and shoved me out of the room. I was trying to unload by the warping mill as usual but she began screaming that the pattern maker had arrived.'

'Well Paton can't do his job without wool, can he?' Eliza said.

'Oh, and what would you know about it, Missy?' As Joe's eyes widened in horror, Eliza turned to see Big Bertha standing beside her, hands on her ample hips. 'Get back to your work you horrible little boy.' As Joe hurriedly manoeuvred his trolley onto the lift platform, the woman turned to Eliza. 'You might think you bagged the best job on the skein winder, but we'll soon see if you can manage some real work.'

Eliza was seething as she returned to her machine. How dare the woman pick on that poor boy. With anger lending strength to her work, for the rest of the afternoon, Eliza wound the wool from the bobbins into skeins at an alarming rate. She was still het up when she saw the tall figure of Mr Carter striding purposefully towards her. Should she complain about the woman's bullying or explain why she'd been working so erratically?

'You'll do yourself a mischief going at it like that,' he frowned. 'In fact . . . look we can't talk here, come into the lobby will you?' he shouted, trying in vain to be heard over the noise. As she followed him out to the clocking on area, where it was marginally quieter, she saw both Mr Grange and Mrs Tucker watching from the office upstairs and had a feeling she wasn't going to like what Mr Carter had to tell her.

Chapter 33

'As I said earlier, to meet this important new order we must increase production in all areas of the mill,' said Mr Carter when they reached the lobby and could be heard above the din.

'But the workers can't work any faster than they have today,' Eliza pointed out, thinking of the exhausted expressions on all their faces.

'I know and plans are being put in place. Starting with the top,' he gestured to the floor above. 'Mr Paton has called for someone to assist his weavers. Being the best pattern maker in the country, his requirements are exacting with only perfection good enough. He is rightly particular who he has around him, and has asked Mr Grange and Mrs Tucker to select a candidate for trial.' He paused and looked pointedly at Eliza.

'Me?' she squeaked.

'Yes, and for what it's worth I agree with them. However, before you can be shown up to his hallowed hall, I have to make it clear that his designs are top secret. So, Eliza Priddle, can you assure me that you have not been sent here to spy on our work processes?'

'Of course, I haven't,' she snorted. 'What a ridiculous notion.' As she stood glaring indignantly, he gave a chuckle.

'I believe you. It's nothing personal but this is a tightly-knit community, and as I'm sure you've found, anyone speaking anything other than the local dialect is considered a foreigner.' As he turned and nodded to the glass fronted office above, Eliza tried to process what the foreman had said. Whilst winding the skeiner had become tedious, she had no desire to be working with Big Bertha.

'The weavers work on piece rates so the more you assist the more they can earn. In turn, this will be reflected in your own wage,' Mr Carter continued. 'I understand you lodge with Rosie and her auntie. As she's not able to work at present, I'm sure that will help with any shortfall in the household funds.' Remembering the way Flo had frantically been trying to juggle the money she and Jen had given her, Eliza stared at him in dismay. Put like that, how could she refuse.

'You'll be pleased to hear Eliza has confirmed she is certainly not a spy, and is willing to move up to the weaving floor, Mrs Tucker,' he said as the overseer scuttled down the stairs. 'Now if you'll excuse me, I need to check the workers' output before the bell rings for the close of day.' As he strode back into the machine room, Mrs Tucker turned to Eliza.

'Although not a skilled position, Mr Paton still insists you sign The Mill's Official Secrets Almanac,' she said, taking an official looking black book from her pocket and opening it at the appropriate date.

'What?' Eliza exclaimed. 'That's taking things a bit far, surely?'

'Indeed, it is not. You need to understand that competition between mills is becoming even more fierce. We are fortunate to have the expertise of a, if not the, leading pattern setter so our reputation is second to none. However, our merchants want assurance the cloth they are purchasing is exclusive and everything you see in the weaving room is top secret. Now sign here and I'll take you upstairs.' After her experience in Lavender House, Eliza was reluctant to put her name on anything, but with Mrs Tucker waiting impatiently, she reluctantly scribbled her name.

'We'll go up before the bell rings and we're mown down by the press of workers clocking off. Having been granted this opportunity, you won't mind staying late, I'm sure. Besides, we don't want the spinners wondering yet why you have been selected over them.'

'But why have I?' Eliza asked as she followed the woman up the stairs.

'Mr Grange seemed to think you suitable. You also have Miss Smith to thank. She has been showing off those fittens you made for her. The evenness of the stitching impressed me. As I'm sure you know, weaving like knitting is all about the rhythm which made me think you might have the qualities Mr Paton is looking for.'

'Oh,' Eliza murmured.

'I must say your lack of enthusiasm surprises me Miss Priddle. Or are you so enamoured with the skeining machine you wish to remain on it for ever?'

'No, it's not that.'

'Well what is it then?' the overseer demanded, coming to a halt outside a heavy door.

'For one thing, I don't know how to weave wool.'

'If you show willing and work hard, you will have the opportunity to be trained,' she replied.

'Also, I don't like the way Big, I mean, Bertha picks on other people, especially young boys like Joe,' she burst out, the memory still fresh in her mind.

'That is unfortunate,' the overseer agreed. 'Whilst I can't condone her behaviour, sometimes it helps to know what might be behind it. In this case, Bertha lost her little boy to influenza. She blames herself because had she been able to afford the services of a medic, it is probable he would have survived.'

'But that's dreadful,' Eliza gasped, Bertha's hostility towards her now making sense.

'It is, and it has left her a bitter woman. Work has become her life and she is now a most accomplished weaver, Mr Paton's right-hand girl as it were,' she stared at Eliza meaningfully. 'I'm sure someone as resourceful as yourself will find a way to work alongside her. It could just be a matter of letting her tell you what to do initially?' She let her question hang in the air for Eliza to digest.

'Well come along then,' she urged.

Eliza couldn't make the overseer out. One minute it appeared she was talking to her woman to woman, and the next she snapped into overseer mode and was unapproachable. Which was frustrating as whilst they were away from the others, she'd been hoping to discuss an idea she'd had about teaching the young girls.

As the bell began to jangle and the machines downstairs ground to a halt, Mrs Tucker pushed open the door and bustled into the noisiest room Eliza had ever heard. The clatter and clacking of the looms was even more deafening than the machines downstairs, making Eliza recoil. There were five big looms and about ten workers in this room, but only Bertha glanced up. She smiled charmingly at the overseer but when she saw Eliza, her eyes narrowed to slits.

'Good afternoon Bertha,' Mrs Tucker called pleasantly as she passed before knocking briskly on another door at the far end of the room.

'Come,' a brusque voice called.

'I have brought the new helper, Miss Priddle, for your consideration, Mr Paton,' the overseer said, her voice respectful.

'Experience?' he asked brusquely, without looking up.

'Miss Priddle is a competent knitter and . . .'

'Knitter,' he barked. 'It is a weaver's assistant I require, Mrs Tucker. You cannot expect me to fulfil my orders with someone who winds wool around sticks,' he exclaimed, straightening up and squinting at Eliza through his gold rimmed spectacles. 'So, you have no experience of weaving then?' he asked, looking her up and down. Irritated by his condescending attitude and not caring whether she was granted the job or not, Eliza straightened her shoulders and stared him straight in the eye.

'Actually, I have, Mr Paton. Prior to coming here, I was a willow weaver. And I didn't need a machine to create my patterns either,' she retorted. In the ensuing silence, Eliza clearly heard the overseer's intake of breath.

'Is that so?' the man replied, giving her a level look. Then he nodded. 'I like a person passionate enough about their work to defend it. Report to Bertha first thing tomorrow and we'll see if you are capable of learning to weave to a pattern on my machines.'

'Yes, sir,' Eliza mumbled. As Mrs Tucker gestured for her to leave, she made her way back through the weaving room.

'Never giving you a start, is he?' Big Bertha snorted, glancing up from her loom.

'Yes he is, so I hope we can get on,' Eliza smiled.

'Hear that Maggie? She hopes we can get on,' the woman sneered. Then her expression hardened. 'I'm Queen and reign up here, so mind you know your place.' Giving a brief nod, Eliza made her way out of the room and down the stairs.

For once there was no need to queue to clock off, the others having left long since. The rain outside seemed to echo her dismal thoughts as, pulling her shawl tighter round her, she hurried past the mill cottages and on up the hill.

To her surprise Rosie was sitting in the lounge, her bandaged hand resting on a cushion. Peter was beside her, periodical in hand. From the clattering and laughing coming from the kitchen, Flo and Jen were dishing up supper.

'Hello,' Eliza said brightly. 'It's good to see you up Rosie, and nice to see you too Peter.'

'Hello Eliza, you're late home tonight. I called by with some Penny Bloods for Rosie.'

'And he's ended up reading every one of them to me,' Rosie giggled, tapping his arm with her good hand. Eliza was heartened to see her cheeks were pink and she was looking brighter than she had since the accident.

'Well, must go, my supper will be waiting,' Peter said, getting to his feet.

'Do come back and read to me again,' Rosie pleaded. 'It gets boring now Auntie's out during the day too.'

'If you really want me to,' Peter sighed, but Eliza could tell he was pleased to be asked.

'That was nice of you to spend time with Rosie,' Eliza told him as she showed him out.

'Funnily enough I enjoyed it. Even the corny storylines,' he raised his brows, then he lowered his voice. 'Do you know her mother still hasn't been in touch. Unbelievable, isn't it?'

'Yes, it is,' Eliza agreed. 'Even if she was unable to come here, you'd think she would have replied to Flo's letter and enquired how she is.'

'Poor old Rosie. Everything alright at the mill?' he asked. 'Only Jen said she saw you disappear with Mr Carter.'

'Trust Jen to make it sound mysterious. Perhaps she should try her hand at writing one of those stories Rosie loves.' She gave a wry grin, then sighed. 'I've to work upstairs with Mr Paton's weavers,' she told him. 'Something to do with this new order. But it's so noisy, I'm not sure how long I'll be able to stand it.'

'Don't knock it, they must think well of you for that's like being promoted. Besides, you could be well out of it,' Peter told her. 'We've to install another two spinners when the mill closes on Saturday afternoon, though where we're going to fit them in, I don't know. Still, orders is orders. See you tomorrow, Eliza,' he said, and pulling his cap further down, he hunched his shoulders and disappeared into the mizzle.

'Oh, has Peter gone?' Flo asked, carrying plates through from the kitchen. 'I was going to invite him to stay for supper.'

'All the more for us then,' Jen grinned, following her through with a dish of vegetables.

'Right young Rosie, now you're stronger you can stay up and have supper with us. I've made your favourite fish pie. Although I think it'll be more a case of hunt the herring, than anything. Still peasants can't be picky as they say. You were late home love, everything alright?' Flo turned her gaze on Eliza.

'I've to start working for Mr Paton's weavers tomorrow,' she mumbled.

'Blimey, how did you manage that,' Jen cried, staring at her incredulously. 'Not that I'd want to work with Big Bertha.'

'Me neither. I'm just to assist the others for this new order, but Mrs Tucker said if I show willing, I could be trained up.'

'As a weaver! Cripes you'll not be talking to the likes of us soon.'

'Don't be silly Jen,' Flo chided. 'It's good Eliza's doing so well.'

'Anyway, it's your fault, Jen. Mrs Tucker saw you showing off your fittens and thought as I could knit, I'd probably understand how weaving worked.'

'Well them fittens as you call them, are terrific. I ain't taken them off all day,' Jen grinned, holding up her woollen clad hands.

'Well Jennifer Smith you can take them off right this minute,' Flo admonished. 'They're all covered in bits of . . . well wool.' Hooting with laughter, they took their seats at the table.

As soon as Eliza walked into the weaving room, Mr Paton turned to her.

'Bertha will show you how I want things done. She is a splendid weaver so you won't get better training,' he said, before darting into his office and shutting the door.

'Right Miss Priddle, listen and learn.' Smiling sweetly, Eliza stood beside Bertha's loom. The woman scowled then began explaining the weaving process, speaking so quickly Eliza could hardly take in what she was saying.

'Warp, runs from back to front of the loom. Starts off on beam, here. Nine hundred and sixty threads. One hundred and twenty cones threaded to get this particular pattern. One hundred and twenty threads per line. Warp comes through these shafts in middle wires. Each one has an eye and needs threading with yarn. Got it?'

Bertha had deliberately tried to confuse Eliza and she knew it. However, determined to show she'd not succeeded,

Eliza nodded then had to concentrate as the woman began babbling again.

'Weft. Shuttles on side here,' she snapped, waving her arm. 'One shuttle for each colour. The worst thing that can happen is for a thread to snap. You have to reverse the process to put the pattern right which means time wasted, money lost. Do not stop halfway through or a line will be left resulting in a substandard weave. You work on until the cloth is finished, understand? Minimum Waste, Maximum Profit, Miss Priddle,' she bellowed, making Eliza jump.

'There, that's your tuition done. I pride myself on my prowess at teaching so all will be clear to you.' Big Bertha crowed, reminding Eliza of how Madam had boasted about her tuition methods. However, the woman turned to Eliza, a gleeful look on her podgy face. 'I'll expect your first piece finished by the noon bell.'

'Right, where's my loom then,' Eliza asked, clasping her hands firmly behind her back so that the woman couldn't see how nervous she was.

'Ooh, hark at Miss Hoity-Toity here. Only thinks she's got her own bloomin' loom,' she cackled. 'Still, I dare say you can afford to buy your own one. Sorry to disappoint you Miss High and Mighty, but you're here to do our bidding.' As Big Bertha stood before her, hands on hips, Eliza didn't know whether to retaliate or run.

Chapter 34

Deciding the woman's venom was best ignored, and conscious of the inquisitive glances being cast in their direction, Eliza hurried back down the long room. However, as she reached the loom nearest the door, an elderly man, skin wrinkled as a walnut but with kind brown eyes, beckoned to her.

'Pay no heed. Her bark's worse than her bite,' his raspy voice wheezed above the clatter of the looms. 'I'm Den, come and work with me.'

'But I don't know how. Bertha talked so quickly, I couldn't understand what she was telling me,' she replied, knowing the trained weavers were paid piece work and not wishing to hold him up.

'Just do as I says and you'll be fine,' he said mildly. 'You can learn the technicalities later. The main thing is to help keep the loom going.'

All morning, Eliza reloaded shuttles with bobbins, picked up, passed and generally did as Den bid, while he operated his loom, seemingly moving to a rhythm of his own. By the time the bell rang for the noon break, the patterned cloth had grown significantly and she felt she'd actually been of some help. However, although the others stopped working and filed out of the room, the man ignored them and carried on.

'Trying to get in Den's good books, are yer?' Big Bertha scoffed as she passed by, but Eliza could tell by the expression on her face that she was impressed by the work on his loom.

'Ignore her,' Den muttered, banging his chest as he was seized by a fit of coughing. Eliza did as he suggested and with a squawk of annoyance the woman stormed from the room, followed by Maggie and the others. Den and Eliza exchanged a grin then turned their attention back to their work.

Despite feeling hungry, Eliza continued to do as he asked, grateful that the noise in the room had diminished.

'Right when we get to the end of this row, we can finish,' Den said, giving his shuttle a final push. Although the clattering ceased, Eliza still felt ringing in her ears and shook her head to try and clear them.

'You'll soon get used to it,' Den told her. 'Cors it's ruined my ears so you'll have to speak up.'

'Oh sorry. I thought the spinners were noisy but this is ten times worse,' Eliza replied. 'Can we go downstairs now?'

'No need. We have our own room in the back,' Den told her, gesturing to a side door. 'Of course, Bertha and the others prefer to mingle with the minions as they call them. Well lord it over them to be precise. Me, I likes a nice bit of peace and quiet,' he winked.

'May I join you?' Eliza asked. 'Or would I be impinging on your peace?'

'Impinging eh? Now there's a fancy word. Come along,' he said, showing her through to a small but clean room housing a round table with chairs neatly set beneath. Pulling out two, he gestured for Eliza to take one then settled himself onto the other.

'I learned it from one of Rosie's Penny Bloods,' Eliza admitted. 'The stories are overly dramatic but it's nice to pick up new words. You stop learning these things when you leave school don't you?'

'Never went meself. I were needed at home. We had hand looms there see, and then after Dora and I married we continued in our little cott.'

'Jen was saying they all got broken up,' Eliza said. 'That can't have been nice.'

'It wasn't. But by then Dora were taken, and well at least working at the mill gets me out. It can become lonely when you've been used to sharing your life with someone,' he sighed. 'Thirty years we were wed.'

'That's a long time,' Eliza murmured, opening her snap box and taking out a crust with a scraping of jam. 'My grammer and gramfer were married for ages too.'

'I were lucky, Dora were a lovely woman. Now, cloth ears, a wheezy chest and paltry pay packet is all I've got to show for a life on the loom,' he added, staring into space.

'Oh, aren't you eating anything?' Eliza frowned, suddenly noticing he had nothing with him.

'Always get up too late to make something,' he shrugged. 'Still I had a bowl of porridge to break my fast.'

'Please share mine. Flo, she's my landlady, always makes plenty,' she said, breaking her crust in half and holding it out.

'I couldn't,' he demurred, his eyes lighting up despite his words.

'Please do. You've been so kind showing me what to do. I was all for heading home earlier.'

'Don't let them get to you,' he told her when he'd finished munching his bread, and licked the jam from his lips.

'If you don't respond, there'll be no point to her taunting and Bertha will give up. With her being Mr Paton's assistant, the rest follow what she does. It's a shame, beneath that hard veneer, there's a nice woman struggling to get out.'

'Perhaps it's time she tried a bit harder,' Eliza muttered, recalling what Mrs Tucker had told her. 'I mean what was the point of her describing all the weaving procedures if I was only going to be picking up and passing all day. Not that I mind doing that,' she added quickly in case he thought he ungrateful.

'That were Bertha's way. Never one to waste a chance of showing off,' he grinned. 'You stick with me and I'll show you more of the procedures as we go along. It's quite involved but satisfying when you see the cloth growing.'

'That loom Mr Paton was threading up yesterday looked very complicated, does it take long to learn?'

'Mr Paton, being the pattern maker, does his own designs.

And very precious he is about them too. The rest of us do as we're instructed.'

'Do they change every week?' Eliza asked.

'Heavens no girl, all that rethreading takes time and it would cost a fortune. They only get changed when a merchant requests a new design. Talking of which there's an important one visiting this afternoon so best to keep your eyes down and your hands working,' he advised. 'That were right nice of you to share your lunch, but we'd best get back,' he said struggling stiffly to his feet and placing his chair neatly back under the table.

Sure enough, halfway through the afternoon, the door opened and Mrs Tucker showed a distinguished looking gentleman into the weaving hall. Dressed in a coat of the finest cloth and full of self-importance, he strutted down the room, sharp eyes staring intently at each loom as he passed. Then without knocking, he swept into Mr Paton's room followed by the overseer.

'I thought Mr Grange would have brought him upstairs,' Eliza said, once the door had closed behind them.

'Mrs Tucker has the right breeding and knows these people expect to be treated with respect. Grange would be demanding orders as soon as they walk through the door. And the only ones he'd get would be his marching ones,' he grinned, then thumped his chest as he was struck by another bout of coughing.

'Shall I go and get you some water?' Eliza asked.

'No food or drink allowed in here,' Den wheezed when

the fit had passed and he could speak again. Eliza stared at him. 'Don't worry about me, I'm used to all the fluff and stuff landing on me lungs,' he said, resuming his rhythm.

Later that afternoon, the door opened and everyone bowed their heads over their loom. However, as the pompous merchant strutted back down the room, Mrs Tucker in his wake, Den was seized with another fit of coughing. The man frowned in his direction then his glance slid sideways and Eliza's heart almost stopped beating as she recognized the face with its hair greying at the temples and glittering eyes. Although the charming persona he'd displayed at Lavender House was distinctly missing.

'Your face seems familiar girl,' he boomed, eying her closely. Then he bent his head to glimpse her feet beneath the loom and she was thankful for the cover her voluminous white apron afforded. The scuffed, down at heel boots were a far cry from the shiny, high heeled ones she'd been wearing the time she'd had the dubious pleasure of having to entertain him.

'Dunna know why that should be, sir,' she mumbled, keeping her head lowered as she replied, in the slow burr of the Sedge Moor dialect.

'I hardly think Miss Priddle could have moved in such illustrious circles as yourself, my Lord,' Mrs Tucker simpered.

'No, of course not. Don't usually forget a pretty face though,' he muttered, as frowning thoughtfully, he strode from the room.

Although Eliza tried to settle back to her job, her nerves

were so frayed she became all fingers and thumbs. Would the man remember where he'd met her? And if he did, would he tell Madam? The sudden jangling of the bell made her jump, so that Den reached out and stilled her arm.

'Calm down or we'll have a snapped thread,' he warned. 'Yer bin like a bundle of nerves since that merchant spoke a yer.'

'Sorry,' she muttered, wishing they could stop work like the others on the floors below.

She tried to concentrate but the incessant clattering of the looms and heat of the early evening sunshine streaming through the glass of the tall windows were making her head throb. How she longed to be outside in the fresh air. A vision of herself standing beside the withies with Clem traversing the peaceful waters towards her popped into her head and she sighed.

How she hated working inside this vast vacuum of a building with its incessant clamour of machines and air laden with puffs of cotton that caught in her throat. Despite Den's kindness, after just one day on the weaving floor, she knew it wasn't for her. But Flo had been juggling Peter to pay Paul as she put it, and relied on Eliza's rent. Although Rosie was making a good recovery and could manage some light housework, fearing her mother might still turn up with 'the oaf' in tow, Flo had temporarily cut her own working hours, not liking to leave her by herself for long. She flinched as Den suddenly leaned closer.

'Go on home afore you do yerself a mischief, I'll cover for you,' he wheezed. 'I need to tighten the belt on here anyways,' he said, when she hesitated. Smiling her thanks, she slipped from the room.

Outside, she peered around but there was no sign of any coach waiting. Breathing a sigh of relief, she walked over to the leat. Other than the weavers, the workers had long since left and she stood listening to the water babbling and the twittering of birds as they sought their last meal for the night. It was such a contrast to the thundering machines in the weaving room, it took her a few moments to regain her equilibrium. Then knowing Flo would have supper waiting, she hurried up the hill, looking over her shoulder every so often to make sure no one was following.

The shadows were lengthening by the time she arrived at the cott. As had become his custom, Peter was just leaving.

'Hello stranger,' he said. 'How are you getting on in the Hallowed Hall?'

'Don't ask,' she groaned.

'Surely it can't be that bad,' he frowned, studying her closely.

'I might as well be nocturnal the hours Mr Paton makes us keep. He's so determined his order will be fulfilled on time, he doesn't care if we die in the process,' she sighed. Knowing Peter worked hard as well, she didn't add that she was exhausted and thoroughly fed up with the constant ringing in her ears and fibres that choked her throat. 'Anyway, enough about me. How are you?'

'Just dandy,' he chirped and it was then she noticed his eyes were shining and his smile seemed wider than usual.

'Been reading to Rosie, have you?' she asked casually. The flush creeping up his cheeks, confirmed her suspicions. 'Sweet on her, aren't you?'

'I didn't mean for it to be like this. But she's so lovely and . . .' he shrugged helplessly.

'It's alright Peter. No hard feelings, in fact I'm pleased for you both.' The look of relief on his face made her smile. Peter was a nice young man but that was as far as her emotions extended.

'I'm glad I've spoken to you Eliza as I want to ask Flo if I can walk out with Rosie, when she's better of course.'

'I'm sure she'll have no objections. Now I must go in. I'm famished.'

'It's frog in a bucket,' he called. 'It was meant to be toad in the hole but Flo didn't have any sausages or eggs for batter so she improvised.'

Shaking her head and wondering just what she was getting to eat, Eliza let herself inside. Work might be a challenge, especially so today, but living here with the others was never dull or predictable.

'There you are,' Flo greeted her. 'Jen's helping Rosie to bed. She's had a good day but tires easily. You're late again.'

'I know and Den let me slip away before the others,' Eliza sighed, shrugging off her shawl. Although May had brought warmer weather during the day, there was a nip in the air by the time she left work.

'Well, I've kept your supper hot so sit yourself down. You'll never guess what you're having?'

'Frog in a bucket,' she laughed.

'Blimey how did . . . oh, you've seen Peter. Did he say anything about, well anything?' the woman asked, eying her curiously.

'Oh, you know Peter, he talked about work as usual,' she laughed, then seeing Flo's worried look, smiled. 'He told me he was fond of Rosie, if that's what you mean.'

'And you don't mind?' Flo asked.

'I'm pleased for them Flo. I like Peter but that's it. Now for heaven's sake, what on earth is frog in a bucket.'

'Hang on and I'll get it for you,' the woman grinned. 'Here you are,' she said bustling back and setting a plate before Eliza.

'Only you, Flo,' Eliza giggled, staring down at the shaped mound of shredded cabbage with two blackcurrants for eyes that nestled in the skin of half a baked potato.

'Well, we might have to make do, but we can jolly well do it in style,' Flo chuckled. It was so infectious that Eliza found herself joining in. As laughter racked her body, she felt the cares of the day lift away. Their merriment was interrupted by a loud hammering on the door. Eliza froze. Surely that merchant hadn't followed her after all?

'Who the bloomin' 'eck's that?' Flo muttered, going over to the door and pulling it open. 'Well look who the wind's blown in and not before time too.'

'Oh Flo, you don't know what an awful time I've had,' a high-pitched voice wailed.

'Can't be worse than what poor Rosie's suffered,' Flo

snorted, opening the door wider to let the woman in. Although she looked tired and her clothes were creased, with her fair curls and azure eyes there was no doubting who she was. And from the large bag she was clutching it was evident she'd come to stay.

Chapter 35

'Mother?' Rosie cried, dashing down the stairs, closely followed by Jen.

'My baby, you can't know what a terrible time Mummy's had,' Edith wept, and heedless of Rosie's bandaged hand, threw herself at her daughter. Rosie winced but the woman was so busy bewailing her lot, she didn't even notice.

'Control yourself Edith,' Flo said, gently prising Rosie from her grip. 'Can't you see your poor girl has hurt her hand?'

'Oh dear,' Edith muttered. 'Still it's nothing compared to the bruises I have. You should see them, bigger and blacker than the hobs of . . .'

'That's enough,' Flo admonished. 'Ever the victim, Edith. Well you've only yourself to blame, while poor Rosie here really has suffered. Oh, you poor thing,' she murmured as she saw the tears welling in the young girl's eyes. 'Jen get Rosie a powder, Eliza you take Rosie upstairs and put her to bed. I'll see what's to be done with this sister of mine,' she said, glowering at the woman.

As Eliza led the trembling girl up the stairs, she heard Edith lamenting again. By the time Rosie was snuggled under her cover, Jen had appeared with her powder.

'Come on sweetheart, you drink this,' she coaxed, lifting the mug to her lips.

'She didn't even ask how I was,' Rosie sobbed. 'And now my hand really hurts.'

'The powder will help with that and make you sleep too,' Jen murmured, easing her gently back against the mattress and pulling the cover right up under her chin. 'I brought some more fibres home, so in the morning we'll stuff them in your pillow and make it plump as a mother hen. Now close your eyes and dream of that handsome man coming to whisk you away on his white charger,' she crooned.

They sat in the growing darkness, until Rosie's gentle snuffles reassured them the powder had done its job. Downstairs they could hear the two women arguing.

'I can't believe Edith didn't ask how Rosie was?' Eliza whispered.

'I can't believe she didn't come as soon as she heard about the accident. I mean what kind of mother is she?' Jen spat. 'I'm glad Rosie's got Peter now ... oh crikey,' she spluttered, turning to Eliza in horror.

'It's alright, I met Peter earlier and he explained. And no, I don't mind,' she added, pre-empting the next question. It was then they realized the quarrelling had stopped and Flo and her sister were talking, if not amicably at least civilly.

'I bet she's wheedling her way round Flo, persuading her

to let her stay,' Jen muttered. 'Well, she can't, there's not enough room.'

'But it's Flo's house and up to her to decide,' Eliza sighed.

'I'm too crackered to worry about it tonight, I'm going to turn in. First though, I must empty this bloomin' lot,' Jen muttered, standing over her bed and shaking out the yarn that, being above her wastage allowance, she'd hidden. 'It's their fault. The faster you go the more mistakes you make.'

Eliza couldn't argue with that, and as she lay in the darkness her thoughts started running amok. If Edith stayed there wouldn't be enough room for her as well. It was already squashed enough in the tiny cottage as it was, but despite the woman's self-centred ways, the fact remained that she was Rosie's mother. Besides Eliza hated the mill and, after her encounter with the merchant, didn't want to risk going back. Weaving thread wasn't for her, and it wasn't as though she'd be letting them down, for she'd spent the day doing the donkey work. She hadn't actually learned anything.

From the snippets she'd overheard when the two women had retired to Flo's room, it sounded as though Edith was thinking of reapplying for her old job as a spinner. That might help Flo's budget, but where would that leave her?

She lay back and closed her eyes, and for the second time that day the image of the Droves flashed into her mind. How she missed the big skies, the open spaces, even the murky green waters of the rhyne. Most of all she missed the feel of working the willow as she created something of use. Despite what Mr Paton had intimated, it was proper weaving, the feel, the texture, the rhythm. Although she no longer had a home to return to, she was seized with a strong desire to see it again, visit the graves of her mother and grandparents. Suddenly an image of clear blue eyes and a cheeky smile materialized and Eliza sighed. Clem, how she missed her good friend and how she wanted to see him again. As Eliza lay there wondering if she dared return, she heard her grammer whisper.

'*The rhythm of life can turn full circle if you only let it.*'

'Thank you, Grammer,' she murmured, smiling into the darkness. How comforting to know the wise woman who'd raised her was still looking out for her beyond the grave. And it wouldn't do any harm to go back and look, would it? Just to see how things were.

Before she could change her mind, Eliza tiptoed over to the cabinet, pulled out her bag and quickly packed her few things. She dressed quietly then crept down the stairs. Pulling a scrap of paper from the shopping pad, she scribbled a note thanking Flo for everything. She wished them all well, for in her heart she knew, that despite the woman's failings, it would be good for Rosie to have her mother staying. Placing it on the table along with enough money to cover the next two weeks' rent, she fought down the pangs of sorrow at leaving such wonderful friends and stepped out into the chill of early morning.

Eliza had no idea how to get to Sedge Moor from here, or indeed how far it was, and hoped when she reached the crossroads someone would point her in the right direction. As she breathed in the fresh air, she felt a flutter of excitement. She was going home. Alright, it was no longer her home, but the thought of going back to the place where she'd been brought up filled her with such joy her feet fairly fled over the cobbles.

Then she heard the sound of hooves behind her and turning saw Tricky and Dicky pulling the wagon up the hill. She waved and Bob drew up alongside.

'Mornin',' he greeted Eliza brightly. 'Goin' ter be another good one an' all. Yer goin' the wrong way for work, ain't yer?' Then he saw her bag and raised his brows.

'Morning Bob,' she replied. 'Mill work isn't for me so I've decided to leave.'

'Yer be wanting another lift?'

'I may be if you can tell me where you're going,' she said, peering over her shoulder.

'Like that, be it? Well, I can take yer as far as Taunton if that be any good.'

'Yes please,' she grinned, her heart leaping, for that wasn't too far from her old home.

'Climb up then,' he invited.

Hardly able to believe her luck, Eliza clambered onto the seat, placed her bag at her feet then pulled her shawl tighter round her.

'Surprised yer didn' wait 'til pay day afore goin',' Bob commented, as they made their way out of the village and turned onto a wider road.

'Why, I didn't even think,' she exclaimed. Perhaps that would have been more sensible for having paid Flo two weeks' rent, she would be going back with less than she'd started out with.

'Yer don't seem the same maid I dropped off,' Bob said, frowning. 'Yer was all nervous like a scared baby bird.'

'Bad experience,' she admitted. 'These months in Culme have changed that, but now I'm feeling homesick.'

'Nothin' wrong with that. Home be where the heart is,' Bob told her, reaching into his pocket and pulling out a crumpled parcel. 'Being as this is how we started last time, why don't you open it and see what we've got today.' As Eliza pulled back the wrapping a savoury aroma wafted before her, making her stomach rumble.

'Ah the missus makes the best brawn,' he said, sniffing the air appreciatively. 'No doubt there's a bite of fresh bread too. Well hurry up and pass some over, I ain't half famished. Go on tuck in, 'tis rude to eat alone,' he grinned.

'Well if you're sure, I am rather hungry,' she replied, taking a bite and sighing contentedly. After Flo's improvisations, this was a feast in comparison.

'Should be some puddin' too,' he said, looking at her hopefully some minutes later. Opening the package wider, Eliza saw a decent sized wedge of apple cake nestling in the corner and passed it to him. Smiling, he broke it in two and passed her half. 'Always tastes nicer when you share,' he said when she hesitated.

They trundled along munching in silence, passing a farm with cows on one side and sheep on the hillier ground above.

Wide open spaces and fresh air and decent food, Eliza thought, sighing contentedly.

'Thank you, that was delicious Bob,' she told him, brushing the crumbs from her lap.

'Ay well, my Jeanie be a grand little cook,' he said, grinning happily. 'Mind yer, I was half this size afore we was married,' he added, patting his ample stomach. Eliza smiled. He was evidently happy with his life and she thought how lovely that must be.

'Well please thank Jeanie from me,' she murmured, pulling her shawl tighter around her as she leaned back against the canvas cover.

Her sleepless night and the rocking motion must have sent her to sleep for she was jolted awake by the wagon lurching to a halt.

'Fine company yer turned out to be again,' Bob chided good naturedly. Groggily she peered around and saw they were at the crossroads in the centre of a town.

'This be Taunton,' he told her. 'I've to head to another mill down there,' he said, gesturing towards the canal where the water shimmered in the sunshine. 'That be a dead end though so yer needs to carry on along this road, past the toll house and yer'll reach open farmland. That'll take yer back to Bridgwater.' Then seeing the horrified look of her face, he added, 'But it also leads to all places north and east of the river.'

'Thanks Bob,' she said. He waited whilst she jumped from the cart then threw down her bag and called to the horses. Waving him off, she could hardly believe her luck. The bells in the church tower soaring over the town were chiming ten o'clock, and, thanks to Bob, she was already nearer to home than she'd anticipated.

The weather was warmer now and shrugging off her shawl, she placed it through the handles of her bag, and began walking through the main street. It was lined with old black and white shops of different shapes and sizes, all looking like the upper floors were going to topple into the street. As the shops gave way to brick houses, the toll house Bob had mentioned came into sight and she decided to ask the way to Langport, which was the town nearest her home.

Happy she was heading in the right direction, she continued walking through rolling green fields where cattle grazed. High above, a skylark hovered, its distinctive call a sure sign summer was here. Revelling in being out in the open air instead of cooped up in the mill, she hardly noticed climbing up the steep hill until she reached the signpost at Ash Cross, where she'd been told to turn off towards Wrantage. Although her feet were sore from the sharp stones that pierced her worn boots, her heart was singing as she knelt and drank thirstily from the cool waters trickling into a roadside trough.

Then, with the noon day sun beating down, she continued walking along the dusty road, grateful for the shade of the dense woodland which now grew on either side. How different it was to the sodden fields she'd tramped across when she'd first left the Droves. Although it was only a few months ago, it seemed like a lifetime for she'd experienced so much. Then she saw the wide flat lands of Sedge Moor stretching off into the distance and her spirits lifted.

Quickening her pace, she strode on through a tiny hamlet of ramshackle cottages where the only sign of life was a dog dozing beneath a tree. Once the trees began to thin out, happiness flooded through her when she recognized the wooded slopes of Worth Hill rising from the levels. Excitement mounting, she ran down towards the open moor then promptly stopped as she spotted the drove which led towards her cott. Would anything have changed? she wondered. She laughed, for nothing ever changed in the Droves. Then she remembered that everything had changed.

Despite that, it didn't stop her heart lurching when she saw the pollarded willows standing firm in the green waters of the rhyne. The sun was lower in the sky now and a breeze had blown in from the river, but she was too excited to stop and pull on her shawl.

Drawing nearer to the cott she'd lived in for seventeen years, she saw the cattle grazing the land, keeping down the weeds. Then her eyes widened with astonishment for the withies were healthy with new growth. The new owner must have planted new sets. Would he tell her off for trespassing?

But she was too tired to worry. Her feet were blistered and her legs ached from walking for most of the day, but it didn't stop her hurrying towards the big oak. As she dropped to her knees beside the three graves, bearing the names of Della,

Mary and George, her eyes widened in surprise. Not only had they been tended but there were fresh marsh marigolds in her little jug. So, someone had moved into the cott, she guessed, her heart lurching at the thought.

'*Welcome home.*'

Of course, it could have been the wind in the willows, yet her heart told her it wasn't.

'Yes, I've come back to see you but obviously I can't stay now,' Eliza told them, her gaze straying to the cott. The willows seemed to be trying to tell her something, their leaves rustling furiously as she got to her feet and moved slowly towards the buildings.

She stared up at the chimney, half expecting to see smoke spiralling from it, but the air was clear. Apart from the green moss on the thatch having grown wilder, everything looked the same as it always had. The wriggly tin sheet was covering the entrance to the barn and behind it she could see her vegetable plot was flourishing. Heart hammering, she knocked on the door and waited, but there was no reply.

Unable to leave without knowing, Eliza gingerly pushed open the door and peered inside. The furniture was the same and everywhere looked neat and clean with the fire laid ready to light. Someone was obviously living here.

'Hello?' she called, staring towards the stairs. But the only reply was the timorous echo of her voice. Realizing she was being horribly rude intruding, she turned to leave then she saw the letter propped up against the jam jar on the table. The envelope bore her name in bold copperplate writing.

Chapter 36

Dropping her bag to the floor, Eliza ran over and snatched it up, her heart flipping when she saw it was sealed with the Seymour Crest. Tearing the envelope open, she gasped when banknotes fluttered onto the table. Hastily, she pulled out the single sheet of thickly embossed notepaper but as she read the contents her blood began to boil.

My dear

It would appear that what your grandfather told me is true. Father thinks that under the circumstances it would be better if I were sent away to recover from what, I'm sure you will agree, has been a most disagreeable shock. It is imperative the truth never comes to light for the resulting scandal would cause us all here unnecessary grief and might even kill Mother. Father has generously sent the enclosed to ensure the secret remains where it should and I trust it will recompense for any inconvenience caused.

Sincerely yours

T

'Inconvenience. How dare he,' she screamed. Nothing about how she was feeling, the heartache their relationship had caused her. Nothing about her at all, in fact. He hadn't even addressed the letter to her personally or signed off with his own name. How could he be so self-centred, so callous, so shallow? Incensed, she screwed his note into a ball and hurled it across the room. That he thought she could be bought off with a pile of banknotes showed how little he knew her. Well, he could keep his precious money, she thought, stuffing it back into the envelope.

What a narrow escape she'd had. Thank heavens Gramfer had arrived in time to stop the wedding. Of course, the marriage would have been annulled when the truth came out, but by then it might have been too late. They would have . . . well, sealed their union and she might well have been with child. The very thought made her feel sick, and sinking onto a chair, she buried her head in her hands. To think she'd spent so much time waiting for him to call and see how she was, when clearly all along his only concern had been for himself. That she should have a twin so heartless made her shudder. They might share the same hair and eye colour, but she prayed that was all, for now she thought about it, his mood could turn arrogant if he didn't get his own way. They might be twins by birth but their upbringing had been completely different. Recalling Lord Seymour, shudders of revulsion ran down her spine. What if his son turned out to be the same?

'*Yer had a narrow escape there, girl.*' She turned, expecting to see her gramfer in his chair opposite, but of course the room was empty.

'You're right Gramfer, thanks to you, I have indeed had a lucky escape,' she murmured. And having shown his true colours, she would no longer acknowledge Theo as a brother. The door crashing open interrupted her thoughts and she jumped to her feet in fright.

'Clem? What are you doing here?' she asked, her heart thudding wildly as she took in his familiar face.

'I might ask you the same question,' he replied, staring at her as if he'd seen a ghost. Then he frowned. 'You alright, you look kind of shaken?'

'Well, you made me jump you clod,' she replied, trying to regain her composure. Although she'd missed him, his appearance had affected her in a way it never had before. Time seemed to stand still as they stood gazing at each other, then abruptly he turned and nodded towards the scrunched up ball on the floor.

'You've seen your letter then? Not good news, I take it?'

'Theo thought he could pay me to keep quiet about, well everything,' she sighed, sinking back into the chair.

'Thought it was from him,' Clem nodded, placing a loaf of bread and jug of milk on the table, then patting her awkwardly on the shoulder.

'You seem to be quite at home,' she frowned. 'What are you doing here?'

'Heard a scream and came to investigate,' he told her.

'But what were you doing here in the Droves?' she asked.

'Look Red, let me light the fire and make us something to drink and eat. I'm famished and I dare say you are too.' She watched as he strode over to the grate and set fire to the peat. As smoke slowly began to curl, he set the kettle to heat.

'Won't the new tenant mind?' she asked.

'I'm sure he'll understand being as how an old friend has returned,' he muttered, collecting plates and mugs from the dresser. She watched as he sliced the bread, spread it with butter then cut into the wedge of cheese. The smell was irresistible and her mouth watered as he pushed a plate across the table to her.

'But . . .' she began but he shook his head.

'You look all in Red. Let's eat then talk. By then the water in the kettle might be somewhere near warm enough to make tea.' At that moment the fire spluttered, sending acrid smoke billowing round the room. He coughed and waved it out of the door with his hands.

'Chimney still needs cleaning then,' Eliza murmured. 'You'd think the new tenant would have seen to it.'

'Perhaps he's been too busy seeing to the withies,' Clem replied. Something in his voice made her look up from her meal.

'It's you isn't it? You're the new tenant,' she cried, staring at him in disbelief.

'Guilty as charged,' he said, holding his hands up in mock surrender. 'Although to be fair, I haven't actually moved in as such, just use it as a base during the day. I mean, I had no idea where you'd disappeared or if you'd be back. Called by to check you were alright and there you were, gone. Then when the rent man called, well I settled up so you still had a home, should you decide to come back.'

'But it's not my home is it?' she cried.

'Of course, it is,' Clem told her, shaking his head. 'What made you think otherwise?'

'Gramfer told me he'd had to sell the withy beds and well the lease on the cott goes with them,' she murmured.

''Tis true he sold some but he'd never let your home go, Red. You should have known that.'

'But he said . . . oh, I'm all confused,' she murmured, stifling a yawn.

'And exhausted too by the looks of it. Why not turn in and we'll talk in the morning.'

'But I can't sleep here, with you,' she gasped.

'Much as I admit that do sound tempting, I shall away to my own bed back home. Ma would soon box my ears if I acted improperly,' he grinned, once again the cheeky Clem she'd known.

'My head's spinning like a top and my legs are so tired I'll accept your offer gladly, Clem,' she told him.

'I'll beg another loaf from Ma and be back bright and early. After breakfast, we'll take a walk along the withies and have a good chat.'

'Thanks Clem, I'd like that. I've got so many questions I can't think straight,' she murmured, stifling another yawn.

'Go on sleepyhead up the stairs to bedlam.'

Certain she'd be able to think more clearly once she was tucked up in bed, Eliza took herself upstairs. But as soon as her head hit the familiar pillow, weariness overcame her and she fell asleep. She didn't even hear the birds roosting or the mice scrabbling.

By the time she surfaced the next morning, the sun was already filtering through the window, and she could hear Clem moving around in the living room below. Jumping out of bed, she threw on her clothes, ran her fingers through her tousled curls and went down the stairs.

'That looks better,' Clem greeted her.

'Hardly,' she said, grimacing down at her creased skirts.

'Well you look good to me,' he told her, appreciation shining from his blue eyes. Then, as if embarrassed he turned and began pouring tea from the pot into a mug. 'Ma was so over the moon to hear you're back, she sent some of her special ham rounds to celebrate,' he said, setting a plate before her. As she stared down at the glistening crusty cob her stomach rumbled, making him grin. 'Same old Red. Go on, eat up and then we'll walk and talk.'

Breakfast finished, they wandered outside where the sun was shining on the withies, tinging the lush green leaves with a golden hue. Mallards waddled down to the water, fluffy ducklings following in a gaggle, while in the reed beds, buntings chirped their high-pitched twitter. Eliza breathed in the fresh air and sighed contentedly. This was heaven. Why ever had she wasted so much time wondering what was beyond here?

'Come and see what's been happening in your absence,' he said, grinning like a school boy. His excitement was infectious and she couldn't help smiling back as she fell into step beside him. They wandered along the rhyne in companionable silence before reaching the fields beyond.

'Oh,' she gasped, stopping suddenly when she saw the extent of the new planting. Everywhere was well-tended and flourishing with the promise of a good harvest to come.

'I suppose the new owner's done all this,' she murmured, not sure whether to be happy the willows had been looked after or sad they belonged to someone else now. 'Poor Gramfer, he worked so hard.'

'He did,' Clem agreed. 'Look Red,' he coughed, suddenly looking awkward. 'Your gramfer was desperate to sell those withy beds. And you know why. Anyway, I had some money put by and well, I bought them from him. You were beside yourself with grief after he died, on tenterhooks waiting for Theo to come, so there was never the right moment to tell you.'

'Oh my,' she gasped. 'I think I'd better sit down before I fall,' she added, flopping down onto the grass and staring unseeingly at the moors and hills rising beyond. So that was what her gramfer had been struggling to tell her just before he'd died. Recalling that terrible night, she let out a long sigh.

Clem hunkered down beside her and she caught the unique smell that was him. A healthy mix of fresh air, boat and water that was far more enticing than any fancy cologne the men who visited Lavender House had worn. Seeing her expression, he smiled and took her hand in his. It felt warm and comforting.

'I thought you needed a few days to come to terms with things,' he told her gently. 'You'd started making your baskets again and it looked as if you were coping. But when I came back, you'd scarpered and nobody knew where you'd gone. By then it was time for the landlord to call, so like I said, I settled the rent.'

'Then I am in your debt, literally,' she murmured, feeling guiltier by the minute.

'Don't be daft. It might mean the lease is now in my name, but nothing need change.'

'Of course, it must,' she retorted. 'I can't stay somewhere I'm not entitled.'

'But of course, you are,' he said, clasping her hand tighter his gaze boring into hers. She shook her head, trying to absorb everything he'd said. 'Look I know things have changed but I don't see why we couldn't share?'

'Clem really,' she squeaked. 'We couldn't . . .'

'I wouldn't be living in the cott with you, silly,' he interrupted, grinning at her indignant expression. 'Unless you wanted me to, of course.'

'Oh, you're impossible,' she groaned. Yet seeing his earnest expression, a glimmer of hope began to flicker. Perhaps she needn't leave the only real home she'd known. How ironic, she been desperate to get away and now here she was back again, desperate to stay.

'We'd have to make it a formal arrangement,' she told him.

'Make it as formal as you like,' he shrugged.

'No, I mean it. I'd pay you rent,' she replied. Then she

remembered how she'd left the last of her wages for Flo. 'Oh, but I don't have any money left, apart from the notes Theo sent and I'd burn them rather than use them.'

'Do you still have, er, feelings for him?' Clem asked, his voice low as he gazed out across the water.

'Oh yes,' she replied.

'I see,' he murmured.

'No Clem, I don't think you do,' she growled. 'I admit I was attracted by this handsome stranger, thought I loved him even. Ironically, he turned out to be my twin. But do you know what really gets me about all this?' she asked, turning to face him.

'Go on,' Clem urged.

'That once Theo found out the truth, he turned his back on both Gramfer and I. He didn't even come here to discuss matters. Just sent a callous letter that didn't even address me by name for heaven's sake. Self-preservation was all he had in mind. He thought to salve his conscience by giving us a few paltry banknotes,' she exclaimed.

'By the thickness of that envelope, I'd guess it was more than a few paltry notes, Red,' he said, quirking his brow.

'Even so, the principle's the same and I'm not touching them ever. Like I said before, I've a good mind to burn them on that smoky old peat fire,' she cried. To her surprise, he burst out laughing.

'Still the same 'urdy head. But I wouldn't do that Red. You never know what the future holds, so set them aside for a rainy day, eh?'

'Blimey Clem, you sound just like Gramfer,' she exclaimed.

'Well someone's got to look after you,' he said, his voice low. Suddenly the easiness between them was gone and they sat in awkward silence. Unable to bear it any longer, she sprang to her feet and began walking back to the cott. 'Where are you going?' he called.

'To get my bag. I can't stay here now, can I?'

'But why Red?' he asked, catching her up and putting out his hand to detain her.

'Well for a start you own the withy beds, and you've paid the rent on the cottage so you're the rightful tenant.'

'But I explained about the rent and I only purchased half the withy beds. The rest were still your gramfer's so now he's . . . I mean,' he shrugged.

'You mean now he's no longer here, the other half are mine?' she asked, staring at him incredulously. Flames of hope flared, then died. 'But as you say they won't generate anything until the end of the year and that's six months away,' she muttered, her spirits sinking as quickly as they'd risen. 'Well, I'll just have to come back then.'

'Still the same rash Red as ever,' Clem groaned, shaking his head. 'That's what I was trying to think out. Although Longstones have placed their order for laundry baskets with someone else now, word has it they're not happy with the workmanship,' he said, stopping as they reached the cott. 'You've got last year's crop, so if we can get them to deal with us again, we'd be in business and you'd have a means of paying this rent you're insisting on. And all without touching those banknotes.'

'Do you think Longstones might?' she mumbled, staring at the ground.

'Worth a try. You were grieving for your gramfer and besides it wasn't as if you left any baskets unfinished,' he pointed out. 'If Longstones were to reconsider, we could work together as a team again like we did with the vegetables.' Although he spoke lightly, she could tell by his expression that her answer really mattered to him.

'You're on partner,' she declared, her spirits rising once more.

'Right, I'll go and see them right now.'

'No Clem,' she cried. 'I'll speak with them,' she told him, gratified to see his look of surprise turned to one of respect.

'Well, well, the girl has grown up,' he grinned. 'Tell you what, I'll take you there in the trow, but I won't come in,' he added quickly when she opened her mouth to refuse.

'Thank you, Clem,' she replied, a frisson of excitement rippling through her. 'Let's go right away.'

Chapter 37

As first the Longstone brothers were sceptical, voicing many reasons why a young girl like Eliza couldn't take on the contract for making their baskets.

'But it was me who made them after Grammer died,' she told them. The two men stared at each other in surprise.

'Well, nobody told us that,' Ernest Longstone frowned.

'May I ask who you thought made your baskets and ensured they reached you in a timely manner, then?' Eliza asked, determined not to be beaten.

'Guess we never gave it a thought,' Walter said, scratching his head with his pencil.

It took a bit of negotiation but when the brothers saw that Eliza was sincere about staying in the Droves, they agreed to reinstate half the original contract immediately with the promise of further orders if they were satisfied.

'With your delivery timings, that is,' Ernest Longstone told her. 'We have no doubt about your quality of basket-making. They're the best in the district. Of course, your grammer Mary was a fine teacher.'

'She was,' Eliza agreed. 'Thank you, I won't let you down.'

'I'm sure you won't. However, a word of warning. There can be no further chances,' Ernest told her, getting to his feet to show her out. 'Your gramfer was a fine man. We were sorry to hear of his passing.'

'Thank you,' she murmured.

'No need to ask how you got on,' Clem said, as she climbed back into his trow. 'Your smile's brighter than the sun.'

'I'm so happy,' Eliza sighed. 'And something Ernest said, got me thinking. If we get snowed under with orders, I can always teach some of the local children basket-making.'

'That's my Red, always running before she can walk,' Clem grinned, as he pulled on the oars.

'I'll have to check on the stock of withies in the barn when we get back,' she told him, her head buzzing with plans.

'I think you'll find everything satisfactory,' Clem told her. 'I'll leave you doing that whilst I finish my deliveries for father, then bring back some provisions. It's your turn to cook supper and your larder's as empty as a cuckoo's nest.'

'Don't worry, once I've sorted out what withies I need, I'll give everywhere a clean. Although it all looked neat and tidy when I got back, thanks to you,' she added quickly, seeing him frown.

As soon as Clem had dropped her off, Eliza ran down to the old oak and knelt beside the graves.

'You could have told me it was Clem who'd bought your withies, Gramfer,' she cried. 'I'd quite forgotten you promised to leave them to me and that on my last birthday you intended giving some to Clem and me if we . . .' she stopped, remembering that was when Gramfer had thought they were going to marry. 'Well don't worry, we are going to work together so your precious beds will continue. Although I have to admit, Clem's been doing a good job looking after them. Still, I guess you already know that. Anyhow, I've got the order from Longstones back so I need to get on with making some baskets.'

As Eliza got to her feet, the willows rustled their leaves and she felt a halo of warmth and approval enfold her.

Sliding back the wriggly tin covering the entrance to the barn, Eliza stepped inside. As the familiar smell of tannin assailed her senses, she felt as if she really had come home. Then as she stared around, her eyes widened in amazement for not only had Clem brought in all of the last season's withies, he'd stacked them neatly according to their size. The abundant stock would make any number of large laundry baskets and any other orders she obtained this year.

Finally, as her gaze came to rest on her lapboard and the old flat iron, she was seized by the sudden desire to feel the familiar tools in her hands once more. Snatching up a handful of withies, she seated herself on the old matting and began fashioning a base. She stared out onto the waters of the rhyne, where the withy beds glinted yellow in the sun, and sighed contentedly.

She was still reeling from the shock of finding out it was Clem who'd bought the withy beds. And that she'd inherited the rest. Seemingly in a flash her life had turned around again, and Clem's proposal that they work together was a pleasing one.

> *One cane round, neat and tight,*
> *insert a decent border.*
> *Upset tight, wale alright,*
> *to keep my stakes in order.*

Unbidden the familiar words sprang to her lips and, as if in harmony with the joyful birds outside, she began to sing. After the racket of the mill machines, this was sheer bliss. She'd thought the spinners were bad enough but the clatter and clamour of the weaving looms was unbearable. No wonder the workers often ended up deaf or at the very least hard of hearing. By contrast, the only sounds here were of the wind blowing through the willows and the wildlife in the countryside. How could she have ever thought life here was dull?

Once she'd finished up-setting the uprights around the base, she began weaving in and out. Lost in the rhythm of her work, she didn't hear the footsteps approaching.

'Well, as I live and breathe.' She looked up to see Old Man Conger grinning in the doorway. 'If the wanderer ain't gon' and returned.'

'Good morning,' she called cheerily.

'Heard yer singin' and says to meself, ah the girl be back. Are yer stayin'?' he asked candidly, pushing his cap to the back of his head.

'I hope so,' she told him truthfully.

'Long enough to make me a couple of traps? Thems

yer make be the best, but by 'eck them eels put up a fight.' Remembering the man always paid cash, she nodded.

'I can make a start on them right away.'

'Be back tomorrow then. I were right sorry to hear about your gramfer. Salt of the earth he was,' he told her gravely.

'Thank you,' she murmured, dashing a tear from her eye as the man strode away, boots crunching on the dry path. Although Gramfer had been gone a while now, grief still caught her unawares and seemed more acute now she was home.

Selecting three of the thicker withies, she made a split in the centre of each of them. Setting these together and inserting another three horizontally through the holes, she took up a thin willow and began the figure of eight weave that would become the base. *Over and under with another two, pull up the sides*, she intoned softly. As the basket began to spread out in the familiar pattern, she took the weaver over and under singly and was just inserting the spokes when she heard the sound of oars on the water. Heart thumping wildly, she placed the trap on the stool and hurried outside, squinting in the rays of the lowering sun as Clem jumped from his trow.

'Now if I thought you was rushin' just to see me, I'd be one happy man. But knowing you and your stomach, you're just keen to find out what provisions I brought back,' he said, sighing dramatically.

'Don't tease Clem,' she chided. 'Besides I've got an order from Old Man Conger so if you get the food unloaded, I can get the first trap finished.'

'Blimin' 'eck the woman's giving me orders now.' But his

grin told her he was only joking. 'How did he know you were back?'

'Heard me singing.'

'Surprised he didn't run a mile then,' he chuckled, his grin growing wider as she pulled tongues at him. 'It's good to hear you that happy again,' he said, leaning over and lifting a bag from his trow.

'I'll call you when supper's ready.' She watched as he strode towards the cott, a contented feeling spreading through her. Fleetingly, she wondered if this was how Bob felt, then quickly dismissing the thought, she returned to her work. Although Clem was generous, if she could show him that she was serious about paying her rent, she'd feel a lot better.

She worked on until Clem called that their food was ready. Even the feel of the cold floor through the thin matting didn't bother her now, she thought, stretching her stiff limbs and hurrying indoors.

'Quite like old times,' Clem said, through a mouthful of pastry as they sat at the table, their supper spread out before them. Then the fire billowed out acrid smoke and he coughed, waving his hands in front of his face. 'I really must get that swept and soon.'

'It's strange,' Eliza said, staring at him. 'I've only been away a few months yet it feels much longer.'

'I dare say you've seen a bit of the world in the meantime,' Clem replied. Although his voice was casual, his clear blue eyes bore into her. Clearly, he was eager to hear what she'd been doing.

'Well you always said I needed to experience life outside the Droves,' she said brightly, not wishing to be drawn into a discussion. It wasn't the time to share her experience of Lavender House. Although she hadn't actually done anything wrong, it wasn't an experience she wished to dwell on. At first, she'd thought it was the men using the girls to satisfy their own desires, but now she could see it was a two-way arrangement, with the girls obliging the men in order to fulfil their desire for money. However, it wasn't a way of life she could comprehend and as soon as Old Man Conger paid her, she would pass over the rent money she'd earned honourably.

'So, what have you been up to? Apart from planting new sets?' she asked, realizing he was still watching her closely and keen to change the subject.

'Catching the odd hour's sleep here and there,' he shrugged. 'It's been a busy time juggling the withy beds around making deliveries for Father. But I've managed, and as you can see, the willows look healthy. Hopefully we'll reap the benefits literally at harvest. That's if you're sure you're staying?' he asked, quirking a brow.

'Why wouldn't I? Especially now I've got Longstones to reinstate their order?' she asked.

'Just thought you might have found life beyond the Droves more exciting.' So, he wasn't going to let the matter drop.

'Well, it was certainly different. I ended up working in a mill, would you believe. All that noise from the machinery, wool fibres floating in the air,' she shuddered. 'Do you know some workers actually go deaf? I did meet some lovely people who were happy with life though,' she added so he didn't think it was all bad.

'Anyone special?' he asked casually as he stared down at his plate.

She shook her head. 'What about you? Been seeing Bethan?'

'Once or twice,' he admitted.

'Oh,' she murmured, a sharp pang shooting through her so that it was her turn to look away. They finished the rest of their meal in silence, each lost in their own thoughts.

'So, how are things going to work now?' she asked when they'd both finished eating. What she wanted to ask was whether he was walking out with Bethan seriously, but courage failed her. 'Like I said, I'll pay you rent, but what about day-to-day arrangements?'

'Don't look so worried Red. Being as how you turned down my original proposal, I'll settle for working together as partners.'

That was nearly a year ago now, she thought, then realized Clem was still speaking. 'You can live here in the cott, tend the vegetables and make baskets to pay your way. I've every confidence you'll get Longstones to revert their total order to you, for they like your work, and will soon realize it's more cost-effective to purchase baskets that will last.'

'But what about you?'

'I'll continue working on Father's barge during the day and tend the withy beds in the evenings. Although the cattle are out grazing, the bindweed needs hoeing before it takes hold. Then I'll return home to sleep.'

'But what will you do about food?'

'If you can prepare meals for us to share, that will save me precious time. We can then discuss progress we're making or any problems over supper in the evenings. How does that sound?'

'As if you've worked everything out just as you want it,' she smiled.

'Let's call it a compromise,' he smiled wryly. 'So, do we have a deal partner?' he said, holding out his hand.

'We do, partner,' she said, shaking it. And although she was happy, she couldn't help feeling something was missing.

'Now I'm off to check those beds, and I dare say you need to finish those traps.' He got to his feet and headed for the door.

'Yes, and with any luck we'll be having fried eel for supper tomorrow,' Eliza told him as she followed him outside.

Before Eliza went back into the barn, she walked down to the big oak and knelt beside the graves.

'You'll be pleased to know Clem and I have come to an arrangement. We're going to be partners,' she murmured. Although there was no wind, the willows began to sway, their leaves dancing as if they were happy.

'Working partners,' she added. The willows fell still. 'We're going to share the chores and I'll be making baskets to pay the rent, so that's good isn't it?'

The willows stayed silent and although she waited and listened, there were no answering voices either. All she could feel was the air heavy with disappointment.

Chapter 38

For the next few weeks they worked to the plan Clem had outlined. Each day Eliza would take herself off to the barn and weave the willow she loved. She was happy being her own boss again, working in quiet and peaceful surroundings, and in her own time, although she was careful to ensure the baskets for Longstones were perfect and completed promptly. Old Man Conger having been pleased with his traps, spread the word she was back and more orders started to arrive which she was able to fit in around Longstones' requirements.

She didn't miss the mill at all, although she found herself wondering how Flo, Rosie and Jen were. As for Lavender House, well she'd consigned that experience to the back of her mind. Along with Theo. She was happy to be home and moving forward with her life.

Clem also seemed happy with their arrangement, although from time to time she'd catch him watching her over the top of his mug or out of the corner of his eye. As if he wanted to say something. Although they'd resumed their former easy-going relationship, she was worried he was going to ask more about her time away or talk about Bethan.

She'd have a pot of tea and bread or cake ready for them to share when he'd finished his deliveries. They'd sit together on the bank of the rhyne looking out over the water, catching up on the news of their day. Then whilst she went off to tend their vegetable plot and start supper, he'd hoe the weeds from the withy beds. Under his attention and care they were thriving and as long as the weather held, they were hopeful of a good harvest.

Later, the living room would ring with their laughter as they shared their meal. But in the privacy of her bedroom, she couldn't help wondering what it would be like to further their relationship.

'Just like an old married couple.' Clem grinned, one evening when they'd just finished the manchit she'd baked.

'Yes,' Eliza laughed, gathering up their dishes and wondering if now was the time to ask him about Bethan, for it had occurred to her that if he was seeing her, they couldn't be spending much time together. However, when she returned, he was thoughtfully studying the jam spoon he'd carved.

'Actually, I've been thinking . . .' his voice trailed off.

'Dangerous habit, Willow Man,' she teased.

'It'll soon be your birthday, won't it?' he murmured, looking serious. Before she could respond something in the fire shifted and the room filled with acrid smoke.

Coughing and spluttering Clem jumped up and threw open the door. They watched in silence as the smoke poured from the room and curled out over the rhyne. By the time the room had finally cleared, the shadows were lengthening.

'You'd best let the fire go out and I'll get that chimney swept first thing in the morning while the weather's still fine. If you can have some old rags spread out in front of the grate, to catch the worst of the mess, that'll help.'

'Of course,' she replied. It was only when he'd jumped into his trow and was pushing off that she remembered their unfinished conversation.

Feeling strangely restless, she ignored the dirty dishes and walked down to the old oak. Being September now, the evening air had a definite nip to it and she knew Clem was right about the chimney. Soon they'd need the fire lit constantly for heating the cott as well as the kettle.

'You'd be pleased if you could see the withy beds, Gramfer,' she said, dropping to her knees beside the graves. 'They are really thriving under Clem's care.'

'*Of course, they are.*'

'*We always said he was a caring man.*'

'And he's a good friend too.' She waited but all was quiet.

'So, you'll need to catch this when I shove it down the chimney,' Clem told her, holding up the huge bunch of holly he'd tied to the end of a rope. 'The prickles should sweep all the soot and debris down into the grate. Make sure you stand well back or you'll get covered,' he warned.

'But don't you want me to steady the ladder first,' she asked, as he began to climb.

'If you must,' he muttered, but she could see he was pleased. 'Remember, as soon as I call you must go inside.'

'Yes partner,' she called, but he ignored her and continued

climbing. She watched as, holly in hand, he steadily clambered onto the moss-covered thatch and as soon as he called, she ran inside. However, she'd only just reached the door when there was the sound of scrabbling and a dull thud, followed by silence.

Turning she saw Clem had fallen and was lying still on the ground.

'Clem,' she screamed, throwing herself down on the grass beside him. 'Clem answer me,' she shouted. But his eyes were closed and blood was seeping from a gash on his cheek.

'Wake up Clem, please,' she cried, cradling his head in her lap. 'Oh, Clem you must wake up. I love you and can't live without you.'

Slowly his eyelids fluttered open.

'Who are you?' he groaned, his eyes closing again.

'It's me Eliza. Do wake up, please. I'll get Bethan . . .'

'Why the heck would I want her?' he asked, his eyes snapping open. 'Blimey Red, I have to bash me own brains out before you see sense and then you go and mention Bethan. It's you I want, always have,' he murmured, smiling groggily up at her. Her heart singing, Eliza leaned forward and kissed him tenderly on the lips.

It wasn't just the cott and withies that had drawn her home, it was him, Clem. The man she loved. And he loved her. Like the heroine in one of Rosie's stories, she'd had to go away in order to discover real love was here beside her all along. And unlike Flo, her man was waiting for her, even if she'd been too blind to realize.

Epilogue

The morning sun blazed like a fiery ball, tinging the withies that stood sentinel straight alongside the dyke with a rosy hue. The smell of pommy drifted across the land where the cattle had been introduced to clear the ground. Aller Moor, with its holes cut by peat cutters, smiled down on the little party below.

Eliza, wearing the new top she'd dyed and fashioned from this season's flour sack, smiled lovingly at her husband. Clem pulled her closer and they both gazed proudly down at their firstborn. A lusty cry filled the air as water from the rhyne was blessed then sprinkled over his forehead. Eliza cuddled her son tighter while the proud father gazed in wonder at the two most precious people to grace his life.

'Let this child be named George Clement Galton. May he be blessed with health and happiness and grow up to know only love and kindness.' Although the morning was still, the willows began swaying, their leaves swishing as if they were happy and dancing for joy.

'Well George Clement, it's time for you to meet your grandmother and great grandparents,' Eliza smiled and taking her husband's hand, they made their way to the big oak.

As they stood before the three graves beneath the old oak Eliza held out her son.

'Meet your new grandson and great grandson, George Clement, the future custodian of your precious withy beds.'

'Of course, he would have been two years old by now, if only Eliza had seen sense and listened to us, George,' Clem sighed dramatically. 'Still at least she got there in the end.'

From high above, they heard a loud chuckle.

'*Ah, she always were an 'urdy head, our Eliza.*'

'*Take care of them both Clem.*'

'*Be happy.*'

As if joining in the merriment, the willows waved their branches, shaking their leaves vigorously until they rustled like the rattle Eliza had woven for her baby.

At that moment, young George let out an indignant cry and Clem smiled ruefully.

'I can see I'm not going to get any peace now, you're as demanding as your mother,' he groaned, his beaming smile belying his words. 'Come on then, time to eat.'

Eliza placed him tenderly in the baby basket she'd spent ages weaving, intoning loving blessings between each round of willow. Then taking one handle each, the little party turned and made their way into the cott that was now their family home. A new generation that in the fullness of time would tend the withy beds, ensuring the cycle continued.

The rhythm of life could indeed turn full circle if you only let it.

Acknowledgements

To the staff at The Willows & Wetlands Centre, Stoke St Gregory, for a most interesting tour and basket-making demonstration, plus their patience in answering my numerous questions.

To the staff at Coldharbour Mill, Uffculme, for the very informative guide around the historic mill and detailed explanation of all the machines and wool processes.

To my brilliant agent, Teresa Chris, who so often imparts that little extra 'gem'.

To the wonderful staff at HarperCollins, HQ, especially Kate, Vikki, Laura, Sarah and all the other unseen heroes who work behind the scenes to ensure my stories are the best they can be. I'm truly grateful for all your hard work and friendly responses to my queries.

For my friends at Budleigh Writers' Circle who continue to listen to my latest offerings then offer their constructive feedback. Your encouragement is appreciated.